CUBE 6

CUBE 6

A Novel

THOMAS W. GRIFFIN

W

WATSON PRESS

SEATTLE

Watson Press

© 2003 by Thomas W. Griffin All rights reserved under International
and Pan-American Copyright Conventions.

www.watsonpress.biz • www.thomaswgriffin.com

Griffin, Thomas W.
Cube6 : a novel / Thomas W. Griffin—1st ed.
p. cm.

ISBN 0-9726585-5-6

1. Serial murders—Fiction. 2. Seattle (Wash.)—Fiction.
3. Journalism—Fiction. 4. Analgesics—Fiction.
5. Pain—Alternative treatment—Fiction. I. Title.

PS3607.R546C83 2003   811' .6
QBI33-868

Cover art by Julie Scott: www.juliescott.com
Book design by Whittington & Co: www.whittingtonandco.com

Published in the United States by Watson Press.
First Edition

9 8 7 6 5 4 3 2 1

To Charles Ward Griffin

"At least do no harm."
Hippocrates

Chapter 1

I t rains a lot in Seattle. Approximately thirty years ago, Seattle's mayor found himself staring out of his office window at yet another storm rolling in from the Pacific. The city was in trouble and so were his chances for re-election. The economy was drowning and the rain was killing the tourist trade.

With an uncharacteristic flash of insight he decided to hold a contest to replace Seattle's nickname, "Rain City." The contest was organized, the names were submitted, and the mayor reviewed the entries with much public fanfare. A ninth grader from Garfield High School won the event with "The Emerald City," a phrase she borrowed from the movie *The Wizard of Oz*. It seemed to embody all the positive aspects of the Pacific Northwest without bringing to mind the dreaded "R" word. Unfortunately for the soon-to-be-defeated mayor, the change had little effect on tourism. But since that time businesses all over town were named and renamed the Emerald City this and the Emerald City that.

The Emerald City Motel was one of a number of dingy, older motels located near Seattle's Sea-Tac International Airport on Aurora Avenue South. In a neighborhood that had seen better days, this particular establishment was a hangout for druggies, bikers, prostitutes and their pimps. It was known for its low hourly rates and its steady clientele.

Normally quiet at 11:30 in the morning, the motel parking lot and registration office were buzzing with activity. Two uniformed policemen were in the registration office talking with the desk clerk. Another cop was out in the drizzle putting up yellow tape that warned all passers-by not to trespass on the crime scene. Room 221 was cordoned off. There were three blue-and-white patrol cars and a television news broadcast van in the parking lot, and more were on the way. Pedestrians were starting to gather.

Detective Karen Able had just returned to her office from the police department's gym, her fiery red hair still damp from the shower. Before she sat down a desk sergeant entered her office without knocking and told her of an apparent homicide at the motel.

"Shit, just what I need," she said. She was already working on two similar murder cases and so far her investigations weren't leading anywhere.

Able closed her file, fluffed her damp hair one more time, and headed down to the police parking garage in the basement of the Public Safety Building. When she drove her unmarked patrol car out onto the city streets, rain started sheeting down her windshield. She slammed on the brakes when a bicycle messenger darted out in front of her, and then sped up on the sidewalk and around the corner. By the time she finished the twenty-minute drive through heavy morning traffic she was still a little jumpy from her three morning cups of Starbucks coffee. After parking her car in the Emerald City Motel parking lot she ducked under the crime scene tape and met Detective Sergeant Gilbert Anderson at the door to 221.

"Hi, Karen."

"How's it going, Gil?" Karen looked through the open door into the room. "Looks like we have another one."

"I'm afraid so," he answered. "The maid discovered the body when she came in to clean the room about forty-five minutes ago. She opened the door with her passkey and only took a few steps into the room before noticing the body on the bed. She says she immediately left the room and notified her boss at the reception desk."

"She didn't touch the corpse?" Karen asked.

"She says not. She returned with her boss a few minutes later. Neither of them touched the vic. He says she was obviously dead so he didn't feel for a pulse. They went back to the office and he called the police."

"Yeah. Then what?"

"Two patrolmen arrived a few minutes later. One of them checked the vic to make sure she was dead while the other secured the crime scene. Because of the similarities to the other prostitute murders, the desk sergeant called us." Anderson ran his fingers through his rain-moistened hair. "So far as we know," he continued, "The maid, the desk clerk and the patrolman were the only ones to contaminate the crime scene. The vic was posed on the bed just like the others. The photographer and the people from the crime lab have been called, but they haven't arrived yet. The room hasn't been touched since we got here."

Gil Anderson was a Swede, one of a number of Scandinavians on the heavily Scandinavian Seattle police force. He was a big man and his rumpled clothes never seemed to fit quite right. He had been on the force for eighteen years and had only another two more to go before retirement. The deep furrows in his forehead never smoothed, and the dark bags under his eyes never went away. He was convinced that he had seen every human depravity that there was to see.

"What about the night clerk?" she asked. "Have you had a chance to interview him?"

"We're trying to locate him," he said. "He went off duty at 7:00 this morning. The room was rented for the entire night, an unusual event in this place. Most of the rooms are rented only by the hour." Anderson checked his note pad. "It was registered to a Carol, no last name, apparently a regular customer. There were nineteen other registered guests last night, all of them regular customers. We're trying to locate them as well."

"Give me some time to look at the room and go over the body, and then I'd like to talk to the manager myself," Karen said. She pulled a pair of latex gloves out of her purse, pulled them on, ducked under the yellow tape and entered the room.

The motel room was vintage '70s, complete with its original orange shag carpeting. The room was neat and, other than the body on the bed, showed no obvious signs of being disturbed. There was no evidence of a struggle. Detective Able began her examination of the room beginning with the peripheral areas.

The bathroom looked as if it had not been used, the toilet still had a paper band around the seat. The closet and dresser drawers were empty. The television remote control was on top of the TV next to a card listing a selection of X-rated pay-per-view movies. The drawers in the bedside stand contained only a Bible, and the clock-radio on top of the stand was broken. The only thing out of place was the naked body of a black woman in her mid-twenties on top of the undisturbed bedspread. She was lying on her back, apparently asleep. Her feet were propped together with her toes up, heels out. Her head was placed on the still-covered pillow, and her arms were folded across her chest mummy-style with her hands covering her breasts.

"Where are her clothes?" Detective Able asked.

"We have patrolmen searching the motel grounds, the dumpster and the surrounding areas, so far nothing," Anderson replied. "Robbie's coordinating the search. They aren't in the room."

Detective Able began her examination of the body.

✸

Approximately nine miles to the north of the motel, Jon Kirk was sitting at his desk in the newsroom of *The Seattle Times*. It was in its usual state of controlled chaos. Clacking keyboards, ringing telephones, shouted conversations, and constantly moving people all contributed to a sense of unrestrained commotion. Jon was one of twenty-three reporters and clerks on the city beat, and at thirty-something years old he was a rising star on their ever-growing staff.

Jon was talking on the telephone when Vicki, the city editor's secretary, approached him from behind and tapped him on the shoulder. He turned his head and smiled as he continued to talk. He'd just returned from Thursday's half-price newspaperman's lunch at The Thirteen Coins and his black wavy hair was still tussled by the effects of the Seattle winter wind and rain. It had been a wet winter, wetter than usual, and he was glad to be back inside.

Vicki gave him a nudge and said, "Thornton's been looking for you; they just found another one." She looked at Jon a moment before adding, "You'd better get in there."

Jon finished his telephone conversation with an, "I love you too," hung up the phone and made his way through the newsroom. Dean Thornton, the city editor, was standing alone in his doorway as Jon arrived. The editor's office was located in a far corner of the room and was walled off from the rest of the space by transparent floor-to-ceiling glass partitions; it had all the privacy of a specimen case. Thornton glanced up as Jon approached and scowled at him. He motioned him inside with a flourish.

"Come in, Kirk. I hope you enjoyed your lunch."

"I did. I'm sorry if you had trouble getting ahold of me earlier."

Thornton shut the door. His office was a mess. A bulletin board on the back wall of the room overflowed with scribbled notes, some of which were tacked to the wall. Several cardboard boxes containing documents waiting to be filed sat next to already-full file cabinets. Papers were scattered all over his large desk; books were stacked three rows deep against the wall. Only the computer and computer table escaped the clutter.

"They found another prostitute this morning," he said, "This time at a place called the Emerald City. It's one of those sleazy motels down on Aurora."

"Was she posed like the others?" Jon asked.

"Yeah," he answered. "Just the same. I couldn't find you so I sent Lizzy over there."

"Lizzy?"

"Yeah Lizzy, why?"

"She's a little young for this type of assignment, isn't she?"

"She's ambitious and aggressive, she's over twenty-one and she'll fill you in."

"Whatever you say."

"The body's on its way to the Harborview morgue, and following notification of the next of kin an autopsy will be scheduled. I want you to be there. Vicki made the arrangements."

The color drained from Jon's face. "Come on, Boss," he said, "You know I hate autopsies. If you want Lizzy involved in this thing let her do it. She loves the blood and guts stuff. If it's anything like the last two, they aren't going to find anything anyway."

Thornton leaned into his desk toward Jon. "What is the matter with you, Kirk? This is the second prostitute killed in a month, the third this winter. That makes it serial murder. Do the names Ted Bundy and the Green River Killer ring a bell? Seattle's had more than its share of these guys."

Thornton's booming voice could be heard through the glass walls of his office. "Vicki pulled a lot of strings to get you a seat at this table, and I want your ass over there. Sooner or later they'll find the causes of these deaths, and I want you to be there when they do."

"But. . . ."

"No buts. Listen, we all appreciate the work you did with the first two murders. Stick with it and who knows," he said. "You might score another *New York Times* byline with this one." His eyes narrowed. "It's still your story." Then he added, "And you'll be at the autopsy if you want to keep it."

Jon brushed his fingers through his wavy hair. He looked at Thornton for a moment and then promised, "I'll be there."

"See that you are," Thornton said as he reached for a bottle of aspirin. Jon walked out of his office.

Thornton shook three Bufferin tablets into his hand. He reached into the small refrigerator next to his desk, poured some club soda from a can into a glass and grimaced as he swallowed the tablets with the carbonated mineral water.

Six weeks ago, almost to the day, the first murder had been discovered. An eighteen-year-old prostitute had been found posed in a mummy-like position, naked on a motel room bed. Her name was Janet Bandon, she was white and, as the autopsy would later show, she was a heroin addict. The clerk at the motel remembered renting her a room, but no one saw her enter or saw who was with her. There were no signs of violence and, although there was a lot of speculation, the autopsy and subsequent toxicology studies had failed to find a definitive cause of death. No incriminating evidence or fingerprints were found at the crime scene. There were no leads to follow and no suspects.

Several weeks later another prostitute had been found, naked and posed in the same position. Again no cause of death had been identified.

Outside Thornton's door Vicki was sitting at her desk filing her fingernails. She eyed Jon as he walked past.

"I just got the call," she said. "The autopsy's scheduled for nine tomorrow morning."

"Thanks a lot," said Jon.

"Better luck with this one," she said with a smile.

Jon gave her a fake smile in return. When he reached his desk, he picked up the telephone and punched in Lizzy's cell-phone number. She answered on the second ring.

"Hello."

"Liz, it's Jon Kirk."

"Oh hi, Jon," Liz said. "Did Thornton find you?"

"He found me," Jon answered. "And he filled me in. Are you still at the motel?"

"I'm still here."

"Good. What's going on down there?"

"It's a madhouse. There are police, television crews, reporters, and a whole bunch of other people all over the place. The police haven't given any official statements yet, but I pretty much know what happened."

"OK," Jon said. "So what happened?"

"This one was black," she answered. "She was posed just like the others. We have photographs of the motel room door with the crime scene tape around it, and another one of the coroner's men carrying the body out of the room to their truck. Thornton probably won't let us use that one. The body was found by a cleaning lady, but I haven't been able to talk to her yet. The motel manager gave me an interview, but it wasn't worth much. I'll be finished in an hour or so if I don't have to wait here for the official police statement. The police aren't talking to anybody yet."

"An hour you think? After you finish why don't we meet at the Blue Moon and go over this stuff."

"Who's buying? You or me?"

"I'll buy," he said.

"I'll see you there around 4:00."

"Call me if you're going to be late."

"Bye."

Jon hung up the telephone. Dean Thornton was right. Seattle did seem to have more than its share of serial killers. There was the Green River Killer, the Renton Ripper, Ted Bundy, Dave Maryatt. Now there was this guy, *The Prostitute Killer, The Sea-Tac Slayer, The Invisible Man.* He would need to come up with something better for tomorrow's headlines.

Jon's head hurt and he needed a cold beer. He left the office, turned on his cell phone and drove his car through city traffic to the Blue Moon Café.

✳

The Blue Moon Café really wasn't a café at all; it was a well-known watering hole located on the fringes of the University District. Seattle's blue laws forbade bars, so establishments like the Blue Moon had to keep up the pretense of serving alcoholic beverages as only a sideline to their food. It was one of those dark, intimate places conducive to quiet conversation. A row of booths and tables lined one side of a long, somewhat narrow room with a bar and a row of bar stools on the other side. Over the bar a sign read:

BEER,
HELPING UGLY PEOPLE
FIND SEX SINCE 1853

Bobby Arnold had started tending bar at the Blue Moon before Jon Kirk knew how to walk. They had known each other since Jon's college days as a journalism major at the University of Washington. Jon sat at the bar talking to Bobby, drinking a Redhook. Bobby stood behind the bar wiping an invisible watermark off its surface with a dishtowel. Four university students with very good fake ID cards sat together in a corner booth. They were drinking beer poured from a pitcher. Two regulars were playing darts.

"Lizzy's late," Jon said. "It's 4:00 and she was supposed to be here by now. She must be finished at the motel."

"She's probably hung up with a crowd of admirers. You know Lizzy and men."

"I know Lizzy," Jon said. He took a big gulp of his beer.

"You ought to pay more attention to her," Bobby said.

"What do you mean?"

"Well, I happen to know she has a thing for you."

"Really."

"She thinks you're cute, or at least she thinks that a certain part of your posterior anatomy's cute."

"Cute?"

"That's what she said."

"You sure?"

"Would I lie?"

"Come on, Bobby, she's barely out of school. She's just a little young for me, don't you think?"

"You *know* what I think."

"Yeah, right, that's all you ever think."

Jon took another drink of his beer. He was working out an angle for his story in his head. It had to be ready for the morning edition. Bobby stepped away and started washing some glasses in a sink behind the bar.

"Bobby," Jon said.

"What?"

"You been following the prostitute murders?"

"A little."

"Tell me, you have any theories? I need a little help. I've got to write something before the morning edition deadline."

Bobby gave him a half smile. "They're paying you, they ain't paying me. Write it yourself."

"Thanks a hell of a lot," Jon said. "I thought bartenders were supposed to have all the answers."

"That's what they say." Bobby continued washing his glassware. Jon drank some more of his beer.

The front door opened, light flooded the darkened interior, and Lizzy walked inside. The dart players interrupted their game, turned and watched the sun silhouette her figure in the doorway. Jon looked at his watch. He picked up his beer, ordered one for her and stood to greet her. "Hi, Lizard, where've you been? You were supposed to meet me at 4:00." They walked over to one of the booths.

"While you've been sitting here socializing with that old geezer reprobate bartender, I've been working," she said. "I got some good stuff."

Bobby brought Liz's beer over to the booth. "Liz, you're looking mighty fine today," he said. "The cold winter air must agree with you. It put a glow in your cheeks." Bobby looked over at Jon and winked. "Here's your beer. Anything else I can do for you?"

Jon answered for her, "No, Bobby, you've done enough for one day." He turned to Liz and said, "OK, what do you have that the TV guys don't have? In less than an hour everyone in Seattle will know that we have a new serial killer in our midst."

Bobby walked back behind the bar.

Lizzy took a drink of her beer and played with a strand of her windblown hair. "The police identified the victim," she said. "Her name was Carol Williams. She was twenty-three years old and she was posed naked like the others. There was no blood or other evidence of violence or a struggle in the motel room. Her clothes are missing." Lizzy paused to take another sip of her beer. "And for the exclusive part, I tracked down her mother. She agreed to talk to me and we had a phone interview."

"Are you sure it's our exclusive?"

"Yes," she answered. "The police said that Williams had been working the streets since she was thirteen, and that she was from the Hilltop neighborhood in Tacoma. I called all the Williams listings there until I found the right one. After we finished she said she was going to drive to Federal Way to stay with a friend, so I assume no one will be able to track her down right away. Not until after the morning edition, anyway."

"Did she know about her daughter?" Jon asked.

"She does now. I had to tell her." Lizzy paused for a moment. "That was not easy. She cried a lot, but she didn't seem surprised. She seemed to want to talk about it."

"Ok. Finish your beer and let's write it up."

Liz sat back and looked down her nose at Jon. "What's this 'let's write it up' stuff? I found her. She's my story. You can write about the autopsy."

Bobby was watching them from his side of the bar. He grinned a sly grin as he finished washing the glasses.

Chapter 2

Harborview Hospital and Medical Center broods over the city from its elevated position on the east side of the interstate highway like a medieval fortress. One of those old, Depression-era, art-deco structures typical of public buildings constructed in Seattle during the first half of the twentieth century, it is owned by the county. During its former incarnation as King County Hospital it served as an institution of last resort for Seattle residents down on their luck. Whispered stories of human experimentation on the psychiatric ward and benign neglect in the geriatric wing are legendary, and they can be heard to this day during quiet conversations in out-of-the-way gathering places. It is an institution haunted by its history, and some say by more than that.

When the advent of Medicare and Medicaid mitigated the need for charity hospitals, the county leased its nearly bankrupt facility to the University of Washington. The university transformed it into a trauma center, which soon became a national leader and trendsetter in its field. The 911 concept was developed at Harborview. Subsequently, in an effort to capitalize on the center's success, county public health planners sought to centralize all trauma-related activities in one location, and they relocated their medical examiner's office in the Harborview complex. With an eye toward the practical, they placed it a quick, two-floor elevator ride below the busy trauma center, and immediately adjacent to the hospital's very large and active morgue.

Jon Kirk drove his Explorer toward Harborview with an unsettled feeling in his stomach. His hands moist on the steering wheel, he had difficulty concentrating on the heavy downtown traffic as he approached Pill Hill. After he arrived and parked his car he asked the large woman at the information desk for directions to "the place where they do autopsies."

Hospitals are sensitive about autopsies. Sensitive about the fact that death is a part of their business, they bury morgues deep in basements and away from their paying customers. Jon waited at the information desk until a security guard was summoned to escort him through a labyrinth of hallways and a maze of staircases. It was already 9:20. Jon was late.

Dr. James Allison was the county medical examiner. A large man who stood at least six foot four, he had strong arms and hands. Allison had achieved some local notoriety through the publication of a book containing graphic photographs of some of Seattle's more famous murder victims. A member of the medical school faculty, Allison was renowned for his lectures on forensic pathology. His annual talk entitled "Gross Things I Have Seen During my Twenty-Year Career as a Medical Examiner" was a well-attended favorite.

Allison and his assistant were already gowned, gloved, and working in the autopsy suite when Jon arrived. Franz List's piano masterpiece The Mephisto Waltz was blaring over the sound system, only partially masking the sounds from the bone cutter as it crunched through the victim's ribs. Detective Able was gowned, gloved, and standing by Dr. Allison's side as an observer. From behind her mask she flicked a glance in Jon's direction when he was ushered in.

The autopsy suite was large. It had three post-mortem examination stations, each with its own stainless-steel dissection table, a set of bright surgical lights, a bank of X-ray view boxes, an instrument stand, and provisions for suction and fluid drainage. The walls were tiled, as was the floor. Tradition dictated that bodies in the morgue were referred to as patients. Last night's patient was on the middle table. The other two dissection stations were empty. The room was cold. What can only be described as the smell of death hung in the air.

After Jon thanked his security guard escort for the third time, an orderly directed him to a small changing room, where he dressed in a set of surgical greens and shoe-covers. "Here, you'd better put this on," the orderly said. He handed Jon a plastic face guard.

"What's it for?" Jon asked.

"Doc Allison said you're going to be standing close to the table. It'll protect your eyes and face from any contaminated bodily fluids accidentally splashed in your direction."

Jon suppressed the rising nausea as he put on the face guard. Once gowned and gloved he was directed back to the autopsy suite, where Dr. Allison paused to welcome him to the group.

"Mr. Kirk, it's nice to see you again. I'm glad you could join us," said Dr. Allison. "This is my assistant, Mark Groudine, and the lovely young woman on my right is Detective Able. She's the lead investigator on this case."

"Hi, Karen."

Karen looked at Jon through her protective visor and answered, "Hello, Jon."

Dr. Allison interrupted their eye contact. "I see you two have already met. Come in closer, Jon, you can't see anything from way back there."

The instrument table on the assistant's left contained the usual sets of surgical knives, forceps and retractors, and in addition there were saws, tissue spreaders, a hammer, and other specialized equipment useful for autopsies. Jon felt a little lightheaded as he edged closer to the table.

Dr. Allison addressed Jon as he said, "The patient's name was Carol Williams. She was twenty-three, and came from Tacoma. She had two brothers and a sister. One of her brothers is dead, thought to be killed in a gang-related conflict by a gunshot wound in the chest. He was one of my patients. The other brother is in prison.

Her sister left the state some time ago, and her current whereabouts are unknown.

"As you know, Carol came to us from a Sea-Tac area motel. She'd worked as a prostitute in the Seattle region for the past ten years, good longevity for a woman in her profession. She's a known intravenous drug user. This information, by the way, is courtesy of Detective Sergeant Washington and the Seattle Police Department. I like to get to know my patients before I operate on them."

Jon was concentrating on his breathing.

Dr. Allison continued, "We've completed our inspection of her skin and found no signs of trauma except for these five curious small bruises you can see here on her chest and the outside of her right thigh. She displays the stigmata characteristic of intra-venous drug use, namely, needle tracks over veins in her arms, over the backs of her hands, on her ankles and over the dorsal aspects of her feet. Samples of blood, and oral, vaginal and anal contents have been sent to the lab for analysis, as have samples from under her nails and those combed from her hair, both scalp and pubic. As you can see, we've opened her with the usual chest-to-pubis incision, and Mark was cutting her ribs with these big bone cutters to remove her sternum just as you came in." His hand came down and rested on the edge of the open cavity.

"Move in a little closer so that you can see better," Allison invited. Jon stayed where he was. Tiny beads of sweat broke out on his forehead.

"Mark, would you give those spreaders another crank or two so we can get a better look in there?" Allison asked his assistant.

"Jon, you're looking a little pale," Karen said. A malevolent half-smile glittered behind her surgical mask. "Oh, I just remembered. You've got a thing about blood."

"I'll be fine," Jon said.

"Are you sure? Sometimes people are bothered by the smell when they open the gut." Karen's eyes twinkled. "It's getting warm in here, don't you think?"

"I said I'll be fine."

"This liver looks a little large to me," said Dr. Allison as he pulled it dripping out of the abdominal cavity. "Weigh it for me, would you, Mark?"

Jon hit the floor with a dull thud.

＊

Jon's cell phone rang. "Hello?" It was Detective Able.

"Where are you?" she asked.

"I'm in the hospital cafeteria drinking coffee," Jon answered.

"Don't go anywhere; I want to talk to you. I'll meet you there in a few minutes." Karen hung up the phone.

Jon and Karen had been seeing each other for most of the past six months. Their work on a prior case had developed into a somewhat stormy on-again-off-again relationship. Lately it was off again. Jon was fidgeting with his cup of coffee when Karen saw him from the doorway of the cafeteria. She walked with purpose over to his table and sat down.

"What a wuss! Maybe you should try another line of work. You didn't hurt yourself, did you?"

"I'm OK," Jon replied. "I didn't eat any breakfast and I got a little lightheaded, that's all."

"Right," she said. "Where've you been, anyway?"

"What do you mean?" he mumbled into his coffee as he took another drink. Her eyes were angry, penetrating. He did his best to avoid them.

"Six months of loving, laughing, fighting, and fucking, and then you don't know what I mean? I don't think so." Her voice was brittle.

"Come on, Karen, hold it down. People are listening." Jon looked around the room. "That redheaded temper of yours is going to get us in trouble again."

Karen took a deep breath and then let it out slowly. "My boss warned me about you, you know," she said. "He told me that all you cared about was your goddamned newspaper stories. He said you could be very persuasive when you wanted something. Boy was that an understatement! I should have listened to him."

"Our relationship had nothing to do with those stories or the information you gave me and you know it," he protested. People at other tables were looking in their direction. "I got a little side-tracked with the prostitute murders, that's all. You know you mean a lot to me." He met her eyes with his gaze. They were cold, unblink-ing; then they softened a little. She looked away.

"Goddamn it, Jon, don't say things like that unless you mean it."

"Shhh," he said. He again looked around the room. People turned away to avoid his gaze.

"What about that last night? At the Olympic Hotel," she half whispered. "You really wanted the forensics on the Bandon case, didn't you? You needed them for your stupid exclusive. You pumped me for that information all night long, remember?" She stared at him for a moment; then her features softened again. "Do you remember what you said, your promise?" She paused to search his eyes. "What was that all about, what happened?" She paused a moment more. "Too much pumping?"

Jon looked down into his coffee. "I guess I got busy," he said. "I had to file the story. Then . . . I don't know."

"Bullshit!" she said a little too loudly. The rest of the cafeteria was quiet. Others in the room pretended they weren't listening. "You got scared. We got close and you got scared." She leaned toward him, waiting for a response.

Jon looked at her for a moment before answering. "We weren't ready."

"I was," she answered.

Jon began fidgeting with his coffee cup. "It's difficult for me," he started to say. "Your job and my job, well. . . ."

"Well what, Jon?" When no answer came after a few moment she looked away and then changed the subject. "At least you didn't miss much down in the morgue. Doc Allison couldn't find what killed our latest vic. She was just like the others. Whatever killed her did-n't leave much of a trace."

Jon was ready for this conversation. "Any hope for an answer from the lab work?" he asked.

"We'll get the lab work back the day after tomorrow, but don't expect it to show much. Allison thinks she was HIV positive, but that didn't have anything to do with her death."

"Wouldn't he at least speculate?"

"Not even that. He has no idea what killed her."

"But he'll keep looking?"

"He's a bulldog, and I know he won't quit until he figures it out." She smiled for the first time since entering the cafeteria as she said, "Go down there and talk to him yourself if you wish."

"No, thanks. I've had enough of the morgue for one day."

"Actually, I have too," she answered. "I've been up all night with this thing."

"I'm sorry you didn't get any sleep." After a short pause he added, "I don't suppose you turned up any new witnesses, or any-body else who saw or heard anything at the motel?"

"Pumping me again?" She leaned back and crossed her arms.

"I thought we were discussing the case."

She looked at him a moment before she continued. "We don't have any new witnesses. There were at least twenty-five people around the motel last night. None of them knows a thing. Or if they do, they won't talk about it."

"What about the clothes?"

"You heard about that too? Not a trace."

"So where does that leave us?"

"I'm not sure where it leaves you, but it leaves Seattle PD nowhere. We're not any further along with this case than we were with the first two."

"At least you have a little more evidence to sift through," Jon said.

"Having more vics only makes it harder. Jon, this is now official-ly a serial murder; all the usual motives are out the window. Believe me, we're nowhere. We've got nothing. My boss did contact the FBI Behavioral Science division to start a psychological profile. Maybe that'll help."

Jon sat back in his chair. He wondered how far he could push it. "Would you call me with the profile when you get it?" He winced a little.

"Why should I?"

"Because I'm a nice guy?" He tried a smile.

"You're as mercenary as ever."

"No I'm not. It's just that sometimes our jobs . . . you know, a newspaperman and a cop . . . I really did get busy, and. . . ."

"I'm busy, too, Jon."

"Please don't hold it against me."

"You'll have to convince me," she said.

Karen got up from the table and left the room. As soon as she rounded the corner she slapped the wall with an open palm. "Why do I do this to myself?" she growled out loud. She leaned her forehead against the wall and slapped the wall again, not as hard this time.

A little girl holding onto her mother's hand stared in her direction. "Mommy, what's wrong with that lady? Is she crying?"

"Don't look at her honey. She's sick."

Karen pulled herself together and headed for the elevators.

Jon knew about serial murder psychological profiles. He had written a piece on the subject once for *The Seattle Weekly* before he'd left that organization to work in his current job at *The Seattle Times*. He didn't think the profiles were all that helpful; they always said the same thing. The killer would be a white male is his late twenties to early fifties. He would work an inconspicuous job, and he would be a loner. He would have had a troubled childhood, and would have had difficulties with one or both parents. Possibly he would have been physically or sexually abused. Jon needed more specific information.

He reached into his pocket, took out his cellular phone and called the city editor's desk at the *Times*. "Vicki, it's Jon Kirk. Is

Thornton there?"

"Yes," she said in a long drawn-out voice.

"Is he still pissed at me?"

"Yes," she said in the same long drawn-out voice.

"Put him on anyway," he said. "Please."

Jon told Dean Thornton about the autopsy, neglecting the part about his early exit. "He has no idea what killed her. It was a very thorough autopsy; it lasted for hours. We should have the lab data back the day after tomorrow. I found out that the police have contacted the FBI to get a psychological profile on the killer; I think I can get a copy." Pause. "That's right. It's probably worth a separate piece of its own." Pause. "I'll be in the office later today to file the story." Pause. "Don't worry, I'll finish it in time for the evening edition."

Jon hung up the phone. He should have known Karen would attend the autopsy.

＊

Liz Carlstrom sat at her desk in the newsroom working at her computer, putting the finishing touches on her story for the morning paper. The newsroom was busy, people were rushing back and forth between desks with their usual level of urgency. Telephones rang and faxes rattled. When she finished she leaned back in her chair, arched her back and stretched. Several of the men in the room noticed. Jean Viereck, the paper's gossip columnist, was discussing one of her "He Said She Said" stories with Vicki at her desk. Lizzy stood up and walked over to join them. Jean was talking about one of Ginny Wright's infamous Seattle Art Museum parties. "You should have seen Bob Leventhal last night," she said. "He was in one of his story-telling moods. He even tried to grab my ass. I got enough material for a week of columns."

"Hi, Liz," Vicki said. "What's up?"

"Would you mind telling Thornton that I finished the story? It's in the computer. Try to get him to review it as soon as you can, will you? I'd like to get out of here."

"Hot date tonight?"

"One can only hope."

"Bye, girls, I'm out of here now," Jean said. She stood up and headed toward the door.

Lizzy watched her walk away and then said, "Say, Vicki, what do you know about Jon Kirk?"

"What do you mean, what do I know about him?"

"Is he seeing anybody? I mean is he serious about anyone?"

"Jon? Are you kidding? He hasn't been serious a day in his life. Why do you ask?"

"No reason," she said.

Vicki arched an eyebrow and smiled just a hint of a smile. "Looking for another notch on your garter belt?"

"How'd you know I wear a garter belt?"

"Be gentle," Vicki said. "He's a sensitive young man."

They both laughed as Lizzy walked back to her computer.

Chapter 3

Detective Sergeants Gil Anderson and Robbie Washington were sitting in a comfortably shabby conference room in the Seattle Public Safety Building. Robbie, with his tailored suit and six-foot-three athletic frame looked more like a successful professional athlete than a city detective. Gil looked like a cop. His copy of *Penthouse* lay on a corner table, and he and Robbie were in the middle of a heated discussion about the future of the Seattle Supersonics when Detective Able walked into the room and sat down. "Well, it's official. We're now a task force," she said.

"Whatever that means," Robbie added. He was squeezing a tennis ball in his left hand as he talked. He reached over and placed a folder on top of the *Penthouse.*

"The mayor supposedly is going to announce it this afternoon," Karen continued. "We're to report to Captain McCabe in homicide."

"Well, I guess it could have been worse," said Gil. "It could have been Callaghan. Kevin loves the spotlight. You just know what it would be like with him in charge."

"A Swede, an African-American, and a woman," Robbie said, "How very Seattle, how very post-WTO politically correct."

Karen stood up and walked over to the blackboard. She divided it in half with a vertical chalk line. Then she labeled the left-hand column with VICTIMS, and the right-hand column with PERPETRA-

TOR. "Let's get to it," she said. "So what do we have so far?"

"Not much," Gil answered, "But more than we had a couple of days ago. The medical examiner's report's been completed, and as you know there were no signs of serious external trauma, only the needle tracks."

Gil picked up the report from the table and read from its contents as he spoke. "The mucous membranes in the vic's nose and mouth were intact, and samples from those areas were negative for toxic substances. Apparently she wasn't killed with a toxic inhalant. She had some mild to moderate liver damage, some lung scarring from old infections and pneumonia, and some evidence of pelvic inflammatory disease."

"Pelvic inflammatory disease?" Robbie asked.

"VD," said Gil. "According to the lab, she had antibodies to both the AIDS virus and hepatitis, neither of which were the cause of her death. The toxicology screen was positive for heroin and cocaine, probably crack, but there wasn't enough in her system to come close to killing her. There weren't any traces of poisons or other lethal agents anywhere. Doc Allison lists the cause of death as cardio-pulmonary arrest, underlying cause or causes unknown." He looked up from the report.

"That wasn't much help," Robbie noted. "It's almost exactly the same as the reports on the other two, even down to the heroin and coke."

"While he wouldn't put it in his written report," Gil continued, "Allison told me that he's fairly certain all three of the women were killed in the same way, probably with an injectable agent that spontaneously degrades over time. The injection sites would have been obscured by needle tracks from their prior intravenous drug use."

"Very clever," Karen commented.

"While he first thought that an air embolism, injecting air in the veins, might have been the cause of the deaths, he now rejects that method as being too unreliable. He currently favors the theory of an unknown drug or substance that isn't detectable by the standard toxicology screens, possibly one that breaks down into undetectable byproducts."

"The perp may have offered the women drugs, and then inject-ed them with their own help and cooperation," Karen said. "Or maybe they even did it themselves."

Then Robbie asked, "Does Doc Allison have a list of drugs that break down into undetectable byproducts? It would sure help our search if he did, especially if the drugs are hard to get."

"He's researching the subject as we speak," Gil said.

"At least we've confirmed that all three women were probably killed in the same way, whatever that is, and that the killings were probably done by the same person or persons," Karen added. She wrote under one column on the blackboard:

<u>VICTIMS</u>   PERPETRATOR
Women
Prostitutes
Drug addicts
No trauma or violence
Possibly unknown injectable
    poison

"What about the bruises?" Robbie asked. "Allison found small bruises on all three vics."

"All prostitutes have bruises," Gil answered.

Karen said, "Robbie, you told me earlier that forensics might have some information for you. What have they got?"

"The lab found a usable print on one of the vic's long, fake fin-gernails," said Robbie, "and it doesn't belong to her. The last two times the bodies were completely clean."

"Our first break," Gil said.

Robbie continued, "It was a good one and they hope to have a match by the end of the day. They also found a few carpet fibers in her hair that didn't match the carpeting in the motel, and traces of semen in both her vaginal and rectal cavities, possibly from more than one person. They're typing or doing whatever they do with the DNA.

"The crime scene was pretty clean, just like the other ones. I think the women were probably killed somewhere else and then moved to the motel rooms. There were prints all over the room and doorknobs of course. Probably none of them are useful."

Karen added the words *possibly moved after death* to the VICTIMS column. "Any new information from the other motel customers or the night clerk?"

"We located all but one of the hookers. So far it's a total bust; they're not talking."

"You'd think they'd be more cooperative," Karen said. "Any one of them could be next."

"Hookers never cooperate," Gil said. "They're all running scared."

Robbie continued, "The night clerk's name is Allan Pinkerton. He's out on parole for burglary; it's his second offense. He says Carol Williams rented the room and that she was alone, as she always was, when she picked up her key. He didn't see or hear anything. I think he's telling the truth. He has no reason to lie."

"What about the psychological profile?"

"The Captain's got it."

"Well, it's a start," Karen said. She looked at Robbie and then Gil in turn. "That's it for today. We'll meet here every morning until this thing's solved, or until they replace us."

"We'll get him," Robbie said. "Even if the fingerprint doesn't pan out, we'll get him. He'll make a mistake sooner or later."

"Lets hope it's sooner," Karen said as she left the conference room. She shut the door and walked to her office. She knew the semen could belong to anyone, and that the fingerprint could have come from anywhere. Time was working against them. The killings would go on.

Karen sat down behind her desk and rubbed her temples, and then she fumbled through her desk drawer for an aspirin bottle. She shook two tablets out of their plastic container and swallowed them dry. She called the Captain and asked if she could pick up the FBI psychological profile.

*

Captain Bill McCabe's office looked like a Seattle Mariner's retail outlet shop. He had fifteen years of team-autographed base-balls on shelves to the right of his desk and a Ken Griffy Jr. jersey on the wall to his left. He kept his prize, the last baseball Randy Johnson pitched as a Mariner, in front of him to remind him of bet-ter days. Trading Randy Johnson had been a dumb idea. You can bet the Yankees would never have traded Randy. They let him get away once; they'd never do it again. McCabe was sitting in his chair look-ing at that baseball when Karen entered the room.

"Hi, Karen."

Karen walked in and closed the door behind her.

"Have a seat," he said. "Here's the first draft of the profile." He tossed it on the front of his desk. "They'll update it as they get more information."

"You mean after he kills again, don't you?" Karen picked up the folder.

"Yeah," he said, "After he kills again. Unfortunately, that's the way it works."

Karen looked through the contents. "Anything useful in here?" she asked.

"Not really, but you get to talk about it anyway. The mayor's holding a press conference at the DA's office this afternoon at five o'clock. He wants you up front and center. TV people will be there."

"That sounds like him," she said. "Prime time."

"Of course," he answered. "You know the mayor, and you know the drill." He ran his fingers through his thick white hair. "I'll intro-duce you and then you'll tell them that you're actively investigating several leads. Tell them your task force is working on a psychologi-cal profile. Don't let them know that the FBI prepared it for you unless they ask."

"You want me to imply that it came from the department?"

"Of course not. Just don't say anything about it at all. Let them draw their own conclusions."

Karen looked at him for a moment and then said, "Right. Make the mayor proud and all that.

"What about the Q and A?"

"Just use your head. We aren't going to answer questions about the details of an ongoing investigation. After it's over, leak the contents of the profile to the press so that our perp can read about it in the morning paper. If it's accurate maybe he'll get a little nervous and make a mistake."

"Let's hope so," she said. "We need a little help."

"Don't worry about it, Karen" he said. "You'll find the perp." McCabe tried to give her a confidence-building smile.

Karen looked at the folder in her hand marked Confidential, FBI Psychological Profile. She remembered when the FBI had recruited her after she'd finished her criminology degree at the University of Virginia. She'd been flattered, but she hadn't wanted to spend her life moving from duty station to duty station, especially on the East Coast. She loved the Northwest, and after four years away from the high mountains and Puget Sound, she couldn't imagine living anywhere else. She'd returned to Seattle and joined the SPD.

She removed and scanned the single-page document inside the folder. "It looks like whoever wrote this is intrigued by the lack of a cause of death," she said. "They want us to send some tissue samples to their lab for further analysis."

"The Feds always think their lab's better than ours," McCabe answered. "Who knows, maybe it is."

"They think the killer works in a technical or medical job, and they say he's smart, probably with an IQ of at least 130, maybe higher."

"We're up against a genius. Great. Just what we need." Captain McCabe was talking to the baseball sitting in front of him. He leaned forward and looked up at Karen. "These next few weeks aren't going to be easy, you know. We're all going to feel a lot of pressure."

"I already feel a lot of pressure," she said.

"Good! It'll give you an edge." He paused a moment before adding, "And Karen, I don't have to tell you to be careful with the press. They'll take advantage of you if you let them, especially that friend of yours from the *Times*."

"I'll be careful," she promised.

"Good luck."

Karen got up and left the room. She went back to the task force conference room and added to the list on the blackboard:

VICTIMS	PERPETRATOR
Women	Male (20 - 50 years old)
Prostitutes	Smart, maybe genius
Drug addicts	Technical or medical job
No trauma or violence	White
Possibly unknown injectable poison	Loner
Possibly moved after death	

✳

The press gathered, the mayor introduced McCabe, McCabe introduced Karen and Karen went through her routine. The conference didn't take long because there really wasn't much to say. Everybody who was anybody in the reporting business was there. The most recent killing firmly established that Seattle was dealing with another serial killer. The women had been posed identically, and they were most probably killed by a single person. The causes of the deaths would not be released at this time. The task force had started its work and was actively tracking down any and all leads. A psychological profile of the killer had been constructed by the FBI.

Jon Kirk was watching Karen's performance from the second

row. The lights were bright and the room was hot. She was getting grilled as if she were a piece of meat slowly turning on a spit over an open fire. The TV reporters did most of the grilling. They asked leading questions designed to make themselves look clever on the evening news. Jon thought TV reporters were a bunch of prima donna assholes. He approached Karen when it was over.

"That looked like fun," he said.

"Not really," she answered. She started to walk away.

Jon walked with her. "I thought you did a good job."

"Tell it to that bitch from KING TV." Karen squished up her face and whined in a high, mocking voice, "This killer's terrorizing our city. We can't waste any time. Do you feel comfortable directing this important task force? How much experience do you have with this sort of thing?" She made a growling noise in the back of her throat. "I should have punched her out."

"Yeah, that question was out of bounds."

"You bet it was, and it'll be on the evening news." She ran her fingers through her hair, combing a few errant strands away from her face.

"Forget it," he said. "You handled it well." Jon looked around the rapidly emptying room. The sound crew was starting to pack up their equipment. "Listen, why don't we go somewhere for a drink or something?" Karen didn't answer. She stopped, looked at him for a second and raised an eyebrow. "How about the Blue Moon," Jon said. "I'll buy."

"How about the Olympic?"

"The Olympic Hotel?"

"Why not?" she asked. "Nervous about being there alone with me again?" She smiled a sly smile. "I don't bite."

Jon said, "Actually, as I remember it, you do bite; but I'm not nervous." He smiled back at her. "I'll get my car and pick you up at the front door."

Jon left the room, picked up his car and drove to the front of the Public Safety Building. It was one of those blustery evenings that drove Seattle's more affluent residents to Palm Springs for the winter. Mist hung on the night wind, and visibility was reduced to less than a block. It was a made-to-order bad hair day.

Karen didn't seem to notice the weather, even though she didn't have a raincoat. She walked to Jon's car, climbed inside, and fastened her seatbelt. Jon drove north on Fourth Avenue.

"Windy outside, isn't it?" he said.

"Sure is," she answered.

They drove on in silence.

"You handled yourself well up there on the podium," Jon said after awhile. "You looked really comfortable, Seattle's best dressed cop."

"I'm glad you thought so," Karen said.

"No, really, you did."

"I sure didn't feel comfortable. This suit isn't my style. It makes me feel stiff." Karen was wearing a blue suit and a white blouse with a designer scarf tied around her neck. Her skirt was knee length and she wore medium heels. "Excuse me a minute," she said.

Karen wiggled out of her jacket and threw it in the back seat. Then she took off her scarf and opened her blouse at the neck. Finally she kicked off her shoes, slid down in the seat, reached up under her skirt, and pulled off her pantyhose. "I hate nylons," she muttered. She balled up her pantyhose and tossed them into the back seat with her jacket. She put her feet back in her shoes.

Jon almost ran into the car in front of him. He looked at her with his mouth open.

"What?" she asked. "It's not as if you haven't seen my legs before."

"Right," he said, attempting to focus on his driving.

Jon drove to the University Street entrance of the hotel. He gave his keys to the valet and escorted Karen from the car into the lobby. She had retrieved her jacked and scarf, but not her pantyhose. The hotel had a large, ornate lobby with a small bar tucked in behind its elegant Georgian Room restaurant. They sat down at one of the dimly lit tables.

Karen spoke first, "I suppose you still want that psyche profile so you can beat your TV competition to the punch." McCabe had suggested that she leak it to the press but she wanted Jon to work for it.

"Come on, Karen," Jon protested. "We're not here just for the story."

"So you don't care whether I give you the profile or not?" she asked.

"Of course I want the psychological profile, but that's not the only thing I want." He looked into her eyes. "You mean a lot to me."

"So you said the last time we were here. And you said it in the cafeteria the other day."

Jon started to fidget in his seat. "You know," he said, "Sometimes I don't understand why you say the things you say."

"There's a lot you don't understand," she answered.

"And what do you mean by that?"

"Well, for starters, we're two different people. I'm a morning person and you'd sleep in every day of the week if you could. I'm a runner and your idea of exercise involves lifting a beer bottle from the table to your mouth. I'm a vegetarian; you're a carnivore. I have strong emotions. . . . "

"You have a temper," Jon interrupted.

Karen paused. "When I say I love you, I mean it."

They sat there in silence, looking at each other. A waiter came over and took their drink orders.

After what seemed like a long time Jon finally said, "Listen Karen, we started off all wrong last time. I. . . ."

"Forget it," she said. "Let's change the subject. I brought the profile with me. I can't give it to you, but I can tell you what's in it." Karen removed the FBI folder from her briefcase, opened it, and held up a single sheet of paper. Jon stared at the back of the document.

"You have to understand that this is a work in progress," she said. "A psychological profile's only a guide and it's never finished.

But they have proven to be helpful, particularly with serial killers."

"I understand."

Karen read from the paper, "According to this we're dealing with a single perpetrator, a male, probably white, probably between the ages of twenty and fifty."

"And he's a loner who was abused by his step-parents," Jon added. "They always say the same thing. Is there anything specific in there?"

"He's a technical person," Karen continued, "And he probably works around chemicals or drugs. He's meticulous and deliberate. He plans his murders in great detail. And he's smart, very smart. He's careful and he won't make many mistakes."

"I assume I can't quote you on this," Jon said.

"Please quote a usually reliable source in the Seattle Police Department."

Karen started to say something else when her cell phone rang. It was Detective Sergeant Washington. "We got an ID on the fingerprint," he said. "It belongs to Dr. George Holyoke, a professor at the Medical School. He lives in the Laurelhurst District, 4701 Northeast 39th Street. He fits the profile. We went over to talk to him, but we missed him. We have someone watching the house."

"I'll meet you at the station," Karen said. "Wait, I forgot, I don't have my car. Is there someone nearby who can pick me up? I'll be at the University Street entrance to the Olympic Hotel." She looked over at Jon, rolled her eyes and shrugged. Then she spoke into the phone again. "OK, thanks."

Karen broke the connection. "Something's come up and I have to go," she said to Jon.

"You got a break in the case?" he asked.

"I can't talk now. We'll talk later." She paused for a moment. "I'll call you." The look on her face was difficult to interpret. Karen stood up and walked to the door to catch her ride. She left Jon alone with his thoughts.

Chapter 4

Jon woke up to the rain. The sound on his windows reminded him of the previous night. He was thinking about Karen, or maybe he'd been dreaming. He wasn't sure. In any case she seemed to have worked her way into his head, into his house, and back into his bedroom. He wasn't sure what to think about that. Leon, his basset hound, was still sleeping on the foot of his bed. He moved his tail when he felt Jon stir.

Jon got up, nudged his dog off the bed, dressed, checked his e-mail, and then took Leon out for his morning walk. Once around the block was enough for Leon. After they finished Jon and Leon climbed into his Explorer and drove off for breakfast.

Jon headed south on McGilvra and then west on Madison to the nearest McDonalds. Jon pulled up to the microphone in the drive-through lane and asked for an Egg McMuffin. Leon punctuated the request with a woof. "Hi, Leon," a voice said over the intercom. Leon was a regular customer. Jon pulled up to the pickup window. When an unwrapped Egg McMuffin appeared in an outstretched hand, Leon extended his long neck from the backseat window and delicately snatched it away. He gulped it down with a smack. Then Jon drove to Starbucks, where he ordered a double espresso for himself. He was on his way back to his house to drop Leon off when his cell phone rang.

"Jon, it's Lizzy. That was a nice piece in this morning's paper on the psych profile. Thornton likes it."

"Thanks, Lizard, and I liked your piece. You handled the conversation with the victim's mother very well. Tastefully done." Leon started scratching himself behind his ear in the back seat. "But you didn't call me for that, did you? What's up?"

"I got a copy of the Carol Williams autopsy report," she said. "I thought you'd want to see it so I faxed it to you at the office. It's almost identical to the other two. Allison couldn't find a cause of death."

"Thanks," he said. "I talked to Doc Allison yesterday and he told me as much. He thinks the women were killed with some sort of injection, some sort of poison that leaves no trace. There was no evidence of a fight, no violence. Someone just quietly put them to sleep, a regular sandman."

"Hey, that's good," she said. "The Seattle Sandman. Thornton'll love it."

"It isn't bad, is it," Jon agreed. "OK, Liz, I'll use it. Now why did you really call?"

"Well," she paused, "I was talking with a friend on the police force last night. He gave me some interesting information."

"How interesting?" Jon asked.

"Very interesting. He told me they found a fingerprint on Carol Williams' body."

"Really?"

"Yeah, and there's more. They identified the print. It belongs to a professor at the University of Washington, a Dr. Holyoke. He works in the medical school. The police went over to his house last night but he wasn't there. They've started a search."

"You're sure?"

"Of course I'm sure. I take good care of my sources."

"What'd you do to get him to talk?"

"I, ah, put him in an interesting position. I'd be willing to come over and show you how it's done if you really want to know. Maybe tonight?"

"Maybe. Let's think about it."

"Whatever you say, Jon."

"OK . . . ah . . . listen, I think I'll head over to the med school and check out this guy Holyoke. I probably won't make it in to the office this morning. Let's talk later."

"OK, Jon."

"Bye, Liz."

"Bye, Jon."

Jon dropped Leon off and then headed out toward the med school. He called Karen using his speed dial function to reach her on her direct line.

"Seattle Police Department, Detective Able."

"Karen."

"Jon, what a pleasant surprise."

"I hope you don't mind me calling you at your office."

"Not at all."

"I wanted to tell you that I woke up thinking about you this morning," he said. "I couldn't get you out of my head."

"Really," she said. "Now why do you suppose that happened?"

"I wish I knew."

"There may be hope for us yet," she said. "Tell me about it."

"I'd love to, but I don't have time right now. Right now I need a favor."

She didn't respond right away and then said, "You woke up thinking about me and now you need a favor."

"That's right. Tell me, what do you know about Dr. George Holyoke?"

"Holyoke! How'd you find out about him?"

"I can't reveal my source, but. . . ."

"Goddamn it, Jon."

Click. The phone went dead.

Jon pulled the phone away from his ear and looked at it. He arched his eyebrows and slowly shook his head, then he dialed the *Times*. Vicki answered the phone on the first ring and passed him on to Thornton. He told his editor about the autopsy report and about Lizzy's information from the police department. He said he was planning to spend the morning at the medical school, and that he and Lizzy would file their takes on the Holyoke story in time for the afternoon edition. With luck, the television broadcasters would read about it in the evening paper.

"Lizzy must have a great source," Thornton said. "I hope she keeps him happy."

"She told me she had it under control," Jon replied.

"Don't forget the deadline. I'll see you this afternoon." Thornton hung up the phone.

Jon drove on to the medical school.

*

The University of Washington Medical Center is the largest building in Seattle. It measures over a quarter-mile long, and its various wings rise between nine and twenty-eight stories high. There are three floors below ground, and several additional sub-basements in some sections. The building stands as a monument to ex-senator Warren G. Magnison and his particular brand of pork-barrel politics. Built in unplanned segments as grants and other federal funds became available over a period of three decades, the building is a mish-mash of architectural and construction styles. It houses a vast warren of hallways and dead-end corridors leading to uncounted classrooms, offices, hospital beds and laboratories. It is difficult, and sometimes impossible, to walk from one end of the building to the other on a single floor. Jon Kirk was hopelessly lost.

Jon had called the medical school dean's office and been told that the division of news and information services would handle all questions regarding Dr. Holyoke. It had soon became clear that he had not been the first to ask about Holyoke that morning. He'd made an appointment to meet Kay Masters, the director, in her office on the third floor of the "C" wing. He couldn't find the office, he couldn't find the "C" wing and he wasn't sure about the third floor.

When Jon reluctantly asked directions from a woman in a white coat he was told that the third floor was really on the first floor, and that the first floor was two floors underground. The "C" wing was not between the "B" and "D" wings, but was off by itself. She led him to the door labeled News and Information Services and he realized that he'd walked by it at least three times. He went inside and a secretary escorted him to an inner office.

"Hello, Mr. Kirk, I'm Kay Masters, Director of Health Sciences News and Information Services. I understand you're a reporter with the *Times*. The Dean told me you were coming."

Jon had never been to the medical school press services center before. The complex of offices was big, as big as the newsroom at *The Seattle Times*. The medical school obviously took their interactions with the press very seriously.

"Nice to meet you, Ms. Masters."

"Please follow me," she said.

Kay Masters led Jon to a small conference room. She was a woman in her late forties with a no-nonsense demeanor and dressed in a no-nonsense business suit.

"You want to talk to us about Dr. Holyoke," she said after they were seated at a conference table.

"That's correct," Jon answered. "I haven't been able to reach him. You don't happen to know where he is, do you?"

"I'll tell you the same thing that we told the police earlier," she said. "Dr. Holyoke is on a three-month research sabbatical. He's due back here any day now. As a matter of fact, he's overdue. We really don't know much more than that." She smiled a demure smile. Very professional.

"Then I'd like to talk to some of his associates, if you don't mind," Jon said. "I need to gather some background material for a story."

"Oh, I'm afraid we couldn't recommend that, Mr. Kirk. As a matter of fact, we would prefer that all press contacts with our faculty and staff go through our offices. We want to minimize the dissemination of inaccurate information. You understand."

"Ah, I'm not sure that I do." Jon shifted in his seat.

"Well then, let me explain. The Dean has instructed all of our faculty and staff to refer all inquiries from the press regarding this matter directly to me."

"So we play by your rules or not at all. Is that it?" Jon asked.

"They're not my rules, Mr. Kirk. They're the Dean's rules. I'm just a university employee doing my job. If it were up to me I'd let you have free access to anyone you wanted to talk to."

"I'm sure you would." Jon said. It was his turn to smile a false smile. "What can you tell me about Dr. Holyoke?"

"Dr. Holyoke teaches anatomy," she said. "He's been with us for twenty-one years and he's one of our best professors. He's board certified in pathology, and is the chairman of our Anatomy Department. His special area of expertise is neuro-anatomy. He came to us from Duke University as an instructor and he worked his way up to the top of our academic ladder in only seven years."

"Seven years? That's quite an accomplishment. How'd he do that?" Jon asked.

"By publishing over two hundred research papers in scientific journals," she answered. "That's an average of ten per year, or a little less than one research publication per month."

"That's remarkable."

"It's awfully good, but it's not remarkable," she said. "All of our big producers average approximately one research paper per month. It's what we do."

"That's a lot of research."

"That's how we survive. The state of Washington pays less than ten percent of our costs. We're a state school in name only. Research grants and income from the clinical practice of medicine pay the rest of the bills."

"And the publications?"

"We need publications to keep the research funding coming

our way."

"That's interesting. I had no idea that that's the way it works." Jon sat back in his chair. "What kind of research does Holyoke do?"

"Primarily pain research," she answered, "Neuro-pathways and that sort of thing. He's been involved in a number of projects over the years, but the physiological mechanisms related to pain and its control are his primary interests. He was instrumental in organizing and starting our clinical pain center."

"How do you do pain research?" Jon asked. "It sounds, uh, painful."

That drew another patronizing smile. "They use animals, of course. He's investigating a new class of pain control agents, ones that won't depress the central nervous system. His research holds great potential.

"But before I get off track, I want to be sure to mention that Dr. Holyoke's an excellent teacher. He teaches gross anatomy and human dissection to our first-year medical students. He's won the Outstanding Teacher Award six times in the last twenty years, more times than any other faculty member."

"It sounds like he walks on water," Jon said.

"Well, not quite, Mr. Kirk. His contributions to medical science, medical education, and our school have, however, been significant. Neither the Dean, nor I, can imagine his involvement with these prostitute murders in any way. He's been an exemplary faculty member."

Jon heard a faint rattling sound on the windows. It was windy and the rain had started again. He hoped he hadn't left his windows open. "What about his family?" he asked.

"He's not married, and as far as we know, he lives alone. I don't think he's ever been married. He doesn't often attend university social functions. I don't think he's even a member of the faculty club."

Jon tapped his finger on the table. "Any hobbies or other outside activities or interests?"

"We don't know much about his private life," she said. "It's really none of our business." She paused, and then added, "One thing though, he's a major collector of primitive art. His collection of art and artifacts from Brazil is supposed to be world class. I don't know much about it, but his donations to the Burke Museum of Primitive Art here on campus have been spectacular.

"Is there anything else, Mr. Kirk?" She glanced at her watch.

"You said you don't have any idea where he went on his sabbatical?"

"We have no idea where he is."

"OK, I don't want to take up any more of your valuable time, Ms. Masters, but I wonder," Jon said, "have any other reporters talked to you about Professor Holyoke or the murders?"

"No, you're the only one. As I said, all contacts with the press are routed through my office, so I can tell you with certainty that no other reporters have contacted us regarding this subject. It's another advantage of our system."

"Well then," he said, "Thank you for your time."

"Please call anytime, Mr. Kirk. It's been a pleasure to meet you." She gave him her card.

They both stood up and Masters escorted Jon out of the office complex. As soon as he was out of sight Jon removed his cell phone from his pocket, and punched a speed dial number.

"Lizzy, you wouldn't believe this place. It's huge. They employ more people to deal with us than we have reporters. It's unbelievable."

"I've heard about it," she said. "They have to protect their image, feeding at the public money trough and all."

"Did you finish your draft of the Holyoke story? So far we've been the only ones to contact the medical school, other than the police."

"It's finished and filed, Thornton loves an exclusive."

"Well I've got more," Jon said. "Holyoke's worked here twenty-one years. That would make him in his late forties or more probably, in his early fifties, the upper end of our psychological profile. He obviously works in a technical job, and he's smart. The woman I spoke with here described him as a loner who doesn't participate in social activities. He fits the profile of our Sandman like a glove."

"I'll add it to my story," she said. "Thornton'll love the tie-in with the psych profile, but you know him. He'll want the legal department to look at it before we print it."

"Your story?" Jon said. "I spent all morning getting this stuff. It's our story. And since I'm the one who came up the Sandman name, I'll put that in my story."

"Fine," she said, "It's our story; we're partners. Just remember that when you file your story. From now on we give each other credit where it counts, in the byline, OK?"

"Whatever. Now I need some help with something else. I need to talk to one of Holyoke's associates. Could you get on line and find a listing of Holyoke's research papers? Print out all the stuff he wrote in the last three years. I'm interested in the names of his co-investigators. I'll talk to any of them."

"I'm way ahead of you," she said. "I have the articles right here. Just a minute. . . . OK, he wrote a lot of stuff and worked with a lot of people. All of these research papers have a lot of people listed as co-authors."

"Probably so that they can all get publication credit and get promoted," Jon interrupted. "I get the feeling that publish-or-perish isn't just a game around here. Are there any names that stand out?"

"I see several recurring names listed on these papers, but Janet Saunders' name appears more than most. It looks like she's a professor in Holyoke's department. Do you need any more?"

"Thanks, Liz, that's all I need for now. I'll look at the other names later."

"I'll make a list. Just don't forget where you got it."

"No problem."

Jon broke the connection. Then he called the medical school information operator. He was informed that Dr. Saunders' office was in the NN wing of the health sciences building, room 110 in the Anatomy Department. Jon began his search for the NN wing.

✳

The Anatomy Department was on the first floor in the old part of the medical center, two floors below ground. It was dark and the halls needed painting. Steam pipes, hot- and cold-water pipes, and assorted conduits ran openly along the ceiling. There was a faint but penetrating smell of formaldehyde in the air. He knocked on Dr. Saunders' open door and walked inside.

The office was small, no more than eight feet by ten feet, and it was cluttered. Janet Saunders was sitting at her desk smoking a cigarette. She looked to be a woman in her mid fifties.

"Dr. Saunders, my name's Jon Kirk. I'm a reporter for the *Times.* I hope you don't mind my barging in on you unannounced like this. I'd like to talk to you for a moment if you have the time."

"I don't mind at all. It's nice to meet you, Mr. Kirk."

There was a 'No Smoking' sign pinned to the wall above her desk. She noticed Jon look at it, then at her cigarette. "What can they do, I have tenure." She snuffed her cigarette out in an overflowing ashtray.

Jon walked farther into the room. "I need some information from your associate, Dr. Holyoke. Do you know where he is?"

"What a coincidence, that's just what the police asked me this morning. I have no idea where he is. I wish I did. I'd tell him to get his ass back here. The little prick was due back last week and I've had to cover his classes for him while he's gone." Dr. Saunders motioned for Jon to sit in a chair.

Jon sat down. "You know him well?"

"I know him very well."

"The police want to talk to him about the prostitute murders."

"You don't say."

Jon paused for a moment and then said, "Do you think he's the kind of person who'd get involved with that sort of thing?"

"Get involved? I'm not sure I know what you mean, and the police certainly weren't forthcoming. But I can put two and two together, and to answer your question, I wouldn't think so," she said. "His students would tell you he's a little sadist, but serial murder seems a bit far-fetched."

"I thought his students loved him," Jon said. "That's what Kay Masters told me."

"I'll bet Kay Masters doesn't know you're down here." Saunders stared at Jon for a minute and then continued, "George is an esteemed scientist. He's also an esteemed teacher. He teaches gross anatomy to first-year medical students, and his classes have become somewhat of a right of passage into our esteemed profession." She paused for a moment. "The gross anatomy class is the first prolonged exposure to death and the dead for almost all of them. God knows they'll see a lot more of it before they're through. George teaches them how to deal with it."

"I'm not sure I understand," Jon said.

Saunders removed a cigarette from her pocket and started to fondle it. She didn't light it. "George teaches his students how to disassociate their emotions from their future work. He teaches them how to be professionals. He does it by providing a prolonged, incremental exposure to all parts of the human body."

"The dead human body, I assume," Jon interjected.

"The Dean wouldn't have it any other way," she said. She lit the cigarette and exhaled a blue cloud over her shoulder.

"The anatomy department provides one cadaver for every six students at the beginning of the year. Each student spends four hours a day, three days per week, for two full academic quarters becoming intimately familiar with every cubic centimeter of his or her cadaver. George makes certain of that. The students dissect them as a team, one organ system at a time, until there's virtually nothing left. As the human form disappears, so does its humanity. Emotions and flesh are segregated. The student becomes desensitized." She took another deep drag from her cigarette. "George is the master of his art. You ought to catch his act."

"No thanks," Jon said. "I have a thing about blood and dead

bodies."

"Whatever," she replied. "Most students arrive here with quite unrealistic expectations about the medical profession, you know."

"In what way?"

"Many plan to save humanity and all that. How naive! It is our job to take these idealistic young adults and turn them into the greedy, self-serving, money-grubbing physicians that they'll soon become. After we beat them down, we repackage them in our own image. We've been fine-tuning our medical education system for the past hundred years, and we're good at it. You really should see George work. He is one of our best."

The smoke and formaldehyde were giving Jon a headache. Saunders' irritating, raspy voice didn't help either. "Could you tell me a little about your research?"

"My research or his research?"

"I thought you worked together."

"Sometimes, not always."

"Kay Masters told me he's sort of an expert on pain. Tell me about his pain research."

"Cats," she said. "He uses cats."

"Cats?" he questioned. "What does he do with cats?"

"Believe me, you don't want to know."

"Do you work on the cats?"

"No. I worked with him on several research projects in the past, and I helped him bring in a lot of grant money. That's why the Dean puts up with me and leaves me alone. But I don't do cats."

Jon had more questions, but he needed fresh air. He needed it right away. He looked at his watch.

"Thank you very much, Dr. Saunders. You've been very helpful. I'm running a little behind, but I'd like to talk to you again in the future if you don't mind. Here's my card. If you hear from Holyoke, I'd appreciate a call."

"Sure, you and those two guys from the Seattle police department. I assume you can find your way out," she said.

"No problem."

Jon turned to leave and hurriedly walked down the hall in the wrong direction. Janet Saunders watched him until he was out of sight.

Chapter 5

John sat behind the wheel of his Explorer. He was in the medical school parking lot across from the emergency room entrance. He had finished his call to Lizzy to update her on the Holyoke business and he was just sitting there, thinking, watching the rain wash over his windshield. The faint smell of formaldehyde had seeped into his clothes. The glass started to fog so he opened a window to clear the air. He fished around in the glove compartment for some aspirin but all he found was an empty plastic bottle.

He finally started his engine and drove back through light afternoon traffic to the *Times* building. By the time he got there Lizzy had filed her article. Jon quickly wrote and filed his. He used The Sandman label. The evening edition would be on the street in less than an hour and the television stations still hadn't a clue about the Holyoke story. It was satisfying to beat the electronic media for a change. He made a mental note to watch the eleven o'clock news to see if they gave the *Times* credit, and to see whether or not they picked up on The Sandman label.

The noise and controlled chaos of the newsroom slowly ebbed as Jon sat at his desk well into the evening. Reporters and staff left the building as they finished their work for the day. By nine o'clock the quiet, nearly empty room was drained of its normal vitality. Jon had caught up on a backlog of e-mail and was working on a companion piece about Holyoke for the morning paper when the direct line on his telephone rang. When he answered he heard a mechanical-sounding voice. It spoke without inflection.

"Is this Jon Kirk?"

"Yes."

"The reporter Jon Kirk?"

"Yes, who's this?"

"I'm The Sandman."

Jon sat up in his chair. *A crank call,* he thought. It had to be, but why the disguised mechanical voice? His heart started to race.

"Jon, are you there? I rather like that name. The Sandman, I mean."

His throat went dry and the palms of his hands started to sweat. "What do you want?" he asked. He was breathing too fast.

"I just wanted to let you know that I admire your work. I'm a fan."

"What do you mean?" Jon fumbled around with his tape recorder. He slapped in a tape and turned it on. It was already attached to the phone.

"I like the way you write. Your articles seem to have captured the essence of my work. They might even help explain to the world what I'm trying to do."

"What *are* you trying to do?" Jon asked.

"Come on, Jon, I'm The Sandman." The phone went dead.

Jon's hands were shaking when he hung up the phone. He felt the adrenaline pumping in his veins. He pushed the rewind button and then the play button on the recorder. A mechanical voice repeated, *'The essence of my work. They might even help explain to the world what I'm trying to do. What are you trying to do? Come on, Jon. I'm The Sandman.'*

Jon listened again, then he switched off the recorder. He pushed star-six-nine on his telephone, the code to retrieve the number of the last caller. The LCD read PAY PHONE. "Damn." Then he called Karen's direct line at the Police Department.

"Seattle Police Department, Detective Able speaking."

"Karen, it's me."

Click.

"Damn!"

He called her again. The phone rang five times and then switched to the SPD voice mail system. He left a message on her voice mail. "Karen, it's Jon. I just got a call from a person who identified himself as The Sandman. He must have read my article in the evening paper. It could have been a crank. I don't know. The call was made from a pay phone. I recorded part of the call. Call me. I am not making this up." He hung up the phone.

Jon sat there until his hands stopped shaking. He stared at his computer screen; there was no point trying to write. After The Sandman's phone call he couldn't get his mind back into his article. Was it Holyoke; was he The Sandman? Jon looked around at the familiar faces of the few other reporters who were still there in the room with him. He sat at his desk for a while longer and then picked up his telephone. He dialed Lizzy's home number. She answered after several rings.

"Hello?"

"Liz?"

"Yes." There was a little bit of a giggle in her voice.

"It's Jon."

"Oh. Hi, Jon, what a surprise." He thought he could hear someone in the background, maybe some stifled laughing.

"I'm sorry to bother you this late after work," he said. "Are you busy?"

"Not at the moment," she answered. More giggling.

"You're sure."

"Positive."

"Then I need to talk to you about something. What are you doing later tonight?"

"Nothing that can't be changed," she said. "Why? What's up?"

"I'll tell you about it when I get there. Is twenty minutes OK?"

"Give me thirty."

"Thanks, Liz. "I'll see you in half an hour." Jon hung up the telephone. Then he turned off his computer and left the office.

Jon walked to his car. The night air smelled clean. The smell of formaldehyde was gone. The light from his headlights glistened off the wet pavement as the Seattle winter mist turned to rain. It took him only fifteen minutes to drive the short distance from his office to Lizzy's apartment in the Fremont District. The apartment building was a fourplex and Lizzy lived on the second floor.

The rain was really coming down now. Jon parked his Explorer on the street and jogged up the stairs to the front door. He rang the buzzer under Lizzy's name. "You're early," she said through the speaker. She admitted him to the front hallway.

A tall man, an athlete type, was leaving Lizzy's apartment just as Jon stepped into the hallway. They passed each other without speaking. Lizzy stood in her open doorway and greeted him.

"Jon," she said, "you're all wet. I'll get you a towel." Jon walked into the cozy, warm apartment and Lizzy shut the door. "Sit down on the couch. Don't worry about the furniture, it's rented. I'll be back in a minute." Lizzy put her hand on his shoulder and then ran it down the length of his arm before she turned and walked out of the room. She was wearing blue jeans and a sweatshirt with the words Seattle Seahawks written across the front. She was barefoot.

Lizzy returned with the towel. "Sit still while I dry you off." She fluffed his hair with the towel, and then patted his shirt. "It's miserable outside," she said. "You should have worn a coat."

"I'm OK," he said.

She finished drying his hair; then she combed it back in place with her fingers.

"If you want to change out of that wet shirt, I have a sweatshirt in my bedroom that should fit."

"No thanks, Liz. I'm not that wet."

"Are you sure?"

"I'm positive."

"OK, if you're sure." She tossed the towel in a chair, walked around to the front of the couch and then curled up on the end opposite from Jon. "So tell me," she said, "What's so mysterious that you couldn't talk about it over the phone?"

"I got a phone call from The Sandman, or at least from a guy who called himself The Sandman."

"You're kidding!" Her eyes sparked. She sat up in her seat.

"I wish I were," he said. "I got most of it on tape. I'll play it for you tomorrow."

"What'd he say?"

"He said he liked The Sandman label. He likes my work. He said something about explaining to the world what he's trying to do."

"I wonder what he thinks of my work," she said. "Do you think he's for real?"

"Probably not, at least I hope not. But it kind of shook me up anyway."

"I'll bet it did," she said. "Maybe it was Dr. Holyoke."

"Now there's a pleasant thought." Jon shivered.

She studied him for a moment and then said, "You look like you could use a drink. Let me get you something. How about some wine, or something else?"

"Thanks Liz, but I don't think so. Not tonight."

"At least let me help you relax." She stood up and walked around the couch until she was behind him. Then she placed her hands on his shoulders and with her thumbs began to knead the tense muscles of his upper back. She continued talking. "It really could have been Holyoke, you know."

"I suppose, but there's really no way to tell. Umm, that feels good." Jon arched his back a little. Then he continued. "He used some kind of a mechanical device to disguise his voice, and he made the call from a pay phone."

Liz massaged his temples and then combed his wavy hair with her fingers.

Jon felt the tension drain out of his body. He pushed his head against her fingers as her fingernails scratched against his scalp. When she knotted her fingers in his thick hair and gently pulled, a pleasant warmth seeped into and over him. He closed his eyes.

"Jon, you still there?"

"I'm here," he said. "You're really good at this."

"I know." She smiled to herself.

"Holyoke's a bit of an enigma," Jon said. "He doesn't socialize much with the people over at the med school, and they really don't know much about him outside of his work."

"That fits the psych profile." She continued to work the muscles of his neck.

"I wish we knew more about him. If I'm going to tell his story, I need to get inside his head."

Lizzy shook him gently by the shoulders. "Who's going to tell his story?"

"I mean, we. We need to get into his head if we're going to tell his story." Lizzy's hands went back to work. "At any rate, we need to get more information," he said.

"Listen, sometimes you'll write the story, sometimes I'll write it, and sometimes we'll write it together, but we share the credit, remember? That was the deal." Lizzy smoothed his shirt over his shoulders and fluffed his hair again. "How was that?"

"Awesome. You have a great touch."

She put her lips close to his ear and said, "It was only a sample." Then she smoothed his shirt one more time and backed away.

Jon turned around and smiled. He stood up and walked over to the front window. He looked outside. "It's still raining out there," he said. "There's no moon." He was talking more or less to himself. Finally he turned around to face Liz. "Listen, I was working on a sidebar article for the morning edition when I called. I wasn't getting anywhere, and then I had this wild idea. Are you up for a little adventure?"

"Always," she purred.

"Then how about a little breaking and entering?"

"What? Are you kidding?" She arched her eyebrows.

"Listen, the cops are looking all over the city for Holyoke, right? They can't find him. They don't know where he is and we don't know where he is, but we sure as hell know where he isn't. He isn't at his home. They already checked that out." Lizzy just stared at him. "He can't be there. He's much too smart for that."

"So," she said.

"So," he answered.

"So we break in to his house?"

"Sure. Why not? Let's find out who this guy really is. Go get your flashlight."

Lizzy smiled as she said, "This is going to be fun."

✳

The rain outside had again turned to mist. They got into Jon's car, drove down Ralston Street and then cut through the University on their way to Holyoke's house in the Laurelhurst District. He lived in a 1920s vintage, brick, Mediterranean-style home. Jon drove his Explorer around the block twice and checked out the neighborhood. Other than a few parked cars, the street appeared empty.

"Do you see anybody?" he asked.

"No," she answered. "It looks OK. But I hope the police aren't staking out the place. We wouldn't see them if they were."

"They're not going to waste their time and people waiting for him here," he said. "They know he's too smart to come back home after he's murdered three women."

Jon slowly drove into Holyoke's driveway and turned off the engine in front of the garage; it was detached from the house and located near the back of the lot. He and Lizzy sat for a moment and looked around the back yard through the car windows. The car doors were still locked. Low-hanging clouds completely obscured the moon. Their car was barely visible from the street, and then only from one narrow angle of view. It was already late, and there were only a few lights on in the neighborhood. The house and yard seemed quiet.

They got out of the car.

Lizzy stopped still. "Did you hear something?" she whispered.

"Shhh," Jon whispered back. He paused for a moment to listen. "I don't hear anything. There's nothing there. Let's go."

They quietly walked together up the brick steps from the driveway to the back porch, looking around to make sure no one was watching them. Holyoke's house was dark. They couldn't see anything from the back door.

"What do we do now?" Lizzy asked in a hushed voice.

"Ring the back doorbell."

"Are you kidding?" she said, too loudly.

"Shhh."

"Are you kidding?" she whispered.

"Why not?"

She looked at him for a moment and then said, "What the hell." She rang the doorbell.

They were both poised and ready to sprint off the porch, but nothing happened. There was no movement. There were no lights. There was no answer. The house was still.

She rang it again; this time she pushed it twice. "There's nobody home," she whispered. "Are you going to pick the lock?"

"Not exactly." Jon turned his back to the door and in one quick movement smashed one of the glass panes with his elbow.

"Jesus, Jon."

"Shhh," he whispered. The house was still quiet.

Jon reached inside the window and felt for the lock. There was no deadbolt. He turned the lock and opened the door. Again they listened. There was no movement. There was no sound.

They went in.

Jon shut the door behind them. Through the gloom they could see that they were in the kitchen.

"What are we looking for?" she asked.

"Holyoke's soul," he whispered.

"What?"

"I don't know, maybe something incriminating. Information for the story. We're trying to get into his head, remember? Just keep your eyes open."

They turned on their flashlights. The narrow beams pierced the dark. A rack full of knives sat next to an espresso maker on a counter along the far wall. A microwave hung from some cabinets above the counter. There was an almost-full floor-to-ceiling wine rack next to a refrigerator at right angles to the counter, and a sink at right angles to that. They checked the refrigerator and it was almost empty. There was nothing unusual or out of place in any of the drawers or cupboards.

They walked through the kitchen into the dining room, and then from there through French doors into the front hall and on into the living room. Nothing seemed out of place or out of the ordinary. Then they walked to the back hall and peered past a door into the basement. Its blackness swallowed their flashlight beams whole.

"If I were a serial killer, I'd keep the bodies down there," Jon whispered.

"Quit it," Lizzy said. She punched him in the arm. They shone their flashlights as they walked down the steps into what looked to be a large, open room. Their lights scanned the darkness. Something popped into Lizzy's beam. She screamed a short, muffled scream. She dropped her flashlight. Jon held his steady. A decorated human skull looked back at them with empty eyes.

The waxy-yellow skull sat on a black pedestal. The eye sockets were empty, the nasal cavity was decorated with a shell ornament, and its natural teeth had been pulled and replaced with pointed dog teeth. There was a triangle with a third eye carved into the bone on the top of the skull. "It's his art collection," Jon said. "The woman at the university said he collects tribal art." As their flashlights traversed the darkness they saw wooden tribal masks hanging on the walls and mounted on pedestals throughout the room.

"Would you look at that!" Jon shone his light on the full-sized effigy of a human male painted with muted colors and decorated with feathers and small seashells. It was standing against the far wall. The figure was depicted naked in a fighting pose with a spear in its hand. "Look at the size of the schlong on that guy."

"What's the matter, Jon? A little penis envy?"

Jon turned his flashlight away from the figure and back to the stairs going to the main floor. "Come on, Lizzy. There's nothing else down here."

Holyoke's bedroom was on the second floor and was as unremarkable as the rest of the house. Jon poked through his dresser while Liz looked through his closet. His clothes were conservative and tended toward the informal. He apparently liked earth tones. They found nothing of interest in either of the other bedrooms.

His study was another matter. "Look at this," Lizzy whispered. She shined her flashlight on piles of papers covering most of Holyoke's desk. "It looks like he was working on something." She propped up her light and started to read the material. "These are all medical articles on pain."

"I forgot to tell you," Jon said. "Holyoke does pain research. He experiments on cats."

"Nice," she said. "Just the kind of thing The Sandman would do in his spare time. Help me look through this stuff." Lizzy took the papers from the desk and sat on the floor in a corner of the study. She started to read.

Jon first looked through the desk drawers, and then through a filing cabinet. Neither was locked. The desk held nothing but the usual pens, paper and paperclips. There was a bottle of eighteen-year-old Macallan single-malt scotch in the bottom drawer, along with a glass. The bottle was half full. The file cabinet contained files of articles clipped from medical journals. Most were related to the treatment of pain or pain research in some way or another. The articles went back all the way to the mid nineteen-seventies. Jon thumbed through the files in a random manner.

Holyoke's computer was sitting on a stand next to his desk. There was a printer and a scanner on a table next to the computer. A sophisticated stereo system including a CD burner and a CD collection was contained on four shelves built into the opposite wall. Most of the music was either classical or tribal.

Jon searched through the office for another fifteen minutes while Lizzy kept reading.

"Jon, you should look at this," she said. "Parts of these articles are underlined and there are notes all over the margins." She flipped through the stack she was reading. "They deal with pain management in primitive cultures, from all over the world. They talk about surgery without anesthetics, natural pain relievers from exotic plants, and all kinds of other stuff. It's a little weird."

"This whole place is a little weird," Jon said.

"It's actually a lot weird." Lizzy stretched her back.

"Have you found anything in there related to his research at the university?" Jon asked.

"You mean about the cats?"

"Yeah, I guess so."

"Not a thing," she said. "Just these reference articles with notes in the margins."

Lizzy stood up and put the papers back on the desk, then she looked at her watch. "Let's get out of here," she said. "We've been here over an hour."

Jon also checked his watch. "Ok. Let's go."

They straightened up the study and walked down the stairs back to the front hallway. They retraced their steps through the kitchen and left the house the way they came. Jon shut the back door and locked it by reaching inside through the broken pane of glass. They were walking down the back steps towards the driveway and Jon's car when two bright searchlights blinded them.

They froze.

"This is the police, put your hands on your head and stay where you are."

"Shit," Lizzy said. "This is going to look great on my resume."

✸

Two uniformed policemen circled Jon and Lizzy and approached them from the back. They pulled their hands behind their waists and clicked on a set of handcuffs each. Then they patted them down, conducting a superficial body search.

"Hey, watch the hands," Lizzy protested.

"Shut up," said a gruff male voice.

There was a dark sedan parked behind Jon's Explorer. They were led to the car. Detective Sergeant Gil Anderson was standing beside the passenger-side rear door. He opened the door and instructed Jon and Lizzy to get into the back seat. The inside of the car was dark and they were still night-blinded from the searchlight. Sergeant Anderson placed his hand on each of their heads in turn, and then guided them into the car. He shut the door and walked away.

Lizzy and Jon tried to look at each other, blinking. A figure in the front seat turned around and the interior light went on. "Well, well, what have we here? A couple of felons?" It was Karen Able. "Let's see, there's breaking and entering, destruction of property, interfering with an ongoing police investigation, obstruction of justice, tampering with evidence. There must be more. Did you take anything out of the house? Maybe a body cavity search at the station would be in order."

"Hi, Karen," Jon said.

"You know her?" Lizzy asked.

"We're old friends."

"Shut up," Karen said. "Maybe you ought to use your one phone call to wake up one of your newspaper's high-priced lawyers. I'm sure he'd be happy to come down to the station to bail you out."

"Karen, we. . . ."

"I said, shut up," she interrupted. "What in the hell did you think you were doing? What were you thinking? How could you be so stupid?"

"It seemed like a good idea at the time," Jon answered sheepishly.

"Idiots," she said. "We've been watching this house since yesterday. You drove by our stakeout twice before you decided to break in. I don't think you guys are cut out for this kind of thing. You could really get in big trouble for this, ya know. It's a good thing they called me and told me it was your car. It's a good thing they had the patience to wait until I got here."

"We were just after some background material," Lizzy said. "Wouldn't you like to know what we found?"

"Nothing that we haven't already found twice," Karen said. She glared at Lizzy. "Turn around so that I can reach your hands." They both turned around. Karen reached over the seat and unlocked their handcuffs. "I'll decide what to do about this tomorrow."

"Didn't you get my message?" Jon asked.

"I got it," she said. "We'll talk about it tomorrow. For now, just go home."

"For Christ's sake, Karen, I got a call from The Sandman."

"I am angry right now," she said enunciating each word carefully. "Come by my office tomorrow. We will talk about it then." As an afterthought she added, "And bring the tape with you."

Karen motioned for Jon and Lizzy to get out of the car. Lizzy got out first. When Jon started to move Karen grabbed his shoulder. "Who's the anorexic young chippie?" she asked quietly. Then she turned around and faced forward before he could answer.

Karen waited until John got out of the car; then she backed out into the street and drove away.

"So what do you think about Holyoke?" Jon asked.

"It's pretty weird in there," Liz answered. "I think he's our man."

Jon looked at his watch. "I can still get it in the morning edition." He looked over at Lizzy. "The TV guys are gonna shit."

Chapter 6

Paul Ramit's alarm clock started to ring. It was Friday, and it was five o'clock in the morning. Ramit was dean of the University of Washington Medical School, and weekday or weekend, workday or holiday, his alarm clock always rang at five o'clock AM sharp. Dean Ramit was a very precise man.

This particular day was like every other. He turned off the alarm after only one ring. He was immediately wide-awake. He got out of bed, pulled the covers back in place, placed the pillow in its proper position, and smoothed out the bedspread. He would change the sheets and remake the bed later. He changed the sheets every day.

Ramit showered, shaved, brushed his teeth and used the toilet. The whole series of procedures took only ten minutes. He was careful not to wake his wife, sleeping in her bedroom across the hall. When he finished he put on his terrycloth bathrobe and his slippers. Then he quietly walked downstairs to the front porch where he retrieved his morning paper.

The timer on his coffee maker was programmed to make four cups of coffee, the minimum, at 5:10 AM. He had ground the whole coffee beans himself the night before. It was the only way he could ensure freshness. He drank Starbucks' Sumatra Blend. He liked its bold taste.

He brought his folded-up paper into the kitchen and poured

himself a cup of coffee. He carried his coffee over to the kitchen table, sat down, unrolled his paper and then started to read. He saw the following headlines in *The Seattle Times*:

Med School Prof Linked
to Prostitute Murders

Professor George Holyoke, a prominent member of the University of Washington faculty and Chairman of the Anatomy Department, is sought by the Seattle police for questioning in connection with the so-called Seattle Sandman prostitute killing.

Dean Ramit read the rest of the article slowly and carefully. When he'd finished he called his assistant, Bob Rust, to schedule an emergency meeting of the Medical School Executive Committee. He also called Kay Masters, director of News and Information Services. It was 5:20 AM. He completed his conversations in a calm, precise tone of voice. He then toasted his usual one piece of whole-wheat toast, which he ate unbuttered, finished his one cup of coffee, and went back upstairs to his bedroom to dress. After changing the sheets and remaking the bed, he left for work at precisely forty-five minutes past five.

❋

Jon Kirk's telephone rang at 5:30. He reached across the bedside stand in a daze, accidentally knocked the clock on the floor, and answered the phone. He pulled the receiver to his ear under the covers.

"Mr. Kirk, did I wake you?"

"Wake me? Of course not, I've been up for hours," he said grogily. "Who is this and what do you want?"

"It's Kay Masters from Health Sciences News and Information Services. I read your article in the paper this morning. It was really quite sensational. I found it to be quite informative. Really," she said.

"Thanks so much," he said. Jon stuck his head out from under the covers. He reached down to pick the clock up off the floor. Leon, who had been sleeping beside the bed, licked his hand.

"Would you mind telling me where you obtained your information?" she asked.

"What?"

"Would you mind telling me where you obtained your information for the story?"

"Yes, I'd mind," Jon said. "Freedom of the press and all that." He was still trying to focus his eyes.

"Alright, Mr. Kirk, I understand your need to protect your sources, but what about that bit about the pain research on animals. Did that come from us?" she asked. "I thought we had an agreement about independent conversations with the faculty."

"Oh my god, it's 5:30! You called me at 5:30 in the morning to ask me that? Get a life!"

"I called you at 5:30, Mr. Kirk, because the dean called me at 5:20. He was angry, and that makes me angry. I don't think you understand the amount of trouble you've caused. You've really been quite irresponsible. I'd hoped we could work together. Now I'm afraid that will not be possible. Please do not attempt to talk to any of our faculty directly, and please do not call my office again." Masters hung up the phone.

Jon groaned. He slid the telephone receiver back onto its cradle, pulled his pillow up over his head, and tried to go back to sleep. He tried to get the image of Kay Masters out of his head. His phone rang again. He grabbed the receiver and yelled into the phone.

"What!"

"You certainly are cheery this morning. A regular bundle of sunshine." It was Karen Able.

Jon looked at his clock. It was 7:30. He must have fallen back asleep. "I'm sorry, Karen. I got a call at 5:30 and I thought she was calling me back. I didn't realize that two hours had gone by, and that you weren't her."

"I see," she said, an icy tone to her voice. "Be at my office before noon. Bring your tape recording of the man who says he's The Sandman with you."

"If you say so." Jon looked at his clock. "Is 11:00 OK?"

"Yes. Be on time." Karen hung up the telephone.

Jon rolled over and called his office. He told Vicki that he had to go to the police station, and that he wouldn't be in until the afternoon. Then he pulled his pillow back up over his head and tried to fall asleep. The telephone rang again.

"Goddamn it!"

*

Karen Able sat at her desk thinking about The Sandman task force meeting earlier that morning. Doc Allison had made no real progress on the causes of the prostitute deaths. He'd sent tissue samples taken from the victims to the FBI for their further analysis. Allison had agreed that the feds might be able to identify something that had been overlooked by the standard toxicology screens. Karen hoped for the best, but didn't expect much.

The task force had discussed The Sandman's call to Jon Kirk and agreed that it most likely was a fraud. But serial killers had been known to reach out to members of the press. The police shrinks said it was about wanting publicity and sometimes a subconscious desire to get caught. The members of the task force were anxious to listen to the tape and to hear what Jon had described as The Sandman's mechanical-sounding voice.

The main topic of discussion at the meeting, however, wasn't the tapes. Instead it concerned the continuing search for Dr. Holyoke. Primarily through cancelled checks and credit card receipts, Robbie had constructed a reasonably reliable trail for Holyoke up until the time of the first murder. Holyoke must have then decided to conceal his whereabouts because the trail had become difficult to follow, and after the second murder it disappeared altogether. The stakeout at his house reported no activity.

The chart on the blackboard now read:

VICTIMS	PERPETRATOR
Women	Male (between 20 and 50 years old)
Prostitutes	Smart, maybe genius
Drug addicts	Technical or medical job
No trauma or violence	White
? Unknown injectable poison	Loner
	? Contacted press
? Moved after death	? Likes publicity
	? Professor George Holyoke

Captain McCabe had attended the meeting and had scheduled another prime-time press conference later in the day. Because they'd been scooped again by the morning *Times*, the electronic media was pushing for something visual. McCabe would again bring the proceedings to order, but this time he said it was to be strictly a Karen, Bill, and Robbie show. Both McCabe and the DA felt that showcasing the task force would put more pressure on the perp and possibly force him into a mistake.

Everyone was now calling the killer The Sandman.

Jon arrived at the police station at 11:00, uncharacteristically on time. Karen had decided to make him wait. After a long twenty minutes she opened her door.

"Come in, Jon. That was quite a stunt you pulled last night."

"Hi, Karen."

"Do you know how lucky you are that the stakeout was under my control?" Karen locked eyes with Jon. "You could have caused some serious trouble for yourself, not to mention the trouble you caused me."

"I'm sorry."

"Sure you are. What if Holyoke had been home? He could have justifiably shot you on the spot."

"I said I'm sorry," Jon said. "Besides, we knew he wasn't home."

"How'd you know that?"

"We rang the back doorbell. Nobody answered."

"Great. That's really brilliant." Karen rolled her eyes. "Did you really think he'd come to the door?" Jon gave her a blank look. "I think you'd better leave the detective work to us."

Karen gestured for Jon to sit in a chair. She sat on a corner of her desk. He tried not to look at her dangling legs. She continued, "We had to tell my captain about your escapade last night you know. Lucky for you he has no interest in prosecuting you or your girl-friend, Elizabeth Carlstrom."

"Liz works at the paper," Jon said. "She's not my girlfriend; she's a reporter. We were just working the story, nothing else. We didn't take anything from the house."

"It's still breaking and entering. You're fortunate he's such an understanding guy."

"I guess we are." He paused. Then he said, "Karen, thanks. I know you fixed it for us."

"You're right; I did, and you're welcome." she said.

"And like you said, I guess we're not cut out for that kind of work." Jon tried to look apologetic. Karen wasn't buying it.

"Did you bring the tape?" she asked.

He reached in his pocket and pulled out an envelope. "Here." He handed it to her. "The tape only covers a part of the conversation," he said. "I didn't get the machine on in time to catch the beginning. I wrote down what I could remember of the missing parts."

"We'll check it out," she replied. "It's probably just a hoax, but you never know." She leaned forward a little. "I read your article this morning," she said. "Holyoke sounds like one sadistic son of a bitch. What kind of a person tortures cats and calls it pain research?"

"Maybe a serial killer," Jon said.

"Maybe," she echoed. She put the envelope with the tape in it down on her desk. "Someone's sure to ask me about it at the news conference this afternoon."

"News conference?" Jon questioned. "I hadn't heard." It took all his willpower to keep his eyes on her face and off her legs.

"That's because you were sleeping in this morning when it was announced," she said. "It's at the DA's office, same time, same station. I'll be wearing my best duds."

"Pantyhose and all?" he asked. "If you need them, I think they're still in my car." Now he made a point of looking at her legs. He tried a hint of a smile.

Karen hopped off the desk. Jon stood up. He looked into her eyes but he couldn't quite read what was there. "Listen," he said. "Let's meet each other tonight after your press conference. We can go to the Olympic again. We have a lot to talk about."

She returned his gaze. Then she answered, "What are you after this time?"

"I'm not after anything," he protested. "We need to straighten some things out, that's all. We were interrupted last time, and we can start where we left off."

"Jon, where did we leave off?"

"Why do you always have to make this so difficult?"

"Let's not talk about it here," she said. "This is a police station."

"Then how about at the Olympic?"

She paused a moment or two and then replied, "I don't think so, Jon. Maybe some other time."

"Come on, Karen," he said, "we need to do this. Meet me at the Olympic and we'll see where it goes."

"And what do you mean by that?"

"I don't mean anything by that."

"This is impossible," she said. "I can't go. Not today." She paused for another moment and then said, "Why don't you ask your friend Elizabeth?"

"Fine." Jon sounded abrupt. "Are we through here?" he asked. "I need to get back to the paper."

"Maybe I'll see you this afternoon at the press conference," she said.

"Anything's possible." Jon turned and left the office.

Karen shut the door behind him, turned around and then kicked her chair across the room.

※

Jon climbed into his car and drove to the Blue Moon Café. A cold draft of air blew inside when he opened the front door. Bobby Arnold was surprised to see him. "You're here a little early, aren't you?" Bobby asked. "Shouldn't you be working or something?"

"It's almost five," Jon answered. "And you can skip the lecture. Do you mind if I turn on the TV? I need to watch the news conference on channel eleven. It starts in a few minutes."

"Help yourself," Bobby said as he walked back to the bar. He brought a Redhook over to Jon without being asked.

Jon took a drink of his beer and then turned on the TV. He switched the channel from ESPN to channel eleven. He had decided earlier to skip the press conference, rationalizing to himself that it would be a made-for-TV event dominated by TV reporters. Besides, after meeting with Karen in her office, he thought he'd seen enough of her for one day. She'd left him more than a little confused.

Jon finished adjusting the TV just in time to see Captain McCabe make his introductory remarks. When he turned the proceedings over to the task force the camera focused on Karen. She was wearing her blue business suit and the lights from all the cameras highlighted her red hair.

"She looks good up there, doesn't she?" Jon said.

"She looks like a cop," Bobby answered.

"Why do you say that?" he asked.

"Oh, I don't know. She just has that look. You can always tell."

"I can't always tell," Jon said. They watched together for awhile in silence.

Karen told the assembled media that the investigation was progressing as expected. They were still attempting to locate Holyoke for questioning. The officials at the medical school were very cooperative. The SPD was following all leads. Yes, they had identified Holyoke's fingerprint on one of the bodies. No, they hadn't yet identified the causes of the deaths. Blah blah blah . . .

"These press conferences are worthless," Jon said. He drank the rest of his beer. "How about another one?"

"You all right?" Bobby asked. He brought him another beer. "You look a little down."

"I'm alright."

Bobby looked him over. "Shouldn't you be over at the DA's office asking questions instead of sitting here watching the show on television?"

"Long night last night," Jon answered. He took a drink of his beer. Bobby looked up at the TV. "Say Bobby, you ever go out with a cop?" They were both watching Karen spar with the press.

"No, never." After trying to read Jon's face he said, "Where's this conversation going?"

Jon took another swig of his beer. "Tell me, are you philosophically opposed, or was it just a lack of opportunity?" He was watching Karen answer a particularly stupid question from a KOMO reporter.

"Philosophically opposed," Bobby said. "I don't go out with women who carry guns." He paused a moment and then added, "Is this about the good-looking red-haired cop up there?" Bobby gestured in the direction of the television. "If it is, be careful. You'd be much better off with Lizzy. Just straightforward sex."

"Lizzy, huh."

"Yeah. She has a body that won't quit. You're passing up a good thing with her, you know."

"Right."

Jon drank the rest of his beer in silence. He watched until the show was finished, and then he removed his cell phone from his pocket. He speed-dialed Karen's number. He wanted to compliment her on a good performance.

Chapter 7

Saturday nights in Seattle are no different than Saturday nights in any other major American city. The streets are busy, the restaurants are full, and the theater crowds are out dressed in their finest. It's a festive occasion, especially after a long, dreary week of rain.

This Seattle Saturday night people on the streets were a little more wary, a little more careful. They stayed in groups, and they could be seen discretely looking over their shoulders on occasion. The news of the serial killer had been on the radio and on all five local TV stations. It was in both newspapers and on the national wire services as well. The Sandman was out there. He was living amongst them and they knew it. They had been there before, first with Ted Bundy, and then with the others. The Sandman would kill again.

Annabel Young had lived in Seattle most of her life. She was a pretty girl with bright red, naturally curly hair. Five feet two inches tall, she weighed only eighty-five pounds. Her small, delicate frame and her childlike, innocent nature made her popular with a particular type of man. She would dress up in little-girl clothes when they wanted her to, and they often wanted her to. She was a professional, and she had learned the skills of her trade at an early age. She was fourteen years old.

Annabel knew about The Sandman. All of the Seattle area prostitutes did. Maybe she was a little more cautious than usual, but deep down inside she felt safe, and that was because Billy Sea took care of her. He fed her, clothed her, gave her shelter, and he gave her the drugs that made her feel good. He gave her drugs to help her start her evenings with the proper attitude, and he gave her different drugs after she finished her work for the night. He also gave her a razor to take along on her tricks, just in case. Annabel owed her life to Billy Sea. He had helped her escape the prison of Seattle's foster care system, and she was grateful to him for that.

Billy Sea was a businessman and he intended to protect his investments. He didn't fool around with knives or razors; he carried a gun. He wasn't about to risk one of his girls on the street while this crazy bastard Sandman was running about. That's why he was particularly happy to get a call from one of his trusted contacts at the Hotel Siena, an upscale, hip, downtown establishment. A well-heeled guest had requested a girl, a particular kind of girl. And he wanted her for the night.

Billy watched Annabel put on a pretty, light-blue dress and then brush her hair. After he dropped her off on the corner of Fourth and Seneca she walked the remaining quarter block from his car to the hotel. Barelegged, she was glad to get inside and out of the cold Seattle misty night air. Annabel walked across the lobby and rode the elevator to the fourth floor. She walked to room 487 as she'd been instructed. There, standing in the hallway, she casually brushed the water droplets from her hair and shoulders and smoothed out her dress. Then she took a deep breath, put on a smile and knocked on the door.

The door opened inward. The man standing there was tall. He was wearing a blue blazer, white shirt, gray pants and no tie. He looked clean and well groomed, and she noticed that he had large, powerful hands. She was relieved to see that he looked nothing like the pictures of Dr. Holyoke that were all over the news. Annabel liked working in the downtown hotels. The customers there were clean.

"Hello. Please come in. I've been expecting you." He stepped to one side and gestured for Annabel to enter.

She took the room in with a glance. It was a mini-suite painted a bright cheery yellow, with a cream-colored carpet and a matching bedspread on the large king-sized bed. There was a vase on the coffee table in front of the couch filled with long-stemmed coral-colored roses that hadn't opened up yet. It was an expensive-looking room. Billy would have arranged a price, but if this john liked her she might be able to talk him out of a generous tip. She planned to make him like her. Fourteen-year-old Annabel immediately took charge.

"Hi, my name's Annabel. What would you like me to call you?" Annabel let the door close behind her as she walked past her customer and into the room. Then she turned to face him.

"Why don't you call me John," he said.

She looked up at him and giggled. "That's original." He was big, but he didn't look threatening. She thought he might even be a little bit shy. "Now that you have me, what do you want to do with me?" It was a line she had picked up from her favorite movie, *Pretty Woman.* Men usually liked it.

"I'll have to think about that," he said.

He smiled at her and walked over to a chair by the window and sat down. There were two overstuffed chairs by the window with a small, round table between them. There was a bottle of white wine on the table with two glasses. Annabel walked over and stood in front of him. Sitting, he was almost as tall as she was standing.

"Do you mind if I take off my shoes, John?" Annabel kicked off her high-heeled shoes and wiggled her bare toes in the carpet. "That feels better." Now their eyes were almost at the same level. She looked in his eyes. She kept her girlish smile painted on her face.

"What now?" she said.

"Oh, I don't know. Let's just pour some wine and see what happens. Would you like some?"

"Sure," she said. "I'll pour." She filled the two glasses half full. "First one for you, and then one for me."

"Are you sure you're old enough?" he asked.

"It may not be legal, but I like it anyway." That was another one of her all-purpose lines. Billy had taught her that one.

"You know you're very pretty, a very pretty little girl," he said.

She looked over and smiled at him.

"How old are you?"

She handed him a glass of wine. "How old do you want me to be?" she answered.

He smiled back at her as he said, "I'd like you to be the little girl that you are." He paused and then added, "And I'd give you back the childhood that you missed if I could; but that's not possible, is it, Annabel?"

"Whatever you say, John." She smiled. She brought her wine glass up to her lips, threw back her head and drank all of her wine in two or three gulps. Then she locked his eyes with her own as she put her index finger in the nearly empty glass, scooped up the last few drops, put her finger in her mouth, and seductively sucked the liquid slowly from her finger.

He sipped his wine, never blinking, never taking his eyes off her. "You can be very sexy when you want to be, can't you?" he said. "What's next?"

"That's up to you." She felt completely in control.

"Well now, we'll have to think about that," he said. She answered his comment with a coy little shake of her head, swinging her red curls. "I'm kind of new at this," he continued. "I guess I'm a little nervous." He looked down at his glass. "This wine isn't quite what I need. I brought along something else that might help."

He reached inside his coat pocket and removed a syringe still in its plastic container, and a medical-looking vial of clear fluid.

She stared at the syringe.

"Dilaudid," he said. "Medical quality. The most powerful narcotic on the market. You can have some if you wish."

Annabel continued to stare at the drug. She could see nothing else.

He pulled a second syringe out of his pocket. "It's really good stuff. Would you like to try it?"

She continued to stare. "I don't know," she said hesitantly.

"It's OK," he said. "I'll tell you a secret." Then he leaned over to her and whispered, "I'm a doctor. Really."

A look of uncertainty swept across Annabel's face. She was losing control of the situation. Billy had told her to always stay in control. But she wanted the Dilaudid. She really wanted the Dilaudid.

She watched him stand up from his chair and take off his coat. He removed one of the syringes from its plastic container. It was the type that already had the needle attached. He took the vial, turned it upside down and pierced the rubber seal on the cap with the needle, gently thrusting it into the clear liquid. Annabel watched as he expelled air from the syringe into the vial, and then drew back two milliliters of fluid through the needle into the syringe. He withdrew the needle and held it up in the air in front of him so that he could look at it as he gently pushed the plunger in the syringe. He carefully expelled all of the air, and he continued to push until the tiniest drop of fluid appeared at the end of the needle. Annabel watched the small drop appear. She was transfixed.

He reached into his pants pocket and pulled out a length of surgical rubber tubing. He offered it to her. "Do you want to go first?" he asked. "Here, let me help. Slip off your pretty dress and lie down on the bed."

Annabel obeyed. She gracefully pulled her dress up over her head. She was wearing blue bikini panties under her dress, and nothing else. She walked over to the bed, climbed up on it, and lay down. She arched her back, deftly removed her panties, and then positioned her legs on the bed with one knee slightly crossing the other. Her skin looked pale against the cream-colored bedspread. It had a slightly bluish tinge. She smiled her practiced, girlish smile, fluttered her eyelashes, and then offered her right arm.

He again reached into his pocked and this time removed some surgical gloves. He put on the gloves. Annabel gave him a quizzical look. "Old habits die hard," he said.

He stretched the surgical tubing around her small arm above the elbow. Her veins filled with blood. He could see the marks from previous injections. He expertly inserted the needle into a vein, drew back on the plunger until a small quantity of blood was visible in the syringe, and then removed the surgical tubing. He smiled at her while he injected the first milliliter of fluid.

After a second or two, a look of surprise filled her face, then a look of panic.

She tried to move. She tried to say something, but nothing came out. The tone went out of her muscles. Her body went flaccid. Then her breathing stopped although her heart continued to beat. She was completely still. The expression drained from her face.

He looked at her and shook his head. He touched his forehead with his fingers as if to rub a headache, but then drew his hand away when he felt the latex of his glove against his skin. He bent forward placing his head nearly over hers. He looked in her eyes. "I'm sorry. I really am," he said. "I'd hoped it wouldn't work out this way. I'd hoped it would be different this time.

"I know you're scared, and I'm sorry about that, too. You can't move because your muscles are paralyzed. That's why you can't breathe. The drug does that sometimes. That's the part I still have to work out. But I promise you won't feel any pain. At least I've figured out that part." He spoke in a soothing voice.

He efficiently removed a pair of pliers from his coat pocket. The jaws were wrapped with tape. He put them to work. He grabbed a bite of her skin, squeezed hard, and then he twisted. Then he did it again. He looked in her eyes. Her pupils didn't constrict. They didn't dilate. They didn't move. She did not react.

"There, I told you that you wouldn't feel any pain." He put the pliers back in his coat pocket. He scanned her body up and down. "Your life's been full of pain, hasn't it?" he said. He stroked her hair.

"I really am sorry about this, you know, but you had no real future anyway. You would have been miserable, and you would have ended up like this sooner or later no matter what happened. Just a life full of pain and suffering. I'm saving you from that. When the world thanks me for what I've done, I'll tell them about you, Annabel. I'll tell them how brave you were."

He injected the second milliliter, removed the needle and held his gloved finger over the vein. There was no bleeding. There was no change. Her heart just stopped.

"Goodnight, Annabel," he said in a soft, quiet voice.

Now he had more work to do. She was already on the bed, and it was made up like it was supposed to be made up. Her head was on the pillow but it was crooked, so he straightened it out. He had to straighten out her legs, too. He balanced her feet together with her heels out so that her toes pointed up, and then he crossed her arms over her chest, placing her hands on her breasts. He closed her eyes. He again checked for bleeding at the injection site. There was none. He smoothed out the bedspread around her.

Next he went over to the table and wiped his fingerprints off his wine glass. Then he gathered up Annabel's dress, panties, and high heels and put them in his duffel bag. He had a few more chores to complete before he checked the room to make sure that it was clean. Then he put on his long overcoat and a wide-brimmed hat. He took off his surgical gloves and replaced them with leather gloves. Finally he checked himself in the mirror, and then he left the room the way he'd come in.

✻

Jon Kirk was asleep on his bed when his telephone rang. Leon was asleep on the floor. It was seven-thirty on Sunday morning. He opened his eyes and fumbled his way to the receiver, answering it after four rings.

"Hello?"

"Jon, is that you?" He heard a familiar, mechanical-sounding voice.

Jon sat up in bed. He was wide awake. Leon's ears perked up as much as a Basset hound's ears can perk up, but he didn't move his head.

"Are you there, Jon?"

"I'm here."

"Good. Listen to me. I killed again, Jon. I murdered someone last night. I'd hoped it would turn out differently, but it didn't."

Silence.

"Jon, are you with me?"

"I'm with you. Why are you telling me this?"

"I like you, Jon. I like the way you write. You understand me, and I want to give you an exclusive, a scoop as it were."

"I don't understand you."

"You understand more than you know," he said. "We'll talk again. Soon."

The line went dead.

Jon quickly called Karen's home telephone number. Leon stood up and started to whine. He had to go outside.

Chapter 8

Karen had just completed her Sunday morning run. She normally ran seven miles. It was better than church. It was better than sex. Well, not really, but it was better than church. It was exhilarating. She was on an endorphin high when her telephone rang.

"Hello?"

"Karen, it's Jon"

"Jon," she said in a sparkly voice. "What a surprise. What are you doing up at seven-thirty on a Sunday morning?"

"The guy who says he's The Sandman called again," he said. "This time he called me at home."

Her voice dropped into a serious tone. "Are you sure it's the same person?"

"It sounded like he was using the same device to disguise his voice."

"When did he call?"

"Just a few minutes ago." He paused. "Karen." Jon's voice was a little shaky. "He said he murdered someone last night."

"What?"

"He said he killed someone."

"Did he say anything else?"

"Nothing about the murder, only that he called to give me an exclusive story."

Karen paused a moment and then said, "Let's treat this like it's the real thing. I'll alert the patrolmen in south Seattle. They'll check on the motels. You'll need to come in this morning."

"You name the time. This guy creeps me out."

"Can you make it by 8:30?"

"How about nine?"

"I'll see you in the office at nine." She paused and then said, "Jon, take care." She hung up the phone.

*

Later that morning Pat Bridges, a maid at the Hotel Siena, was working at her assigned area on the fourth floor. After replenishing the supply of linens on her cart, she knocked on the door to room 487. When she heard no answer, she unlocked the door and announced herself, "Maid service." There was no response. Pat put a rubber doorjamb in place to hold the door open and then carried her vacuum cleaner into the room.

At first she didn't notice Annabel Young's body on the bed. Even after she saw it, it took a moment or two for her to realize what had happened, that someone had been killed, that a child had been murdered and posed on one of her beds.

Pat froze. She felt a scream well up in her throat. It came out first as a whimper and then as a cry before it fully crescendoed into an uncontrolled panicked screech. She couldn't stop screaming until some minutes later when the men from hotel security reached her and escorted her out of the room.

*

Jon was sitting in Karen's office, sharing a cup of bad coffee with her when she got the call.

"My God . . . Hotel Siena? . . . What's the room number? Four what?" Karen glanced up at Jon. "Ok, I got it," she said, scribbling on a piece of paper. "Notify Robbie and Gil. . . . Yes, yes, call them at home. I'll get there as soon as I can." She hung up the phone.

"They found the body," she said. "This time it's a little girl."

"Jesus Christ!"

"Jon, your caller's the real thing. This guy's forming some kind of a bond with you."

"Jesus Christ!"

Karen stood up. Jon stood up too. "I've gotta go," she said. "It's a fresh crime scene. You can't come." Karen grabbed her coat and put it on. "I'll call you later on your cell phone." She rushed out of the room.

Jon sat back down. "Jesus Christ," he whispered to himself. He sat still for a moment. Then he removed his cell phone from his pocket and called Lizzy's home number.

"Lizzy, it's Jon."

Jon told her about The Sandman's call. He told her about the body at the Hotel Siena, and about Karen's admonition not to go. She still had to dress so they agreed to meet at the crime scene in half an hour.

Jon grabbed his jacket and hurried out of the office. He jumped into his car and narrowly missed a taxi as he drove out of the Public Safety Building's parking garage. He straightened the wheel, turned left and then sped off in the direction of the hotel. He worried about what he was going to tell Karen when he got there.

＊

Detective Able and Detective Sergeants Anderson and Washington were working the crime scene at the Hotel Siena. They had sealed the fourth floor after asking the hotel guests to either stay in their rooms or vacate them as quickly as possible. Additional police were arriving by the minute.

Police scanners had picked up the news and the word was out that The Sandman had killed again. The hotel lobby was already starting to fill with reporters, photographers, and video cameramen. A television news broadcast van was parked sideways along Fourth Avenue, almost blocking the road. Counting the hotel staff, guests, and various gawkers and passers-by, the spectacle was getting out of hand.

Jon had been at the hotel for twenty minutes before he spotted Lizzy entering the lobby. She told him she had double-parked on Fourth. "The police aren't allowing access to the fourth floor," said Jon. "Everyone's trying to talk their way past elevators and stairs. Even the freight elevators are blocked."

"I thought that we'd get a jump on these bozos," Lizzy said. "Sorry it took me so long to get here. What now?"

"I've got an idea," Jon answered. "Follow me."

There were two elevators at the end of the elevator bank that led only down to the underground parking garage, and they weren't guarded. Jon and Liz rode down to the level A garage. On the far side of the parking structure there were two police officers shining their flashlights into and under parked cars. A police car blocked the entrance into this part of the garage. Karen and Jon worked their way from the elevator to a metal door marked STAIRS. They quietly opened the unguarded door into the stairwell and then just as quietly walked up the stairs, past the police who were guarding the door in the lobby, and then on up to the fourth floor.

Once on the fourth floor they moved toward a buzz of voices coming from the end of the hallway. They found several policemen talking with each other. Robbie Washington stood out from the group, he was taller and better dressed than the rest. He was the first to spot them. "Goddamn it!" he exclaimed. "You can stop right there. How'd you get past the guards?" The others stopped their conversation and looked.

"We told them we were with Detective Able," Lizzy replied. "They sent us right up."

"Uh huh," he said. He took a step in their direction and pointed his finger toward the middle of Jon's chest. "Wait here." Then he moved back towards the entrance to the hotel room and yelled in the door, "Karen, we've got a couple of party crashers out here. It's our friends from the *Times*, Jon Kirk and his girlfriend."

"Jon and who? A girl?" she asked. "How'd they get up here?"

"Beats me. What do you want me to do with them?"

"Keep 'em there. I'm almost finished. I'll be out in a few minutes."

Robbie looked back at Jon and Liz, "You heard her," he said. "Stay right over there and don't get into any trouble." Then he turned his back to them.

Lizzy leaned toward Jon and whispered, "The boss'd love a picture of those cops by the door with the number 487 on it. What do you think?" She fingered the camera in her purse.

"Probably not a good idea," Jon answered. "The flash."

Lizzy slid down the wall to sit on the hallway carpet and Jon joined her. They waited there for awhile. Finally Karen's voice came from inside the hotel room, "Robbie, send 'em in. Tell them not to touch anything."

Robbie turned his attention towards Jon and Lizzy. "You heard her. Go on in." He motioned for them to go into the room. "Don't touch anything," he said. "If it were up to me I'd throw your asses back down the stairs." They went in.

The room was crowded. A police photographer was snapping photos. Two men were lifting fingerprints from all hard surfaces. Annabel Young's small body looked ghostlike on the top of the bed. Karen was fastening plastic bags over the victim's hands with rubber bands.

Karen looked Lizzy up and down. "Oh, it's you." She turned toward Jon and then back to Lizzy. "Come in, take a good look. You wanted to see what serial murder looks like. Well this is it. This could have been you at Holyoke's house."

Lizzy walked over to the bed to look at the body. Jon held back. He looked a little pale. Lizzy spoke first. "This is the way all of them were posed, isn't it?"

Karen answered, "Just like this, all of them. Hands crossed on their chests, eyes closed." She finished bagging the hands and then continued, "The Sandman's trying to tell us something here. These poses mean something. We just aren't smart enough to figure it out."

"She looks like a mummy, ready to be wrapped," Lizzy said. "Could that mean anything?"

"Who knows," she said. "Look at this." She pointed to several prints visible in the powder that the technicians had sprayed on the headboard.

Jon came closer. "Are those Holyoke's?" he asked.

"We'll know soon enough," Karen answered. "Whoever he is, he's announcing himself." She turned and walked away. "Come with me," she said. "I want to show you something else."

Karen led them into the bathroom. "Look at the mirror. Don't touch anything." There was a full handprint in the middle of the mirror plainly visible in the fingerprint powder. "He left it there on purpose. He knew we'd find it." They stood crowded together in the small room staring at the handprint.

"And another thing," said Karen. "This is an upscale hotel, it's in a different area of the city, the vic was an expensive hotel hooker. It's exactly the same but completely different." She paused a moment. "What does all this tell you?"

"Copycat murder?" Jon asked.

"It's possible, but I doubt it," Karen said. "The victim's posed too perfectly, just like the others. It'd be difficult for someone else to get it exactly right just from reading the paper."

"Maybe he wants to get caught," Lizzy said. "Don't all serial killers want to get caught? Deep down inside they all want to tell their story, don't they? They want us to know how smart they are. They want to take credit for what they've done. They crave the limelight."

"I certainly hope so," Karen said. "We could use the help."

The group walked back to the bedroom. Karen went over to say something to one of the lab technicians. The police photographer had finished and was putting her equipment away. When Karen finished her conversation she sat down in one of the overstuffed chairs and pulled off her latex gloves. She looked up at the ceiling and said to no one in particular, "What kind of a twisted fuck would do something like this? For Christ's sake, that girl's only fourteen or fifteen."

Gil Anderson entered the room. The bags under his tired eyes looked darker and puffier than usual. He walked over to Karen. "I just finished the interview with the hotel's chief of security," he said. "We have pictures of The Sandman. We have him on video."

Karen sat up in the chair. Nobody else moved or spoke.

"His face?" Karen asked.

"Not so far," Gil replied. "But we haven't reviewed all of the tapes yet. I've only seen the one from the registration desk."

"What else do they have?"

"Everything," he said. "They have the best surveillance system I've ever seen. They have cameras at every entrance, at the reception desk, in the lobby, the elevators, the hallways, the kitchens, everywhere. Everything's covered except the room itself. We should have The Sandman on video from the time he entered the hotel until he entered this room. We should also have him as he leaves."

Lizzy interrupted from across the room, "Mind if we look at the tapes?"

Gil turned around, "Reporters!" His lip curled. "What're they doing here?"

"The Sandman called Jon this morning," Karen said. "He told him about the murder. He was invited. But now that I think about it, I'm not really sure why she's here." She nodded towards Liz. "Why is she here, Jon?"

"Cut it out, Karen," he replied.

"So what about the tapes?" Lizzy reiterated.

"Don't push it," Karen said.

Gil turned his attention back to Karen. "The security staff is making copies of all their tapes. Their equipment's better than ours. We have a man watching to preserve the chain of evidence. He'll take the originals and the copies with him when they're finished."

"Good, we'll look at them back at the station," she replied. "Are you guys about finished?" she asked the lab techs. One of them was packing away equipment while the other called the coroner's office to find out what was taking them so long.

Jon whispered to Liz, "Go into the bathroom and get a photo of that handprint. Don't use the flash."

Lizzy slipped into the bathroom and shut the door.

Robbie Washington walked into the room and joined the conversation with Karen and Gil.

"We got all that we're going to get from the hotel staff today," he said. "None of the day shift people saw The Sandman. We have the names of the night shift."

"Where'd he get the prostitute?" Bill asked.

"Probably one of the bellmen, maybe the bell captain," Robbie said. "We're checking it out."

Karen's cell phone rang. Conversation stopped while she answered it. "Yes . . . yes . . . right . . . OK . . . thanks, Ben." She broke the connection. "They identified the prints," she said. "They're Holyoke's."

Lizzy walked out of the bathroom and Jon grabbed her by the arm. "We've got to go; we've got work to do." He turned as he walked out the door. "Thanks, Karen. I know you didn't have to do this. I'll call you later."

Two men from the coroner's office entered the room. One was pushing a gurney with a human-sized, heavy, black plastic bag on top.

"She's over on the bed," Gil said, as if they couldn't see her for themselves.

They zipped Annabel Young into the body bag. Then they transferred her to the gurney and wheeled her out the door to the service elevator. Members of the press were waiting on the first floor in a feeding frenzy. The lobby erupted when the elevator door opened.

*

The newsroom at the *Times* was relatively quiet, as it was most Sunday afternoons. Jean Viereck was writing her gossip column and she looked more than a little hung over from the social events of the previous night. Thornton's office was empty. Jon had just filed his story for the Monday morning edition. Lizzy had already filed hers and left for home. News of the Hotel Siena murder was all over the local radio and TV news shows. CNN carried the story on cable, and Jon was sure it would make the national broadcast networks by evening.

Jon sat at his desk, staring into the distance, doing nothing. He didn't feel like going home. He didn't feel like being alone. He couldn't get the sound of The Sandman's electronic voice out of his head. He was totally lost in thought when Karen walked up behind him and gently put her hand on his shoulder.

"I thought I'd find you here," she said. "Is Liz around?"

Jon turned around. "Hi, Karen. No, Lizzy's not here. She left a long time ago. You might be able to reach her at home. Here, let me give you her number." He leaned forward to write her number on a scratch pad.

"Actually, Jon, I came here to see you, not Liz." she said. She walked past his chair and leaned against his desk. "It's been a long day and I felt like some company."

"I know what you mean," he said.

"Some days . . . the job . . . I don't know. I called you at home and you weren't there, so I thought I'd take a chance and stop by. I hope you don't mind. The security guy downstairs let me in when I flashed my badge."

"I'm glad you came," he said. "It's this Sandman thing. He works his way into your mind. I don't know that I like being his personal press agent."

"I wouldn't like it either," she said. She sat down on the desk. Her leg brushed against his knee. "He's going to call you again, you know."

"Yeah, I know."

"You need to be ready for him this time. Do you have a recorder on your home phone?"

"No, just here at work."

"You should get one. It could be important."

"Good idea," he said. "I'll get one tomorrow."

They looked at each other without speaking for several seconds. Karen broke eye contact first. She scanned around the newsroom from her position on Jon's desk. Jon continued to look up at her from his chair. The room was almost empty. She felt a little silly. When she looked back at him and said "Jon," he said, "Karen" at exactly the same time. They both laughed.

"This is a little awkward," she said. "I hope I'm not interrupting your work."

"I finished a long time ago," he answered. "I just didn't want to go home."

"Me either."

They paused a moment longer and then Jon said, "Come on, let's get out of here." He stood up, took her hand and gave it a tug. She slid off the desk. "Why don't we go to a movie or something."

"That sounds good," she said. "I haven't been to a movie in a long time. Let's find something totally mindless."

"How about a Schwarzenegger flick."

"I think that qualifies as something totally mindless."

Jon reached around behind her to turn off his computer. Their bodies touched, just for a moment. Then he quickly backed away. He looked out the window. "It's raining again," he said. He could see Puget Sound in the distance. Water was sheeting down the glass. A neon sign flashed on at The Navy Surplus Store.

"Of course it is," she said. "It's winter in Seattle. What'd you expect?"

He continued to look out the window. "Don't you ever get tired of the rain?" He shifted his gaze back to Karen.

"I love the rain," she answered. "It's clean. We could walk to the movie, you know. The Cineplex is only a few blocks away."

"We'll get wet," he said.

"So what," she replied. "It'll feel good."

"It's cold out there."

"What's the matter? Afraid to get all wet and slippery?" She flashed him a smile. Jon arched his left eyebrow. They walked out of the room together and into the rain.

Chapter 9

Captain McCabe was sitting in his office looking at a copy of the morning Seattle *Times*. A photograph of a palm print on a bathroom mirror filled most of the top half of the front page. The accompanying story about the Hotel Siena murder was by Jon Kirk and Elizabeth Carlstrom. He wondered how the hell they got the photo. He'd have to talk to Karen about that. Oh well, if that picture didn't spook Holyoke into a mistake, nothing would. There was little doubt that he was The Sandman.

The Sandman story was his second piece of bad news that morning. The newspaper also reported that Ichiro wanted to renegotiate his contract with the Mariners. He'd been named Most Valuable Player by the American League two years ago, and now he wanted a salary commensurate with his superstar status. Alex Rodriguez had left the Mariners to sign with the Texas Rangers for 252 million dollars. Who could blame him? A quarter of a billion dollars was a lot of money. Now Ichiro would want the same thing. Ever since they'd traded Ken Griffy Jr. the Mariners had been a little short on star power. McCabe looked up longingly at the Ken Griffy jersey on his wall. Trouble always came in threes, and he wondered what else the day held in store.

McCabe didn't feel like answering the telephone when it began to ring. It rang four times before he picked it up. It was a representative from the FBI calling to tell him that they had made some progress in their search for a cause of death in The Sandman murders. He apologized for taking so long to get back to McCabe, explaining that Dr. Allison's first sample had been contaminated, probably by an inexperienced tech at the FBI lab. Traces of an unknown drug or drugs were found in the second set of tissue samples from all three victims. Although only small quantities of the substances were available, testing suggested that they were related to the tropical poison known as curare. The FBI man told him that curare was a plant-extract poison from the Brazilian rain forest, and that jungle tribesmen had used it for centuries on the tips of their arrows and spears. It worked by causing muscle paralysis, and victims died by asphyxiation. When McCabe asked about the psychological profile he was told that it had been updated and expanded to include a search for people with active interests in or contacts with primitive cultures and medicines.

McCabe hung up the phone, walked out of his office and joined Robbie, Gil and Karen in their morning task force meeting.

Karen had a television and videotape player set up in the conference room. The monitor was playing a composite tape made from the hotel surveillance tapes.

The Sandman first entered at 5:17 PM through the Fourth Street entrance. He was wearing a full-length raincoat and a fedora that obscured much of his face. He identified himself as Gary Reed to the hostess at the registration desk. He had a reservation, and he gave her an American Express credit card with his name on it. He brought only a small duffel bag, which he carried to his room without the assistance of a bellman.

Annabel Young entered the hotel at 10:46. She walked through the lobby and took an elevator directly to room 487. At 11:52 the Sandman left his room, dropped his key in the fast checkout slot at the reception desk, and left the hotel. He was wearing the same long coat and hat that he wore when he came. The security technicians at the hotel said that room 487 had then remained undisturbed until the maid entered the next morning.

The group was watching the tape for the second time. McCabe commented that the perp had done a good job of hiding his face from the cameras. "He knew he was being photographed," Gil said.

"There weren't any usable fingerprints on the key or the door-knob," Robbie said. "See, he was wearing gloves when he dropped the key into the checkout slot."

"Do we have a sample of his handwriting from the registration form?" Gil asked.

"Unfortunately, no," Robbie answered. "He asked the hostess to fill in the card for him, claiming he had injured his hand." Robbie paused for a moment and then said, "No handwriting sample, no prints on the key, but prints all over the bed and on the bathroom mirror. The operator said he made one phone call to the evening-shift bell captain, but there weren't any prints on the telephone. What's wrong with this picture?"

"He's a very careful man," Karen said. "It's inconceivable that the prints were a mistake, especially the one on the mirror."

The videotape ended with the perp walking out of the Fourth Street entrance of the hotel. "Well that shoots another one of my pet theories all to hell," Robbie said.

"Which one?" asked McCabe.

"The one where he kills his victims somewhere else and then moves them. That's obviously not the case. He has to kill them in the room. I wonder how he does it."

"Doc Allison's theory about intravenous drugs seems to be the most plausible explanation," McCabe said. "Needle tracks would have hidden the injection site. How else could he have done it without causing a ruckus?"

"Smoke and mirrors," Robbie said.

"We need some more evidence. All we have is theories."

"And Holyoke's fingerprints," Robbie added.

Gil Anderson spoke next. "We haven't been able to locate the bell captain yet. When we find him we'll want to ask him about his telephone conversation with The Sandman. He must have asked him to arrange for the prostitute."

"Holyoke registered under the name Gary Reed," Karen said. "Do we know anything about that?"

"Not yet," Bill said. "We're working on it. He made his room reservation the morning he checked in. He either constructed a false identity, which would have taken some time, or he stole the credit card before he called in the reservation. It won't take long to sort it out."

"Let's watch the tape one more time," Karen said. "How tall do you think he is?"

✳

Jon was sitting at his desk in the newsroom, writing at his computer. The usual newsroom scene was happening all around him. Years of practice had taught him how to wall off the continuous background activity from his consciousness while he concentrated on his work. Lizzy walked up behind him and slid her fingers through his hair. He involuntarily relaxed his shoulder muscles, shut his eyes and tilted his head back against her hands.

"Umm, this could be habit forming," he said.

"It's supposed to be." She continued to kneed his scalp.

"I think you've found my weakness."

"One of many, no doubt." Liz withdrew her fingers and walked around to the right side of his desk. "Any word on Holyoke yet?"

"None," Jon said. "Not a trace."

"Don't you think it's a little odd he just disappeared like he did? Where does he get his money? We know it's not coming from his credit cards or bank account."

"He's good," Jon said. "He's smart and he's careful. I think he could hide out for quite awhile if he wants too. We won't find him until he makes a mistake."

Lizzy looked over his shoulder at the computer screen. "How's the story coming?"

"It's getting there. I can't get the image of that dead girl out of my head. It's haunting me."

"I know what you mean." Lizzy sat down on the edge of his desk. "Listen, I just heard that the FBI updated their psych profile. They think The Sandman has an interest in primitive medicines and cultures. Sound familiar?"

"It certainly does. I'm getting to like your source on the force."

"There's more," she said. "They found something in the tissue samples Doc Allison sent to them. My contact doesn't have access to the report itself, but I bet you could get a copy from Karen if you really tried."

Jon started to smile. "And what would you suggest I try?" he asked.

"That little-boy grin you have on your face right now ought to work," she said. "Try flashing it to her during the autopsy this afternoon. I'm sure she'll be there. She'll be putty in your hands." The smile dropped from Jon's face like a stone dropped from a bridge. "You are going to be there, aren't you? Vicki twisted a lot of arms to get us a spot at the table."

"Uh, sure," he said. "I'll try to get there."

"It's scheduled for three o'clock. The boss wanted to make sure that you knew about it."

"Uh, I might be a little late," Jon said. "Don't wait for me. I'll get there as soon as I can."

Lizzy slid off his desk. "I've been thinking about that handprint on the mirror," she said. "Does it make any sense to you? Why would he leave it there on purpose? The way he poses the bodies, he doesn't need another calling card."

"I've been thinking about that too. It's hard to know what motivates a man like that. Who knows why he does what he does."

"We'll figure it out," she said. "Don't forget the autopsy. I'll see you at three."

Lizzy briefly tussled Jon's hair again before she walked out of the newsroom. Jon watched her as she left. He smoothed out his hair, and then he called Karen.

Karen wasn't busy and she was in a chatty mood when he called. She didn't mind talking about the psychological profile and laboratory report from the FBI. McCabe had told her to leak the information. She told Jon about the toxins and their possible relationship to curare, and she told him about the psych profile and how it fit Holyoke like a glove. It wasn't enough. Jon needed more information. After he hung up he searched the newspaper's old files for articles about plant toxins and primitive medicines. He was looking for an expert in the field who could give him some help. He came up with the name Dr. Katherine Monahan.

Dr. Monahan knew about natural poisons and drugs. She knew about curare. She was a naturopath, and she actually used some of those types of agents in her medical practice. She lived on Orcas Island, near Seattle just north of Puget Sound. When Jon called her she said she would prefer to meet him in person rather than talk at length over the phone. She was absolutely firm about the face-to-face meeting. He called Kenmore Air and chartered a floatplane to leave for Orcas in the morning.

✳

Jon had good intentions about attending the autopsy. He called Dr. Allison to let him know that he was coming, and he left for Harborview Hospital at 2:15 so that he wouldn't be late. He knew that his problem with blood and dead bodies was just a mental thing, an issue of mind over matter, and he was determined to will himself through the procedure this time. He bravely entered the elevator, rode it down to the basement, exited the door, walked down the hall, opened the door to the autopsy suite, felt the chill and smelled the smells of the morgue, stared into the room for a moment, swallowed hard, turned around, closed the door, walked back to the elevator, rode back to the lobby, and walked out of the hospital to his car. Although it was cold and rainy outside, he couldn't stop sweating.

Jon sat in his car for awhile. He didn't want to return to the office while the autopsy was in progress. He called his voice mail for messages. There were none. With nothing to do but wait until the autopsy was over he drove to the Blue Moon Café. Bobby Arnold looked up from washing glasses when he walked in. Jon took a seat at the bar. "How about a Redhook?" he asked.

"You're spending too much time in here," Bobby said. "Pretty soon you'll look like those guys over there." He pointed in the direction of a pair of rummies at the end of the bar.

"I'm supposed to be at an autopsy at Harborview, but I hate those things. Does that sort of stuff bother you?"

"Nope." Bobby brought Jon his beer.

"Well, it bothers me. I've got to figure out a way to get over it."

"Mind over matter," Bobby said. "There was this time I went out with a female Cat driver. She drove a big rig, a D-9. Never heard of deodorant. I picked her up after work. Never shaved her pits either. I found out about that later, but that's another story. Anyway, what was I saying? Oh yeah, the next time you need to do something that really makes your stomach crawl, just focus your mind on something else."

"Like what?" Jon asked.

"Focus on something pleasant. Think about something that makes you feel good. Focus on something warm and fuzzy, like pussy for instance. Give it a try. It works for me."

Jon took a swig of his beer. He looked at Bobby over the rim of his beer glass. Bobby had gone back to washing the glassware when he asked, "Bobby, do you ever have a thought that gets stuck in your head? I mean, no matter what you do, you can't seem to get it out?"

"Sure, all the time, especially with women," Bobby said. "Why don't you just call Lizzy and get it over with. You'll both be better off."

"That's not what I mean. And besides, I call her all the time. I work with her for Chrissake."

"And that's not what I mean," Bobby said.

"Yeah, I know. Listen, I need to work out a problem. It has to do with The Sandman murders. Karen let us into the Hotel Siena crime scene and. . . ."

"Wait a minute. Karen let you and who into a hotel room?"

"She let me and Liz into the room."

"Karen, you and Liz in the same hotel room."

"Yeah."

"There's going to be trouble."

"Oh, come on."

"Listen, I know what I'm talking about. There's a storm on the horizon."

"Let's get back to the subject, shall we?" Bobby looked at him, shook his head and shrugged. "Well anyway, we were in the hotel room where The Sandman committed his last murder. I'm sure you read about it."

"I did, and a masterful piece of journalism it was, too. You and Lizzy make a great team."

"Right." Jon ignored the comment. "Anyway, the problem is the handprint."

"The one on the front page?" Bobby asked. "The one that belonged to that medical school professor?"

"Yeah, Dr. Holyoke. *Anyway!* There was this naked body on the bed, a prostitute. The room was neat. The covers on the bed weren't even mussed. We know The Sandman made a phone call, but there weren't any prints on the phone. Yet there was a full palm print in the middle of the bathroom mirror." Jon swallowed the rest of his beer. "We know The Sandman carefully plans and executes his crimes. He doesn't make careless mistakes. Obviously he meant for the police to find it. But why? Why plant it there on the mirror? What's the purpose?"

Bobby looked at Jon for a moment or two and then said, "You don't see it, do you?"

"See what?"

"Come on, Jon, use your head. Think out of the box. He meant for the police to find it because he's not Holyoke. Holyoke isn't The Sandman."

Jon stared at him for a moment. "What did you say?"

"Holyoke's not The Sandman. Do I have to spell it out for you? Holyoke's dead."

Jon thought about that for awhile. Holyoke had to be The Sandman. The fingerprints fit and the psychological profile fit. Everything fit. Bobby brought Jon another Redhook, and Jon drank about half of his beer before speaking again.

"If Holyoke's dead, how did the hand print get on the mirror?"

"Jesus, Jon, use your imagination."

Jon took another drink of his beer, and then another. "I think I'd rather not," he finally said.

Chapter 10

It was nine-thirty and the plane was late. Jon was standing alone on a dock at the south end of Lake Union waiting for the Kenmore Air chartered floatplane to pick him up. The flight from Seattle to Orcas Island was scheduled to take about fifty minutes. He knew Thornton would be pissed about the expense when he saw it at the end of the month, but it was the only practical way to get there.

Jon looked around the horizon for the plane. The sky over the lake was empty. He sat down on the wooden dock, got out his cell phone and called Karen.

"Seattle Police Department, Detective Able."

"Hi, Karen."

"Jon!" She sounded surprised and a little startled. "I cannot believe you took advantage of me by taking a photo of that handprint! I took some real shit for that. Ask me again sometime to let you on to a fresh crime scene!"

"Oh that," he said. "I'm sorry."

"Sorry my ass!"

"I didn't mean to get you into trouble or anything."

"You didn't get me into trouble! That's not how things work around here. And actually, as it turns out, it's not bad for the case. I just wish you'd asked my permission first, that's all. I felt like a fool when Captain McCabe called me about it."

"OK, next time I'll ask."

"Sure you will," she said. "Anyway, what's up?"

"Oh nothing much, I'm just sitting around at Lake Union waiting for an air charter to get here. I'm heading up to Orcas Island to interview a source for a story. I hope they didn't forget me. The plane's a little late."

"I'm sure they didn't. It should be a good day for a flight."

"I hope so." Jon was watching a pair of sailboats as they tacked into the wind. "It's a little windy out here." He heard some rustling of papers on Karen's end of the phone. "I had fun at the movies with you the other night," he said.

"So did I," she answered. "We'll have to do it again."

"There's nothing like a good hot dog with lots of spicy mustard."

"And some popcorn."

"And a Coke."

"The company wasn't bad either," she said.

Jon heard the sound of an approaching airplane. "Hear that?" The throaty sound of a nine-cylinder radial engine reverberated through the air. "The plane's on it's way in. I'm going to have to go in a minute.

"Listen, are you doing anything tonight?" he asked

"I don't think so," she answered. "Want me to check?"

"Sure, if you want to. Maybe we could go to dinner or something. Someplace nice."

"I'd like that," she said. "Why don't you call me when you get back? We'll make plans then."

"It's a deal. We'll talk as soon as I get back in town. See you later."

"Bye."

"Bye."

Jon first spotted the plane as it descended over Gasworks Park out of the north. The yellow-and-white Kenmore Air Beaver dropped down over the top of the tacking sailboats and landed with a splash, then it taxied through the boat traffic over to the dock. Jon waved to the pilot as he jumped out of the plane and stepped across the pontoons. He opened the door to the passenger cabin and then held the plane next to the dock as Jon climbed up the pontoon steps and into his seat. Jon buckled his seatbelt. The pilot let go of the wing strut, pushed away from the dock and climbed up into the cockpit. Jon watched as he went through his pre-flight checklist. The pilot then started the engine, advanced the throttle and taxied out behind the sailboats. The water blurred and then fell away as the fifty-year-old airplane took off and then banked to the north.

Jon watched the city pass beneath him during the climb. He saw the medical school to his right and wondered about the animal research going on in the labs. He wondered about Holyoke, and he wondered about the cats. If Holyoke wasn't The Sandman, who was, and why did he use Holyoke's fingerprints? It still didn't make a lot of sense. He made a mental note to discuss it with Karen when he got back. The plane droned on.

Jon leaned his head against the window. As he drifted into that hypnotic state somewhere between wakefulness and sleep, Karen found her way into his mind. Karen was strong, and she was beautiful, and she was smart, and she had great red hair, and then the plane bumped as it transitioned from a climb into level flight. At fifteen hundred feet it flew over the limits of the city. The gray waters below and the gray clouds above formed a corridor for the plane to follow on its course toward the horizon. Jon thought about Karen during most of the fifty-minute cruise at altitude. He was looking out of his window when the plane almost imperceptibly began its slow decent. Orcas Island was out there somewhere beyond the mist.

＊

The waters of Westsound Bay were smooth when the plane landed and taxied toward the only dock in sight. Katherine Monahan was waiting there for him. "I saw the plane as you passed by Mount Constitution," she said. "Welcome to Orcas Island." She extended her hand.

"It's nice to meet you, Dr. Monahan," he replied. Jon shook hands with her. She had a firm, confident grip. "I appreciate you taking the time to talk to me."

"How could I refuse such an interesting proposition," she said. "It's not every day I'm asked to help with a serial murder investigation. Please walk with me up to the house. And please, Jon, call me Kate."

"All right, Kate."

Jon and Kate walked up a wooden stairway from the dock to the bank, and then up a path surrounded by dense vegetation. The path led to a Victorian house overlooking the water.

"It's beautiful, isn't it," Kate said as she looked out over the bay. "I love it out here."

"It looks peaceful. It's a world away from Seattle," Jon said.

Kate Monahan was in her mid fifties. A naturopath and an expert in herbal medicines, she had a large following and was known throughout the Northwest for her garden of medicinal plants. The state medical society did not approve of her or her activities. They considered her brand of alternative medicine to border on quackery. She considered them to be small- and narrow-minded.

At the house Kate led Jon into a classical Victorian parlor. "May I get you some tea?" she asked. "It's herbal, I grow it myself."

"I didn't know you could grow tea in the Northwest," he said.

"When I first moved here I was told that this climate and altitude wouldn't support a tea garden, but I found that not to be the case. With a little research and a little work, anything's possible. I have access to a large greenhouse on the mainland that grows all sorts of things. Would you like to try some?"

"No thanks," Jon said. "I'm not a tea drinker."

"A pity," she said. "It's really quite good." Kate smoothed the wrinkles out of her ankle-length skirt as she sat. "Now what can I do for you?"

"As I told you over the phone, I'm working on a story about The Sandman murders. We may have found out how he killed his victims."

"And you think I can help?"

"I hope so. The FBI thinks that the cause of death in these cases might be some type of plant poison, possibly something related to curare. I'd hoped you could tell me something about it."

"Well, I'm not sure. A lot of poisons come from plants. Your question covers quite a lot of ground. Could you be a little more specific?"

"Sure, let's start with curare. It's a poison isn't it? I really don't know much about this stuff."

"It's a poison. It's also a medicine. As you know, it comes from South America. Indians make it from a black resin extracted from the *Strychnos toxifera* tree. They use it to poison arrow points, especially those on the arrows and darts used with blowguns. These cultures still exist in some parts of the Amazon Basin."

"So I've heard," Jon said. "How does it work?"

"It combines with the cholinergic receptors of motor end plates to produce depolarization and inhibit neuromuscular transmission."

"What?"

"It causes paralysis."

"Oh."

"Among other things, it paralyzes the muscles used for respiration. The cause of death is asphyxiation. It would be a particularly horrible death. Air hunger's a terrible thing."

"Then death wouldn't come quickly?" Jon asked.

"No. Although incapacitation is almost instantaneous, death would take some time. You'd be paralyzed as soon as the drug entered your blood stream. You wouldn't be able to breathe, but your brain would function normally for some time. Your mind would race in a panic while your body just lay there, totally motionless. Finally the oxygen would run out. You'd probably lose consciousness after three or four minutes. It would take several more minutes for you to die."

"Lovely. No wonder people were wary of the Amazon tribesmen. What about other drugs related to curare?"

"There are lots of them," she said. "Probably its most lethal relative is curarine. That's an extremely poisonous alkaloid obtained from curare, but there are others. Many haven't even been cataloged. Western medicine still has only a rudimentary understanding of the drugs developed by primitive jungle cultures. We have a lot to learn."

A long-haired Persian cat padded into the room. He looked at Jon and then jumped up into Kate's lap. Jon could hear him purr from five feet away.

"How would anyone around here get access to these kinds of drugs?" Jon asked. "It's not as if they're sitting around on pharmacy shelves."

"It's not as difficult as you might think," she answered. "As I said, curare can be used as a medicine. It's used in low doses to treat the muscle spasms and the rigidity of diseases such as tetanus. Succinylcholine is a short-acting cousin that's used by anesthesiologists as a muscle relaxant during surgery. Most physicians and pharmacists would have access to these drugs. Of course, you could also import them directly from South America."

"Could just anyone import them? I'm hoping to develop a list of potential suspects. But if they're readily available to any physician or pharmacist, I guess it'll be a long list."

"I'm surprised that it's still an issue. I thought the police had already identified the killer. Isn't George Holyoke supposed to be The Sandman?" she said. "He certainly would've had access to those agents."

"I'm not totally convinced it's that simple," Jon said.

"Things never are with George."

Jon tilted his head. "Do you know Dr. Holyoke?"

"Yes, I know him. He called me for help with a research project. He was interested in Amazon Basin drugs and folk medicines. I thought that's why you wanted to talk to me."

"I didn't know you knew him. I called to learn about curare and those other drugs you told me about."

"Holyoke heard stories about exotic drugs used by tribesmen deep in the Amazon rain forest. We've all heard about them."

"What kind of drugs?"

"All kinds, really. A lot of psychoactive drugs, and a lot of drugs that promote healing and relieve pain. George was interested in pain and pain control. There are rumors of medicines in the Amazon Basin that block pain signals *before* they reach the brain."

"Why is that important?"

"Most drugs control pain by suppressing pain centers in the central nervous system, in the brain. Narcotics, such as morphine and heroine, effectively suppress these pain centers, but they supress the rest of the brain as well. Patients become obtunded. Moderate overdoses can lead to coma. Larger overdoses can kill.

"But imagine if you were somehow able to block pain signals in the peripheral nerves *before* they reach the brain. Pain control would be complete. There would be no central nervous system effects, no drowsiness, no obtundation, no coma, no overdose deaths. Cancer patients, for instance, wouldn't have to feel dopey all of the time. They wouldn't suffer the isolation of a dulled brain. They'd be able to interact with their families and the world around them in a normal way. Indian shamans and witch doctors tell stories about such drugs."

"Why would these drugs would be valuable?"

"Are you kidding? No one would ever need to be in pain again, ever. Such drugs would have tremendous commercial value. However, they could also pose great dangers."

"What do you mean?"

"Pain is an evolutionary defense mechanism. It lets us know when we're in trouble. It stimulates us. It keeps us alive. There are those who would say that without pain there could be no ecstasy. Besides, these drugs could have their own side effects."

"What sort of side effects?"

"Pain is a sensory signal. Nerves carry both sensory signals and motor signals. Motor signals cause muscles to move. If *all* signals in a nerve were blocked—motor signals along with sensory signals—

there would be no pain, but there would be no movement either. Paralysis would result. Curare is interesting because it selectively blocks motor signals. By that I mean that it causes paralysis, but it does not block pain. Some other compounds related to curare block *both* pain and motor signals. Holyoke was searching for a drug that would block *only* pain signals *without* blocking motor signals. No pain and no paralysis. Talk about a miracle drug."

Kate scratched her cat behind its ear. He rolled over onto his back and started to play with her finger. She played with the cat for a few moments and then looked directly at Jon.

"If these drugs exist," she said arching her eyebrow, "they would likely be derived from plant resins. They could even appear to be similar to curare on a toxicology screening test."

"Are you saying that anything made from these plant resins could look like curare in a lab test?"

"Not everything, but certainly some could. It's ironic that drugs that are so closely related could have such opposite effects."

"That's interesting," Jon said. "Do you know if Holyoke found such a drug?"

"No, I don't know. But I don't think so. At least he didn't tell me about it."

"If he found such a drug, could he have used it to murder those four women?"

"If it killed them it wouldn't have much value as a pain reliever. Why bother to develop such a drug? There have to be easier and cheaper ways to kill people."

"I don't know," Jon said. "It's hard to get inside the mind of a serial killer."

"I guess you're right," she said. "It's just that George certainly seemed rational when he talked to me. It's still hard for me to think of him as a murderer."

Jon's watch started beeping. "We'd better wrap this up. The pilot gave me strict orders to return to the plane on time. He has another charter this afternoon."

"Then we'd better get you back to the dock," she said. Kate looked him in the eyes. Her soft demeanor suddenly became cold and penetrating. "You know, there are still a lot of secrets locked up in the Amazon jungle. There is much that we don't know. There's much we aren't meant to know. Some say our civilization isn't ready." Then her features softened again. "I personally think it's just that most of us are too arrogant to look."

Kate scratched her cat behind the ear again, and then she pushed him off her lap and onto the floor. She stood up. Jon stood up too. "Let's walk through my garden on the way back to the plane. You'll never see another like it. Some of these plants hold the keys to the future of medicine."

"Thanks for your help, Kate. I really appreciate it." They walked out of the house and into the garden. "By the way, is there any possibility that Amazon Basin plants could be grown here in the Northwest?"

"Not without a serious greenhouse or some significant genetic engineering."

"Thanks again," Jon said.

They descended down toward the dock. A tall stone wall contained the large garden. There were two gates, one near the house and one overlooking the water. There were exotic looking plants on all sides of the path connecting the gates. Kate pointed out some with medicinal value as they went through.

When they reached the dock she said, "I've enjoyed meeting you, Jon. Thanks for making the effort to come out here to meet me." She shook his hand. "Have a safe flight. And, Jon, I'd appreciate it if you wouldn't use my name in print. I like the peace and quiet I've found up here. I enjoy my privacy."

"No problem," he said.

Kate waved after he climbed into the plane and shut the door. The fog had finally cleared and the sun was shining. It turned out to be one of those rare Northwest days that were pictured on the tourist postcards. Jon felt the sun on his face and it warmed him.

As the pilot pushed the throttle forward and the plane climbed up over the magnificent island scenery, Jon's thoughts began to drift from exotic tropical plants in the Amazon rain forest to Holyoke, to The Sandman, and then to Karen. Holyoke and The Sandman could wait. He decided that he would call Karen as soon as he got back to Seattle.

✳

Jon called Canlis Restaurant on his cell phone as soon as his plane landed. Canlis is one of Seattle's oldest and most upscale eating establishments. With its fabulous view over Lake Union, it's also one of the most romantic places in the city. Jon made reservations for two, and after protracted negotiations with the person on the other end of the line, he was promised a small, semi-private table overlooking the lake. Then he called Karen.

Karen's phone rang five times, and then switched to her voice mail. Jon left a message. He told her about Dr. Monahan and the drugs, and then he told her that he'd been thinking about her all day. He said that he had a romantic evening planned. Their reservations were at nine-thirty. He suggested that she meet him for a drink at his house before dinner. He would be working late at the paper, but the key to the front door was in its usual place. Leon would be there to greet her, and he would call her on his way out of the office. He said that he couldn't wait to see her in a cocktail dress, with or without panty hose, and then he said something about her red hair falling over her white skin onto the black dress. Finally he told her that he missed her, and then he hung up the phone and drove back to his office at the *Times*.

Jon was busy working on his next Sandman article trying to ignore the usual newsroom scene around him when Vicki walked over to his desk.

"How's it coming?" she asked. "Deadline's in an hour, isn't it?"

"Yeah, in an hour, and it's coming fine." He continued to type as he talked.

"Did you learn anything up on Orcas?"

"As a matter of fact I did," he said. "How'd you know I went up there?"

"I heard you chartered. The boss isn't going to like that. You should've taken the ferry. And I know everything, you know that." Vicki looked over his shoulder and tried to read what he was typing.

"I met a doctor up there," he said. "She's a naturopath. She helped me understand how The Sandman kills his victims. It turns out she knew Holyoke, and even helped him with some of his research."

"Are you writing about that?"

"Yep," he said. He continued typing.

"Do you think Holyoke's The Sandman?" she asked.

"I don't know." He sighed. "Why are you pestering me?"

"I'm not pestering you." She feigned a look of hurt on her face. "I just stopped by to tell you that Detective Able called. She said she'll meet you tonight at your house. You were on the telephone when I took the call."

Vicki waited for a reaction.

Chapter 11

Karen left work at five-thirty, early for her. She stopped at Nordstrom on her way home to pick up some shampoo, some cream rinse, and a new lipstick. The sales clerk talked her into some matching nail polish as well. She checked her cell phone for messages after she walked outside, and then drove home to her apartment in the Capital Hill neighborhood.

Karen's apartment was in one of those comfortable older buildings on Tenth Street. After she arrived she stripped out of her work clothes, put on her running clothes and left for a leisurely three-mile jog through the neighborhood. The air was crisp and clear; the sun was low; and after two miles she could taste the salt on her face. After she finished her jog she walked another half mile to cool down, and then returned to her apartment for a shower.

Jon was working late, trying to ignore Jean Viereck's loud voice in the background. She was bitching to somebody about Dean Thornton, the other reporters she had to work with, her working conditions, the ownership of the *Times*, and life in general. Jon had filed his story on medicines and poisons from the rain forest and their possible tie-in to The Sandman murders. He was working on a sidebar article about Holyoke and his research when Lizzy walked over to his desk. She stood beside him, draped her arm over his shoulder in a familiar sort of way and looked at his computer screen. She was on her way out of the office.

"How's it coming?" she asked.

"Not bad," he answered. "This guy Holyoke's a unique piece of work. This thing almost writes itself."

"Well, don't work too hard." She fluffed his hair and started to walk away.

"I've been working too hard all day," he said. Then before she could get too far away he said, "Hey." Lizzy turned around. "How about one of those scalp rubbing back rubbing things that you do before you leave?"

"Poor baby, are you all tensed up?" She made a pouty face and started to walk backward towards the door. "Stop by my place after work if you really need some stress relief." She laughed as she continued walking. She turned toward the door and left the newsroom. Jon went back to his computer.

Karen finished her shower by turning off the hot water. She left the cold water on a few moments longer. She stood under the icy cold stream as long as she could stand it, and then stepped out onto her tiled bathroom floor. The cold water had tensed her skin and made her feel fresh. She stood in front of her full-length mirror for a moment.

Karen grabbed a towel, toweled off and then wrapped the towel around her damp hair. She put on a terrycloth bathrobe and walked barefoot out into her bedroom. Next she sat down on the edge of her bed and set a box of Kleenex and Q-tips down next to her. She pulled a tissue out of the box and tore it carefully in half, then each of those pieces in half again. She took one of the quarter-pieces and folded it in half over and over until it wouldn't fold anymore. Then she stuffed that wedge of tissue between her big toe and her second toe. She repeated the procedures until all of her toes were separated by little bundles of tissue. She opened her new bottle of nail polish, pulled her heels up on the bed and applied the polish to her toenails, first one foot, then the other. Then a second coat on each toe, and then a clear top coat on all of them. Next she painted her fingernails. After she finished, she walked around her apartment with her toes and fingers spread apart, waving her hands back and forth, waiting for the polish to dry. She again noticed herself in the mirror and rolled her eyes. She duck-walked back into her bathroom, found her hair dryer and plugged it in. With the setting on cool, she turned it first on her fingernails, and then on her toenails in turn. She took the Kleenex wads out from between her toes. Then she dried her hair, applied a touch of eye shadow and put on her new lipstick.

Karen selected a little black cocktail dress. She had a pair of high-heeled shoes that went with her dress and flattered her legs. She looked at the panty hose in her lingerie drawer, paused for a moment or two and then grabbed a pair and put them on, careful of her fingernails and toenails. She slipped into her dress, walked back into the bathroom and combed her hair. She noticed that her red hair did fall over her white skin onto her black dress in a pleasing sort of way. She put on a pair of soft slippers, planning to put her high heels on at the last possible moment. They were so uncomfortable. Then she checked herself in the mirror one last time and left for Jon's house.

Jon had owned his 1930s vintage house in the Madison Park area for almost a year. It was a small, two-bedroom bungalow, and like everything else in Seattle, it had cost too much. He liked it because of its location near the old Madison Park Village with the quiet bars, restaurants, and shops. Karen had no problem finding it; she had been there before.

She parked her car on the street, walked up to the front door, fished the key out from under an upturned clay flowerpot, and let herself it. Leon greeted her with basset-hound eyes and a wagging tail. She shut the door behind her and walked into the living room. The house was as she remembered it, only neater. Jon must have tidied it up in anticipation of her visit. She walked into the kitchen, got some ice out of the refrigerator and poured a glass of water. Then she drank the water as she walked around the house waiting for Jon.

She wandered into the bedroom, peeked into the closet, and then walked back to the living room. Leon followed her as she went. When they reached the living room Leon jumped up onto the couch and Karen settled in on the end nearest the table holding Jon's telephone and answering machine. There was a flashing red number 1 in the machine's indicator window.

Karen hadn't noticed the flashing message indicator when she'd first entered the house, but it must have been there. She hadn't heard the telephone ring. She pushed the play button, thinking maybe Jon had left a message for her. He'd said he would call as he left the office. After she pushed the button a computer generated voice from the machine's speaker said, "You have one new message." The machine then went on to play it for her:

"Jon, it's Gina. It's been awhile. Weren't you supposed to call? You've probably been busy with all this Sandman stuff. I've loved your articles. They're wonderful. How'd you get to be so smart, anyway?

"Listen, I've been thinking about you for a few days, and I thought it might be fun to have dinner together at my place again. It's kind of lonely around here with all this dreary weather, and you know how much I love to cook. I'll make you your favorite lemon pie. Then again, maybe you'd like something else for dessert? Call me. Love ya. Bye."

Karen's muscles tensed. Her face flushed. Leon hunkered down in the corner of the couch, aware that something bad was unfolding. "God damn it, Jon. Shit," she screamed. "Shit! Shit! Shit! Shit!" She screwed up her face and mocked, "How'd you get to be so smart anyway? You know how much I love to cook. I'll make you your favorite lemon pie. Love ya!" She looked heavenward. "Shit!" She turned around once, then kicked the table holding the answering machine with her leg-flattering black high-heeled shoe. The table leg broke, the telephone and answering machine bounced against the wall, the table tipped over, and the lamp on the table slipped to the floor. Leon was now cowering on the other end of the couch.

Karen looked at the mess she had made. Then she very quietly, and in a drawn-out voice, said "Shit."

Jon saw Karen's car parked in front of his house when he drove into his driveway. It was eight-fifteen, and he calculated that he had plenty of time to take a quick shower, shave, change clothes, have a drink with Karen and make it to Canlis by nine-thirty. When he walked in the front door Karen was sitting demurely in her little black dress on the couch next to Leon. Leon was wagging his tail. Neither one of then got up to greet him.

"Hi, Karen. Sorry I forgot to call," he said. "I'm glad you're here. You look great."

"Thank you," she said. She smiled a serene smile. The table leg was propped up so that you could hardly tell it had been broken. The lamp was in its proper place on the back of the table. The telephone answering machine was on the front of the table and a red number 1 was blinking in the message window. Karen had a glass of wine.

"I can see you made yourself at home. Will you excuse me while I take a quick shower? I'll just be a few minutes."

"I'll be fine," Karen smiled.

"I'll be right back," he said. He walked into his bedroom, took off his clothes and threw them on the bed. Then he walked into the bathroom and turned on the water. After a quick shower he toweled off, wrapped the towel around his waist, shaved, and returned to the bedroom to get dressed. Karen was waiting for him, sitting on the foot of his bed. She was sitting with her hands folded in her lap, her legs crossed right knee over left, her right shoe off her heel and hanging from her toes, and her right foot rhythmically moving up and down. She smiled at him.

"Karen," he said half laughing. "Couldn't stay away from me?" He noticed that his clothes were now neatly folded on the foot of the bed next to her.

"Jon, who's Gina?" she asked with a quiet voice. She stood up and walked toward him. Jon stood still.

"Uh . . . I'm not sure," he said.

She stood in front of him, put the painted fingernail of her index finger teasingly against his skin just above his navel and ran it up to his mid chest while she said, "Are you sure you're not sure?"

"Uh, I'm. . . ."

"Because I'm sure," she yelled. She grabbed his arm, turned her back, and in one long sweeping motion threw him over her hip onto the floor with a whap.

"Ooooff" he managed to say. When he caught his breath he looked up at her and said, "That hurt!"

"I hurt, too," she said. Then she walked out of the room and out of the house.

✳

The phone rang four times before Jon answered it.

"Hi, Jon, it's Liz."

"Lizzy. What's up?"

"Nothing at all, really. It's just been one of those days, and it's starting out to be one of those nights. I've been sitting here, and I don't really feel like an evening alone. You know what I mean?"

"Do I ever," he said.

"So I was wondering, do you think you'd like a little company, that is if you're not busy?"

"I don't know, Liz. I did have plans for this evening, but at the moment they don't seem to be working out."

"Then live a little," she said. "Let's do something. Just give me a moment to throw on some clothes."

An image of an unclothed Lizzy briefly flashed through his mind. "OK, sure. Do you want to go out for a drink or something?"

"Oh, I don't know," she said. "Why don't you come over to my place and we'll take it from there. Do you think you can find it?"

"No problem."

"I'll see you in a few minutes then."

"Great, I'll be over in a bit."

"Bye."

"Bye."

Jon hung up the phone. He was sitting on his couch in his living room with Leon's head in his lap. He could feel his back stiffen. It hurt like a bitch. He couldn't believe Karen had just flattened him like that. He'd wanted the evening to be special. He had a headache, and he felt confused. He felt like he needed some company. After a few moments of just sitting there he stood up and then left for Lizzy's apartment.

Lizzy lived in a fourplex in the Wallingford District. Jon parked his car in front of her building. He got out and then jogged up the stairs to her front door. He tested his back and it seemed to be getting better. He rang the buzzer under Lizzy's name and was admitted into the building. Lizzy was waiting for him by her open door when he arrived at the top of the stairs. "What a pleasant surprise," she said. Lizzy invited him in. Then she walked over the fireplace to put another Presto Log on the fire. As the fire flared, Jon could feel its warmth fill the room. After one sunny day Seattle's cold dreary winter rains had returned. It was probably snowing in the mountains.

"Could I offer you a glass of wine or something?" she asked. "I have a nice Oregon pinot."

"That would be great," he said. "The fire's nice."

Liz brought a wine bottle and two glasses into the living room. She handed the bottle and a corkscrew to Jon and asked him to open it. He sat down on the couch, removed the cork and poured a glass for each of them. "This looks good," he said.

"It's one of my favorites," she answered.

Lizzy kicked off her shoes and curled up at one end of the couch with her feet tucked under her. She was wearing a loose-fitting blouse and a long skirt.

They each drank some of their wine. She waited for Jon to speak first.

"I was over at the Blue Moon yesterday," he said. "Bobby's got an interesting theory about the fingerprints in the hotel."

"So we're going to talk about The Sandman murders?" she asked.

"We have to talk about something."

"Then what does Seattle's most quoted bartender have to say about that subject?"

"He says that Holyoke's not The Sandman."

"OK, I'll bite," she said. "Why not?"

"The handprint's too obvious to be anything other that a plant. He thinks that Holyoke didn't leave the print. He thinks that Holyoke's dead."

"Cute," she said.

"Yeah, isn't it," Jon answered.

"Let me see if I understand this," Lizzy said. "The Sandman, whoever he is, killed Holyoke for some reason or other, severed his hand and then planted his fingerprints at the murder scenes. That way the police would think that Holyoke committed the crimes. They would search for Holyoke, who's really dead, while the real killer remains free to work his will whenever he pleases. Do I have it right?"

"That's about it," he said, "at least according to Bobby Arnold."

Lizzy stared at him for awhile. "Well, at least it's imaginative."

"You don't think it's plausible?"

"It's plausible, but really, Jon, realistic? I'm afraid it sounds more like the plot from some rookie mystery writer's first novel, not a reasonable explanation of the facts." She paused. "I think you've been watching too many movies. We must make it a point to find something more interesting for you to do in the evenings."

Lizzy drained her wine. Then she got up and walked over to the fireplace to add a third fake log to the fire. Jon watched her walk. "Do you mind if I turn down these lights?" she asked. "The fire's so pretty, and the lights break the mood." Lizzy switched off the lights completely. The glow from the fire highlighted her silhouette. Jon took another sip of his wine. The wine made him feel pleasantly warm. The fire made him feel pleasantly warm. Lizzy made him feel pleasantly warm. He was getting pretty warm.

"That's better," she said as she walked back to curl up on her end of the couch. The firelight danced across the walls.

Jon tried to return to the subject. "Do you have any plausible explanations for the handprint on the mirror?" he asked.

"Not as interesting as yours," she said. "But if I were you, I'd keep that theory to myself for awhile. It's not quite ready for prime time." She picked up the wine bottle. "May I pour you some more wine?"

"Certainly."

She poured the wine, first in his glass and then in hers. Then she returned to her end of the couch and tucked her feet back under her long skirt.

"You know, Liz, I was thinking about you today."

"Oh really?"

They looked at each other for a few moments without saying anything.

"You know," Jon said. "I really did come over here to talk about Holyoke, but you look really great in the firelight, and I. . . ."

"You what, Jon?" She looked at him and giggled.

"You know," he said, "this should be a lot easier than it is."

"Oh, it's easy enough," she purred. She slid over to his end of the couch.

*

Jon drove home with a smile on his face. There was no traffic. He was pleasantly tired, happy, and completely relaxed. His back felt great. It was two o'clock in the morning and he was totally spent. He smiled to himself as he thought about his evening of lovemaking with Liz. It had left him running on empty. Leon greeted him with a wagging tail after he unlocked his front door. He went inside, turned on the lights and sat down on the couch with a plop. Leon jumped up beside him. They sat there for a few moments, and then Jon's telephone rang. The sound of The Sandman's mechanical voice slipped into his head. He answered the phone with a sense of trepidation.

"Hello?"

"Jon, it's Karen."

"Karen! Why are you calling me this time of night? Need some more judo practice or something?"

"I'm sorry. I know it's late." She paused. "Listen, I feel really bad about what happened earlier this evening. I hope I didn't hurt you. It's just that I have this temper. . . ."

"Temper? Jesus, Karen, if that was just your temper I'd hate to be around when you really get mad. Jealousy does *not* become you."

"I know," she said. "It's just something that I can't seem to control. It pops out and I can't seem to do anything about it. Anyway, I'm really sorry I broke your table."

"What table?" He looked around the room.

"I couldn't sleep. That's why I called," she said. "We need to talk."

"Then we'll talk sometime," he said.

"Ok, let's talk." Karen took a deep breath. "Here we go. You remember what you said to me in the hotel? Well, I think it's about time we talk about that."

"Karen, it's late." Jon rubbed his forehead.

"You act as if it meant nothing. Maybe it didn't. But you have to understand how that makes me feel."

"I didn't ever mean to hurt you," he said.

"You haven't made it easy for me, you know."

"I know. I'm sorry." He couldn't think of anything else to say.

"And our jobs only make it worse."

"I didn't mean to put you in the middle," Jon said.

"We have so many conflicts; it gets all confused."

"It doesn't have to be that way, does it," he said with a sleepy voice. He stifled a yawn.

"I hope not. I've been thinking about it all night," she said. "We're two adults. We need to do something about this, so I thought, what the hell."

"What the hell," Jon said.

"That's why I'm on my way over. I'm glad you weren't asleep."

"What?"

"I just jumped in my car and pointed it in your direction. I'm glad you're awake."

Jon was suddenly wide awake.

"I hope you're not too tired. I have a surprise planned for you."

Jon sat up on the couch.

"I want to see if we can begin where we left off. I'll see you in ten or fifteen minutes."

"Ten or fifteen minutes," he echoed. Karen had already hung up the phone.

Jon panicked. He jumped off the couch. Leon fell on the floor.

He ran to the bathroom and took a two-minute shower. He brushed his teeth for another thirty seconds, gargled with Listerine, the mint kind, and then got dressed in a fresh shirt and jeans. Five minutes later his doorbell rang. It was Karen.

Jon opened the door. Karen was standing on the porch. She was wearing a long, soft coat to protect her from the rain. "Hi, Karen, you can come in if you promise not to hurt me." Leon wagged his tail.

Karen walked in the door. He closed the door and turned around. She locked his eyes with hers as she let her coat slide off her shoulders. She wasn't wearing anything, not a thing, nothing at all.

Jon tried to be cool. He tried to maintain their eye lock, but he blew it. He broke her gaze and quickly scanned her body. "No pantyhose?" They both giggled. He grabbed her hand and they walked together into the bedroom. *Think about her legs*, he thought to himself. *Think about her long, strong, beautiful legs. No, don't think about Viagra, you don't have any. Think about her powerful thighs and her long, strong, beautiful athletic legs.*

It was going to be a long night.

Chapter 12

"Kirk, you look like hell," Dean Thornton announced to the newsroom as he walked by Jon's desk. "By the way, that was a nice piece you wrote yesterday. It had real punch. I hope somebody at SPD takes the time to read it. They might learn something."

"Thanks, Boss," Jon said.

Thornton made a grunting sound and then walked into his office.

Jon was working on another Sandman piece for the evening edition. He was having difficulty concentrating on his work. Memories from the previous night seemed to wash over him in waves, and every few minutes he'd chuckle to himself with a Cheshire cat grin on his face. Vicki was watching him from her desk on the other side of the room. Curiosity was killing her. She picked up her telephone and called him on the office intercom.

"You're looking very self satisfied this morning," she said. "Was she anyone I know?"

"I don't know what you're talking about," Jon replied.

"Of course you don't. That's why you can't wipe that silly smile off your face. Poor boy, she must've kept you up all night."

"You don't know the half of it." Jon chuckled again.

"Come on, Jon, spill your guts," she said. "Was it that policeman who called yesterday? You know I'll find out sooner or later anyway. It might as well be today."

"I don't think so," he said still smiling.

"My, aren't we being stubborn this morning," she said.

Jon laughed as he hung up the phone.

He turned back to his computer and tried to finish his work. After a few minutes of just sitting there he realized that it was hopeless. He wasn't in a serial killer frame of mind. He decided to finish it later. He sighed a sleepy sigh, turned off his computer, and then got up to leave the newsroom for an early lunch. He was walking through the newsroom when a sweaty deliveryman from the Same-Day Bicycle Delivery Service passed him on his way out.

By the time the bicycle messenger found his way through the room over to Vicki's desk, Jon was on his way down to the lobby. The messenger asked her to sign for a package. She looked at the address and then signed in the appropriate place. The same-day-delivery package was addressed to Jon Kirk. Vicki smiled. She tried to catch Jon by calling the guard stationed at the entrance of the building. Bob Blethen had worked as a guard at the paper for years. He had tried other jobs, but nothing ever seemed to work out. He caught Jon just as he was about to leave through the front door.

"Jon, Vicki says you have a package waiting for you upstairs. You must've just missed the messenger. She wants me to tell you it's from your secret admirer."

"Oh really." *Which one*, he wondered.

"She says she's holding it at her desk for safe keeping."

"Did she say if there was a return address?"

"Just a minute." The guard called Vicki and asked her about a return address. "She says no. Is there anything else you want me to ask?"

He thought about it for a moment, and then said, "No. Tell her I'll be right up; and Bob, tell her not to peek." Jon walked back to the newsroom.

Vicki was sitting at her desk, talking to Dean Thornton. Jon waited for Thornton to finish his conversation before he approached.

"I hear you have a little something for me," he said.

"Have you been a good boy?" she asked. "No, don't answer that. You'd probably lie to me anyway."

"I wouldn't lie to you, Vicki."

"Right," she said in a deadpan voice. She reached below her desk and brought out a package wrapped with bright red wrapping paper. It was about the size of a shoebox.

"Aren't you going to open it?" she asked.

"In front of you, God, and everybody?"

"You know I'll find out what's in there anyway."

"Sooner or later," he said.

"Sooner or later," she replied.

"Oh, what the hell." Jon shook the box. He could feel something solid move inside. He smiled at Vicki. She smiled knowingly back at him. He opened the package. There was a typewritten note on top of some shredded paper. Jon took the note out of the box and started to read.

Vicki said, "Read it out loud." Jon rolled his eyes at her and read to himself.

Jon Kirk
Investigative Reporter
Seattle Times

Dear Jon,

Here we are in contact again. I was going to call, but somehow this seems more appropriate. As you know, I am an admirer of yours, and I'm quite impressed with your work. I have become one of your many fans. It is with this sense of appreciation that I wish to offer you some constructive criticism. I hope you don't take it the wrong way.

You're getting off on the wrong track with this case. Your last article on the South American poisons was way off base. Unfortunately, you have been misled by the obvious. Let me give you a hand.

Sincerely,

S

Vicki strained over her desk to see what was inside while Jon removed the top layer of shredded paper.

"Jesus Christ," he exclaimed. He reeled back on his heels and dropped the package in surprise. Its contents fell out onto Vicki's desk with a thud. The shredded paper and box fell onto the floor. Jon froze. He wanted to look away from the severed human hand laying palm up in front of him, but he couldn't.

Vicki screamed a short, clipped scream. Thornton came bounding out of his office. He was joined by a gathering crowd of reporters from the newsroom. "What the hell?" He looked at the hand on Vicki's desk. "This is a crime scene," he said. "Everybody back. Don't touch anything." He addressed Jon. "Did that bicycle delivery kid bring this thing in here? Where is he?" He looked around and then yelled at the crowd. "Somebody find that kid."

✳

The police arrived and were escorted up to the newsroom. Thornton met them at the door. Security people from the newspaper had already evacuated most of the employees from the area. Vicki was in Thornton's office, talking on the telephone. Jon was standing beside one of the windows, looking outside. Thornton brought one of the policemen over to talk to Jon after they secured the crime scene.

The policeman addressed Jon. "You were the one who opened the package?"

"Yeah."

"Come with me." They walked over to Vicki's desk.

"Is this where you dropped it?" The policeman gestured toward the hand on the desk.

"Yeah."

"Did you touch it?"

"I might have brushed against it when I removed some of the packing, but I didn't pick it up. Nobody's touched it since it fell on the desk. It hasn't been moved."

The hand was lying exactly where it had been dropped. A small pool of fluid had formed on the desk from drainage from its severed wrist.

"What about the note?"

"Nobody touched it but me."

"I can vouch for that," Thornton said. "I've been here since it happened, and nobody's disturbed anything on or around this desk."

"OK," the cop said to Jon. "Why don't you go get a cup of coffee or something, but don't go too far. The Sandman task force is on its way over and they'll want to talk to you."

Jon walked back over to the windows overlooking the street. The sky was slate gray and it was drizzling. He watched as Detective Sergeants Washington and Anderson got out of their car and walked to the entrance. He watched Karen as she drove up, double-parked, and then hurried toward the building. He watched as television broadcast vans marked KING BROADCASTING, KOMO NEWS, and KIRO TELEVISION parked in the street and disgorged their complement of reporters and cameramen. He looked up and watched a helicopter arrive; he knew there would be more.

Karen, Robbie and Gil arrived in the newsroom at the same time. Robbie and Gil joined the other two policemen. Karen met with Thornton. In the middle of their conversation Thornton pointed in Jon's direction. When she finished she approached Jon at the window. He was staring outside.

"I heard the package was addressed to you. You OK?" she asked. She gently touched his arm as she spoke to him. She smiled with a soft smile.

"Yeah, I'm OK" he replied. Then he said, "Are you OK, I mean with everything? With last night?" He turned to search her eyes for an answer.

"I'm OK," she said. "I want this, but it does get complicated, doesn't it?"

"It's the story of our relationship."

"It's the story of my life," she said. "But at least now we know where we're going."

"I hope so," he said. "We do if this Sandman business doesn't get out of control." He looked back out of the window. She glanced over at Robbie and Gil and then back at Jon.

"How do you feel?" she asked.

"I really don't know."

"Well you're in it now," she said. "The phone calls were one thing, but this is something else altogether. He's trying to take control." She gently touched him again. "Jon, this is dangerous."

Jon stared out of the window as he spoke, "I was afraid you'd say something like that."

"Come on." She gently tugged on his arm. "Let's get this over with," she said.

Karen and Jon walked over to Vicki's desk. A police photographer entered the room and joined them. She began snapping photos. After the first pictures were taken Robbie picked up the note and put it in a cellophane bag. He was wearing latex gloves. He sealed the top and handed it to Karen. He then examined the severed hand.

"The hand's moist and the skin is well preserved," he said. Robbie smelled the puddle of fluid. "It smells like formaldehyde." He continued his examination. "The wrist end is cut smooth, not jagged or chopped. It looks like it's been surgically removed."

Gil was looking over his shoulder, "Whoever did this knew what he was doing."

"It belonged to a white male," Robbie said. "This isn't a working-man's hand, no calluses. The fingernails are trimmed."

"It's a doctor's hand," Jon said.

"A doctor's hand," echoed Robbie. "Why do you say that?"

"It just is. It belongs to George Holyoke. Check the fingerprints."

Gil challenged him, "How could you know that?"

"My bartender told me," Jon said.

"Right," Gil said. "Are you sure it wasn't your astrologer?"

"It's true, you can ask him."

Karen interrupted the discourse before it went any further. She'd put on latex gloves and had been reading the letter. "I think we can assume that *S* is the Sandman," she said. She turned to Jon. "The letter's fairly typical for this type of perp. He feels superior. He's obviously well educated, and he wants to tell us how clever he is and how stupid we are. *Let me give you a hand.*" Then she looked directly at Jon. "This letter's significant. This package was addressed to you for a reason. He's chosen you for some purpose."

"Oh, goody."

"Jon, you need to be careful. It isn't uncommon for serial killers to make personal contact with a member of the press. Sometimes they form an ongoing bond, even after they get caught."

"If they get caught," Jon said.

"Oh we'll catch him," Gil said. "Don't you worry about that."

"Yeah, well what about the Green River Killer? Thought you had him too, didn't you?"

Karen again interrupted before it could go any farther. "I think he feels close to you. He even corrected you when he thought you were on the wrong track. It's our first real break."

"My buddy, The Sandman," Jon said.

"There's no doubt he'll contact you again."

"Wonderful, I wonder what he'll get me next time. Only forty five shopping days left till Christmas."

"Don't be a smartass," Gil said.

"Are we about done here?" Jon asked. "The formaldehyde's starting to get to me. I need some air."

"Go ahead, take off," Karen said. "I'll call you later. Keep your cell phone on."

He was on his way out of the office when Thornton spotted him. "Kirk," he yelled.

"Yeah."

"Are you doing this story?"

"It'd be better if it came from Lizzy," he said. "I'm too close. I'll find her and work it out. Call if you find that delivery guy." Jon walked out of the office.

Jon left the building to go to his car. Reporters and cameramen were still milling about outside. Guards were keeping them away from the doorway, and Thornton would see to it that they stayed away until after the evening edition was on the street. He knew how to protect an exclusive. Jon climbed into his Explorer and called Lizzy. She answered her cell phone.

"Lizard, where are you?"

"Jon, is that you? What's this, Lizard, where are you?"

"Huh?"

"How about, hi, Liz. You were great last night; or at least, thanks for the evening, Liz. Not, Lizard, where are you."

"Then you haven't heard," he said. "The Sandman sent me a little present this morning, Holyoke's hand. At least I think it was Holyoke's. We'll know for sure later today when they check the fingerprints."

"You're kidding!"

"I wish I were. It came by bicycle delivery. Vicki was watching when I unwrapped the thing."

"Ugh."

"It was a mess."

"How'd Vicki take it?"

"OK, I guess. Karen and the task force are still in the newsroom. Television news crews are all over the street. So where are you?"

"Workin' out. I've got to keep these washboard abs you seem to like so much in primo shape."

"Listen, we need something for the evening paper and I can't do it. I'm too close. You want the severed hand story?"

"You kidding? Sure!"

"You'll need to interview Vicki and the rest of the crew in the newsroom."

"You don't need to tell me how to do my job."

"Sorry." He paused and then continued. "Electronic media types will be all over the place. They'll have rumors and what they can squeeze out of the cops, but nothing much else. You can interview me when I get back. It should be your exclusive."

"Do I owe you something for this?"

"Let's just call it even."

"Deal."

"Deal. Listen, while you're back at the office, I'm going to go over to the med school. I want to find Dr. Saunders."

"What a story. Thanks, Jon."

"And Liz, you were the greatest last night. Thanks for the special evening."

"My pleasure," she said.

"See you later." Jon hung up the phone.

*

The traffic was light as Jon drove towards the medical school. The thought of visiting the anatomy department again unsettled his stomach. He called Saunders, but she was busy with a class. His plan was to make his way to her office and then wait for her there.

After he parked, he was able to find NN110 and the Anatomy Department with less difficulty than he anticipated. As expected, Dr. Saunders was not in her small office. The double doors to the human dissection laboratory were open and the smell of formaldehyde emanating from the room was strong. Nausea coursed through him.

Jon looked inside the double doors. The anatomy laboratory was large. It had a polished cement floor, tiled walls, and bright fluorescent lighting. There were twenty-six dissection cubicles around the periphery of the room separated from each other by stainless steel partitions. The cubicles were approximately ten feet wide and fourteen feet long. They were open at the central end.

Each cubicle had a rectangular dissection table at its center with a partially dissected human cadaver top. There were six students in each cubicle working on the cadavers. Dr. Saunders was writing something on the blackboard in the cubicle marked Cube 26 when she noticed Jon near the double doors. She motioned for him to come in.

"Mr. Kirk, nice to see you again," she said in a loud voice. She walked over to greet him. "I'm glad you came. I need a break." Saunders pulled a pack of cigarettes out of the pocket of her lab coat, selected one and lit it. She inhaled deeply and then blew a smoke ring in the air.

"Is this the class that Holyoke taught, the one you told me about?" Jon asked.

"The very one," she answered. "Now I'm stuck with it. Let me show you around."

Jon felt trapped. She led him over to the nearest cubicle. There was a sign on a small blackboard near its entrance that said Cube 26. Below the sign was written *Dolly*.

"There are one hundred fifty-six students in a freshman class," she said. "Six students for every cadaver." Saunders held her cigarette in her mouth when she talked. It bobbed up and down, shaking ashes onto the floor. "At the beginning of the freshman year, each group of six students picks their cadaver from a central holding tank. When they first see them, the cadavers are completely wrapped in cloth. The wrap helps to reduce the students' stress level when they see the tank full of floaters. It also helps to keep the cadavers moist when they're out in the air. The students then transfer their cadavers to their dissection cubes and begin work."

Saunders took a last big drag from her cigarette and then put it out on the wall. She dropped the extinguished butt in the pocket of her white lab coat. "Come and look at this table." She shooed the students away. "These dissection tables are really formaldehyde tanks with movable tops. The cadavers rest on an internal metal shelf that can be raised to serve as a dissection stand, or lowered to immerse the bodies in the formaldehyde solution. This is how it works."

There was a partially wrapped body on the dissection stand. Its head was wrapped in a brown-colored bandage, as were its legs. The body was lying on its back. The chest and abdomen were open, with the skin folded back over the cadaver's sides from a central, mid-line cut. The intestines were gone, dissected away. Dr. Saunders stepped on a pedal at the base of the table. The tabletop and the cadaver recessed inside a tank filled with fluid. Once in the lowered position, Saunders closed a stainless steel lid sealing the cadaver in the tank. "And that's how it works," she said. She opened the lid, again stepped on the lever, and the cadaver smoothly emerged out of the fluid so that the students could continue their work. Jon looked green as he watched the formaldehyde solution drain out of the open body cavities. He felt more than a little nauseous and shaky.

Saunders looked at him and said, "Let's go back to my office. The students will be OK on their own for a little while."

Saunders continued talking as they walked, "At the beginning of the year, students place their cadavers face down and dissect the muscles of the back. Rather than unwrap the cadavers they cut through the cloth, exposing only the area that they're dissecting. It was Holyoke's idea. That way they're exposed to the bodies just a little bit at a time. After a few weeks, they turn the bodies over and begin dissecting the abdominal cavity. The chest and extremities are next. Finally they unwrap the head and begin on the face." Saunders stopped to light another cigarette. Then they walked into her office and sat down.

She changed the subject. "Any news of Holyoke?" she asked.

"That's what I came here to talk to you about. I believe you were right about Holyoke and the prostitute murders. The police are fairly certain he didn't commit them. Unfortunately, they have reason to believe that he might have met with some foul play."

"It wouldn't surprise me," she said. "He was a foul little man." She deeply inhaled and then put the half-smoked cigarette out in her overflowing ashtray, exhaling as she asked, "What happened to him?"

"They're not sure, but I doubt if he's still alive. He may have been killed by the real Sandman, or maybe someone else."

"Really."

"We haven't a clue about a motive. Do you know of anyone who might have had a reason to kill him?"

"Me," she said, "and maybe a hundred other people. The list would be long. You either love him or hate him, or sometimes both."

"A hundred people who might actually do him in?"

"Oh, not really, I suppose," she said. "I don't know of anyone who would actually do it. It's just that he could be a very irritating, frustrating little man when he wanted to be."

"Holyoke was conducting pain research with medicines extracted from South American plants," Jon said. "We think they may have been used in the murders. Do you know anything about that?"

"Not really. As I told you, he used cats for those experiments. I don't do cats. It was all very mysterious. Why don't you look at his research records?"

"What research records?"

"He must have kept records of his research. It's standard practice. They must be around somewhere."

"Any idea where?"

"Nope. But if you find them, let me know. I'd love to know what the old fart was up to."

"Thanks, I'll check it out."

Saunders removed her pack of cigarettes, looked at it and then put it back in her pocket. "Listen, I'd like to talk to you some more about this, but I really should get back to my students. They'll get into another fascia fight if I leave them in there alone much longer."

"A fascia fight?"

"Yeah. Fascia is human subcutaneous tissue, you know, fat. If I turn my back, students rip it out of the cadavers and throw it at each other. It's kind of disrespectful of the dead, but on the other hand it helps desensitize the students. It wouldn't be too bad except that it's greasy and it leaves spots on the walls when they miss each other."

"You're kidding."

"Nope. There are one hundred and fifty-six of the little bastards out there. Can you believe it? There are too many damn doctors in the world. The dean won't cut down our class size because he's afraid he might offend some alumnus and lose some funding. It's all about money. It's always about money."

"Listen, I'd really like to ask you some more questions."

"Call me tomorrow," she said. "We'll talk then."

"OK, but how about just one more? When you were showing me the dissection station, the sign read Cube 26. I assume that's the number of the dissection cubicle. Under the sign it said *Dolly*. What was that all about?"

"Tits."

"What?"

"It's about tits. Dolly's the cadaver's name. The students named her Dolly because she has big tits." Jon just looked at Saunders. "They named her Dolly after Dolly Parton. All the cadavers have names. It's a tradition around here. Let's see, there's Mongo, Gabby after Gabby Hays (no teeth); Captain Hook with one hand; Charlie, I have no idea why they named him Charlie; Al Gore, he was stiff as a board when they pulled him out of the tank; Olive Oil and so on." Saunders looked in the direction of the lab. "I've really got to go. As I said, call me tomorrow. We'll talk then."

Saunders stood up. She fingered the pack of cigarettes in her pocket and then left her office to return to the anatomy lab. Jon felt like he needed a shower.

Chapter 13

Jon turned off the water, pulled back the plastic curtain, and climbed out of the shower. It was one of those old-fashioned combination bathtub-showers. The tub was small and slippery, and there was barely enough room for one, much less the two of them. Standing still was difficult; moving around was dangerous. And they had done a lot of moving around. Jon held Karen's hand as she stepped over the edge of the tub onto the tile floor. He offered her a towel, grabbed one for himself, and then they toweled each other off. Karen wrapped her towel around her body and tucked it in above her breasts; Jon wrapped his around his waist. They both radiated warmth as they walked through the hallway into the living room.

Jon and Karen sat with each other on the couch and listened to the soft sound of the Seattle rain outside the windows. Seattle rain has a texture all its own, a texture halfway between rain and mist. The Seattle mist-rain had enveloped Jon's small house like a cloud. A fire was crackling in the fireplace.

"Are you warm enough?" Jon asked.

"Um-hum," she said as she snuggled in closer to him.

Jon held her for awhile. "How nice," he said. "It almost makes you forget about this afternoon."

"Almost," she said.

They cuddled for awhile longer. The fire crackled as the rain slid down his windows in rivulets.

"You know," he said, "I can still see that hand on Vicki's desk when I shut my eyes. That and the handprint in the hotel."

"Something like that stays with you for awhile."

"Not too long I hope."

"It's always too long, but it'll fade with time," she said. "Believe me; I know about these things."

Jon was leaning against the corner of the couch. Karen's back was against his chest and the back of her head nestled in the crook of his neck. His arm was around her waist. She shifted her position so that they fit together like the proverbial spoons in a drawer.

"I've been wondering," Jon said. "This whole thing's so weird. Why'd he pick me?"

"Publicity," she answered. "Your stories brought him national attention; after all you made *The New York Times*. He likes that in some perverse sort of way."

"If he wants publicity you'd think he'd pick someone from television."

"You gave him his name," she said.

"You think that's it?"

"Maybe. Or maybe he knows you or at least has met you. He could be anybody. These guys know how to hide and blend in."

"Now that's a comforting thought."

Karen shifted her position to snuggle in a little closer. Jon curled around her. They sat together for awhile and watched the rain on the windows.

"Still thinking about The Sandman?" she asked.

"Yeah," he answered. "I don't think that profile's going to help us find him."

"You don't think much of psychological profiles do you?"

"Not really."

"You should. They're useful when they predict behavior. The FBI's sure to update The Sandman's after this hand episode."

"He doesn't seem that predictable," Jon said.

"It may seem strange," she answered, "but he fits a pattern. There's a whole group of these guys who seem to get their kicks from severing body parts. Sometimes they mail them, sometimes they save them, and sometimes they even eat them. Hands are a bit unusual though. Usually it's internal organs or heads."

"Well there's a mood breaker."

Karen sat up and turned her body around so that she could look in his eyes.

"I meant it when I said you'll hear from him again you know, maybe soon."

"I hope he won't send any more body parts."

"He might. He probably has the rest of Holyoke somewhere. Oh, I forgot to tell you. We got a positive ID. It was Holyoke's hand."

Jon sat up so that he could better look at Karen. Now they were sitting face to face.

"I talked to one of Holyoke's associates at the medical school this afternoon," he said. "Janet Saunders."

"I know that name," Karen said. "I think we interviewed her after we found Holyoke's print on the third body."

"You'd remember her if you'd ever met her," Jon said. "Anyway, Holyoke wasn't as universally liked as the school's PR office would have you believe. Nonetheless, Saunders didn't know of anybody who disliked him enough to kill him."

"That doesn't surprise me," she said. "I don't know how Holyoke's presumed murder ties in with The Sandman anyway. We don't have a motive."

"I think it's somehow related to his research."

Karen shifted her position of the couch. "You mean the business with the cats?"

"The drugs from the South American plants," he answered. "When The Sandman called he told me that I was off base about the plants. He said the same thing in his letter with the hand. I think he's trying to steer me away from something."

"You could be right."

"Saunders says Holyoke would have kept research records. Did you guys look at them?"

"We never found any research papers. We searched through his offices and computer files both at home and at the medical school. There's nothing there."

"That's a little strange, don't you think?"

"Of course it's strange. What are you getting at?"

"This was more than a research project to him. It was his life. There ought to be something, some reference to it somewhere. After all, Lizzy and I did find the background reference material at his house."

"I've been meaning to talk to you about that," she said.

"A minor indiscretion."

"Breaking and entering? Hardly."

Jon shifted his position on the couch again. Karen stood up and walked over to the fireplace. She looked into the fire as she spoke. "Jon, where's this going?"

"You mean The Sandman case?"

"No, I mean where are *we* going."

Jon squirmed a bit in his seat. Karen kept her back to him, waiting for his answer. "We discussed this the other night, didn't we?" he asked.

"Yes, we did; but that was the other night." She stared at the fire. "Tell me how you feel." She turned to face him. "I need to know how you feel now."

"I'm not very good at this," he said.

"I don't need you to be good at it," she replied. "I just need you to do it."

Jon steadied himself against the corner of the couch. He looked at her, hesitated a moment, and then started to speak, "Well, I. . . . What I want to say is," he paused, "I uh," he paused again. Then he interrupted himself. "This is really hard for me."

"I know," she said. "It used to be easy. Now it's not so easy. That's an improvement." Karen moved from the fireplace in his direction.

Then she knelt down so that one knee was on the floor and the other was up in line with her chest. She wrapped her arms around her upright knee. She leveled her eyes on the same plane as his.

"I, um. . . ." He started to squirm again. He moved his arm from the couch to the corner table and inadvertently bumped the answering machine with his elbow. The answering machine slid sideways and the table leg Karen had pieced together collapsed. As the table tipped over forward the lamp on the table fell back against the wall, crashed to the floor and broke in several pieces. Karen rolled backward. Leon ran out of the room to hide under the bed. Jon looked at everything piled in a heap next to his couch. "Oh, *that* table."

Karen looked up at him from the floor. She was sitting with her legs out in front of her and her hands behind her, propping her up. Her eyes were wide. "I'm sorry," she said. "I broke it the other night when I lost my temper. I propped the leg together and forgot to tell you to glue it."

Jon started to laugh. Karen looked up at him for a moment longer and then joined in the laughter. "It's getting late," he said. "Stay here with me tonight."

"Umm, I'd love to," she said.

"Let's finish this discussion later."

"It's a deal. We'll work on it tomorrow."

Karen climbed up on the couch. She put her arms around his waist and her head against his chest. She gently hugged him.

"I can hear your heart," she said.

After a few minute's silence Jon said, "Karen, I'm so sorry for the hurt that I caused you. I. . . ." She reached up and touched her index finger to his lips. "Shush," she said softly.

Chapter 14

The morning Sandman task force meeting was in progress in the usual location. Gil and Robbie were sitting at the table. Karen was standing beside the blackboard. McCabe was sitting in a chair in a corner of the room. He had attended the meetings on a regular basis ever since the discovery of Annabel Young's body. The mood was glum. For the first time since the task force had formed the group felt as if they were losing ground. The Sandman, it appeared, was winning.

Karen had just erased several lines from the chart. It now read:

VICTIMS	PERPETRATOR
Women	Male
Prostitutes	Smart, maybe genius
Drug addicts	Technical or medical job
No trauma or violence	White
Unknown injectable	Loner
poison	Likes publicity
	Leaves false clues
	Communicates through J. Kirk
	? Killed and mutilated Holyoke

"Look at this stuff," Karen said. "We're no farther along than we were when we started.

"Sure we are," McCabe said. "Holyoke may not be The Sandman, but they're tied together somehow. That's progress. Now we have to find the connection."

"I suppose," Karen said.

McCabe moved his chair in the corner. It made an annoying sound as it scraped on the floor. "Has Doc Allison finished his written autopsy report yet?" he asked.

"Yeah," Gil said. "Give me a minute." He pulled the report out of his tattered briefcase. "Here it is. It's not too much different from the others," he said. "Death was due to cardio-pulmonary arrest of undetermined cause. She was a drug addict like the others, and had the usual needle tracks. She tested positive for hepatitis C, and was HIV negative. There was no evidence of trauma."

"What about the bruises on her right side?" Karen asked. "I saw two distinct bruises on the right side of her chest at the autopsy. There were some odd serrated marks on her skin too."

Gil leafed through the autopsy report. "He mentions the bruises and the marks, but he doesn't comment on them," he said. "He must have thought they weren't important."

"I'll ask him about it," Karen said.

"What about the tissue samples?" McCabe asked.

"No results yet," Gil answered. "He's still testing. He's using the same tests the FBI used in their crime lab. He's hoping to find something, but it'll take a day or two for the tests to be completed."

"It sounds like more of the same," Robbie said.

"I'm afraid so," Karen agreed.

"All the news isn't bad," Gil said. "We found the bell captain, the guy who talked to The Sandman on the hotel telephone. His name was Patrick something or other. He arranged for the prostitute."

"What'd he have to say?" McCabe asked.

"He was very cooperative," Gil said. "We didn't even have to threaten him with aiding and abetting."

"I'll bet he was," McCabe said. "I hope you scared the shit out of him."

"Get anything useful?" Karen asked.

"A little. The guy in room 487 was very specific in his tastes. He wanted a young, girlish prostitute, and he wanted her for the night."

"Anything about The Sandman's voice?" Robbie interjected.

"Nothing special, no accents or anything like that. He spoke in a normal male tone, not high or low. He didn't sound nervous or anxious."

"Where'd the bell captain get the girl?" McCabe asked.

"Through Billy Sea, a local pimp."

"I'd like to talk to Mr. Sea," Karen said. "Maybe he's dealt with our perp before."

"Me, too," Robbie said. "Five minutes alone with him should do it."

"I don't think that's such a good idea, Robbie," McCabe said.

"I hate pimps," Robbie replied. "They seduce these kids into prostitution, and then dump 'em when they're all used up. He's as guilty as The Sandman as far as I'm concerned."

"That won't get us anywhere," McCabe said.

"What about Holyoke? What's his tie-in?" Gil asked.

"We don't know," Karen said. "The substances the FBI lab identified have to be related to his research in some way. We need to learn more about it. Jon Kirk at the *Times* has researched the subject pretty well."

"I've seen you and Kirk together a lot lately," Gil said. "Anything going on there we should know about?"

"Watch out for Kirk," McCabe said. "He's a mercenary son of a bitch. He'll use you any way he can to get what he wants."

"And what he wants is a story," Robbie added.

"I can take care of myself," Karen said.

"I know you can," McCabe replied. "I just don't want you to get hurt."

"Maybe I should have a talk with him," Robbie said.

"Come on you guys. I don't need any big brothers. I'm a big girl.

Let's get back to Holyoke and The Sandman."

The door opened and the desk sergeant poked his head in the room.

"We just picked up Billy Sea. We got him for carrying a concealed weapon, a semi-automatic pistol. He's on his way to the holding cell. I thought you'd like to know."

✳

Robbie and Gil went down to the holding cell together. It was a twenty-five by fifteen foot cinderblock room with a steel bar front wall and a solid steel door. There were benches along each cinderblock wall, and one in the center of the room. The benches, walls, floor and ceiling were all painted the same drab color of gray. Five prisoners sat around the room. Billy Sea was sitting on a bench by himself, away from the others. He was wearing a black sport coat over a blue silk shirt opened at the neck. At five foot nine, he was the shortest man in the room.

"Hey, Billy, is that you?" Gil said.

"Fuck you."

"Come on, Billy, it's time to talk."

"I got nothin' ta say."

"You tell him, Billy," said a grisly old man with a gray beard in the corner.

"Did I say you could talk?" Gil said to the old man. He didn't answer. "Then shut the fuck up.

"Get over here," he said to Billy. "You know the drill. We're going for a walk down the hall."

Billy walked over to the cell door. Gil unlocked the door, grabbed Billy by his coat and pulled him roughly out into the hall. Robbie clasped his large hand over Billy's arm.

"Hey, be careful," Billy said. He stood there while Gil relocked the door.

Gil fixed Billy's gaze with his own before he spoke. "Let me introduce myself. I'm Detective Sergeant Gil Anderson. I'm the good cop."

"And you know what that makes me," Robbie said as he glowered down at him. He was at least a head taller than Billy.

The three of them walked down the hallway to the interrogation room. Gil opened the door and shoved Billy inside. The two detectives followed him in.

The interrogation room was one of six at the Public Safety Building. It was small, about twelve by twelve feet, and equipped with the usual two-way mirror and video recording equipment. The walls were cinderblock and the floor was tile. It had a heavy metal door with a lock. The room was made to look uncomfortable and it had the feel of a jail cell. Karen and her boss were watching the interview from behind the two-way mirror.

"Sit in the chair over there," Gil instructed. Billy sat down. Gil sat in a chair facing him with his back to the door. There was a table between them. It was bolted to the floor. Robbie walked over to a corner behind Billy, behind his line of sight. He leaned against the wall. Gil started the interview.

"Looks like we got you on a concealed weapons charge, Billy," Gil said. "A semi-automatic Glock. That's a nasty gun, especially for an ex-con."

Billy didn't say anything.

"What do you need a gun like that for? Don't tell me it's for plunkin' rats."

Billy still didn't say anything. Robbie walked up behind him and cuffed him on the side of his head with the heel of his hand. Billy's head lurched forward.

"Answer the man," he said.

Billy turned around and looked at Robbie, then at the camera mounted near the ceiling in the corner of the room, then back toward Gil. Robbie walked back to his corner. "Don't look at the camera Billy," Gil said. "It's turned off. No little red light. We can do anything we want in here and nobody's going to know."

"Protection," he said. "I need the gun for protection."

"Ya know, Billy; you're not too smart. That gun's going to earn you a trip back to the joint. You liked it in Walla Walla, did you?"

"Hey, The Sandman's out there. There's a lot a weirdos out there. Maybe even terrorists. I gotta protect my girls."

He heard Robbie's sarcastic voice from behind him. "You did a great job of that."

He turned around again to look at Robbie, and then back toward Gil.

"Tell him to stay away from me," he said to Gil. Robbie laughed a deep laugh. "Alright, alright," Billy said. "Whatdaya guys want?"

"Not you," Gil said. "We don't give a shit about you. As dumb as you are, you'll be back here soon enough anyway."

"Tell us about Annabel Young," Robbie growled. "You sent her over to Hotel Siena to get killed."

Billie turned around. "What the fuck you talkin' about?"

Robbie took several quick steps forward and hit him again in the head with his open hand. Billy saw it coming, but there was nothing he could do about it. This time his head lurched forward and smashed into the table. Robbie grabbed Billy's hair, pulled his head back, bent over and put his lips close to Billy's ear. He spoke in a quiet but determined voice while he held his head back by the hair. "The Sandman killed Annabel Young. You made the arrangements. We want to know about that." He shoved Billy's head forward as he let go of his hair and walked back to the corner of the room.

"I don't know nothin' about it," he said in Gil's general direction. He rubbed his forehead. "Some guy wants a little girl type at the hotel for the night. I sent Annie over. That's all. I don't know nothin' bout the murder. She had a razor."

"What about The Sandman's other victims," Anderson asked. "Were they your girls, too? Was Carol Williams your girl?"

"No man, they weren't my girls."

"Robbie," Gil said.

Billy heard movement from somewhere behind him. He ducked

his head and flinched in anticipation of another blow.

Karen and Bill McCabe were watching the interrogation from behind the mirror in a viewing room. The door to the viewing room opened. A sergeant stuck his head in the door and told Karen that she had a phone call. It was from Dr. Allison. She told him that she would be right out.

"What do you think, Cap?" she asked.

"I think we aren't going to get much more out of him. He probably doesn't know much anyway."

"Tell me if he says anything." Karen left the room to take her call. She walked down the hall to the sergeant's desk.

"You can use this one," the sergeant said as he pointed toward a phone. "It's line four, the one that's blinking." Karen picked up the phone.

"Dr. Allison?"

"Detective Able, I recognize your voice."

"We've been waiting for your call," she said.

"We finished our toxicology tests. We identified the same type of compound in Annabel Young that the FBI found in the other victims. There's no doubt now about the cause of death."

"Well that's something," she said. "It keeps the pattern consistent. Finally a little progress in this case. Is there any more?"

"Not much," he said. "The compounds are definitely related to curare, and they probably have at least some of the same properties. Unfortunately, we don't have much of the drug to work with. The tissue concentrations were minute. We don't have near enough to do a detailed analysis."

"That sounds like a problem."

"It's a big problem. We can't even tell for sure if the same drug was used in all four of the women. They're all related to each other, it's the same type of compound, but they may or may not be the exact same drug. We don't really know."

"I wish we knew more," she said. "This is one of the few solid clues we have in this case."

"I'm afraid that's all I've got," he replied.

"You knew Dr. Holyoke, didn't you?" she asked. "Could these drugs be related to his research?"

"I knew him, but not well, and I don't know anything about his research. I'd have no way of knowing if these drugs are related or not."

"Thanks anyway," she said. "Let me know if anything else turns up."

"OK, I'll talk to you later."

"Bye," she said. Karen hung up the phone. Then she called him right back to ask him about the bruises, but his line was busy. She left a message on his voice mail.

Chapter 15

I t was Saturday and it was a big day in the anatomy lab, the biggest day of the year. Students had anticipated this moment since classes first started. After hundreds of hours of dissection, and many more hours of study, it was finally time for the 156 students of the freshman class to meet their cadavers face to face. The period of anonymity was over. It was picture day in the anatomy lab.

Having started on the cadavers the previous quarter, the class had finished the bulk of their dissections. Their work on the chests, abdominal cavities, and extremities was complete. Now it was time to unwrap and expose their cadaver's heads. Tradition held that each group of students would have their pictures taken with their cadaver on the day the faces were finally unveiled. Dissection of the heads wouldn't actually start until the following week.

The anatomy lab had been converted into a make-shift photography studio for the occasion. A high-backed wooden chair was placed at the far end of the room. A curtain was placed behind the chair as a backdrop. The setting for the photos had been the same each year for as far back as anyone could remember. Tradition held that the chairman of anatomy would take the pictures. With Holyoke missing the duty fell to Janet Saunders. These photos from picture day provided a secret record of accomplishment for generations of physicians from the school.

Each dissection group would take their cadaver and place it in the chair. The six members of each cube would then pose behind the chair for a group photo. Some of the poses were serious. Some of them were funny. Dr. Saunders stood by a 35-millimeter camera on a tripod. Cubes 1 through 5 had already completed their portraits. There were twenty-one groups to go. Saunders was taking a cigarette break while the next group of students moved their cadaver into position. The desensitization process had worked.

The Cube 6 team pulled their cadaver, Captain Hook, out of his humidor and carried him around to the chair of honor. It took only two students to carry the body. A third mopped up the fluids that drained onto the floor during the move. Captain Hook was easy to move because the students had already removed and dissected all of his internal organs. His chest and abdomen were empty, so was his pelvis. His arms and legs had been skinned. His muscles were separated from each other, but were still attached to his bones in their proper locations. He was really just an empty shell.

Photos were taken either with the skin flaps open, exposing the empty body cavities, or, more modestly, with the skin flaps closed. Some students dressed their cadavers in coat and tie, or even a hat. This group had decided to pose Captain Hook *au natural.* They sat him up in his chair, opened his skin flaps and then slowly unwrapped the cloth bandage from around his head. All eyes were focused on his face.

Hook's cheeks were hollow as expected, due to the shrinkage of his subcutaneous fat. One eye was open and one eye was partially closed. His exposed cornea was opaque. The formaldehyde had tanned his facial skin and caused his lips to retract away from his mouth, exposing his teeth. His thin gray hair was stuck to his head. The students looked him over for a moment or two, and then moved behind him and smiled. They posed. Nothing happened. They waited for Dr. Saunders to take their portrait.

Nothing. Dr. Saunders just stood there. Her cigarette fell out of her mouth and onto the floor, still lit. After a moment or two she crushed the cigarette with her foot. She snapped the photo and asked the students to wait for a moment. Then she took another photo for good measure, and then one more. The students watched her as she silently walked toward them for a closer look. She took a moment or two to be sure. Then the students of Cube 6 heard her say, mostly to herself, and only half out loud, "Well I'll be God damned."

＊

Jon Kirk was sitting on his couch watching the Huskies play football when his telephone rang. It was Saturday and he was enjoying his day off. It had been a long week. After five rings he answered the phone. The Huskies weren't doing all that well anyway.

"Hello."

"Mr. Kirk, it's Janet Saunders at the medical school. I hate to bother you on a Saturday, but something's come up."

"What's that?" he asked matter-of-factly. He was not in the mood to talk to Janet Saunders.

"We seem to have found the missing Dr. Holyoke, or at least what's left of him. He's here at the lab."

"What?"

"Do you remember Captain Hook, the cadaver with the missing hand in Cube 6? The students unwrapped his face today. Well guess what?"

"Jesus Christ. Have you called the police?"

"Not yet. With the exception of 156 freshmen medical students, you're the first to know. I thought you might like to come down here and talk to some of them before Kay Masters and the police bottle them up for the duration."

"I'll be right there. Don't let anyone leave." Jon hung up the phone.

Jon jumped off the couch and nearly tripped over Leon as he ran to the door. He ran to his car and then climbed in behind the steering wheel. He made a U-turn as he pulled away from the curb, drove to Madison, and then headed west toward the University. He'd been in his car for less than a minute and was ripping through the city at least thirty miles an hour over the speed limit when he speed dialed Lizzy's number. "Liz, drop whatever you're doing and meet me in the anatomy department at the medical school." His voice was a little shaky. "They found Holyoke. He's a cadaver in his own class."

There was silence at the other end of the phone.

Jon continued, "He's been dissected."

"Is this a joke?" she asked.

"No, it is not. Get a photographer to meet us there. And hurry."

"I'm on my way."

Jon broke the connection and then called Karen. He left a message for her to call him on his cell phone. Then he drove into the hospital parking lot, left his car and ran down to the anatomy department. When he arrived the students were standing around in the dissection lab in groups, talking among themselves. Dr. Saunders stood at the door to greet him. Jon was out of breath.

"You certainly got here in a hurry," she said. "I thought I'd wait until you arrived before I notified the police. Now I have no choice but to call them, after I have another cigarette, that is."

"Where is he?"

"Over there." She nodded her head toward the end of the room. "Feel free to talk with the students or do whatever you do. I'll go make my phone call." Saunders lit a cigarette. The pocket of her lab coat was bulging with extinguished cigarette butts.

Jon's eyes slowly shifted from Saunders to the figure in the chair at the other end of the room. The color drained from his face. There sat the almost completely dissected body of Dr. George Holyoke. He sat in a chair with his skin folded back, his chest empty and his abdomen open. Holyoke's opaque eyes stared back at him.

The rest of the cadavers were back in their humidors with the lids shut. Saunders was leaning against the doorway. Jon turned to her and started to speak but nothing came out. He turned again to look at the body. He didn't know Lizzy had entered the room until he heard her speak.

"That's him?" Lizzy asked.

"I guess so," Jon said.

"Why is he in the chair?"

"I have no idea," he said. He addressed Saunders, "Why is he in the chair?"

"Today was picture day. Each year we take photos of the students with their cadavers. They pose them in the chair. It's a tradition," she said.

"You mean you have photos of Holyoke with the students who dissected him?" Liz asked.

"The very ones. It was a great shot. Captain Hook, that's what they call him, is sitting in the chair just as you see him and they're all smiles standing behind him." Saunders blew a smoke ring.

"Could I have a copy?" Jon asked. "I mean, I'd love to have a copy if you don't mind."

"You and the *National Enquirer*," she said.

Jon and Liz took a few steps toward Holyoke's body. Lizzy turned to Jon and whispered in his ear, "You realize this is the story of a lifetime."

"Medical students dissect their professor," he replied softly. He was formulating a headline. "It's one for the books."

"It's a Pulitzer unless we fuck it up," Lizzy said.

The *Times* photographer banged through the double doors and joined the rest of the group. "Jesus Christ!" She immediately began taking photographs of Holyoke, the students and the dissection laboratory.

Jon addressed Lizzy as they both continued to stare at the cadaver, "Get as many statements from the students as you can before the police get here. They'll throw us out as soon as they arrive. And tell that photographer to finish up and get out of here before they confiscate her film."

Saunders was listening to their conversation. She walked over to her camera, rewound the film, removed it from the camera, and put it in a pocket in her jeans. Then she inserted a fresh roll and snapped off five or six photos of the body. "The police should be here soon," she said.

"Could you point out the students that worked on Holyoke?" Lizzy asked.

"They're the ones over there near the Cube 6 sign," she answered.

Liz walked over to the group, introduced herself, and began her interviews.

Jon had a thousand questions for Saunders. Who had access to the anatomy dissection laboratory? How were the bodies switched? When were they switched? What happened to the body that was supposed to be in Cube 6? Did she have any ideas about who could have done it? Who had access? What happened to Holyoke's organs after they were dissected? Before he had a chance to ask any of them he heard Robbie Washington's voice from the laboratory entrance.

"What the fuck?"

Robbie, Gil Anderson and two uniformed policemen were standing in the doorway. Two members of the hospital security team were with them.

Jon looked at Robbie and then gestured toward the corpse; "It's George Holyoke."

The police were all staring at the body.

"What're you doing here?" Gil asked Jon. The others were still staring at the corpse.

"Working," Jon replied. "Where's Karen? Shouldn't she be here?"

"I don't know," Gil said.

Robbie replied to Jon's question while still looking at Holyoke's body, "She's up in the mountains hiking or something. She'll be back later today." Then he noticed Liz interviewing the students. "Hey you, quit that. Come over here," he said in a loud voice. "This is a crime scene." He didn't notice the photographer, who had put her camera away and was sitting with the other students as if she belonged there with them.

Saunders put her cigarette out on the wall and added the butt to the collection in her pocket. She addressed Robbie and Bill. "My name is Janet Saunders." She extended her hand. "I'm the acting director of this lab. I'm the one who called the police."

"I'm Detective Sergeant Robbie Washington and this is Detective Sergeant Gil Anderson. We're members of The Sandman task force," Robbie said.

"And these are the young men and women of the freshman class." Saunders gestured toward the students with a sweeping motion.

Robbie turned his attention back to the group across the room. "Young lady," he said to Liz, "I said get over here."

"Thanks for calling," Gil said to Saunders. "We got here as quick as we could."

Robbie glared at Liz, "Miss Reporter, Jon's girlfriend, if you don't get over here now I'm going to haul your ass in for tampering with a crime scene."

Lizzy asked one more question, waited for a reply and then walked over to join the group. "What's the problem?" she asked. "I didn't touch anything."

"I want you two out of here, now," he said. "And whose camera is that?" Robbie gestured toward the camera on the tripod.

"It's mine," Dr. Saunders answered. "I took some photographs." She lit a cigarette and blew smoke in Robbie's general direction.

"I'll have to confiscate that film. It's evidence. You'll get it back later," he said.

"Sure," she said with her cigarette hanging from her mouth. "Here, I'll get it for you." Saunders rewound the film, removed it from the camera and gave it to Robbie.

Gil and the uniformed policemen had walked over to take a closer look at the cadaver. "What the hell's going on around here?" he asked.

"Picture day," one of the students replied.

"That's our cue," Jon said. "Time to leave. Thanks, Janet. I owe you big time. Come on Liz, we know when we're not wanted." Jon and Liz turned to leave. The photographer stood up to go with them. She put her backpack on. Robbie stopped her.

"No students leave until we interview you."

"I'm just going to the bathroom," she said. "I'll be right back."

"We may want to talk to you two later, too," Gil said to Jon and Liz.

"We'll be at the *Times* all afternoon," Jon answered.

They all three walked out.

＊

Liz was still typing at her computer in the newsroom when Jon walked over to her desk. The newsroom was quieter than usual, even for a Saturday. Thornton was in his office reading Jon's piece on Holyoke and the anatomy lab. Lizzy was writing her story of the student interviews. Jon rubbed her shoulders from behind.

"How are you coming?" he asked.

Lizzy looked up at him over her shoulder. "It's getting there," she said. "I really want this to be good. Have you heard anything on the news yet?"

"Not yet, at least not on KIRO radio. I'd think they'd have it if anybody had it. It's still our story."

"Look at him in there." Liz nodded toward Thornton. He was rereading Jon's story. "He loves it. He's in hog heaven. I wonder if he'll let us use the pictures."

"Not a chance," Jon said. "He said they were tabloid stuff. He'd never print a photo of the cadaver. He'll use one that shows what the lab looks like, maybe the one with the med students milling around."

"Too bad," she said. "Now go away and let me finish. We still have deadlines around here you know."

Jon walked over to Thornton's office and knocked on the door.

Thornton looked up at him through the glass, and then motioned for him to come in. Jon opened the door.

"So what do you think, boss? It's incredible isn't it?"

"Incredible is not the word. It's bizarre. It's downright creepy. It's unreal."

"It's the story of the year."

"It's the story of a lifetime." Thornton stood up to get some mineral water out of his refrigerator. He washed down two aspirin tablets. "How's Lizzy coming? We've got to get this stuff out."

"She's almost finished," Jon said. "Have you decided on the pictures?"

"We can't use them. They're great, but they're not our style. Kids look at our paper, and they don't need to see a half-dissected corpse on page one. We'll use one of the general shots on our web page."

"Done," they heard Lizzy say from her desk.

"You know you're going to get a lot of attention with this stuff," Thornton said, "*New York Times, Washington Post,* national attention. Don't let it go to your head." Thornton typed a command on his computer and started to read Lizzy's story.

"So, boss, all of this national attention's got to be good for the paper."

Thornton looked up from his computer to look at Jon. "So?"

"So how about a raise?" Jon asked.

Thornton gave him a disgusted look, said nothing, and then returned to his computer.

"Oh, well, it was worth a try." Jon left his office.

Chapter 16

J on and Lizzy had their exclusive, and the next morning all hell broke loose at the med school. Telephones rang off the hook. Switchboards were overwhelmed. Police cars, television broadcast vans, and various other vehicles blocked the street. Police were everywhere. The students of the freshman class, who had been sequestered on Saturday, were being interviewed for the second time by a team of policemen from SPD. Even though it was Sunday, members of the faculty were milling about, talking. Faculty lists compiled by department were being reviewed by the police. Reporters were everywhere talking to anyone who would talk to them. Protesters advocating various animal rights causes occupied the lobby. A group from PAWS was blocking the entrance to the anatomy department, demanding the release of all research cats. The congestion and confusion made it difficult for emergency vehicles to reach the emergency room. Business as usual was impossible.

The dean had called an emergency meeting of MSEC, the Medical School Executive Committee, to try to deal with the problem. MSEC was the governing body of the med school, and it was made up from the academic departmental chairmen and the assistant and associate deans. Kay Masters from News and Information Services addressed the all-white, all-male committee. She considered the situation nothing short of a public relations disaster.

"Gentlemen, gentlemen, would you please be quiet," she said. "We're not finished yet." The group was restless. The nineteen committee members sat around the large table in the plush Turner Conference Room. Masters sat at its head. Committee members were busily talking among themselves. "I'm going to play another tape from a program that aired this morning," she said. "This one's from FOX news."

A technician put the videotape in the player. They had already watched tapes from the broadcast networks and from CNN. The FOX tape was the last, and the members of the committee watched it in glum silence. Masters addressed the group when the tape was finished.

"OK, now you know what they're saying about us. Our procedures are sloppy, we're insensitive, we're ghoulish, we torture little furry animals, we're disrespectful of the dead, and we're a bunch of arrogant bastards. But you gentlemen knew that anyway, didn't you." She paused for effect. "We're the top story in every newspaper, on every news broadcast, and on every talk show in the country. We need some serious damage control here."

Phil Ruben, the chairman of radiology began to speak, "I just want to say that. . . ."

Masters interrupted him, "Shut up, Phil. Just listen for a change. The dean's already in Olympia so he can work the governor and our friends in the legislature tomorrow as best he can, but he's pretty sure he's going to get clobbered. They'll want his head. Our budget, and that means your money, Phil, is in real jeopardy. We're a public institution, and we can't tolerate this sort of publicity. We can't change what happened, but we can try to put a positive spin on it. Here's what we're going to do."

The room was again silent. The members of MSEC were not accustomed to being addressed with such abruptness. Masters switched on an overhead projector to display an outline of her plan.

"Number one," she said. She referred to the page projected on the screen. "No one talks to members of the press except me.

There'll be no exceptions. My staff will arrange all press contacts.
Refer all inquiries to them.

"Number two. . . ."

＊

The press conference in the district attorney's office was
jammed with reporters. The podium sat on its elevated platform,
and was surrounded on three sides by cameras, video recorders and
other broadcast equipment. The room was much too small for the
size of the crowd. In addition to the local media the room was filled
with representatives from national news organizations, and
reporters from British Columbia. Captain McCabe made his introductory remarks before turning the event over to Karen. She was
planning to read from a prepared statement and then open the proceedings to questions.

"Yesterday afternoon, Professor George Holyoke was found
dead in the human dissection laboratory at the University of
Washington Medical School. He had been sought by the Seattle
Police Department for questioning in relationship to The Sandman
murders. As has been previously reported, his fingerprints had been
found at two of the crime scenes, and several days ago his severed
hand was discovered by a reporter at *The Seattle Times* building."
Karen looked up and into the crowd surrounding the podium. She
felt hundreds of eyes looking at her. She continued reading.

"Professor Holyoke served the University of Washington as
Chairman of their Anatomy Department for over a decade. He also
served the school as director of the student anatomy laboratory in
which he was found. The circumstances of his discovery have been
widely reported, and I won't repeat them here. I'm here to try to
answer your questions. I'll answer them as best I can, but please bear
in mind that this is an ongoing investigation, and that I won't be able
to provide you with all of the information that you might like."

Karen again looked up from her prepared text. Bright lights

were shining on her from three sides. The room was hot and she felt uncomfortable. Hands were up all over the room. Reporters were shouting at her. She called on a reporter from ABC News.

"Detective Able, as I understand it Dr. Holyoke taught human anatomy and dissection to the students in the anatomy lab where he was found. Is it true that he was dissected by his own students?"

"Not exactly," she said. "He taught anatomy to prior classes of first-year students. He disappeared before this year's group started their work."

"But they did dissect him, didn't they?"

"Yes, they did."

Someone shouted a question from the side of the podium.

"How far did they get? I mean, how much of him did they dissect?"

"I'm not qualified to answer that," she said. "You'll have to ask the medical examiner."

More hands went up in the air. More questions were shouted. Karen called on a reporter from British Columbia.

"Detective Able, would you speculate on how professor Holyoke's body ended up in the anatomy department? And then as a follow-up, when did it get there?"

"We know Holyoke's body was there on the first day of class. The students will testify to that. They would have known if the bodies had been switched after they started their dissections. That places him there before the second murder, so the fingerprint in the Carol Williams case was planted."

Karen paused a moment. She brushed a few strands of hair away from her face, and then continued. "Bodies are donated to the medical school throughout the year. They're received by the medical examiner's office, inspected, flushed with formaldehyde, and then wrapped in protective gauze. They're then transferred to a holding tank in the anatomy department where they are immersed in a formaldehyde solution. The students select their bodies from the tank and then bring them to their individual dissection stations at the beginning of the academic year."

"You mean to say that students select their own cadavers from a tank filled with floating bodies?" The question was asked by a member of the local press.

"Yes," Karen replied, "as I understand it that's the way it happens." Karen looked around the room and then continued. "We did a count of the cadavers left in the central holding tank, and there's one more there than there should be. Holyoke was either wrapped, placed in the tank and selected by the students of Cube 6 by random chance, or was switched with the cadaver in Cube 6 after the students had selected their bodies from the holding tank, but before they started their dissections. In either case he was prepared in the same way as the other cadavers."

The room erupted in noise. Sid Andrews' voice could be heard above the rest. He was a television personality from channel nine Public Television News, an affiliate of PBS. Karen called on him. He asked, "How could the medical school people not notice an extra body in their central cadaver holding tank?"

"We don't know," she said. "We're looking into it."

Hands again went up all over the room. It was really getting hot. There were too many bodies in too small a space; and there were all those lights. Karen called on a woman in the second row. "How many people would know how to do this cadaver preparation?" She was a reporter from NBC news. "Doesn't that limit your list of suspects?"

"Dr. Allison in the medical examiner's office is making a list for us. He's getting names mainly from hospitals and mortuaries. We'll combine that list with a list from the medical school and go from there."

"Is it a long list?" asked the reporter from NBC.

"Unfortunately it is. There are quite a number of people with the knowledge to do the cadaver preps. There are 156 medical students in each class; there are nearly eight hundred faculty members of various types in the school, and there are a large number of trained technicians in the labs and in the hospital who have the required knowledge to do the job. That's only our list from the med school. The list will grow when we add in the names provided to us by the medical examiner. The combined list will involve hundreds of people, but it's a place to start."

A reporter from CNN asked, "What about places where this type of work could be done?"

"Theoretically it could be done anywhere there's access to a pressure hose and a drain."

Someone shouted a question from the back of the room. "What about the cause of death?"

"We asked Dr. Allison that question, and he's been unable to determine the cause of death. X-rays revealed no broken bones. The internal organs have been dissected and are gone, and the body's been immersed in formaldehyde for several months. At this late date it's probably impossible to determine precisely what killed him."

Another shouted question, "What about the students who dissected him? How are they taking it?"

"We interviewed them and they all seemed quite professional. None of them are suspects at this time."

"Are they receiving counseling or any other professional help?"

"You'll have to ask the people at the med school about that."

Reporters started shouting questions and waving their hands, trying to attract attention from all over the room. Karen called on another CNN reporter. "How was the body discovered to be Holyoke's?"

"A member of the anatomy faculty recognized Dr. Holyoke after his head was unwrapped for dissection. She recognized his face."

"And the rest of the body had already been dissected, is that right?"

"That's right."

The questioning went on for another hour.

✳

Jon's telephone was ringing again. He had been taking calls all day at his desk in the newsroom. Everyone, it seemed, wanted to talk to him. His newfound celebrity status was both flattering and annoying. The Sandman had picked him as his conduit to the world, and everyone wanted to know about it. They wanted to know what he knew. He had invitations from the Sunday morning news talk shows, and from 20/20 at ABC. As far as he was concerned they could all read about it in the newspaper. He had better things to do.

Jon had called Dr. Saunders at the med school. He wanted to ask her again about Holyoke's research records. If he could find them, they might point the way to the identity of the serial killer.

"Dr. Saunders, it's Jon Kirk. I want to thank you for calling me last Saturday. I really appreciate the heads up."

"What do you want, Mr. Kirk?" she asked. Saunders didn't seem particularly happy to hear from him. Even she was feeling the pressure to refer all inquiries to the News and Information Services office. They couldn't fire her because she had tenure, but they could harass her. To try to keep her in line they had threatened to station a fire marshal outside of her office to keep her from smoking.

"I'd just like a little information," he said. "I won't quote you or write anything that could be traced back to you."

"Are you kidding? They probably bugged my telephone and are tracing this call as we speak."

"I'll cut to the chase. We're trying to locate Holyoke's research records and I wondered if I could come down and look through his office. I know the police have already been there, but they might have missed something. You could leave the door open and be out of the department when I come by. Nobody would need to know."

"I could, but it wouldn't do you any good. The police cleaned it out and took all of his stuff away in boxes. They took his computer too. The room's empty."

"When did that happen?"

"Earlier today."

Jon groaned silently. "I'm sorry to have bothered you," he said. "You've been a great help."

"You're very welcome, Mr. Kirk."

"Thanks again," he said. He hung up the phone.

He put on his jacket and walked over toward Lizzy's desk. "Lizard, you busy?"

"Not particularly, what's up?"

"You up for a field trip?"

"Where are we going?" she asked.

"Back to Holyoke's house. We have some unfinished business to take care of."

"The research records?"

"You got it," he said. "The police cleaned out his office and the records weren't there. They have to be somewhere."

Lizzy turned off her computer. She picked up her coat and joined Jon on his way out of the office. Then she slipped her arm through his and whispered something in his ear. Vicki noticed. She made a mental note to ask Liz about garter belt notches.

Chapter 17

Jon was driving; Liz was talking on her cell telephone, ". . . we already know they took a computer, and a bunch of files . . . OK . . . there was nothing there . . . no research notes, OK . . . thanks, you're the best . . . OK, soon." Liz completed her call to her contact at the Seattle police department.

"What did you find out?" Jon asked.

"They went through all of his books and files, and then experts went through his computers, both the one they took from his office and the one he had in his home. According to my source, they didn't find anything. No research records, or anything else of value to the case. It was a total bust. He also told me there's no stakeout at Holyoke's house now that they know he's dead."

"Dr. Saunders said the research records have to be somewhere."

"If they're not at his house we may never find them. And the police have already combed the place. Why do you think we'll be able to find them when they couldn't?"

"Look, he must've hidden them there. There's no place else. And he had to have hidden them. Otherwise they would have turned up by now. If they were stolen you'd think that there'd be at least some reference to them in one of his computers."

"Why would he have hidden them in the first place? What was he afraid of, and what was he trying to protect?"

"I don't know. It's another mystery we'll figure out when we find them."

"*If* we find them," she said.

Jon repeated his routine and slowly drove around Holyoke's block several times, not completely convinced there wasn't a police stakeout. When he drove into Holyoke's driveway it was dusk, but not yet completely dark. Lights were starting to come on in the neighborhood.

Jon parked his car. The two of them sat there for half an hour just to be sure that they weren't being watched. Then he walked with Liz up the back steps to the back door. The window that he had broken the last time they were there was covered with plywood. "Well, here we go again," he said. He turned his back to the door and broke the pane of glass just above the plywood with his elbow. He then reached inside, turned the lock and opened the door.

"And Detective Able said you weren't cut out for this kind of work," Lizzy said. She poked him in the ribs.

They went inside. The kitchen was neat, just as he remembered it. This time they walked directly to the study, which also was as he remembered it with the exception of the computer. It was gone. The scanner, printer, and CD recorder were still in the study, but the CDs and diskettes were gone. The police must have taken them also. His papers were still in his filing cabinet. Jon opened the bottom drawer of the desk and was not surprised to find that the bottle of scotch was also missing.

Jon and Lizzy began a systematic search of the study. This time they knew what they were looking for and they looked through everything. After more than an hour of going through reams of material, they gave up. The research records weren't there.

"This is a waste of time," Lizzy said. "The police have already done this. They'll probably find his research notes in one of his computers, hidden or coded somewhere, anyway."

"Think outside the box, Liz," Jon said. "You're good at that. Let's start all over. What are we looking for?" Jon slowly scanned the room.

"Not paper," Lizzy said. "It's unlikely we'll find paper records. The police would have found them if they were in the house. Besides, I can't believe Holyoke didn't keep his research records on a computer."

"Think outside the box," Jon said again. "We're probably looking for something that stores computer files like diskettes, CD's, DVD's or something like that."

"How does this work?" Lizzy asked. She was referring to the old Philips CD recorder.

"I don't know," Kirk answered. "I've never used one."

Lizzy turned the machine on. Lights on the control panel lit up. She pressed the eject button and nothing happened. "Does this thing record on regular CDs?" she asked.

"I suppose so." Kirk was still scanning the room.

"Jon, I'll bet he recorded his research records on a CD. Maybe that's why he has this machine."

"Maybe," Jon said. "Or maybe he just likes to burn tunes. The police took his CD's when they took his computer. If any of them contained his research notes, the police would have found them by now. Are you sure you can trust your source?"

"My source is golden," she said. "They only took the CD's they could find. Let's see, where would I hide a CD if I wanted to make it difficult to find?" she asked. She looked around the room. "In plain sight, of course" she answered herself.

"What?"

"If I wanted to hide data on a CD, or something else like that, I'd hide it in plain sight," she said. "That's always the best way."

"Go on."

"I might put it with my other CD's or in some other obvious place, probably inside a music CD plastic cover."

Jon paused for a moment. "You might be right, but the police probably thought of that too. They took his CD's."

"They took the ones they could find here in the study."

"Maybe he has another stereo in the house? Do remember seeing one?"

"I don't recall."

"Let's check it out," he said. "I'll look upstairs and you look in the basement."

"It was my idea," she said. "You look in the basement. That art collection down there creeps me out. I'll look upstairs."

"Anything you say, Lizard." He smiled at her.

Jon opened the basement door, turned on the light and walked down the stairs. The Brazilian tribesman was still guarding his lair. He looked around the tribal gallery, and then in the adjoining smaller side rooms. There was no stereo. He went through all of the cabinets and drawers. There were no CD's. He walked back to the main floor, looked around, and then called up the stairs to Lizzy. "Did you find anything?"

"Yeah, I found cuff links, Brazilian money and a clarinet, but no CD's. There's no stereo up here either," she answered. "Any other ideas?" she asked as she walked back down to the main floor to join Jon.

"Let's turn off the lights and go home."

Jon and Liz left the house by the back door. They shut the door and Jon stuck his hand back through the broken window to lock it. They returned to Jon's Explorer and climbed inside. "I really thought we'd find something in there this time," he said.

"What now?" Lizzy asked.

"I don't know," Jon answered. "I'm all out of ideas. Let's go over to the Blue Moon for some inspiration." He put the key in the ignition, turned it and started the engine. He turned on the headlights and began backing out of the driveway. Lizzy turned on the sound system. Ella Fitzgerald began to sing *Mack the Knife*.

"Wait a minute," Lizzy said.

Jon stopped the Explorer. His headlights were shining on the garage.

"Listen," she said.

"What?"

"Your Ella Fitzgerald CD."

"So?"

"We didn't check the garage. Do you think Holyoke's car is still in there?" she asked.

They looked at each other. "That's good, Lizard. That's really good."

He turned off his car, leaving his lights on, and they both got out and walked to the garage. It was a double garage, and it had one of those old-fashioned, heavy doors that slid open by pushing it to the side. They opened the left-hand door. There was a 1998 black Jaguar sedan parked inside.

"Ten to one it's in there," he said. "That's where I'd hide it. It's in plain sight." His headlights illuminated the back of the car.

"Well what are you waiting for?" she asked.

Jon tried the driver-side door. It was unlocked. He opened the door and climbed in the front seat. He looked around the dashboard. "It doesn't have a CD player, there's only a slot for a tape," he said.

"Of course it has a CD player," Liz replied. "They all do. Move over. Let me look."

Lizzy stuck her head inside the door. Jon leaned to his right as far as he could to give her a view of the dashboard.

"It's right here," she said as she pointed out the controls for the sound system. "It's the kind that has the changer in the trunk. I once dated a guy that had one of these." She reached below the steering wheel and pushed the trunk release. Then she walked to the back of the car and opened the trunk.

With the trunk light on she could clearly see the CD changer holding six CDs in a stack. She slid back the lid to the changer and pushed the eject button. The stack of six CDs popped out. She pulled the CD's out of the stack one by one. Three were recordings of chamber music, two were Miles Davis jazz recordings, and one was an unmarked read/write Philips CD. Lizzy held the Philips CD up in the air.

Jon softly whistled through his teeth and said, "Bingo!"

"Let's get out of here," she said.

"We'll make a copy and then get the original to the police before they charge us with tampering with evidence."

They shut the car door and closed the trunk. Then they shut the garage door, leaving it the way they'd found it. They hurriedly backed out of the driveway, drove to Forty-fifth Street, and then out of Laurelhurst on to Sand Point Way. They looked at each other and started to laugh.

*

Jon told Karen about the CD. He met her in her office at the Public Safety Building and explained to her how they had found it in Holyoke's car the previous night.

"Damn it, Jon. I wish you hadn't done that," she said. "I thought we had agreed you'd let me do the police work."

"I'm sorry, Karen, but we did find the research records. Actually it was Lizzy that found them."

"I've noticed you've been spending a lot of time with that girl," she said. Jon thought he saw something flash in her eyes as she spoke.

"Come on, Karen, I work with her. She's just a work associate. Besides, this is the tie-in we've been looking for. Maybe these records will explain something. We thought you'd be happy." He knew she'd be pissed.

"You could have called first," she said. "I would have gone out there with you. It doesn't look good to have me covering for you all the time. People around here are starting to notice."

"I said I'm sorry." Jon was sitting in a chair. Karen was pacing back and forth. The CD was sitting on her desk.

"You know you probably messed up any fingerprints that might be on the CD," she said. "Captain McCabe isn't going to like that."

"The only prints you're going to find on that CD are Holyoke's, Lizzy's and mine. What's the big deal?"

"You don't know that. That's the trouble. You're too casual about this sort of thing."

"Sorry," he said again. He looked down at his feet and tried to look remorseful.

Karen stopped her pacing. She sat down in a chair next to Jon. "Have you looked at it yet?" she asked. "The CD, I mean."

"I tried, but it's pretty technical. You'll need an expert to figure it out."

"I'm not going to ask you if this is the only copy because I don't want you to lie to me." She nodded toward the disc on her desk.

"Right," he said.

"Right," she said with a skeptical look on her face. "I get enough crap thrown at me around here without you dishing it out, too."

"Look, Karen, honey, we're all on the same side here," he said. "We need to work together. This guy's crazy, and sooner or later he's going to kill again."

"Don't 'honey' me," she said.

"You're right, of course. I shouldn't have said that. But you said you're putting together a suspect list. That CD may help to narrow it down. Don't try to cut me out, OK?"

"Right," she said again. "But you're the reporter, remember? I'm the cop. You do the reporting. Leave the police work to me. I don't want you to get hurt."

"I'm not going to get hurt." He shuffled in his seat.

"No, you're not, not if I can help it," she said. "I like you the way you are, totally intact with everything working. Now go on, get out of here," she said. "I've got work to do." Then she shooed him out the door.

"Say hi to Captain McCabe," he said to her as he left the room.

✻

Jon put in another call to Janet Saunders. He'd been trying to reach her all day. She hadn't answered her phone and somebody had disconnected her voice mail. Kay Masters was doing her best to restrict press access to med school faculty. This time Saunders answered her phone after four rings.

"Janet Saunders."

"Dr. Saunders, it's Jon Kirk. I wondered if I might be able to meet with you. I think we found Dr. Holyoke's research records and we need some help interpreting them."

There was a pause at the other end of the phone. Saunders weighed the hassle she would get for talking with the press against the temptation she felt to review Holyoke's research records. Temptation won out. "Alright, Mr. Kirk," she said, "but not here."

"How about here at the *Times*? I can reserve a conference room and set up a computer."

"That would be fine. I'll be able to do it this afternoon after work, say around six o'clock."

"We'll have the room ready," Jon said.

"The *Times* isn't a no-smoking building, is it?" she asked.

"We'll take care of it," he said. "I'll see you at six."

"I'll see you then." She hung up the phone.

＊

Janet Saunders arrived at six. Jon and Liz were waiting for her when she arrived. They escorted her to the conference room and then waited outside while she looked through the research records. They were sitting near a window outside of the conference room door. The door was open. It was misting outside and water was streaking down the windowpane. "She's been in there almost two hours," Lizzy said. "Do you think we should ask her how it's coming?"

Through a haze of cigarette smoke they could see Saunders occasionally type on her laptop while she read research data on the larger screen of a desktop PC. The first thing she'd done after asking for an ashtray was to copy the CD into the memory of her computer. Jon was a little nervous about that, but there really wasn't much he could do if he wanted her to review the records for him.

"We ought to leave her alone until she's finished," Jon said. "I hope she doesn't run out of cigarettes before she's done. It looks like she already has nine or ten butts in the ashtray."

Another hour passed. She had worked without a break. Finally she closed the lid to her laptop, stood up and stretched. She walked over to the door. "Hey, reporters," she said in a loud scratchy voice. "Let's talk." She coughed.

Jon and Liz walked into the smoky conference room. "Would you like a Coke or something?" Jon asked.

"What kind of or something?" Saunders responded.

"Only soft drinks."

"Forget it then," she said. "Let's get down to it."

All three of them sat down at the conference room table. Saunders sat in front of the PC so she could refer to the computer screen as she talked.

"I can see why ol' Georgie hid these notes," Saunders said. "They're potentially dynamite, and they could have international repercussions. There was a lot more to George Holyoke than met the eye."

Saunders continued, "We all knew that George was interested in primitive cultures and medicines, but I don't think any of us knew that he was a bioprospector. He hid that one from the University, and with good reason. As it turns out George was living out the romantic dream of every scientist who studies this kind of stuff. He had become a self-taught ethnobotanist."

"Bioprospector, ethnobotanist, what are we talking about here?" Lizzy asked.

"Just as a mineral prospector might search for gold or oil, a bioprospector searches for medicines and other plant products in their native environment. Ethnobotanists study the drugs and plant products used by shamans, witch doctors, and the like, usually they study them in their native environment. Bioprospectors, ethnobotanists, they're variations of the same thing.

"Visions of Indiana Jones come to mind," Lizzy said.

"Maybe a short, pudgy Indiana Jones," she said. "It seems George spent a lot of his vacation time in Brazil. None of us knew about it."

Saunders pulled a cigarette out of her purse and lit it. She talked while she smoked. "Bioprospecting has become somewhat of a controversial subject, especially in South America."

Jon asked, "Why is that?"

"Indigenous tribes have complained that it's nothing less than bio-colonialism, or even worse, bio-piracy. They think bioprospectors are stealing their secrets and their heritage, and then getting rich at their expense. It goes all the way back to the Spanish Conquistadors who learned the secrets of coca and cocaine from these people. They also learned about the anti-malarial agent quinine."

"But the Conquistadors are ancient history."

"Sure, but more recently cancer treatments and pain control medicines have come from the jungle. Seven of the world's top twenty-five selling drugs, with billions in sales, come from plant sources. I'll bet you didn't know that."

"I didn't," he answered.

"South American governments and the native peoples who discovered many of the agents in the first place have been shut out. They feel screwed, and they want a share of the profits."

"That sounds reasonable," Lizzy said.

"Yes it does, and in 1992 the Earth Summit in Rio established national sovereignty over genetic resources. These countries want some control over the drugs and products derived from the plants and animals that live within their national borders."

"What's wrong with that?"

"Nothing, but the US Senate never ratified the biodiversity treaty, so naturally South American countries have been reluctant to have US researchers tromping around in their jungles. That's partly why Holyoke wanted to keep his work quiet."

"Only partly?" Jon asked.

"Yes, the other part comes from the University. There's no way they would let him keep the fruits of his research."

"Even if he did his work on vacations and on his own time?" Lizzy questioned.

"They don't see it that way. If there's money in it, they want it. Based on these notes, I'd guess Holyoke was planning to leave the University in the not too distant future anyway. Maybe he had already left. He didn't trust them, and for that matter neither do I."

Saunders lit another cigarette with the glowing butt of the one she had just finished smoking.

"George spent his time in the Amazon Basin prospecting for the Holy Grail of pain relief, a drug that completely blocks pain signals to the brain without depressing the central nervous system itself. There were rumors that native shamans had knowledge of such a drug, but none of us really believed it. It goes against what we know about the mechanism of action of modern pain medications. Holyoke, however, wasn't dissuaded. Based on these notes, it looks like he may have found it, or come close."

The room was quiet for a moment.

"So Holyoke found a magic potion for pain relief," Lizzy said. "He could have made millions with it."

"It's not that simple," Saunders replied. "Brazil's reluctant to let plant samples out of the country."

"Because we didn't ratify the treaty?"

"That's right, so George decided to smuggle the samples out of Brazil. He established a greenhouse somewhere around here to grow these plants. Unfortunately his notes don't say where. But even if he established a large facility to make this drug, he'd still have a problem. He'd have to patent the medication to be able to capitalize on it, and any patent application would trace the drug back to its native country. The patent would then be challenged by the Brazilian government, and probably by the Andean Pact countries as well. He'd never get it through the government patent office, and he'd never get his money."

"The Andean Pact countries?" Jon asked.

"George noted that Bolivia, Colombia, Ecuador, Peru and Venezuela formed the Andean Pact to control access to their native genetic material, and to require compensation for its use. Brazil has its own laws. Anyway, the only way George could make a buck on this thing would be to try to isolate the active ingredient in the drug, and then to synthesize it in a way that hides its links to the Amazon Basin. He established a large greenhouse to grow these plants in jungle-like conditions, extracted the pain reliever in large quantities, and then worked to isolate the active agents in the extract. He hoped to develop a patentable product."

"Was he successful?" Lizzy asked.

"He did develop a number of synthetic agents, however it's unclear whether or not he completed his work before he died. His notes are incomplete and don't tell us if he was able to test them. This is where it starts to relate to his work with the cats."

"Would somebody have killed him over this?" Lizzy asked.

"Are you kidding? People get killed every day for nothing more than a pair of sneakers."

"It's possible," Jon said. "But then how would it relate to The Sandman? He was Holyoke's killer; at least I think he was. He had to get his hand somehow."

"OK, that's it," Saunders said. "You don't need me for this discussion." She put out her cigarette in the ashtray, picked up her laptop and stood up. "It's late and I'm going home." She started to move toward the door. Jon and Lizzy stood up to join her.

"Be careful with the information in your laptop," Jon said. "You know you're not supposed to have it."

"Give it a rest, Jon; don't be such a worrier," Saunders said. She laughed a short, husky smoker's laugh and then turned around and left the office.

Chapter 18

"That was interesting," Jon said.

"And potentially dynamite," Lizzy answered. "It seems no one really knew the good Dr. Holyoke. He had quite a secret private life."

"Who would have guessed."

"This bioprospecting stuff must tie in to The Sandman murders somehow," she said. "We have to figure it out."

They walked back to the conference room together. Jon picked up the ashtray and emptied its contents into a wastebasket. Lizzy brushed cigarette ashes off the table.

"It does tie in with the information Kate Monahan gave me about Holyoke, only she didn't know he'd found the plant he was searching for," Jon said. "It sounds like Holyoke was a smuggler. He had a plan to make a fortune on a new pain medication. He smuggled the plants in from Brazil. He grew them in a greenhouse, probably somewhere around here. He extracted the painkiller and then planned to synthesize the active ingredients to hide their Brazilian origins. Isn't that what she said? How does that relate to a serial killer?"

Jon took the ashtray with him as they left the room. Lizzy spoke as they walked. "It doesn't seem to relate at all. But then again serial killers aren't supposed to have any of the usual motives for their crimes."

"At least they don't have motives as we usually understand them," Jon said.

"If The Sandman killed Holyoke, it may not have had anything to do with his research. There might be some other connection between them. Maybe there's something at the med school we don't yet know about or understand."

"That group at the school plays their cards pretty close to the vest," he said. "And they'll do their best to keep Saunders out of the loop. If there's something else going on, it's going to be difficult for us to find out about it."

"All we need is a contact," Lizzy said. "Somebody we know. Somebody we can trust."

"Somebody who trusts us."

"Yeah."

"Like your friend at the police station," Jon asked with a sly grin on his face.

"Maybe," she answered. "Or maybe *your* friend at the police station." She grinned back at him. "Vicki's been spreading some very interesting stories about you lately."

Jon rolled his eyes, "She's a gossip," he said. "You know you can't believe anything she says." He tried to look nonchalant.

"Hmm."

They walked by the few reporters working late over to Lizzy's desk. She plopped down in her chair, spun around in her swivel seat and faced her computer. "How should we do this?" she asked.

"I'll do the bioprospecting bit, you do the med school tie in."

"You want me to mention the cat research?"

"Sure, we both can. It'll drive Kay Masters and her friends crazy."

"I don't know if I can do it on an empty stomach," she said. "That stuff about the cats gets to me."

"Now that you mention it, we did miss dinner, didn't we. I'm kind of hungry."

Lizzy spun back around in her chair to look at him. "And you're a man of strong appetites," she said with a smirk.

"Right," Jon answered, "and right now I have a strong appetite for food. How about the Thirteen Coins, it's just around the corner."

"I hate that place," Lizzy said. "It's always filled with newspaper people and drunks. Let's go someplace different. How about Etta's?"

"That's expensive."

"We'll split it."

Jon agreed. They walked out of the *Times* building to Jon's Explorer and drove to the restaurant.

✻

The Pike Place Market is one of Seattle's favorite tourist destinations; it's also a functioning farmer's market. The sights, sounds and smell of the place can make you forget you're in the middle of a big city. It is located at the foot of Pike Street overlooking Elliot Bay, and its vendors hawk their wares to any and all who will listen to their songs. A cacophony of voices fills the air. Fishmongers are the stars of the show. They bring their fish into their stalls at five o'clock each morning, and then sell the freshest fish in the country (so they say) to local fish aficionados and restaurants.

Etta's restaurant is located near the north end of the Market. It's known for its fresh fish, modest prices and Northwest-style cuisine. Jon and Liz drove around the market several times looking for a parking spot. They were lucky and spotted a car leaving directly in front of the restaurant. Jon parked his Explorer and then escorted Lizzy to the front door on his arm. They walked in the door and asked the hostess for a table. After a few minutes, they were seated at a small table for two by a window overlooking the street. They immediately fell deep into conversation about Holyoke and The Sandman.

Marjorie Bathum happened to be eating in the restaurant that same evening. She and Karen Able had been good friends for a long time. Although Marjorie was thirty years older, they shared each other's interests, especially their interests in hiking and the outdoors. Having grown up in a small logging community, Marjorie loved the outdoors. She loved to hunt and fish. She also loved good food, especially seafood. In a city known for its seafood, Etta's was one of the places to go.

Marjorie was sitting with her husband, Roy, watching Jon Kirk at his window table with Lizzy. She had watched them as they walked into the restaurant together, her arm in his. She had watched Jon as he touched her while he helped her into her chair. She watched the way Liz flirted with him. It was so obvious. She watched them as they talked to each other. They were deeply involved in their conversation, unaware of everything else going on around them. Roy noticed that Marjorie was looking past him, over his shoulder.

"Marjorie, what are you looking at?" Roy asked.

"Shush, not so loud," Marjorie said.

Roy shifted in his chair in order to turn around to look. "Don't turn around, they'll see you," Marjorie whispered.

"Who'll see me? Who's back there?" Roy whispered back.

"It's Jon Kirk, Karen Able's friend. He's the reporter. You know, the one I told you about."

"The one she went to visit wrapped in a coat and nothing else." Roy chuckled.

"Shush," she said. "Don't talk so loud. They'll hear you."

"I'm not talking loudly," he said.

"You aren't supposed to know about that anyway."

"Then why did you tell me?"

"Well don't turn around. He's sitting over there with another woman."

Roy spun around in his chair to look at Jon and Lizzy sitting at their table by the window. Lizzy was reaching across the table to give Jon a bite of her food. Roy turned back to face Marjorie. "What a babe. She's really stacked. She's built like a brick shithouse."

"I'm calling Karen," she said.

"Now, Marjorie," he said, attempting to maintain a calming voice. "Wait a minute, honey. We don't know what's going on over there. Maybe it's a business meeting. Maybe he's just working on a story. Maybe she's his sister."

"His sister my ass. Karen needs to know about this."

"Marjorie," he said quietly through gritted teeth.

"Men," she said with a tone of disgust. "You always stick up for each other." She stood up and walked over to ask the hostess for a telephone. She left Roy sitting at the table.

Roy half turned around so that he could see Jon and Liz. They were obviously oblivious to everyone else in the room. They seemed to be deeply involved in an intimate conversation.

*

Karen was sitting in her office, working late. Her experts were taking their sweet time with Holyoke's research records. She couldn't understand why it was going to take at least several days to perform a complete analysis. She was finishing some paperwork when her direct line rang.

"Detective Able speaking."

"Thank God I reached you. I tried your home number and nobody was there."

"Who is this?"

"It's Marjorie."

"Marjorie, I didn't recognize your voice. You sound like you're out of breath. What's up?"

"Treachery, that's what. Jon Kirk's here at Etta's with another woman. I knew you would want to know."

Karen's face started to flush. She felt her pulse race. Her hands became moist as she gripped the phone ever more tightly. "I ahh. . . . Are you sure it's him?"

"Of course I am. Roy and I were eating dinner when Jon came in with this woman draped all over him. Roy says she's a babe."

"Short and blond, in her early twenties," Karen asked.

"That's her. Do you know who she is?"

"I think so," Karen said. "Thanks, Marjorie. I owe you."

"Don't mention it. I'm going to go back in there to see what they're doing."

"I'll talk to you later. By the way, did you happen to see his car parked anywhere around there?"

"Why? What does it look like?"

"It's a black Explorer."

"Just a minute, I'll check."

Marjorie put down the phone and told the hostess not to hang up; she told her that she would be right back. She walked out the front door, looked around and then returned to the restaurant to pick up the phone. "I found it," she said. "It's parked right out in front of the restaurant. Why?"

"Just watch." Karen hung up the phone.

Then she called the desk sergeant. "Sergeant, this is Detective Karen Able in homicide. There's a black Explorer registered to Jon Kirk parked in front of Etta's restaurant. Please send someone over there to find it illegally parked. Have it towed away. There won't be any problem . . . that's right . . . thank you."

✳

Marjorie casually looked over at Jon and Liz as she returned to her seat. "Roy, did anything happen while I was gone?" She was whispering again.

"Not much," he said. Roy started to whisper. "He slipped his hand under her skirt when he thought no one was looking. Too bad you missed it."

"Roy Bathum!" she exclaimed.

Roy was chuckling. "Just kidding," he said.

Jon and Lizzy were still deeply involved in conversation. Although they were sitting at a window table, they barely noticed what was going on around them.

"I wonder if The Sandman killed Holyoke with his own medicine?" Lizzy asked. "And if he did, how did he do it? Holyoke wouldn't have willingly let himself be injected."

"No doubt about that, but Holyoke's murder may not have been related to the others. Maybe The Sandman hadn't planned on killing him. Maybe Holyoke surprised him, or caught him doing something. Maybe Holyoke was just in the wrong place at the wrong time."

"I don't think so," Lizzy said. "I think he specifically wanted Holyoke's fingerprints at those murder scenes."

"Why?" Jon asked.

"I don't know. It has to be related to his research. That stuff they found in the murder victims, it's related to curare, and curare's related to Holyoke's research. Why else would The Sandman use that stuff to kill his victims? It's all tied together somehow."

"OK, you tell me how," Jon said.

"I wish I could," Lizzy answered. "There's a link there somewhere, it's just not obvious where."

Liz glanced out of the window, then back at Jon and then she looked out the window again. "Jon, she said, "have you paid all of your parking tickets?"

"Why do you ask?"

"Look out the window. Somebody's towing your car away."

Jon looked out the window just in time to see a police truck drive off with his Explorer in tow. "God damn it!"

Marjorie was sitting at her table with Roy, watching. She smiled a self-satisfied smile.

Chapter 19

Jon was pissed. He had spent the last several hours tracking down his car and getting it back. The ticket said he had illegally parked in a handicapped zone. He hadn't seen any handicapped parking zone in front of the restaurant. What a screw job. SPD would hear about this. In addition to the seventy dollars he had to pay to get his car back, he had to pay a two hundred dollar fine or schedule a court appearance to contest the ticket. He was still fuming as he drove back to the office from the impound lot. Lizzy had taken a cab back from the restaurant.

By the time he made it to the newsroom Lizzy had already finished and left for home. The place was almost deserted. Janitors were emptying wastebaskets and cleaning the floor. Fred Middleton was busy working on his fishing report. Jon went to his desk, turned on his computer and started to write. The piece on bioprospecting and the Amazon rain forest brought him back into focus. When he finally finished the article he looked at the clock and saw that he had missed his deadline. Thornton wouldn't be happy about that. He turned off his computer and left for home.

Jon arrived to a dark house. It was almost two o'clock and he needed sleep. Leon greeted him with a welcoming woof. It had been a long day. He let Leon outside, walked into his living room and noticed a flashing red 1 in the message window on his answering machine. He pushed the play button and then flopped down on the couch to listen to the message. He was exhausted.

"Good evening, Jon." It was a familiar mechanical-sounding voice. Jon sat up, suddenly alert. "I had hoped to speak to you in person tonight. Oh well, I suppose this will do. You know I'm a great admirer of your work. Your recent piece on the life and death of Dr. George Holyoke was right on the mark. That part about the cat research was marvelous. I'm sorry about the hand. My purpose was to get your attention, but now I admit that it was a bit overly dramatic. I apologize, and I've decided to make it up to you.

"Stay with me now, I'm going to give your career another boost. Don't worry, no more helping hands, just an exclusive. Listen carefully. I suggest that you go to room 108 at the Rain City Motel near Boeing Field. It would be best if you went tonight, the sooner the better, and it would be best if you went alone. No harm will come to you, I promise."

The phone became quiet, and then a different mechanical voice spoke. "End of message." Jon pressed the play button to repeat the message. He was on the edge of the couch. He was wide-awake.

Jon listened to the message again. Then he went to the door and let Leon back in the house. He knew he should call Karen immediately, but he also knew that if he did she would tell him to stay home while she and the other members of her task force investigated the motel room. He doubted he'd be in danger at the motel, and he didn't want to lose the story. He looked up the address, then he went back out to his Explorer and drove off into the night.

The Rain City Motel was a dingy, single-story structure near the north end of the Boeing field runway. It looked like it had been painted yellow at some time in the past, but the soot from uncounted takeoffs and landings had turned it a mostly dirty gray. A small neon sign near the office announced "Vacancy." There were only twelve units, and Jon drove directly to unit 108. There were three other cars in the parking lot.

Jon left his lights on, shining on the door to room 108. He walked over, tried the doorknob and found it to be unlocked. He opened the door and peered inside the room. He could see no activity or other sign of life. He walked inside and left the door open behind him, ready to run. His headlights illuminated the room. He could clearly see a dresser on the left side of the room opposite a smallish double bed on the right. The room was sparsely furnished with only a single bedside stand on the left side of the bed. He saw her right away, and although he wasn't surprised by what he saw, the sight was still unsettling. The pale, naked body of the woman on the bed stood out in contrast to the brown-and-yellow pattern on the bedspread. She was lying on her back. Her feet were propped together toes up, her arms were crossed on top of her chest covering her breasts, her head was on the pillow and her eyes were shut. She was posed exactly like the others.

Jon carefully walked past the foot of the bed to look through the open bathroom door into the bathroom. His body was full of adrenaline, in full fight-or-flight mode. The bathroom was empty. He turned around to survey the bedroom. The room was neat, and there was no sign of a struggle. Other than the outside doorknob, Jon hadn't touched anything.

He returned to his car and turned off the headlights. He needed to notify the police. He knew The Sandman task force would be called to the scene, so he decided to call Karen directly. He removed his cell phone from his pocket and called Karen's home number. Her phone rang four times before she answered it.

"Hello," she said with a soft, sleepy voice.

"Karen, wake up. It's Jon"

"Hi, Jon," she said a little more awake now. "It's after two o'clock. Why are you calling this time of night?" She thought she knew.

"Are you awake?" he asked.

"Yes," she replied. "I'm awake."

"I'm over at the Rain City Motel. It's a little dump near Boeing

Field. The Sandman called. He left a present for me."

Karen was suddenly wide-awake.

Jon continued, "He left a message for me on my answering machine. He told me to go to room 108 at the Rain City Motel, and to go alone."

"And you went?"

"I'm here now."

"You idiot!" She screamed into the phone. "What's the matter with you?"

"There's another body here," he said. "It's posed just like the others."

"Stay there and don't touch anything. I'll be there in half an hour. You are such an idiot."

"Sorry."

"One of these days you're going to get yourself killed." Jon heard the receiver bang back into its cradle.

Jon walked back into the room. He pulled the sleeve of his jacket over his fingers so that he wouldn't leave any fingerprints, and then he turned on the lights. He kicked the door shut behind him. He walked over to the bed, and felt a sense of unease wash over him as he approached the body. It was becoming a familiar feeling.

The woman on the bed was white and looked to be in her mid twenties. The hair on her head was blond, but she was obviously a brunette. Her skin was smooth and pale. There was no blood or other sign of trauma that he could see. She had needle tracks on her arms just like the others. Jon presumed that she was a drug addict.

Jon took a deep breath and then bent over to get a closer look at her needle tracks. He confirmed the lack of blood on her skin. He held his hands behind him to avoid touching anything. The room had become cool during the period of time that he'd left the door open, and he could now feel warmth radiating from her body when he was close to her. She couldn't have been dead for very long. He wondered how long a dead body stayed warm. He knew medical examiners could determine a time of death by measuring core body temperatures. He looked at her face with her head propped up on the pillow. That was when she opened her eyes and looked back at him.

"Shit!"

Jon lunged backwards and his heel caught the carpet, throwing him off balance and onto the floor. He scrambled backwards away from the bed with his hands and feet until he banged into the front wall of the room.

"Jesus Christ!"

He huddled against the wall for a moment and then slowly stood up, still pressing against the wall, staring at the woman on the bed. She didn't move, but her eyes were open.

"Hello," he said tentatively. "Can you hear me?" There was no response.

He slowly walked back toward the bed. She didn't move a muscle. He looked in her eyes. They looked straight up at the ceiling. He looked closer. He thought the pupils might have changed size for a moment ever so slightly. He covered her eyes with his hands for a few seconds and then quickly removed them. There was definite movement. Not much, but definite movement. Her pupils constricted when he let the light back in her eyes.

"Hang on," he yelled.

He scrambled over to the telephone and dialed 911. He told the operator that there was an unconscious woman in room 108 of the Rain City Motel and that he needed help immediately. He dropped the phone, picked up the woman's wrist and felt for a pulse. He wasn't sure he could feel one. He pulled her arms down to her sides and put his ear on her chest. He could hear a slow but steady heart beat. He pulled back to look at her again. She didn't seem to be breathing. He didn't know what to do. He wasn't sure he remembered how to do CPR.

He watched a moment longer and then he saw her chest move ever so slightly. She was breathing, but very shallowly. He hadn't noticed it when her arms were resting on her chest. She was so still.

Anyone would mistake her for dead. He pulled the bedspread from the other side of the bed and covered her with it.

The paramedics were the first to arrive. They pushed him aside as they did a quick bedside evaluation of their patient, started her on oxygen through nasal prongs and started an IV. One of the paramedics asked Jon about the woman's condition when he found her while the other two continued their work.

Karen arrived within minutes of the paramedics. She was surprised to see the ambulance in the parking lot. The door to room 108 was open, and she could see the activity around the bed. She got out of her car, said something into her radio's hand mike and then entered the room. Jon was waiting for her by the door. He looked tired. He had depleted his body's supply of adrenaline.

"Hi, Karen."

"What's going on?" she asked.

"The body I called you about wasn't quite as dead as I thought."

"I can see that," she said.

"When I came in, she was posed just like the other Sandman victims. I went over to take a closer look after we finished talking. I was careful not to touch anything. I was looking right at her face when she opened her eyes. She didn't move another muscle. Her breathing was barely noticeable. I called 911 and here we all are."

"The room's a mess. The crime scene's totally contaminated. What was it like when you got here?"

"Not a thing out of place. The bed was made and the body was lying on top of the covers. The bedspread wasn't even wrinkled."

Karen walked into the room. She watched the paramedics working on their patient for a moment, and then she put on a pair of latex gloves. She opened the closet and looked inside. She looked in the dresser drawers and in the drawer of the bedside stand. All were empty.

She noticed the telephone receiver on the floor. "Did you touch the telephone?" she asked.

"Yes," Jon said. "I used it to call 911."

Karen continued to look around the room. The paramedics were preparing to transfer their patient to a gurney in order to take her to Harborview Hospital. Karen looked in the bathroom and then returned to watch the paramedics wheel the gurney out of the room and into an ambulance. Robbie Washington drove into the parking lot just as the ambulance turned on its lights and pulled out. Two more police cars arrived. The noise and confusion finally brought the night clerk out of his office to see what was going on. Jon spoke to Karen.

"I think he thinks that he killed her," Jon said. "I saved the message he left for me on the telephone."

"We can retrieve it after we finish here," she said.

"I wonder if she can identify him. The Sandman I mean."

"God, I hope so. We'll talk to her as soon as we get the OK from her doctors at Harborview."

Robbie entered the room. Gil Anderson drove into the parking lot. Karen walked over to Robbie and joined a conversation with two uniformed policemen. Another uniformed policeman was talking to the night clerk. Jon left the room to go sit in his car and phone in his story. After he finished he returned to the motel room. On his way back in he saw a KING TV news van drive into the parking lot. There would be others close behind.

"Karen," Jon said. "If you don't need me, it's been a long night. I think I'll take off. Come on over after you finish and I'll play the answering machine message for you."

"We'll need a statement," she said. "I can get it later."

"I'll leave the front door unlocked. I'll be asleep in the bedroom"

"Lock your door. I'll be by in the morning."

Jon left as an additional two news crews arrived in the parking lot.

Chapter 20

Jon pulled out of the parking lot, but instead of going home he drove up Airport Way towards the *Times* building. He had a story to file, and it would be a blockbuster. He listened to KIRO news radio as he drove, and he smiled to himself as they reported that the Sandman had killed again. He would get his story in the morning paper. Thornton loved an exclusive.

Jon drove on, but he couldn't get the motel room scene out of his head. Who was the woman? How was she doing? What could she tell him about The Sandman? He needed more information. After another block or two he decided the story could wait a few hours. He stopped his car, turned around, and then drove through the International District to Harborview Hospital. Once there he parked and found his way to the busy emergency room. He was looking for the woman still officially identified as Jane Doe #1, the first Jane Doe of the day.

The ER was busy as always. Nurses, paramedics, doctors and technicians were everywhere, all dressed in the same surgical green. A cacophony of noises and smells permeated the air. The ER's all too small waiting room with its tattered and tacky furniture was overflowing with people, some well dressed and some dressed for life on the street. An Arab woman was trying to quiet her crying infant. A scruffy bearded old man with no front teeth was sitting next to a teary-eyed young couple. They were holding hands. Three young men in gang colors sat in stone-eyed silence. A man in a business suit stared catatonically out into space. The reception desk at the end of the room served to separate them from the activity beyond.

On the other side of the reception desk several patients lay on gurneys in the hall waiting their turn for treatment. There were twelve patient care stations with their beds and support equipment off the hallway on the left, separated from one another by screening curtains. People dressed in green scrub suits were constantly moving about. Jon saw what he was looking for, a hospital security guard standing outside one of the treatment stations. He walked by the reception desk as if he owned the place and approached a nurse who came out from behind the curtain guarded by the security guy.

"How's she doing?"

"Are you a relative?" she asked.

"No, I don't even really know her. I'm the one who found her in the motel. I called 911."

She looked him over for a moment. "It's hard to tell. Her X-rays are negative and her vital signs are strong, but she hasn't been able to communicate. She may have suffered some brain damage, maybe from a lack of oxygen. Maybe it's something else. Anyway, she's stable now and her lab work looks fine. We're going to send her up to the floor."

"May I try to talk to her?"

"You'll have to ask him." She gestured toward the security guard, and then she scurried away.

Jon walked over and said, "My name's Jon Kirk." He showed the guard his press card. "Detective Able told me that the Jane Doe was coming here. Do you mind if I talk to her for a moment?" He looked in the direction of the closed curtain.

"She can't talk," he said.

"Do you mind if I try?"

"Be my guest. She won't be able to hear you. Leave the curtain open while you're in there."

Jon opened the curtain that partially shielded Jane Doe #1 from the rest of the activity in the ER. She was hooked up to an IV, but the oxygen hose had been discontinued. The heart monitor was also disconnected. She lay on her back underneath the covers on her hospital gurney. She was absolutely still. Her eyes were open. Jon moved closer and looked in her eyes. She was completely expressionless. "Do you recognize me?" he asked. "I found you in the motel room, remember?"

She was silent and didn't move.

"I'm a reporter for the *Times*. I'm investigating The Sandman murders." He paused. "He did this to you, didn't he? It's the drug. He gave you a drug, didn't he?"

Nothing.

"Can you hear me?" There was no response. "The drug paralyzed you, but it shouldn't be permanent. It should wear off in time. You should be fine."

Still nothing.

"Can you blink your eyes? If you understand me, blink your eyes once."

She didn't blink, but Jon thought he saw her eyelids move ever so slightly.

"I think you can hear me, and I think you can understand. I know you can. It's the way the drug works. You must be scared to death."

There was no recognition in her eyes.

"Listen to me. I want to find the son of a bitch who did this to you. I want to make sure that he never hurts you or anybody else again. Blink if you understand."

He watched her eyelids, but they didn't move.

"I need your help. I really need your help." He paused. "You'll help me won't you? You'll help me when this drug wears off?" Another pause. "They say you're stable and out of danger. Try not to worry. They're going to take you up to a hospital room in a little while. Just hang on." He squeezed her hand through the blanket. "I'll see you after they move you upstairs. I'd like to know your name. Try to blink if you understand me."

She didn't blink, but Jon noticed something else. A small tear welled up out of the corner of her right eye. It trickled down the side of her cheek.

"OK, that's enough." The nurse had returned. "We're going to take her upstairs now. She'll be on the fifth floor. You can talk to her later."

Jon smiled at the woman staring up at him. "As the lady says, we'll talk more later. You'll get through this. I promise. I'll come up to see you." He touched her on her shoulder and then as gently as he could, he wiped away her tear. "Don't be afraid," he said as he clasped his hand over hers. He held it until it slipped away as the nurse released the breaks on the gurney and wheeled her patient out into the hall.

Jon had to hurry. He had a great story, he had a deadline to meet, and there wasn't much time left. He was thinking about his headline when he noticed the nurse and her patient disappear into an open elevator. Without knowing exactly why, he jogged to the elevator and joined them through its still open door. "You don't mind if I ride up with you, do you?" he asked.

"Help yourself," the nurse answered. "You can wait in the fifth floor waiting room if you want."

Jon stood next to Jane Doe #1. He again placed his hand over hers and gently held it while the elevator doors closed. He was going to miss deadline for the biggest story of his life.

❋

Jon was sleeping in a chair in the fifth floor hospital waiting room when Karen shook his shoulder to wake him up. The furniture was old and the floor was linoleum.

"I thought you were going to go home," she said. "The nurse

said you've been here all night."

"Last minute change of plans," he answered in a sleepy voice. "What time is it?" Jon looked at his watch. The sun was up. It was ten o'clock. He rubbed his eyes and tried to clear his head. His back was stiff from sleeping in the chair.

"You look like you could use some coffee."

"I look that bad, do I?"

"You don't look bad, just sleepy." Karen couldn't put the thought of Jon and Lizzy eating dinner together out of her mind. She thought she should feel angry, but she didn't. She felt confused. She tried not to let it show.

Jon ran his fingers through his wavy black hair. "How's Sleeping Beauty?" he asked.

"She'll make it. Her name's Sarah Boyd. We're taking real good care of her."

Jon stood up and stretched. "Sarah's a nice name. We had a little chat last night."

"How'd you do that?" Karen asked. "She couldn't talk."

"Last night I asked her if she could blink her eyes. She was able to move them a little. I think she understood me. I'll bet she can tell us what happened to her, and who did it."

"What's this *us* stuff? Why should I let you talk to her? You're just in it for another exclusive, and you haven't done anything lately to deserve that little perk."

"Come on Karen, lighten up a little. I blew the exclusive by spending the night here instead of filing a story. My boss is going to be really pissed when he finds out."

"That's a little out of character, isn't it?" she asked.

"I made a promise last night. I promised her I'd come see her."

"Last night when you talked with her?"

"Yeah, last night when I talked with her. Besides, what's to keep me from just walking into her room like I did last night?"

"You'd never get near her. No more security guards, we have a real cop stationed outside her door. Nobody gets in unless they're on the list."

"Listen, I'm the one who found her. The Sandman called me, remember? I've been invited. I'm in this whether I want to be or not."

Karen looked in his eyes. She paused for a few seconds. She looked outside through one of the hospital windows at the downtown skyline, and then back at Jon. "Oh all right," she said with a tone of resignation in her voice. She shook her head. "Let's go."

✳

Everyone on the floor could hear the racket. The old hard surfaces on the walls and floor of the hallway amplified the sound. It was coming from Sarah's room at the far end of the hall. She was wide awake and it was obvious that she had recovered the full use of her voice. Her doctors had restrained her arms and legs to prevent her from hurting herself as she recovered from her paralysis. She had an IV in her left arm and a catheter in her bladder.

"Get those fucking tubes out of me!" She was screaming at the nurse trying to adjust the flow of fluid in her IV. The nurse wore a nametag that read CANDY. "Untie my hands, God damn it! Let me out of here!"

"Calm down," the nurse said. "The restraints are there to protect you from hurting yourself."

"Fuck you, you fucking cunt! Let me out of here!" Sarah continued to scream at the top of her lungs.

The nurse left the room. Jon and Karen passed her in the hall.

"What's that all about?" Karen asked the guard outside the room.

"Who knows," he answered. "She's been doing that off and on all morning."

"How is she?" Jon asked.

"Loud," he answered. "She's quiet for the moment, but she's been shrieking like a banshee. Good luck in there," he said.

Karen and Jon entered the room. Karen walked over to the bed. Jon hung back by the door.

"Who the fuck are you?" Sarah asked Karen. She pulled at her restraints.

"I'm Detective Able of the Seattle Police Department. I'd like to ask you a few questions if you don't mind."

"I don't talk to cops," Sarah said. She turned her head away and gave another tug at her restraints.

"This is about The Sandman. He tried to kill you last night. He probably thought that he did kill you. We'd like you to help us catch him."

Sarah slowly turned her head back toward Karen. "What the fuck's the matter with you? Are you DEAF?" she shouted the word as loudly as she could. "I told you I don't fucking talk to cops. Now get out of here!" She turned away again.

Jon walked in and stood at the foot of the bed where Sarah could see him. She looked at him for a moment or two before speaking.

"I know you," she said. "You were there last night. You were the one who wiped the tears from my eyes and told me not to be afraid."

"That's right," he said. "I was there."

"Everybody else treated me like a piece of meat. You were nice."

"I'm sorry," he said. "I'm sure they didn't mean it."

"They're a bunch of assholes," she said. "I couldn't talk; I couldn't move; I could barely breathe. You have no idea how helpless I felt. I thought I was going to die. You gave me a little hope. It meant a lot."

"I'm glad," he said. "I found you in the motel after The Sandman tried to kill you. I came to the emergency room to see how you were doing."

"Nobody tried to kill me," she said insistently. "I just got some bad drugs." She started again to pull at her restraints. "I don't know what's worse, being helpless and unable to move, or being helpless and tied to a fucking bed against your will. Why do doctors do that?" She turned her head to face Karen. "Hey, cop, isn't it against the law to tie someone up against their will?" She kicked at her ankle restraints.

Jon continued, "I found you because The Sandman called me and told me where to look. He thought he had killed you. He thought you were dead. Bad drugs had nothing to do with it. Come on, let's talk about it. What do you say?"

She stopped struggling and looked at Jon. "Untie me." She looked him straight in the eye. "Untie me and I'll tell you what you want to know."

"I'll have to ask the doctors," he said.

"Untie me now or you can fucking forget it," she demanded.

Jon looked at Karen. She shrugged her shoulders and looked back at him. Jon reached down to untie her left hand restraint.

"You're a reporter. You told me so last night," she said. "I'll talk to you, but I don't talk to cops." Sarah tilted her head toward Karen. "She has to leave."

Jon addressed Karen. "Is it OK?"

"It's OK for now," she said. "But be careful. I'll be right outside."

Jon continued to undo the left hand restraint. He then undid the restraints on Sarah's ankles and her right hand. She stretched a little, raised the head of her bed with her hand control panel and then stared at Karen, who was still standing in the doorway. Karen left the room.

"OK, she's gone," said Jon. "Now tell me about last night."

Sarah sat up and swung her feet over the left side of her bed. "Excuse me a moment," she said. Then she grasped the IV tubing with her right hand and pulled it out of her left arm. Blood started to leak from the wound created by the IV needle.

Jon flinched. "Jesus Christ," he said. He closed his eyes and steadied himself by grabbing the frame of the bed.

"Don't be such a pussy," she said.

Next she reached down between her knees and picked up her catheter tube. "Look at this fucking thing. They push this tube into your bladder and then squirt in water to blow up a balloon that's attached on the other end. The balloon stays in your bladder to keep the tube from falling out." She grimaced as she pulled it out with a yank. She held it in her hand for a moment, looking at the inflatable balloon on the end. It was still inflated, and it was covered in blood from the trauma caused by pulling it out.

Jon looked at her in amazement. "That had to hurt," he said, still gripping the bed frame.

"I'll be pissing blood for a week," she answered. "I've done it before. Here, help me with this." She dropped the catheter on the floor and put her fingers over the wound in her left arm to stop the bleeding. It was a bloody mess.

Jon just stood there.

"OK. Don't help me." Sarah walked around him to the right side of her bed, took some gauze and some tape out of the bedside stand, wiped the blood off of her arm with the bed sheet and then taped the gauze tightly over the wound. The bleeding stopped.

"What now?" Jon asked.

"A deal's a deal. Now I tell you about last night," she said. Sarah sat back down on the side of the bed. She patted the foot of the bed for Jon to sit next to her. He sat down willingly. The color was coming back into his face. Then she began to talk.

"I was working near the Pike Street Market when this john drives by. He stops and rolls down his window. I walk over to the car and ask him if he's looking to party. He says sure and we make a business deal. Then I get in."

"What did he look like?"

"He was tall, maybe six foot three or four, medium build, not flabby, about fifty I'd say. He was white. He had brown hair, and he was strong. He had strong hands."

"What kind of car did he drive?"

"I can't remember for sure. It was a dark color, maybe a Taurus. Anyway, we drive to the Rain City Motel and I get the key. We go in the room and I ask him what he has in mind. He says to take off all my clothes, so I do."

"Was there anything special about his voice, you know, high pitched, low, gravely or something? Maybe he had an accent?"

"No, it's just a normal voice. He says to me that he's a little nervous. He says he brought some drugs to put him in the mood, good stuff, and he asks if I want some. I say sure. He draws some from a medical vial and gives me the syringe. I shoot some. Then I tell him I don't feel nothing. He says something like, wonderful. He's all excited. He says it works. I say I don't think so and he says I'll show you. He pinches the skin on my leg as hard as he can. See, there's the bruise. Excuse the blood." She wiped the blood from the catheter off her legs. There was a well-demarcated bruise on the inside of her left thigh. "I tell him I don't feel nothin'. I mean I feel him touching me, but it doesn't hurt. Now he's even more excited. He tells me to shut my eyes, and when I do I feel him touching my side. When I open my eyes I see red marks. See, now there's a bruise." She pointed to a bruise on the side of her chest. "I say something like, what the fuck you tryin' to do? He says he's sorry, he just wanted to show me how good the drug was. I say, your drug's not worth shit, where's the rush, and he says try this. He gives me something else from another vial. It feels warm, and all of a sudden I slide off the bed. I can't talk and I can't move. I can hardly breathe. He smooths out the covers and puts me on the bed. He shuts my eyes and I can't open them. I lay there for a long time, and then you came."

"Jesus, that's quite a story."

"Yeah, isn't it."

"Listen, if I brought in an artist would you describe him to her?"

"Not a police artist, and not here. I'm leaving."

"OK, not a police artist, someone else, but you can't leave. There's a guard outside the door."

"You want to bet. Just watch me. I've done it before. It's called leaving a hospital AMA, that means against medical advice. They can't keep you unless you're under arrest for something." She hopped off the bed.

"You'll be in danger," he said. "The Sandman won't want you to talk. You can identify him. He'll try to kill you if you give him the chance. You'll be safer here."

"I can take care of myself."

"You don't have any clothes. You'll be arrested for indecent exposure in that hospital gown."

"Indecent exposure?" She started to laugh. "Give me a break. Better yet, give me your coat."

"What?"

"You heard me, give me your coat. I'll give it back. If you want me to work with the artist you'll give me your coat."

Jon thought about it for a minute and then answered, "Sure, you can have my coat, but you'll never get out of here." She was barefoot and didn't have any shoes. He continued, "But just in case, here's my card." Jon put his card in the pocket of his coat. "If you make it, call me at home tonight. We have more to talk about and I want my coat back."

"Sure," she said.

Jon gave her his coat. Sarah put it on. She blew him a kiss, wheeled around and then marched barefoot out of the hospital room. Jon followed her outside and watched her yell at Karen and the guard and two nurses and a doctor about unlawful imprisonment and holding her in a hospital against her will. She yelled something about you can't hold me, get away from me, don't try to follow me, police harassment and I know my rights. He could hear her yelling as she walked down the hallway, and he continued to hear her voice until the elevator doors shut and cut it off. He shook his head in amazement.

Chapter 21

Sarah Boyd was a big story. She survived The Sandman's attempt on her life, and presumably she could identify him. She left the protection of the Seattle police department and checked herself out of the hospital. She was last seen walking barefoot over to James Street where she hitched a ride and then disappeared. She wasn't just a big story; she was an incredible story. Half the reporters in Seattle were looking for her. Unfortunately, they didn't know where to look.

Dr. Jim Allison knew where to look. He knew where she worked. He knew where she lived. He knew how she worked and how she lived. He knew everything about her. He was a very thorough man. He studied his subjects extensively before he selected them. He knew where Sarah got her drugs, and he knew that if he were patient he would find her there.

Allison was sitting in his rented blue minivan near a group of rundown apartments west of Boeing Field. The streets were deserted. He was waiting. He'd nearly panicked when he'd found out that Sarah had survived. It wasn't like him to make such a careless mistake. It had to be fixed. So he just sat there, watching and waiting. It was cold, it was raining and it didn't take long.

Allison saw a cab stop a block and a half north of the apartments. He raised his Zeiss binoculars to watch Sarah get out of the car and step into the rain. He watched her as she walked down the street and looked over her shoulder to make sure that she was alone. And he watched her as she turned right into a small apartment building and as she knocked on the door. When she entered he knew that she wouldn't be inside for long. Nobody ever stayed long in the crack house no matter what kind of drugs they were after.

Before she reemerged, Allison repositioned the van to the north of the apartment complex. He parked it halfway between the apartment and the corner on the same side of the street. The rain and dingy setting contributed to the gloom of the night, and it hid the driver of the van from outside view. He waited.

After ten minutes or so Sarah left the apartment alone and started walking back the way she'd arrived. As she neared the van the front door opened and a man wearing a long dark coat and a fedora got out. She could sense him looking at her from under the hat as he approached. She was accustomed to men looking at her.

"What the fuck you want?" she asked. He didn't answer. She wasn't afraid. She felt in control. She carried a six-inch knife and some pepper spray in her purse. She tried to look at his face, but she couldn't see it under his hat because it was hidden by the dark and shadows of the rainy night. He continued to move purposefully toward her, and when he was close enough, he looked up so that she could see under the brim of his hat.

"It's you!" She was startled. She shoved her hand in her purse for her knife.

It was too late. He had already plunged the needle into the side of her neck.

She pushed away and took a few steps backward before her legs grew weak. She tried to say something, but nothing came out. She took another few faltering steps and then collapsed in a heap on the sidewalk.

Allison watched her until all movement stopped. Then he grabbed her by her wrists and dragged her over to the van. He opened the side door, threw her inside and climbed in after her.

The rear seats had been removed to make more room in the back. He then slid the door shut behind him. He looked around through the darkened windows to see if anyone had come out on the street. No one was there. The streets were still deserted. He rolled Sarah onto her back and checked her pulse with two fingers on the side of her neck. Finally he put his face very close to hers.

"I know you can hear me, Sarah," he said in a whispered voice. "It's curare. More precisely, it's a shorter-acting close relative of curare. That fine point shouldn't make any difference to you; you're suffocating. You're paralyzed, you're scared and you're suffocating. It won't be much longer now unless I help you."

Allison reached forward next to the front passenger seat and retrieved his resuscitation equipment. He placed the resuscitation mask over her nose and mouth, and then began to rhythmically squeeze the bag attached to the mask. He began to breathe for her. Six breaths per minute. Enough air to keep her alive, but not enough to completely alleviate her hunger for air. After one minute —six breaths—he removed the mask. He saw life return to her body. He saw expression return to her face. He saw terror in her eyes.

"I can bring you life." He put the mask back over her face and squeezed the bag four more times. "Or. . . ." He took the mask away again. Sarah blinked her eyes. The short-acting drug was beginning to wear off. "It's up to you. You'll be able to talk in a minute or two. Tell me what you said about me while you were in the hospital. Tell me the truth. I'll know if you are lying."

Allison removed another syringe from his pocked and showed her the needle. "I'm going to put this needle in your arm. If you lie to me, I'm going to inject the drug." He tied a rubber tube around her arm above her left elbow. He inserted the needle in a vein after it expanded with blood. He then placed the mask over her face and squeezed the bag twice. He took the mask away and watched.

Sarah Boyd was in agony. Her lungs were burning with air hunger. She couldn't scream. She couldn't cry. She could barely move. She struggled to breathe for herself, and her chest moved ever so slightly.

"Good," he said. "Now tell me what you told the police in the hospital. You'll be able to speak in a moment."

Sarah could feel her strength slowly return. She tried to speak. She couldn't draw in enough air in to make her vocal cords work the way they were supposed to. The sound came out in a dry whisper. "Uh . . . a . . . I . . . uh . . . d . . . on't . . . ta . . . k . . . cop . . . s."

"Exhausting, isn't it? I'm sorry, but I couldn't understand you. You're going to have to do better than that." Allison put the mask over her face again. This time only one squeeze of the bag. "Now try it again."

Sarah wheezed the words; "I . . . don't . . . talk . . . to . . . cops." She continued to struggle to breathe.

"There, that's much better. Unfortunately, we still have a problem." He put his face right over hers; "I don't believe you."

Her eyes followed his hand as it moved to the syringe. He pushed in the plunger. Her cheeks sagged, her jaw dropped and the expression fell from her face. Everything was still. She stopped breathing. He looked in her eyes for a moment.

"I'll bet you want this?" He held the resuscitation mask and bag in front of her. He laughed. "Maybe some other time." He tossed the mask and bag on the floor of the van. "Try counting backwards from one hundred," he said. "It'll help pass the time."

Allison climbed into the front seat of the van, and then turned to look over his shoulder at Sarah's flaccid body one more time. Her eyes were dead. He turned back to focus on the road ahead of him. He started the engine, he shifted into drive and then he slowly drove away.

✳

"Shouldn't she have called by now?" Lizzy asked.

"She's not going to call. She never had any intention of calling," Karen said. She turned to Jon. "And you aren't going to get your coat back either."

"I liked that coat," he said.

"It serves you right," Karen said. "You should never have given it to her in the first place."

"Jon, sometimes you can be so naive," Lizzy said.

Jon had told Sarah Boyd to call him at home, and Karen wasn't about to let Jon take that phone call by himself. She had insisted on being there with him. Lizzy also wanted to be there. She needed material for her planned article for the morning paper. The three of them were sitting around Jon's dining room table, waiting for the telephone to ring. Jon felt a little unnerved with the two women in his house at the same time. Bobby Arnold's warning came to mind.

Leon was lying on the floor under the table. He enjoyed being around people. He lifted his head as if listening to the conversation, shifted his position slightly to the left and then passed some gas.

"Jesus, Jon. What do you feed this dog?" Lizzy asked.

"Just the usual," he answered, "Dog food, cheeseburgers, that sort of thing. Anybody want a beer? I'm going to go to the kitchen and get a beer."

"No, thanks," Karen said.

"Me neither," Lizzy said. "I'll try some wine if you have any." Lizzy leaned back in her chair, arched her back and stretched. Then she casually fluffed Jon's hair with her outstretched right hand. Karen felt her chest tighten as she saw Jon lean into her touch before he stood up to leave for the kitchen.

"I'll see what I can find," he said.

Lizzy turned to Karen and said, in a low voice so that Jon couldn't hear, "Cute, isn't he?"

"I suppose so," she said. There was ice in her voice.

"Nice buns, too."

"If you're into that sort of thing." Karen could feel her face flush. Her pulse beat a rhythm in her ears. She tried to smile. She took a slow deep breath. Then she added as calmly as she could, "Are you involved with him?" She searched Lizzy's eyes for the answer.

Lizzy paused for a moment and then said, "Jon? Are you kidding?" She laughed out loud. "I work with him, I don't sleep with him," she lied. "He's a great guy though, don't you think?" She paused again, and then she asked, "What about you? Are you involved with him?"

"Sometimes I wish I weren't," she said.

Jon walked back into the room. He carried a bottle of wine, two glasses and a beer. "So how about those Seahawks?" he asked. Lizzy and Karen looked at each other. They both laughed a nervous laugh. "What," he said. "Did I miss something?" He put the glasses on the table and poured some wine for Lizzy. "Would you like some?" he asked Karen.

"Sure, why not?" He poured the wine. "I heard you had a little problem with the law last night," she said.

"Who told you that?"

"I heard it at the station. People down there think I'm interested in everything that happens to you for some reason or other."

"Now why is that?" Lizzy asked.

"Some asshole had my car towed away and it cost me seventy bucks just to get it back."

"Gee, I'm sorry to hear that," Karen said.

"I was parked in front of Etta's. The ticket says I parked in a handicapped zone."

"You should have seen his face when he saw his car being hauled down the street," Lizzy said through her chuckles.

"It wasn't funny," Jon protested.

"And what were you doing there?" Karen asked.

"In the handicapped zone?" Jon questioned. "There was no handicapped zone."

"We were having dinner," Lizzy said.

"Oh?" Karen questioned.

"A working dinner," Jon added.

"So you were working," Karen reiterated, "at one of the most expensive restaurants in town."

"It's not that expensive," Lizzy said. "And besides, we split the bill." She lifted her wineglass and drank half of her wine.

Karen looked at them for a moment "Do you have the ticket with you?"

"Here," he took his wallet out of his back pocket and pulled out the citation.

"May I see it?" she asked him. When Jon handed her the ticket, Karen pretended to study it. "This is from Officer Rademaker, I can fix this one."

"Thanks, Karen. You just saved me two hundred bucks. I owe you."

"Don't mention it." She flashed a look in Lizzy's direction. Then she took a sip of her wine.

Lizzy interpreted Karen's glance and finished her wine in two quick swallows. "What time is it?" She looked at her watch. "Uh oh, it's later than I thought," she said. "I still have a story to file before deadline. If Sarah Boyd was going to call, she would have called by now anyway." She stood up.

Jon stood as well. "Let me walk you to the door." They walked through the living room to the front door. He helped her on with her coat.

"Jon," Lizzy said quietly. "Karen needs you to be nice to her tonight." She winked at him. "I'll see you tomorrow." Jon opened the door and she hesitated a moment before ducking her head and then making a dash for her car through the pouring rain.

✳

Jim Allison drove his rented minivan north on Airport Way and then on through the International District. He turned right on Madison toward Lake Washington. Allison kept his boat docked on the lake near the Leshi District. It was a twenty-six footer with a cabin.

At the dock he was careful to park his van in the shadows away from the streetlights. After looking around to make sure the area was deserted, he climbed in between the front seats into the back of the van with Sarah Boyd's dead body. He checked her pulse one more time just to be sure. It was still. There would be no mistakes this time. He knew he'd screwed up when Sarah had survived his first attempt to kill her but he told himself that everything was all right now, that it was just a momentary lapse, and that it wouldn't happen again. Everything was back to normal. What was wrong he had put right. He paused a moment to smile a satisfied smile before he continued.

Allison stripped the clothes off her body and put them in a pile with her purse in the back of the van. She'd been wearing jeans, a blouse, loafers and a coat, no underwear. He then covered the body with a tarp, opened the sliding door, pulled her out of the van and carried her over his shoulder to his boat. He was pumped with adrenaline and he barely noticed her weight. After putting her body in the cabin, he walked back to the parking lot and again looked around to make sure that no one was watching. He was alone.

He re-entered the van, pulled Sarah's purse out from under the pile of clothes in the back and dumped the contents on the floor. There was the usual assortment of makeup, tissues, a wallet, pen, nail file, and money plus a six-inch switch blade knife and some pepper spray. He checked the pockets of her jeans and the pockets of her coat. That's when he found the card.

"Shit!" The card belonged to Jon Kirk. It identified him as an investigative reporter for *The Seattle Times*, and it listed his work and home telephone numbers plus an e-mail address. His home number was underlined. Allison's heart started to race. He stared at the card. It was another mistake, another loose end. He'd planned everything, and he'd been so careful. What was happening here?

Then, as quickly as it had surged up, the panic faded away. He waited until his heart slowed to normal. Kirk was not a threat; Kirk and his friend, Liz Carlstrom. He'd take care of them. He put the card in his pocket.

Allison scooped up the clothes, the purse and its contents, wrapped them securely with duct tape and put them in a plastic garbage bag. He then added a one-pound weight and tied the bag shut with a plastic tie. Finally he meticulously wrapped the whole bag and its contents with several more segments of duct tape. After he got out of the van and locked the door, he carried the garbage bag to the boat and tossed it in next to the tarp-covered body. He then climbed into the boat and sat there for a full five minutes to make sure that he was still alone.

He started the engine and untied the lines. The boat slowly idled away from the dock. Once in the clear, he motored to a location on the water about half way between Leshi and Mercer Island, a half mile from either shore. When he arrived he cut the engine and let the boat drift for a while. He listened. The lake was silent.

After exactly twenty minutes he removed the tarp from around Sarah's body. He handcuffed a thirty-pound anchor on a chain to her ankle, pulled her up, and then pushed her over the side. She slid into the water. He threw the weight in after her with a splash and watched her suddenly sink beneath the surface. The bottom of the lake was seventy feet down. He again listened. He heard nothing. He grabbed the weighted garbage bag and dropped it in the water. It was pitch black outside. He was certain no one could see him. After exactly another twenty minutes he restarted the engine and returned to the dock. He felt Kirk's card in his pocket. "Shit!" He walked to the minivan and drove away.

✳

Karen snuggled in close to Jon. Her head was on his chest. He was on his back and he was breathing heavily. The lights were out and Leon was asleep on the floor. Karen's eyes were wide open.

"Jon, are you asleep?"

"Uh, what time is it?" He turned his head to the side to look at the clock. It was 4:45. He groaned.

"Jon." She tickled his ear with her finger. "Let's get up and watch the sunrise."

"It's too early."

She snuggled closer and continued to tease his ear. "Come on, Jon, wake up."

He slowly unfolded himself from her body and sat up against the headboard. He tried to clear his head. "OK, I'm awake," he said with little conviction.

She sat up next to him. "I love sunrises. Let's sit together and watch the sun come up."

"Karen, it's raining outside," he said with a yawn.

"Not above the clouds."

"No, not above the clouds."

"You know," she said, "Things never seem to work out for us quite the way they're supposed to."

"What do you mean?"

"Oh, I don't know. It's just a thought that popped into my head." She slid back down under the covers. He slid down next to her. She cuddled in close. Within a few minutes he was breathing heavily. It was still dark. Her eyes were wide open.

Chapter 22

The story of Sarah Boyd dominated the morning news. The electronic media had reported The Sandman's failed murder attempt, but Jon reported the details from his interview in the hospital. It was another exclusive. His story had hit the streets like a bombshell. Everyone wanted to interview the man who had interviewed Sarah Boyd. Jon had no intention of helping his competition.

As Jon sat at his desk in the noisy newsroom drinking a cup of burned coffee, he read the piece he'd written on bioprospecting in the morning paper. It was published along with Lizzy's as a sidebar article to the Sarah Boyd story. Lizzy sat at right angles from him while he read. "Good stuff," she said to him.

"Mysterious medicines from exotic plants, restless natives, greedy scientists, the rain forest, serial murder, how can it miss?" he said.

"It can't. It didn't."

"Now we need to somehow tie it all together."

"Easier said than done," she said.

"It's a big jigsaw puzzle, and now it seems like we finally have all of the pieces. It can't be that hard to make them all fit."

"Not if you start with the edges and work inward." Lizzy reached over to Jon's desk and picked up his cup of coffee. She took a drink. "Ugh. How do you drink this crap?"

"It's not that bad." He took the cup back from her and grimaced as he took another swallow.

"Not that bad huh," she said.

"You're right. It's awful."

"Let's go over to Starbucks and get some of the good stuff."

"Good idea." He dumped his coffee into his wastebasket and then threw the cup in after it. The two of them walked out of the office together. They talked as they walked.

"How'd it go last night after I left?" Lizzy asked.

"Sarah Boyd never called."

"That's not what I mean and you know it. How'd it go with Karen?"

"It went fine."

"She's in love with you, you know."

"I'm not so sure about that," he said. "A few days ago she almost killed me."

"It's all part of the deal."

They walked the half block to Starbucks and went inside. Liz ordered a latte and Jon ordered a double espresso. They sat at a small table by the window where they could people watch. They both sipped their coffee.

"How are you coming on your think piece?" Jon asked. He took another sip of his espresso.

"It's a challenge. I'm trying to weave a web between Holyoke, smuggling, bioprospecting, The Sandman and the prostitute murders. I'm looking for motives, if there are such things with serial killers."

"Has the boss seen it yet?"

"Not yet," she said. "It's a little long, and it needs a little more work. I was aiming for the Sunday paper. That way I wouldn't have to cut it down."

"You should let him see it. He might be able to help. It's the kind of piece that separates us from the TV guys."

"I'll do that," she said. "I'd like to include the Sarah Boyd material if we get her lab work back before the deadline."

"I assume Sarah's still missing," Jon said

"I haven't heard a word."

It started to drizzle, and it looked as if someone had switched the people-watching show outside their window into fast forward. People were scurrying to get in out of the rain. Jon and Lizzy watched for awhile, finished their coffee and then quickly walked back toward the office. The drizzle stood out on their hair like hundreds of little beads. "Doc Allison was supposed to call me this morning," Lizzy said. "You haven't heard from him, have you?"

"Nope." The rain was starting to trickle down his neck. He picked up the pace.

"I really need that lab work. I need to know if the drugs that were used on Sarah Boyd were the same as those in the others."

"Maybe he couldn't tell. All he had was her blood. He had tissue samples from the first four."

"Maybe," she said. "But I need to find out just the same."

"Do you want me to try to reach him for you?

"I can do it. It's my story."

They reached the *Times* building and went up to the newsroom. Jon returned to his desk. The morning paper was still leaning on his computer with his stories prominently displayed on the front page. Lizzy brushed the water off his hair before moving on toward her own desk. "I'm going to track down Doc Allison and finish this thing," she said. "Blue Moon around five?"

"It's a date. And, Liz, let me know what Thornton has to say about your think piece."

"I will," she said. She turned away and detoured toward the editor's office.

＊

Jim Allison was sitting at his desk in the medical examiner's office. He had already finished the two autopsies he had scheduled for the day. One was a floater and it had been in the salt water of Puget Sound for almost a week. Allison had called down the five medical students taking their pathology service rotation to watch the dissection. The body was bloated and was full of hydrogen sulfide gas. It smelled like rotten eggs. He was disappointed when he was only able to make one of them sick. He wondered what he could have done better when his telephone rang. His secretary told him that he had a call from a woman who declined to identify herself.

"Dr. Allison."

"Yes."

"Some of our investors require a personal demonstration. We're going to need another test subject."

"I'll see to it," he said. He hung up the phone.

✳

Jon watched Lizzy walk away and then he went back to work on a follow-up bioprospecting story. He was writing about drug extraction from tropical plants, and he had a question. He dialed Dr. Saunders' number at the med school seeking an answer. "Hello, Dr. Saunders?"

"Mr. Kirk, what a surprise. My old pal. What can I do for you?"

"You can tell me how Holyoke built a large greenhouse and lab facility on a professor's salary. How much would such a facility cost?"

"It would have cost millions."

"Millions?"

"Yes, several millions. There's the facility with its environmental controls, then the equipment. At least five million, maybe as much as ten, maybe more."

"Was Holyoke a rich man?"

"Not that rich."

"Then who do you think paid for it?"

"I wouldn't have any idea. Obviously someone with a lot of money; someone who wanted to share in the profits."

"OK then, just a couple of more questions," Jon said.

"I'm afraid I don't have time for a couple of more questions right now. Can we talk later?"

"Sure, I'm meeting Liz at the Blue Moon Café this afternoon at five. Would you like to join us?

"The Blue Moon? Is that place still in business? I haven't been there in years."

"It's still there."

"Then I'd be delighted to meet you, Mr. Kirk."

"I'll see you then."

"Goodbye." She hung up the phone.

✳

Dr. Allison was sitting at his desk in his office staring at the telephone while he held its receiver to his ear. He pushed number four on the keypad to replay the message. "Dr. Allison, it's Lizzy at *The Seattle Times.* Do you have the lab results yet on Sarah Boyd? I'm finishing an article on bioprospecting and new drug development for the Sunday paper. I need the results to complete the tie-in to The Sandman murders. I'm working on a motive. Please call me as soon as they are available. Thanks." He pressed seven to erase the message and then hung up.

Sarah Boyd had carried Kirk's card in her pocket. He shouldn't be surprised that Liz called about a connection between new drug development and the murders. Had they figured it out? Sarah had told them something, but what? How much did they know? What had they guessed? Something had to be done. He would correct the situation. He had to. No more mistakes.

Allison returned Liz's call at the *Times.*

"Dr. Allison, thank you for calling me back."

"Oh, you're welcome. I'd never pass up a chance to talk with such a lovely young woman."

"Flattery will get you everywhere," she said. "Listen, I'm finishing a story for the Sunday paper and I need to know the results of Sarah Boyd's lab tests. Are they available?"

"As a matter of fact yes, they are. But it's a little complicated. We found a curare-like substance in her blood, but it's not the same as the substances that were in the other victims. The differences are subtle, but important. I can discuss it with you, but I have an appointment in a few minutes. It'd be difficult to explain it all to you in a short conversation over the telephone anyway.

"Then would it be OK if I dropped by later today to talk to you about it?"

"Yes. I can make room in my schedule. Four o'clock would work."

"I'll see you at four."

"One more thing," he said. "It might be a good idea if you parked in the old underground parking lot on the south side of the hospital. The main parking lot to the north is usually overcrowded and full in the afternoons. Be careful not to miss the sign."

"I'll be there," she said, and then she hung up the phone.

"That'd be lovely," he said into the dead line.

Allison hung up the phone, stood up and walked out of his office. He approached his secretary at her desk. "Andrea, Liz Carlstrom from *The Seattle Times* asked for an appointment with me this afternoon at four o'clock. I don't have anything scheduled for that time do I?" He knew he didn't.

"No sir," she answered. "The afternoon's clear."

"Good, then would you please mark her down."

"Yes sir. Do you want me to call her to confirm?"

"No, that won't be necessary. I told her that I thought the time would be OK." Allison made a point of looking at his watch. It was almost noon. "And Andrea, since there's nothing else scheduled for the rest of the day, why don't you take the afternoon off. I'll handle the phones. I plan to be here in my office all afternoon anyway."

"Oh, thank you, Dr. Allison. I guess I'll see you tomorrow morning."

"Yes, Andrea, I'll see you then." He turned, walked back into his office and shut the door. He sat down behind his desk and looked at the large clock on the wall. Four hours to go.

✳

Jon left his office early for the Blue Moon Café. Bobby Arnold greeted him as he walked in the door.

"The corner booth," Bobby said. "She's waiting for you. I'll bring you a Redhook."

Jon looked back to the corner booth. There were only a few people in the bar. His eyes weren't fully adjusted to the dim lighting but he could see a cloud of smoke hovering in the air. He walked back to the booth. "Dr. Saunders," he said. "I'm glad you could come."

"Nice to see you too. I'd hate to have to buy my own martinis," she said. "As a matter of fact, now that you're here I think I'll order another." She leaned out of the booth so that Bobby could see her. "Bartender, another one of the same." She held her martini glass up in the air. After she was sure Bobby saw her, she sat back inside the booth and lit another cigarette.

Jon sat down across from Saunders. He wondered how long she had been there. There were already three cigarette butts in the ashtray.

"How are things at the med school?" he asked. "Anything new?"

"Fun and games," she said. "The police are still there. They've almost finished with the students, but they have a lot more faculty to talk to. Animal rights activists are doing whatever they can to disrupt the research labs. Yesterday there were white rats running all over the place. I heard several even got into the operating rooms. Let's see, your friends in the press are trying to get Kay Masters in News and Information Services to loosen up a little. That'll never work. The dean's office is doing everything it can to distance itself from George Holyoke. I guess that's just about it, the same old stuff. What's new with you?"

"Just trying to make a living."

Bobby brought Jon his beer and Saunders her martini. He returned to the bar to wait on another customer.

"Where's Liz?" she asked. "I thought she was going to be here too."

"She'll be here in a little while," Jon said. "She said she'd meet me at five." Jon took a swallow of his beer and then looked around the corner of the booth to see if Lizzy had come in. Saunders puffed on her cigarette. Jon slid back in his seat.

"What was it that you wanted to talk about this afternoon?" she asked.

"A bunch of stuff, really," he said. "I was curious about the whole process of bringing a new drug to market."

"It's complicated and it's expensive," she said. "The FDA process is a nightmare. The whole thing can take years."

"How many years?"

"Five if you're lucky. Eight to ten if you're not. First you have to test the drug in animals. Next you do phase-one clinical trials, that's code for human toxicity experimentation. You give the drugs to humans in increasing doses until you cause side effects. It's done not only to determine side effects, but also to determine the maximum safe dose for the drug. If you're lucky, you don't kill too many people. It's the dark side of the pharmaceutical business."

"They actually kill people? That's really a part of testing new products?"

"The drug companies are too smart to do that kind of work themselves. Mostly they farm it out to universities and university hospitals."

"What a story *that* would make!"

"They're supposed to test new drugs only in patients who are going to die anyway, and then only with completely informed consent. At least that's the way it's supposed to work."

"What do you mean?"

"Sometimes investigators bend the rules. There's a lot of pressure to complete the studies in a hurry."

"Because of the expense?"

"Sometimes, but more often its because of the publications. They need results to get publications, because they need the publications to get promoted. It's publish or perish, the university law of the jungle."

Jon took a drink of his beer. "Holyoke didn't need publications, did he?"

"No, he was a full professor, and who said George cut corners in his clinical research trials? I didn't."

"It was just a thought," he said. "What comes next?"

"Phase-two clinical trials test the effectiveness of the drug in specific diseases, and phase-three trials compare the new drug to the best older one. The whole process requires hundreds, and sometimes thousands, of patients. As I said, it's time consuming and expensive."

"Is there any way to short circuit the process?"

"Not legally. At least not in this country."

Jon broke his train of thought when he heard Bobby greet Karen Able. Bobby directed her to the smoky booth near the back. Jon stuck his head around the corner of the booth as she approached.

"Hi, Jon," she said. "Lizzy said I would find you here. It's starting to rain again." She took off her coat, shook it out, and hung it on a peg near the booth. Then she sat down next to Jon.

"Karen, this is Janet Saunders. Professor Saunders works at the med school and did some collaborative research with Dr. Holyoke. Dr. Saunders, this is Karen Able. She's a detective with the Seattle Police Department, and the head of The Sandman task force."

"Nice to meet you, Detective Able," Saunders said.

"Please call me Karen, Dr. Saunders," said Karen.

"OK."

"Can I get you something?" Jon asked Karen as he waved his hand in the air to get Bobby's attention.

"A beer would be fine," she said.

"Bobby, another Redhook," Jon said.

"Coming right up," he answered.

Karen addressed Saunders, "Were you involved with Holyoke's pain research?"

"Not really," she said as she lit another cigarette with the butt of the one she was smoking.

"We were talking about bringing new drugs to market when you came in," Jon said to Karen. "Dr. Holyoke was a bioprospector. He was looking for new drugs in Brazil."

"I know that," she said. "We went through his research notes too." She looked at Jon as she emphasized the "too."

Jon noted her comment and then addressed Saunders, "How close was Holyoke to human testing of his pain drugs?"

"It's difficult to know," she said. "He hadn't made an application to the Human Subjects Review Committee." She took a drag from her cigarette and then a swallow from her martini.

"What's a human subjects review committee?" Bobby asked. He set Karen's beer on the table.

"Human subjects review committees approve all human experimentation. They're supposed to protect patients from dangerous exploitation. They also protect researchers from dangerous lawsuits. It's as much for the protection of the experimenters as it is for the experimentees," she said. "The committees are made up from scientists in the natural and social sciences along with non-science faculty members, university administrators, and people from outside the university such as clergymen and civic leaders. It's a federal policy."

"I hate federal policies. It sounds like a pain in the ass to me," Bobby said.

"Aren't you the bartender?" she asked. "Go get me another martini."

"Yes, ma'am, I'll be back with your martini in a minute."

"Where's Liz?" Karen asked. "She said she would be here."

"I don't know," Jon said. He looked at his watch. "She should have been here by now."

"Here's your martini." Bobby brought the drink over to the booth and then sat down in next to Saunders. She leaned away and looked down her nose at him.

"Is he always this pushy?" she asked.

"Usually," Jon said.

Saunders pulled another cigarette out of her purse. Bobby lit it for her. "My name is Bobby Arnold," he said.

"You know, Mr. Arnold," Saunders said. "You seem to be an intelligent man."

"A very perceptive woman, how unusual," he replied.

She blew a smoke ring into the air. "What do you think about this Sandman mystery?"

"If you eliminate the impossible, whatever remains, however improbable, must be the truth," Bobby said.

"Sherlock Holmes, Sir Arthur Conan Doyle" Saunders said.

"I thought it was Mr. Spock, from Star Trek Six," Bobby replied.

Saunders looked at him, took a deep drag on her cigarette and blew another smoke ring into the air.

Chapter 23

The meeting had been in progress for approximately an hour. Five men and three women in business attire were seated around the mahogany table in the boardroom. The décor was minimalist, and the view from the seventy-sixth floor of the Columbia Tower Building was spectacular. Airplanes flying instrument approaches to Boeing Field could be seen below eye level. No one noticed. Seven pairs of eyes were focused on the chairman. She was speaking from her position at the head of the table. She was wearing a Missoni suit and she had her steel gray hair pulled back close to her head. Katherine Monahan was in charge. She had stepped out of her Orcas Island naturopathic physician persona into something else altogether.

"Compound-13 was a complete success," Monahan told the other board members. "Measurements in laboratory animals reveal a ninety-six percent pain impulse blockade. Measurements of drug levels in the cerebro-spinal fluid were zero, and effects on skeletal and smooth muscles were also zero. The compound has been successfully tested in a human subject with results in agreement with our animal work. Details of the studies are outlined in the booklets in front of you." She paused to scan her audience, then she added, "I can now report that we have confirmed complete pain relief with no observed side effects. Our investors should be pleased."

"I assume that means that phase one of our research is complete," said Judy Runstad. She was a lawyer, a Democratic Party political activist, and she was a close personal friend and confidant of the Governor. Sitting to the chairman's right, she was dressed in a navy Chanel suit.

"Almost," the chairman responded. "I've asked our medical director to identify one more human subject before we close the books on phase one. Some of our investors want to witness the power of our new drug before they ante up the kinds of funds we'll need to complete phase two."

"You're sure the pain blockade was complete?" asked Joshua Green, an influential member of Seattle's financial and banking community.

"There can be no doubt about it. Dr. Allison used the pliers on his test subject. He'll repeat it at the demonstration."

Runstad asked another question. "You're planning for the demonstration to take place at our test facility on the Olympic Peninsula?"

"That's correct," she said. "Dr. Allison has agreed to bring the test subject to our facility there in the next day or two."

Dr. Monahan looked around the table and then continued, "We've developed an enviable record with this project. Even though the time needed for drug identification and synthesis turned out to be longer than expected, we'll still be fifteen percent below budget after this last human subject is injected. Not a bad record considering the sums of money that are involved."

"I'm still worried about the Andean Pact," said Chris Bayley. He was a former prosecutor and his connections were Republican. The sleeves on his pinstripe suit were precisely cut to reveal the lower one-third of his gold cufflinks. "You're certain the drug can't be traced back to Brazil?"

"We're certain," Monahan said. "Our process of synthesis hides all traces of the drug's origin. We'll file a patent application based on our animal tests and then begin our phase-two human tests at our clinic in Milan. The Italians have a reciprocal agreement with our own FDA. Our drug's credentials from synthesis through clinical testing and acceptance will be impeccable."

"Why Milan?" asked Bayley.

"They'll complete the clinical studies much faster than we possibly could in this country. They aren't burdened by our cumbersome informed consent laws. Patients' rights are more open to interpretation in that country."

Clarissa Dyer was sitting on the left side of the table. She was twenty years younger than anyone else on the board. She was from San Francisco, and was president and CEO of her own company. Well connected to the new economy companies of Silicon Valley, she brought her new approaches and attitudes with her to the board meetings. She was wearing a Black Label Armani suit, and her skirt was considerably shorter than the others in the room. She had not yet turned thirty. Her company was quietly but decisively successful, a description that could be applied to her as well. "Was it your idea to use prostitutes as phase-one test subjects?" She glared at Monahan as she spoke.

"I realize some of you are still upset about that," she said. "I apologize for not spelling that out for you ahead of time, but we can't do anything about that now. Those of us who were directly involved judged it to be the most expeditious way to bring our tests to a conclusion. It saved us a lot of time and our investors a lot money. In the long run it'll save lives. And no, that was Dr. Allison's idea."

"I've always liked the idea," Bayley interrupted. "Why are we bringing this up again?"

Monahan continued with her answer. "What would you have us do, Clarissa? Let those women loose to divulge our work? Dr. Allison's ruse has turned out to be an effective cover for our clinical experiments," she said. "As you know, the women were all drug addicts and their needle tracks concealed Allison's veinapuncture sites. Drug addiction is an incurable, terminal disease. Their long-term prognosis for survival is awful. In that sense they're not that much different from the terminal cancer patients that universities use in their phase-one drug tests. Our goal, after all, is to rid the world of pain."

"Be that as it may, I'm still a little worried about Dr. Allison," Dyer said. "He seems to like his work a little too much."

"I agree," said General Garfield Jeffers. He was wearing civilian clothes.

"Is it your plan that he will continue as medical director for phase two?" pressed Dyer.

"Jim Allison's been a tremendous asset to this project," said the chairman. "He's worked closely with Dr. Holyoke on drug extraction and subsequent product synthesis. He and Holyoke became friends, and together they conducted the first human test."

"Too bad Holyoke lost it when the first test subject died," Jeffers said. "I guess he just wasn't cut out for this sort of work. Who'd have guessed he'd have reacted the way he did, refusing to continue the human testing."

Dyer kept her eyes on Monahan, and spoke to her as if she hadn't heard Jeffers' comments. "Allison's creative disposition of Dr. Holyoke was unnecessarily dramatic, and it could have brought undue attention to our work. I'm worried about his judgement. He's slipping, and I think he creates more problems than he's worth. We can't afford any mistakes."

"It's nothing to worry about," Monahan said. She'd tried to keep a don't-ask/don't-tell relationship with the board regarding the details of Allison's work. "We're keeping a close watch on him. We've been monitoring his activities." She shifted her gaze from Dyer to the entire group. "Dr. Allison's future affiliation with our organization will be limited to the final phase-one human test demonstration. He has a flare for that sort of thing, and I'm sure our investors will be impressed. We'll retire him after it's over."

Paul Skinner nodded in agreement. He was the newest member of the board of directors. No one knew exactly what he did for a living.

The room was silent for a moment.

"Congratulations," said Sandy Rant after a pause. He was speaking to Katherine. "You've made us all a lot of money. I assume one of our more public affiliate corporations will carry the ball from here." Sandy was an American lawyer from Hong Kong. His specialty was international finance. He had flown to Seattle after stopping in San Francisco to shop at his favorite men's store, The Hound.

"We've planned for a public offering once the clinical trials are underway in Milan," she answered. "Liquidity for our investors is in sight." The chairman again looked at the faces around the room. "Well, I think that's just about all of it," she said. If there are no further questions or comments, I think we can draw this meeting to a close." She looked into the faces around the room one last time. "I can see that there are no more questions. We stand adjourned."

✳

Lizzy decided to leave the *Seattle Times* building early. She wanted to stop by her favorite wine shop on her way to Harborview Hospital to pick up a particular bottle of Chardonnay. She didn't have plans for the evening, but anything was possible. If worse came to worst, she would drink it herself. She loved Woodward Canyon Chardonnay.

Lizzy bought the wine and then traveled south toward the hospital. She was looking past her interview with Dr. Allison to her meeting with Jon at the Blue Moon. She hoped things would work out for him with Karen, but if they didn't, that would be all right too. She drove by the hospital's front entrance and almost missed the south parking lot. It was separated from the rest of the medical center, and it was difficult to see the entrance in the diminishing early evening light. It was used primarily by doctors and a few hospital employees, and it was identified only by a small, inconspicuous sign. The lot was old, underground and poorly lit. Lizzy drove in through the narrow entrance.

It was almost four o'clock by the time she arrived. The lot was only half full. Lizzy picked a place away from the other cars, parked her car and locked it. She looked around the underground structure for the entrance to the hospital. The air was cold and damp, and the old-fashioned lighting in the garage created contrasting areas of light and shadow. She could hear water dripping somewhere. She was alone.

Lizzy spotted a pedestrian walkway nearly forty yards away on the other side of the garage. She put her keys in her purse and began her walk toward the hospital at a deliberate pace. She didn't want to be late for her meeting with Allison. As she approached the entrance to the hospital she saw a blue minivan parked at an angle and occupying two parking spaces. She hated people who did that, who took up two parking places to avoid getting dings in their paint. As she passed the minivan a slight movement caught her attention just at the edge of her peripheral vision. It was in an area of sight developed by eons of evolutionary adaptation to warn of concealed threats. Her body responded in the way that natural selection had programmed it to respond. Her muscles involuntarily tensed, her head snapped in the direction of the perceived movement and she blinked a few times for a better view. She tensed for fight or flight. She saw a man standing in the shadows near the front of the van. He was perfectly still. All she could hear was the dripping sound.

"Lizzy, it's me," said a familiar voice. "I didn't mean to startle you." He started walking toward her out of the shadows. It was Dr. Jim Allison.

"Dr. Allison, you scared me," Lizzy said, relaxing with relief.

"I'm sorry, I didn't mean to," he said. "I came out here to load some papers in my van." He continued to approach. "I thought I'd make it back to the office before you arrived." He was wearing a gentle smile like a mask.

"That's OK," she said. "I guess I'm just a little jumpy. It's kind of spooky down here and I thought I was alone."

"We are alone." He fixed her in his gaze as he purposely proceeded toward her.

Lizzy looked to her left, and then quickly to her right. Ingrained instinct kept her alert with threat warnings. "I guess it's just the two of us," she said. She forced a nervous smile in return.

Allison kept coming. Lizzy stood still. The space between them closed. He approached within reach. He made a fist with his gloved right hand and then in one swift movement without warning he violently smashed it square into her face with all the force he could muster. Lizzy cried out as she fell backwards to the pavement. Her nose was flattened. Blood was everywhere. It gushed from both her nose and her mouth. Allison was on her almost before she hit the ground. Lizzy tried to lift her head from the pavement. He straddled her body with his knees and hit her again in the face with his gloved fist. Her head bounced back into the floor with a crack. Blood continued to flow. Her body stilled. She didn't move. He looked down at her with curiosity as she lay there motionless on the cement floor. He paused a moment or two, he tilted his head to one side and stared at her again for a moment more; and then he slowly balled his hand back into a fist and smashed it into her face full force one more time. The parking garage was quiet. There was only the sound of the dripping water.

Allison sat back on Lizzy's motionless body. He was breathing hard, he could feel the blood pulsing through his arteries, and he felt the adrenaline. He craved adrenaline but he knew it was his enemy. He stared down at Lizzy bleeding on the cement floor beneath him. Her face was a mangled mess. Her nose was pushed to one side, her mouth was open, and there was blood everywhere.

Allison stood up when his breath returned. He was covered in blood. He took off his gloves, wiped his face and neck with a handkerchief and ineffectively wiped the blood on his full-length raincoat. He put the handkerchief in his coat pocket. He walked the short distance to his van and opened the sliding door. There was a tarp balled up inside on the floor. He removed the tarp and spread it on the ground next to Lizzy. He checked her pulse with two fingers on her carotid artery, and he found it to be strong. "Good," he said. He needed her alive. There would be no more mistakes. He rolled her onto the tarp, onto her stomach. Her face was still bleeding. He threw his gloves and handkerchief down next to her. He took a syringe from his pocket, removed the needle guard and thrust the needle into her neck. Then he pushed the plunger. Lizzy didn't move. After checking again to make sure that they were alone in the garage, he rolled the tarp around her body and lifted her into the back of the minivan. He scanned the area. There was blood on the floor, but nothing else. In the dimly lit garage it looked like an oil stain. He listened. The garage was quiet. Even the water had stopped dripping.

Allison took his long coat off and threw it in the back. After checking to make sure there was no blood on his pants, he climbed into the front seat of his rented van. He backed out of his parking place, exited the garage and drove down James Street to the interstate highway. Traffic was light. He was careful to stay below the speed limit. He proceeded south on the interstate past Tacoma on to Olympia where he turned right on to a narrow two-lane highway leaving the population centers of western Washington behind. He headed west toward the ocean. He had another two hours of driving ahead of him to reach his destination in the Olympic rain forest. Next to the Amazon Basin, it was one of the most heavily vegetated and rainiest places on earth.

Chapter 24

K eyboards were clacking, telephones were ringing, and reporters were either working at their desks or talking in small groups. The newsroom was in its usual state of controlled chaos. Vicki was sitting at her desk outside of the editor's office talking to her boss, Dean Thornton, over the interoffice intercom on her telephone.

"No, she isn't in yet . . . No, she hasn't called . . . I don't know where . . . of course she knows the deadline . . . I *am* trying to find her . . . you'll be the first to know . . . bye."

Vicki hung up the phone. She reached into her purse, pulled out her compact, and checked her makeup in the small mirror. She decided to put on some additional lipstick. She applied the lipstick, checked herself in the mirror one more time and then she walked over to Jon's desk. Jon looked up from his computer screen as she approached.

"Good morning, Jon."

"Hi, Vicki. What's up?"

"Not much. Have you seen Liz?"

"Not since yesterday."

"The boss wants to talk to her." Vicki looked over Jon's shoulder to see what he was writing. It was an article on animal research at the med school. "I wonder where she is," she continued. "She was supposed to have that think piece ready this morning. Dean's starting to drive me crazy worrying about it. You know how he gets."

"Yeah, I know," Jon said.

"He wants to put it to bed for the Sunday edition."

"She should be almost finished. All she wanted to do was to add some material from the Sarah Boyd case."

"I hope you're right."

"Have you tried her at her home?"

"She's not there; at least she's not answering her phone."

"How about her cell number?"

"No answer there either. Should I try your house?" Vicki asked the question with a deadpan expression.

"Nice try. What's the matter, Vicki, running short of office gossip?"

"It was just a thought," she said. "Call me if you hear from her." Vicki turned around and walked back to her desk. Jon looked over toward Lizzy's empty chair.

Jon worked until noon and then he left for a lunch at The Thirteen Coins. The usual groups of reporters from the two newspapers were sitting at the bar. He stayed for an hour, swapped some stories and had a Joe's Special and a beer. After lunch he checked his messages. Dean Thornton wondered if he'd seen Liz. He asked him to call. Jon first tried Lizzy's cell phone. He got no response. Then he called her home telephone number. There was no answer there either. Finally he dialed Dean Thornton's intercom number.

"Dean, it's Jon Kirk."

"Kirk, where's Lizzy?"

"I haven't seen her. She was supposed to meet me yesterday after work, but she didn't show."

"Listen, she was supposed to have that think piece of hers on my desk first thing this morning. It still isn't here and I need it today. She'd better be on her death bed or have some other damn good excuse for not being here."

"I'm sure she does," Jon said. "In the meantime, I'll finish the article. It was almost done anyway. I have her computer password."

"Thanks," Thornton said gruffly.

"You'll have it in an hour."

"Good," Thornton's voice softened, "and Kirk, call me when you find out where she is. I'm worried about her." Thornton broke the connection.

Jon retrieved Liz's article from the computer and went to work. He saw how Sarah Boyd's lab data would have strengthened the piece. He did what he could to polish it, and then he called the medical examiner's office for more information. A pleasant female voice answered the phone.

"County medical examiner's office, Andrea speaking."

"Hello, Andrea, My name's Jon Kirk. I'm a reporter at the *Times*. May I speak to Dr. Allison?"

"Just a minute please."

Jon waited until a somewhat familiar voice came on the line.

"Hello, this is Dr. Allison."

"Dr. Allison, it's Jon Kirk from *The Seattle Times*. We last met during the Carol Williams autopsy."

"I remember," he said.

"Listen, I'm sorry to bother you, but I'm working on a story with Liz Carlstrom related to The Sandman killings. We're looking for some information on Sarah Boyd."

"The lab data? Liz called about that yesterday. I told her that we identified a substance in Sarah's blood that was similar to what we found in the other victims. She made an appointment to discuss it with me."

"When was that?" Jon asked.

"She was supposed to meet me here around four o'clock. She didn't show up."

"And you haven't heard from her since then?"

"No, I haven't. Is there a problem?"

"Probably not. She didn't come into the office this morning, and we're trying to locate her." Then he continued, "Could you tell me a little more about the substance you found in the blood? I'd like to know if it's related to curare."

"It is. And as I told you, it's similar to the compounds we found in the other women."

"Similar? Does that mean it's not the same?"

"Not exactly."

"How's it different?"

"That would take some time to explain. Maybe if you want to drop by later today. . . ." His heart skipped a beat. It was the adrenaline again.

"Maybe some other time," Jon said. "Thank you, Dr. Allison. I think that's all I need for now."

"You're welcome."

Jim Allison sat at his desk, motionless. Obviously Sarah Boyd hadn't identified him or directly connected him to the killings, but just as obviously she had to have told Kirk something. His card was in her pocket. Did Kirk tell Lizzy everything that he knew? What had they guessed?

After the phone call, Jon sat back in his chair for a moment, he ran his fingers through his hair and then he placed a call to the Seattle police department to check on automobile accidents. After that inquiry turned up no leads he decided to call the Seattle area hospitals. Lizzy hadn't been to any of them. Finally he called Karen.

"Karen, I'm worried about Liz. She didn't show up for work this morning. Nobody's seen her since yesterday afternoon. She had an appointment with Doc Allison yesterday at four and didn't show up there either . . . I agree, it's probably nothing, but . . . would you . . . thanks . . . I really appreciate it . . . see you soon. Bye."

Jon tried to go back to work but he couldn't concentrate. He finally finished Lizzy's story in twice the time that it would have normally taken him. After he sent it on to Thornton for editorial review he left the office for the day.

Jon drove over to Liz's apartment. He parked his car on the street, walked up the steps and rang her buzzer. There was no answer. He rang it again, and then after a few minutes he walked back down and around to the back of the building. There were only two cars in the apartment parking lot. Lizzy's parking spot was empty. He leaned against the back of the building, thought a moment and then decided to retrace her steps from yesterday for lack of anything better to do. She had planned to meet Dr. Allison at Harborview Hospital, and then rendezvous at the Blue Moon. He walked back to his Explorer, started the engine and left for Harborview.

Jon drove toward downtown Seattle on Aurora. He again called the area hospitals on his way. He didn't call the police because he knew Karen would notify him if they received any information. When he approached the downtown area he exited Aurora, crossed I-5 and drove up the hill toward Harborview. When he arrived at the old art deco building he drove to the entrance of hospital's new parking garage.

Harborview's parking garage was a six-story structure located to the north of the hospital. It had been built with county revenue bonds and the parking fees generated from the facility had become one of the hospital's biggest revenue source. Jon decided to systematically search the building from the ground floor up to the sixth parking level. He checked out each car as he drove on each floor. Lizzy's car was not there. He stopped when he reached the sixth level and parked. He sat there for a moment. Then he got out of his car and walked to the elevator leading to the hospital. He was on his way to the medical examiner's office.

The hospital no longer seemed as intimidating to him as it once had, and he found his way to the morgue without difficulty. Even the smells of the place no longer bothered him. The door to the medical examiner's office complex was open, and the offices appeared empty. The reception desk was vacant. Jon walked by the empty reception desk to a hall leading to a row of inner offices. He found the office for Dr. James Allison, MD, Ph.D. He knocked on the door. There was no response. He tried the door. It was unlocked. He went inside.

Allison's office was neat. It was more than neat; it was immaculate; it was sterile. Not a thing was out of place. There were no photographs or other personal items anywhere to betray the identity of the occupant. There was a desk, a computer on a computer table on one side of the desk, and a microscope on another table on the other side of the desk. His chair was neatly pushed into its place, and there was a bank of X-ray view boxes on the wall behind the chair. His desk had a small stack of papers on one side, a telephone on the other side, and three odd-looking pieces of equipment lined up in the middle. They looked something like cordless electric shavers. Jon had started to walk around behind the desk when he heard a noise from behind him.

"Excuse me, can I help you?"

Jon turned around. A tall, amber-haired woman in her mid forties was standing in the doorway.

"Yes, my name's Jon Kirk," he said. "I'm looking for Dr. Allison."

"He's not here. He left for the day," she said. "What are you doing in his office?"

"I wanted to talk to him about Liz Carlstrom."

"She's not here either. She had an appointment with him yesterday, but she didn't show up." Allison's secretary stood by the door until Jon took the hint and walked out into the reception area. She followed, and then shut the door behind them.

"You were here yesterday?" he asked.

"In the morning. Dr. Allison gave me the afternoon off."

"Then how do you know that she didn't show up?"

"Because Dr. Allison told me that she didn't show up." She scowled at him. "I don't know that I like the tone of your questions, Mr. Kirk. I think you'd better leave."

"I'm sorry," he said. "I didn't mean to offend you. It's just that Lizzy's an associate, and a very good friend. She's been missing since yesterday afternoon, and I'm trying to retrace her steps. I apologize."

"I understand." She softened her gaze a little.

"Thanks," he said, "and would you tell Dr. Allison that I'd like to see him when he returns? Maybe he could call me later today if he checks in." Jon gave her his card.

"I don't think he'll be back," she said. "He went to a Laryngophonics board meeting and he usually doesn't come back to the office unless he has an autopsy or some sort of emergency."

"Laryngophonics?"

"It's a company that makes electrovibratory devices for people who've had their voice boxes removed. They're called laryngophones. They create voices. Mechanical voices."

Jon was stunned. He stood there mute. The color drained from his face.

"Are you all right, Mr. Kirk?" she asked.

"Yeah, I'm OK," he said after a few more moments. "Is that what I saw on his desk? The laryn . . . what did you call it?"

"Laryngophone. Yes. Those are three of their newest models," she said. "They're trying to come up with a way to get rid of the artificial monotone sound and develop inflections in the mechanical voice. So far they haven't been successful."

"Could you show me how they work?"

"Certainly." She walked into Allison's office and picked up a laryngophone from the desk, held it against the side of her neck and turned it on. She mouthed some words, but Jon heard The Sandman's voice come out of the device. "It works like this," she said through the laryngophone. "The rain in Spain falls mainly on the plain. In Seattle, it falls everywhere." She put the device back on the desk, her face flushed from her little joke.

Jon tried to keep his composure, but he could barely breathe. "I see," he said. "Thank you for the demonstration." He really felt lightheaded.

"Are you sure you're alright?"

"I'll be OK," he replied. He took a deep breath, then another. "Please don't forget to have Dr. Allison call when you next hear from him."

"I'll have him call you," she answered. Then she added, "I hope your friend's alright."

"Thanks." Jon hurried out of the office.

Jon called Karen as soon as he could get a signal. She was tied up in a meeting and couldn't come to the phone. He left a message for her to call him back on his cell phone as soon as possible. Reeling with the possible implications of his discovery, he could not remember exactly where he'd left his car. Without thinking about where he was going he followed signs back to the parking garage. But after walking through the door and letting his eyes adjust he realized he was in the wrong garage. There were hardly any cars in here, and it was dark.

Then Jon's pulse started to race. He could clearly see Lizzy's Honda parked by itself about one third of the way into the nearly empty facility. Jon jogged over to the car and looked inside. There was a bottle of wine on the front passenger seat. He tried the doors. They were locked. He put his hand on the hood. The engine was cold. The car had been parked there for some time. There was no sign of trouble.

Jon tried Karen again. She was still unavailable. He called the main number and was told that she'd be busy for at least another hour or two, and no, they wouldn't put him through or even get a message to her. He had no intention of waiting that long, so he hurried back to his car, which as he remembered it was on the sixth floor at the other end of the hospital. Jon didn't see Lizzy's dried blood as he rushed by, and even if he had, he wouldn't have recognized it for what it was. By this time it looked like any of the other old stains on the dimly lit cement floor.

✻

Allison waited until long after dark before returning to the garage. He timed his return to occur before the evening shift changed but after all other activity in the garage had long since ceased. He parked the rented van away from the other cars, and then removed several rags and a gallon container of cold water from the back. He was dressed in workmen's coveralls. He took the rags and water over to the bloodstains and then he started to work on the dried blood. Very carefully, one small section at a time, he would moisten a rag with the water and then meticulously rub out the stains. When he was finished, when he was satisfied, when all traces of his assault on Lizzy were erased, he put the rags in a plastic garbage bag along with his bloodstained raincoat, and then put that bundle, along with the remainder of the water, back in the van. They would find their way to the bottom of Lake Washington before the night was out. Finally he took a can of motor oil and poured half of it over the site of the previous bloodstain. It was now exactly like any of the hundreds of other oil stains on the floor of the old garage. There would be no more mistakes. Liz Carlstrom was gone. Jon Kirk would be next.

Chapter 25

Captain McCabe had called a special session of The Sandman task force. The meetings were usually held in the mornings, but something new had come up. DNA evidence had identified a new suspect. McCabe entered the room as Robbie and Gil were discussing their efforts to locate Sarah Boyd. The meeting had been going on for some time. Gil was speaking.

"We canvassed the Pike Street Market area without any luck," Gil said. "Our usual informants haven't admitted to seeing her since the day she checked herself out of the hospital. I'm afraid we lost her."

"Where do we go from here?" Robbie asked.

"We can check around the Boeing field and Sea-Tac areas, but I don't think we'll find much. Nobody's seen or heard anything. She seems to have vanished into thin air."

Karen said, "I think she's gone. She either left town or The Sandman got her."

"We should never have let her out of the hospital," Robbie said.

"There wasn't much we could do," she answered. "Boyd knew her rights, and she exercised her right to get out of Dodge."

McCabe entered the conversation. "Karen's right, there isn't much we can do about that now. That isn't why I called this meeting anyway." He pulled his chair up to the table and sat down. "Spokane PD thinks they caught the Renton serial killer. His name is Johnny MacBaker, Jr., Johnny Mac to his friends. They have him in jail charged with the murder of a sixteen-year-old prostitute, but he's a suspect in at least twelve other murders."

"Could he be our guy?" Karen asked.

"It seems so," he said. "He's confessed to every murder within a five-state area, but he seems to know a lot about The Sandman murders, more than the average person would pick up at least. Besides that, he's white, he's forty-seven, he's married and he has five children."

"He fits the profile. Serial killers have been known to operate in more than one place at a time," Robbie said.

"Do we have a photo?" Gil asked. "It's too bad Sarah Boyd's not around for a line-up. She might be able to ID him."

"Baker has been described as a big man with big hands," McCabe said. "The description fits. We'll get his photo later tonight."

"We should check him out in the Green River killings as well," Robbie said. "He's the right age for that one, too, and he was in the neighborhood. I always thought the Green River killings could have been done by more than one perp."

"It can't be this easy," Gil said. "Things are never this easy."

"The mayor thinks it is. He plans to announce the confession at a prime-time news conference."

"How'd they get him?" Karen asked.

"DNA evidence," McCabe answered. He was about to elaborate on his answer when there was a knock on the door. The door opened a foot or so and a desk sergeant stuck his head inside. Conversation ceased while the group listened to the sergeant.

"Detective Able," the sergeant looked at Karen. "I'm sorry to interrupt. Jon Kirk's out here. He's agitated and he says he has to talk to you. He's very insistent."

Gil answered, "Tell him to wait outside until we're finished. Detective Able isn't going anywhere."

"He says it's important. He says to tell you that he thinks Liz Carlstrom has been kidnapped. He also says that he knows The Sandman's identity. Do you want to talk to him?"

"Not really," McCabe said.

Karen stiffened and said, "Send him in."

The sergeant looked at McCabe, saw him nod in acquiescence, and he then left to get Jon.

Jon walked into the room. He eyes flashed back and forth and his body movements were animated as he looked around at the task force group. Karen stood up to greet him. McCabe invited him to sit down at the table. Jon addressed the group.

"Jim Allison is The Sandman." Jon paused for a moment. The room was silent. You could have heard a pin drop. "And I think he's got Lizzy."

Robbie and Gil looked at each other. Karen just stared at him. Finally after several seconds McCabe said, "What makes you say that? And who's Jim Allison anyway?" The furrows in his deeply etched forehead deepened even further as he spoke.

"You can't mean Dr. James Allison, the medical examiner?" Robbie said.

"I know, I know," Jon said. "I realize this sounds really crazy, he's the county medical examiner and all, but he *is* crazy. That's the whole problem. You've got to believe me. He *is* The Sandman. And now he's kidnapped Lizzy."

"Come on, Jon," Gil said. "Slow down. That just isn't credible. I can see that you're upset, but *really*. What've you been smokin'?"

"Just listen to me for a minute," Jon said. "Lizzy disappeared after work yesterday. You guys probably know that, or maybe you don't. Anyway, nobody's seen her since yesterday afternoon. I decided to retrace her steps. The last thing she told me was that she needed to talk to Doc Allison to get some information for a story." Jon looked at a pitcher of water on the table. "Do you mind if I have a glass of water?"

"Help yourself," McCabe said.

Jon poured a glass of water from the pitcher. Karen could see his hands shaking. He drank several sips before he continued. "I called Allison to ask him if he'd seen her. He said that she made an appointment to meet with him yesterday afternoon at four, but that she didn't show up. When I went over to Harborview to check it out, I sort of accidentally found her car in the parking lot. The engine was cold. Allison was gone but his secretary was there. She said Allison told her to take yesterday afternoon off. I found some small devices on his desk that she said were machines to help people who've had their voice boxes removed talk, electromechanical artificial voices. She demonstrated one for me. They make the same sound that The Sandman used to disguise his voice over the telephone when he called me.

"I think Lizzy went over to see Allison yesterday afternoon. He met her there and then something happened. "Allison's The Sandman. I know it. We need to find out what happened to Lizzy. We need to get her back."

Jon was almost out of breath. He looked pleadingly at the group. He was emotionally spent. It was a classic adrenaline drain.

"Jon," Karen said. She put her hand over his. Her eyes were tender and her voice was soft. "We already have a confession to The Sandman murders. A John MacBaker confessed to the crimes earlier today. DNA evidence ties him to the murders in Renton. He fits the profile."

"No." Jon said. "No."

"Believe it," Gil said.

"He's lying," Jon answered.

"The mayor believes it," McCabe said. "He's going public with it this afternoon."

Jon looked at McCabe, then at Gil, then back at McCabe. "All I'm asking is that you check it out. What can it hurt?"

"Maybe we should check it out," Robbie said. "Once they caught him, Baker confessed to everything but shooting the Pope. Besides, I'd love to help the mayor shove his foot in his mouth."

"That's enough of that," McCabe said. Then he addressed Jon. "Suppose you're right. Why would The Sandman snatch a reporter? His specialty is prostitutes. This isn't his MO."

Jon was getting ready to speak when Karen answered. "I think he's changing," she said. "He missed in his attempt to kill Sarah Boyd, and that's not like him. He's very meticulous and he usually doesn't make that kind of mistake. He's been communicating with Jon more and more. Then he kidnapped Liz. Something's happening."

"Then *maybe* he kidnapped Liz," Gil corrected.

"OK, then *maybe* he kidnapped Liz," Karen said, "but let's say that he did. Why is he changing? What's happening here? What's going on?"

"God I hope she doesn't turn up posed on a bed somewhere," Jon said. "I'm the one who sent her to Allison in the first place."

"I still don't buy it," Gil said.

"Neither do I," said McCabe. "Let's not get ahead of ourselves. Jon has a theory, that's all. There's nothing that he says that's even close to any kind of proof."

"Jon's worried about Lizzy," Gil said to Karen. "That's understandable. He traced her to Harborview. He found her car in the parking lot and an artificial-voice machine in Allison's office."

"It's a laryngophone," Jon said. "Allison's secretary called it a laryngophone."

"Whatever," Gil said. "Anyway, a medical device on a doctor's desk is hardly incriminating, and Lizzy's car in the parking lot doesn't mean that Dr. Allison kidnapped her."

McCabe addressed Jon, "You said he freely admitted that Liz had an appointment to see him yesterday afternoon. Why would he tie himself to her like that if he'd kidnapped her?"

"He's smart," Jon said. "Think about it; he's very smart, maybe a genius. He's the right age, he has a medical job, and he certainly has the know-how to prep Holyoke's body and get it into the anatomy lab. He fits the profile almost perfectly."

"It's a stretch," McCabe said. "Allison's almost above suspicion. We all know him personally. We've worked with him for years."

"That's the way it works," Jon said. "These guys blend in. Nobody suspects them of their dual lives. Nobody's above suspicion."

"Serial killers are crazy," Gil said. "You said so yourself. Doc Allison's not crazy. I know him and he's not crazy."

"We can at least check out the, what did you call it, Jon, a mechanical voice," Karen said. "We can call and ask Allison's secretary for a demonstration over the phone. We can compare it to the mechanical voice we have on the voice mail tape."

"It's getting late. She's probably left by now," Gil said.

"Let's try," Karen answered. "Jon, do you know his secretary's name?"

"I think it's Andrea. She said Allison's on the board of Laryngophonics. They make the laryngophone."

Karen left the room for a moment, and then she returned with a tape recorder. She attached it to the telephone. Then she called Allison's office.

"Put it on speakerphone," McCabe said. Karen pushed the speakerphone button.

"Medical examiner's office, Andrea speaking."

"This is Detective Able in homicide, is Dr. Allison in?"

"I'm afraid he's out for the afternoon, may I help you?"

"I'm not sure. I understand Dr. Allison's on the board of Laryngophonics."

"That's right," she said.

"We're conducting an investigation involving someone who disguises his voice over the telephone. It's possible he's using a laryngophone. We wanted to ask Dr. Allison about it. Do you know if he has access to one?"

"He has several sitting on his desk right now," she said.

"Would it be possible for you to demonstrate one for us?"

"Right now?" she asked.

"Please. We'd like to hear it over the telephone."

"I can do that," she said. Andrea retrieved one of the laryngophones from Dr. Allison's office.

"How does this sound?" she asked. She was speaking with the laryngophone.

"That's it," Jon exclaimed.

"Ask her to speak some more," McCabe said.

"Would you please say something else with the laryngophone?"

Karen asked.

"Sure," she said with the laryngophone. "These things can be very helpful to people who've had laryngectomys. The trouble is that they allow people to speak only with a mechanical-sounding voice, and in a monotone. You lose the inflections that are an important part of everyday speech." She continued in a normal voice. "How was that?"

"That was fine," Karen said. "Thank you very much. Please tell Dr. Allison I called."

"I will, and you're welcome," Andrea said. "I'm glad I could be of help. Goodbye, Detective Able." She hung up the phone.

Karen hit the replay button: *The trouble is that they allow people to speak only with a mechanical-sounding voice and in a monotone. You lose the inflections that are an important part of everyday speech.*

"We got it," Jon said. He pounded his fist on the table. "There's no doubt. It's The Sandman's voice."

"Come on, Jon," Gil said, "even if that is the voice you heard, there's no reason to assume that Doc Allison was doing the talking. It could have been anyone. It could have been his secretary."

"We'll check it out," McCabe said. "We'll compare it to the other tape tomorrow."

"But you've already heard the tape. What more proof do you need?" Jon asked.

"We'll have an audio expert do a computer comparison of the tapes and see if they match," Gil said. "We'll have to wait till tomorrow and then we'll go from there."

"Wait?" Jon almost screamed. "We can't wait. He's got Lizzy! Let's go get him!"

"We don't know that!" Gil said. "You're jumping to conclusions."

"We can't go get him, Jon," Karen said. "We don't want to scare him away, and we don't have near enough evidence to get a search warrant. We'll watch him."

Jon started to say something, and then he stopped himself. He drank some more water instead. His hands were shaking again.

"Come on, Jon, let's go," Karen said. She stood up, walked over to his chair and put her hands on his shoulders. "Let's go home. We're finished here anyway."

Jon looked up at her. She was smiling softly. He stood up without saying anything and they left the room together.

"What do you think?" McCabe asked the other two.

"I think she likes that guy a little too much," Gil said. "It's clouding her judgement."

"Doc Allison does fit the profile," Robbie said. "We should at least check him out."

"I'll do it," Gil said. "I'll do it tomorrow."

The three of them stood up and left the room.

✳

Karen followed Jon's Explorer over to his house. She changed out of her work clothes and put on a baggy sweatshirt and an old pair of jeans. Then she started a fire in the fireplace, opened a bottle of wine and curled up next to him on the couch. They were both barefoot, and both of them had their feet tucked under Leon. Leon had a dog's sixth sense, and he seemed to know that something was wrong.

Jon and Karen hadn't spoken much since the meeting in the police station. There really wasn't much to say. All three of them, Karen, Jon and Leon, stared at the fire. All three of them seemed to be waiting for something. Time passed slowly as they sipped their wine.

"It's hard waiting around like this," Jon said. "Don't you think we ought to be doing something?"

"I know how you feel," she answered. "The question is, what? We don't want to do anything that might endanger Lizzy's life, if she's still alive."

"She's still alive," Jon said. "Don't say that she's not. She's alive. I can feel it."

"It's hard not knowing; that's the difficult part," she said.

"Lizzy's alive!"

"OK, she's alive, but we have no idea where she is. We don't know if she's safe. We don't even know whether or not The Sandman has her. We really don't know anything."

"God damn it, Karen, then why don't we find out? It's up to us to find out, don't you think? Nobody else is going to do it. Let's find Allison and find out."

Karen pushed away from Jon. She stared at him for a moment. "Just go over to his house and stomp him or something? Is that what you want me to do?"

"No, we don't need to do that. Let's call him up. Let's find him and just ask him what happened to Lizzy."

"And you'll make him talk."

"Oh he'll talk, you can bet he'll talk, they always do, and I'll be able to tell if he's lying or not, too. There's always a shrug of the shoulders or a slight change of facial expression, a squint, a blinking of the eyes, a false smile, something. It's called a tell. It's better than a lie detector. I see it all the time. If I can watch him face to face, I'll be able to tell."

"Maybe," she said.

Leon jumped off the couch and walked to the front door. Jon got up and let him out. Karen thought for a moment.

"If Doc Allison's The Sandman, he's changing the way he works," Karen said. "If he grabbed Liz, maybe he did it for some reason other than his usual one."

"What are you talking about?" Jon walked back to the couch.

"What if he grabbed her for some rational purpose? What if she knew something that he needed to know? What if she knew something that could expose him?"

"She didn't," Jon said. "She would have told me about it."

"Sure, but maybe he doesn't know that."

Leon scratched on the door. Jon got up again to let him in. Leon ran to the couch, jumped up and curled up into his corner. Jon pushed him back onto the floor and sat in his place.

"If that's the case," he said, "he must think that I know it too, whatever *it* is."

"Then that's how we'll catch him," she said.

For the first time since finding Lizzy's car, Jon's facial muscles relaxed a little bit. He looked in Karen's eyes and she looked back at him. They each took a sip of wine.

Chapter 26

The first thing she noticed was the rain. She woke up to the sound of rain splashing on a glass roof. It wasn't an unpleasant sound, and it was the only sensation she felt at first. Then there was the heat, the heat and the humidity. These too were just sensations really, but oppressive. She just lay there, trying to clear her head.

Her head hurt. Her face hurt. Movement hurt. She was in a bed of some sort. She tried to lay still.

Finally she opened her eyes. One of her eyelids wouldn't work very well. She touched it with her fingers and it was tender. Her left eye was swollen almost shut. She tried to sit up in bed, and did so only with difficulty and a lot of pain. She propped herself up with her arms and she looked around the room. Her vision was blurry. *Where the hell am I?*

The room was constructed like a cage within a larger room, but instead of bars the walls were solid glass or Plexiglas, or something. They were transparent and they extended from the floor approximately thirty feet up to a ceiling of crisscrossing metal struts spaced about a foot apart. The ceiling of the large surrounding room was much higher. The door to the cage was also transparent except for the hinges, the latch and the lock. The whole place was constructed like a fishbowl or a specimen case so that people on the outside could look in.

Lizzy tried to shake off her disorientation. She looked around her cage. She was sitting on a narrow hospital-type bed with side rails. The side rails were down, and the bed could be raised and lowered with a remote control just like other hospital beds. There was a single, large, overstuffed chair in a corner of the room with a movable metal stand next to it. The stand was the kind that they used in hospitals to serve meals.

Lizzy shut her one open eye and gingerly touched it with her right hand. It hurt like hell when she touched it. She tried to clear her vision. She reopened it and continued to scan her surroundings. There was a white ceramic sink and a toilet in the opposite corner of the enclosure with a mirror attached to the wall above the sink. A privacy screen was standing open next to the rudimentary bathroom. Lizzy noticed that there were no bathing facilities. The room obviously was not designed for long-term occupancy.

Then Lizzy looked at herself. She was surprised to realize that she was naked, and that she had bruises everywhere. It hurt when she swung her legs over the side of the bed to put her feet on the tile floor. The floor was warm beneath her feet. She looked around the room to see if she was alone. She was. Her head still felt fuzzy, and she knew that she wasn't thinking clearly. She just sat there for awhile.

As her head slowly cleared she felt pain inside her mouth. When she touched her face she could feel that her lips were swollen and that several of her teeth were loose. She ran her tongue across her teeth. At least one was missing. She felt her nose with both hands. It wasn't where it was supposed to be. It was smashed over to the side. Her left eye throbbed in time with her pulse. She tried to focus, to cut through the mental fog.

She looked towards a table in the middle of the room. *Focus*, she thought. *Forget the pain and focus.* She slowly realized that she was looking at an operating table. She was shut inside a transparent cage of a room with an operating table. The table had arm extensions on either side equipped with Velcro immobilization straps. There were leg stirrups attached to the end of the table, and they too had Velcro immobilization straps. There was a bank of operating-room lights hanging over the table from the metal lattice above.

Lizzy shuddered. The room was completely sterile and white. The tile on the floor was cream colored. The bed, the ceramic sink and the toilet were white. The privacy screen and the chair were both white. The operating table was chrome and white. It would have felt cold and antiseptic were it not for the oppressive heat and humidity.

The surrounding larger room had a much different feel. It was green. She could see the humidity hanging in the air. The floor was mostly dirt, except for metal-grate walkways, and there were large trees and plants extending up to the ceiling, much higher than the top of her cage. There was a path leading away from her door through the trees. The ceiling was made out of greenhouse glass and she could still hear the rain tapping against its panes. As her head cleared she realized where she was. She had to be in Holyoke's tropical greenhouse facility.

Lizzy looked out into the greenhouse forest. She couldn't see the end of it or the outside walls through the dense foliage. It was beautiful. What she could see were three rows of bleacher-type seats immediately outside her transparent cage. She shuddered; she suddenly felt exposed, like an animal in a zoo. She pulled the white sheet off of her bed and wrapped it around herself. The maneuver was painful. All of her muscles and joints hurt.

Lizzy again peered through the leaves of the tropical forest. Nobody was there. She listened. She heard nothing but the sound of the rain. "Help," she said. Her voice was weak. There was no answer. She listened; then she stood up.

Standing tensed her muscles and made the pain worse. She gritted her teeth. She felt lightheaded and had to steady herself with her hand on the bed rail. Then she slowly, carefully and painfully walked over to the little open bathroom. She put her hands on the edge of the sink. She leaned heavily against the ceramic basin and then looked up at the reflection of her face in the mirror. She hardly recognized the person she saw. She stared for a few seconds, and then she looked away. Her lip started to quiver. Tears welled up in her eyes. At first there were only a few, and then more, many more. She started to sob. She cried out a lonely cry. The tears wouldn't stop.

Chapter 27

Karen spent the night at Jon's house. They lost themselves in each other for awhile, but only for awhile. Mostly it was a restless night. They both had difficulty sleeping and Lizzy wasn't far from their thoughts.

Jon was shaving and Karen was getting ready to leave for work when the telephone rang. Karen answered the phone. It was Gil Anderson.

"Hello?"

"Karen?"

"Gil?"

"I figured you might be there," Gil said. "I tried your home number first. Are you sure you know what you're doing?"

"Can it, Gil."

"OK. Whatever you say. You can take care of yourself. Listen, I called to let you know that I talked with Doc Allison this morning."

"And?" Karen was irritated with him. Her private life was private. She could sleep where she wanted, and with whom she wanted. It was none of his, nor Robbie's nor Bill McCabe's business.

"And he says he doesn't know anything about Liz Carlstrom. He says he hasn't seen or heard from her since she called him two days ago. He doesn't know anything about her car in the parking lot, and he doesn't know anything about her disappearance."

"What a surprise. What would you *expect* him to say if he were involved? Anything else?"

"He was interested to hear that The Sandman may have used a laryngophone to disguise his voice. He said he'd be happy to demonstrate one for us. He said that every single person who used it would sound exactly the same."

"Did he sound nervous?"

"No, not at all."

"When are you going to meet with him?"

"Later today. He has a meeting this morning. I'm going to meet him around three-thirty at his house or maybe his office, depending on where both of us are this afternoon."

"So what do you think?"

"I think he's OK. He doesn't sound like he has anything to hide, but I'll check him out anyway. I'll let you know if I find anything."

"Thanks, Gil."

"You're welcome."

"We'll talk later," she said as she hung up the phone.

Jon walked out of the bathroom. He had a towel wrapped around his waist. His hair was still damp from his shower. "Who was that?"

"It was for me," she said. "Gil Anderson talked with Doc Allison this morning. He's going to interview him in person this afternoon."

"I suppose there's no point in asking if I can come along."

"No point at all."

"That's what I thought. What about Lizzy?"

"He asked about her. Allison says he doesn't know anything."

"Right, of course not." Jon combed some of the dampness out of his hair with his fingers.

"Listen, Jon, I've got to go to work. Promise me you'll leave Doc Allison alone. We're doing all that can be done. I don't want you to muck it up."

"I won't muck it up."

"Promise."

"OK, I'll behave myself."

"Promise!"

"OK, OK. I promise."

"I'll call you later if I hear anything. Keep your cell phone on."

"Thanks, I'll keep it on."

"Oh come on, quit pouting," she said. She went over to give him a kiss. When she was close enough she pulled the towel from around his waist. "Nice," she said as she gave him a look of approval. She noticed just a hint of arousal. "Hold that thought," she said with a smile. She kissed him and then left for the day.

✳

Jim Allison was the only person on the elevator. He was on his way to the seventy-sixth floor of the Columbia Tower Building where he was to meet with the chairman and two other members of the board. They wanted to hear about his plans for the Compound-13 drug demonstration. Monahan had asked him to keep his answers short and to the point. He'd decided to humor them and play it their way. He hummed a little ditty from *The Phantom of the Opera* as he watched the numbers climb up to 76 on the indicator above the door.

The elevator door opened and Allison walked the short distance down the gray carpeted hallway to the company conference room. The room was quiet when he entered. The chairman, Katherine Monahan, along with Paul Skinner and Judy Runstad, were seated around the table waiting for him. Allison took his seat and the meeting began.

"Thank you for coming, Dr. Allison." Katherine Monahan said. "We understand that you have a busy schedule and we appreciate your time. We'll be as brief as possible."

"I'd appreciate that," he said. "I have a lot of work to do." He folded his hands in front of him on the table.

Ms. Runstad spoke next. "Dr. Allison, as you know, our investors will begin arriving in a day or two. We've planned for them to stay out at the lodge in the rain forest. The demonstration is scheduled for next Wednesday, and it's vitally important that they come away from that demonstration duly impressed with Compound-13. We intend to ask them for substantial sums of money to support the next phase of our drug development." The company had purchased the old Rain Forest Lodge out on the Olympic Peninsula as a front for their greenhouse and drug development center. It was located off highway 101, about fifteen miles inland from the ocean at the inland apex of the Quinault Indian Reservation, and it was totally surrounded by the dense rain forest of The Olympic National Park.

"Everything's in place," Allison answered. "You won't be disappointed."

The lodge and its access road had been purchased to mask the substantial amount of truck traffic going to and from the greenhouse and research facilities deeper in the forest. The company kept the lodge open for guests and tourists in order to maintain the ruse. They also used it to house visitors to the labs.

"You have adequate supplies of Compound-13 for the test?"

"Yes," Allison replied. "We have more than enough drug. Your lab production facilities are very efficient."

"And the test subject?" she asked.

"She's already on site."

"Good."

"We're planning for a relatively short demonstration," he said. "The subject will be immobilized on a table in the middle of the room when the investors arrive. They'll be escorted to their seats by one of our staff. I will have fully briefed them on the nature of the demonstration earlier that morning. I understand that they have already been updated on Compound-13."

"That's correct," Monahan said.

"You'll be using another prostitute." Runstad said.

"No, not this time," said Allison. "This time we're doing things a little differently." His lips curled into a smile. "This time we plan to use a normal, healthy, human subject, not a spaced-out used-up drug addict. I want to leave no room for doubt in our investors' minds concerning the efficacy of Compound-13. This time our demonstration's going to be special. I think you'll enjoy the show."

Monahan sat forward in her chair. She tapped her pen on the

pad in front of her. She could feel Judy Runstad turn away from Allison and look in her direction. She needed to take control of the discussion. "I understand your rationale, Dr. Allison," she said, "But I thought we'd agreed. You said you'd bring us another prostitute for this test. That's what our investors were told. That's what they expect. They understand that our subject's drug addiction is a fatal disease, that it's the equivalent of an incurable illness such as can-cer, and that our test demonstration is no different in principle than the kinds of tests that are done in university hospitals every day. That's an important point for them. We don't want them to get squeamish about the test or our drug."

"I assure you they'll be impressed," he said. "After all, they're the ones who asked for this test."

Runstad looked back at Allison. Her voice was demanding. "If not a street hooker, who's the subject?"

"Her name is Elizabeth Carlstrom," he said. He kept up his smile. "She's a reporter. She's been writing those Sandman stories for the *Times* along with Jon Kirk."

"What? What stories?" Runstad asked.

Monahan arched an eyebrow. "Liz Carlstrom?"

"You kidnapped a high visibility newspaper reporter?" Runstad almost screeched. "Are you crazy?"

Now his smile was gone. His eyes flashed from person to person. "No," he said, "I'm not crazy." His pupils constricted as they settled on Runstad. "Let me explain it in a way that you can understand. Liz called me several days ago to ask about Sarah Boyd's lab results."

Monahan cut him off. "Dr. Allison is concerned about recent newspaper articles having to do with bioprospecting and new drug development." She looked at Allison as she spoke. "He's afraid they'll somehow point to our project."

"Those people are just guessing," Allison said. "They can't know anything."

Monahan cut him off again. "Jim," she interrupted, "Why don't you tell us how you plan to conduct the demonstration?"

Allison scanned the three people in the room. "There's no real problem here," he said. He was speaking a little too fast. "I have a little interview with Liz planned for tomorrow. Don't worry, I'll find out what she really knows."

"We're not worried about that," Runstad said. "Don't complicate this thing unnecessarily."

"There's no need to worry about Kirk either," he said. "I'll take care of him too."

"Jesus," Runstad said. "What in the hell are you talking about?"

Katherine raised her right hand to silence Runstad, then she addressed Allison. "Jim, there's no way Jon Kirk could possibly know about our project."

"Do you think I don't know that?" he said too loudly. "I'm not a fool, you know." His face was flushed. He put his hands on the table to keep them from shaking. He paused a moment. His gaze shifted from Monahan to Runstad to Skinner, and then back to Monahan. He knew adrenaline was his enemy. He took a deep breath. He let it out slowly. Then he said in a calmer tone of voice, "I'll take care of it."

The room was totally silent for a moment or two. Then Monahan said, "I'm sure you can, and I'm sure you will." She paused for a moment more and then continued, "Just the same, I'd like to talk to Kirk myself. He trusts me, and he'll tell me what I want to know. I'll do it this afternoon, and then you won't have to deal with him. You can concentrate on the matters at hand. Is that acceptable?"

Again the room was silent for several seconds. "Sure," he said. Whatever you say."

"Then thank you, Dr. Allison. You may leave."

Dr. Allison's eyes again flashed from face to face. They all looked back at him stone faced, expressionless and blank. Their expressions betrayed nothing. He started to say something, then stopped himself, paused a moment, smiled at them, turned around and left.

They all waited until the door closed. "He's gone over the edge," Runstad said. "Did you see his eyes? He's completely insane."

"I think we're finished here," Monahan said. "Judy, you can

leave now. Paul, stay here a minute or two, will you." It was a command, not a question.

"Katherine?" Runstad said, rising from her chair, her hands flat on the table.

"Paul, please, escort Judy to the door, would you?" Monahan said. She shuffled through some notes in front of her.

"Do not, for one minute, think you can just . . ." sputtered Judy to Monahan as Paul walked around the table. He held her arm firmly, just above the elbow, and walked her to the door.

Katherine Monahan followed Judy Runstad's departing figure. "Oh, yes I can," she said.

✳

The day seemed to go by slowly in the newsroom. Conversations were quieter, activity was subdued, and everyone was worried about Lizzy. There was no longer any question that she was missing. Jon couldn't concentrate and he left work early. He had his cell phone on and fully charged. He was waiting for a call from Karen. Driving home, he had just turned off Madison onto McGilvra Boulevard when it rang. It was three o'clock.

"Karen?"

"No, it's Kate Monahan. Is this Jon Kirk?"

"Kate! I'm sorry. I was expecting another call. How are you?"

"I'm fine," she said. "It's nice to hear your voice. How are you?"

"I could be better," he answered. He stopped his car in front of his house and turned off the engine.

"I'm sorry to hear that. I'm in town for a couple of days, and I thought we might get together for a cup of tea or something. I've got some time to kill. Are you at your office?"

"I just got home," he said. "Would you like to come here? Where are you now?" He gave her his address.

"I'd love to meet you there," she answered. "I can get there in fifteen minutes or so."

"Good. I'll see you then."

"Goodbye." She broke the connection.

Fifteen minutes later a white Jeep Cherokee pulled up in front of his house. The front door opened and Katherine Monahan got out of the car. She was wearing a loose-fitting white blouse and a full-length denim skirt. Her fluffy gray hair was blowing in the gentle Seattle afternoon breeze. Jon greeted her at his door.

"Kate, it's nice to see you again. Did you have any trouble finding the place?"

"Not a bit," she said. They walked into the house together.

"Why did you say you're in town?" he asked.

"I'm in town for a meeting with some insurance people. It seems they don't feel obliged to pay for naturopathic medical care."

"Maybe I can be of help. I'd be happy to write an article about the problem."

"Thanks for the offer," she said, "But this is a dance we do every year. They say they won't pay. We say they're discriminating against our patients. They argue, we threaten, and then we work it out for another year. It's always this way."

"It sounds awful."

"It's no fun, but since I was going to be in town for the weekend anyway, I thought I'd look you up."

"I'm glad you did," he said. "Please sit down. I'll make some coffee." Jon walked toward the kitchen.

"Thanks," she said. "I'll sit, but I'll pass on the coffee. Do you have any tea?" She primly sat on the couch, folding her hands in her lap. Leon was sitting on the other end of the couch and he gave her a snort when she sat down. He could smell her Persian cat.

"I'm sorry, I don't," he answered from around the corner. "We can go down to Starbucks and get some. It's only a block away."

"That's not necessary. Water's fine."

"Would you like ice?" he yelled out from the kitchen.

"No, thank you," she said. "If you have bottled or filtered water I'd prefer it."

After starting the coffee, Jon returned with her glass of water. He kept his cell phone close at hand.

"Thank you," Kate said as she accepted the water. "You look tired. I hope I'm not interrupting anything."

"Not at all," Jon said. "The coffee will be done in a minute or two. I just need my afternoon caffeine fix. That's all."

Kate looked down at her lap. She smoothed her skirt and then looked back at Jon. "How are things going with The Sandman business? A lot's happened since we last talked up on the island."

"I don't know, Kate. It's getting complicated."

"I suppose it is," she said. "What ever happened to that girl you wrote about? I think her name was Sarah Boyd."

"She dropped out of sight. Nobody's seen her since she left the hospital."

"You were her confidant, weren't you?"

"Sort of. She told me about the attempt on her life. It was pretty strange." Jon's thoughts drifted to Sarah and her story.

"In what way?" Kate asked.

"In almost every way," he answered. "I put it all in the paper. I can send you a copy if you're interested."

"Thanks, but I already read it. I read everything you write." She smiled at him again. "Did she tell you anything about the identity of The Sandman?"

"Just a general description. It wasn't worth much. She disappeared before we could get her to describe him to an artist."

"That's too bad."

"Excuse me a moment," Jon said. "The coffee should be done. I'll be right back."

Jon left for the kitchen. Kate stood up and walked over to look out of the window. It had started to rain again and she checked to make sure that the windows on her rented jeep were closed. After only a minute or two, Jon came back into the living room and joined her at the window with his cup of coffee.

"Are you sure I can't get you some coffee or something?" Jon asked.

"No thank you. I'm fine," she said. She turned from the window to look at Jon. "I enjoyed your articles on bioprospecting."

"It's all related to The Sandman killings somehow. You were a great help with those stories. We're continuing to research the links."

"You and your associate, Liz Carlstrom?"

"Yeah," Jon said. He looked away from Monahan and back out the window. He was staring at nothing. "I don't know if I'm supposed to tell you this or not," he said, "But Lizzy's been missing for several days."

"Good lord, no!"

"She may have been kidnapped, maybe by The Sandman."

"What? How can that be? How do you know?"

"We don't. We really don't know anything, at least not for sure. We don't know for sure if it was him. We don't even know if she's still alive." He continued to stare out of the window.

Monahan allowed for a respectful few moments of silence and then she asked the question that she had come there to ask. "The last time we talked you thought Holyoke was the Sandman. That obviously wasn't the case. Do you have any idea who he is now, The Sandman I mean?"

"I might, and I might not," he said. "Actually the police have someone who confessed."

"You're keeping me in suspense. Who is he?"

"I really shouldn't talk about it. I hope you understand."

"I understand," she said. "I shouldn't have asked."

"With luck, it'll all be over soon," he said.

"I hope you're right." Kate looked at her watch. "Good heavens, I didn't know it was this late." She walked over toward the couch and put her glass down on the coffee table. "If I don't hurry I'll be late for my next meeting with the insurance people. I'd better be running along." She locked Jon's eyes with hers and spoke with a sincere, grandmotherly voice. "I hope things work out for your friend."

"I hope so too."

"We'll see each other again soon." She started to walk toward the door. Jon opened the door for her.

"Goodbye, Kate."

"Goodbye." She walked to her car and drove away. As soon as she was out of sight of the house she called Paul Skinner.

"Paul?"

"Yes?" He recognized her voice.

"Kirk's not an immediate threat. Proceed with Allison, the sooner the better." She switched off her cell phone and drove back to her suite at the Olympic Hotel. She couldn't wait to change out of her frumpy clothes.

✳

Gil Anderson was running way late. He left a message with Karen telling her that he had to delay his planned meeting with Dr. Allison. He then called Allison at his home asking if he could postpone the meeting. Allison told him to call him on his cell phone when he became available. The call came in at six-thirty, and they arranged to meet on Allison's boat as soon as possible. Gil arrived at the boat dock at ten minutes to seven.

It was dark and the rain was really coming down. Lighting in the parking area was poor. Gil parked his unmarked patrol car as close to the boat dock as possible. He turned off the engine, buttoned his coat, turned up his collar, and following Dr. Allison's directions, briskly walked through the downpour to the boats. He was getting too old and too close to retirement for this kind of bullshit. Allison's boat was the one with the lights turned on.

Gil saw Allison sitting in the boat's cabin drinking a cup of coffee. He stepped onto the deck, causing the boat to rock. Allison looked up. He saw Gil and opened the cabin door, inviting him to enter. They greeted each other like old friends. Gil walked into the cabin.

Gil took off his coat, shook off the rain, and hung it up on a hook. The cabin was warm and smelled of freshly brewed coffee. Allison offered Gil a cup and he accepted. Their conversation centered around sports, the weather, and Seattle city politics. Finally Gil came to the point of the meeting.

Gil asked Allison about where he'd been yesterday afternoon and who could corroborate his whereabouts. When he was satisfied with Allison's answer he asked about Lizzy. He saw no sign of unease when Allison repeated the answer he'd given over the telephone saying that he knew nothing about her disappearance. Gil asked about the laryngophone and was told that everyone sounds the same when using such a device. He was promised a demonstration later if he wished. Then he brought up Jon Kirk. They both laughed about Kirk's ineptitude at playing detective. Gil laughingly told him that Kirk had a specific question he wanted him to ask:

"Are you The Sandman?"

Allison laughed. "That's a good one," he said. He didn't look particularly surprised by the question. He reached behind his back still laughing and pulled a five-shot Smith and Wesson thirty-eight-caliber Detective Special pistol out of his belt from under his jacket. Without hesitation or change in expression he shot Gil Anderson once at point blank range square in the chest straight through the heart. Gil fell over backward and died on the spot.

"Yes," he said. "I am The Sandman."

＊

The lake was choppy and there were no other boats out in the bad weather. Rain was coming down hard. He could barely see the lights of the dock from his position in the middle of the lake. He idled the engine and went back in the cabin. Gil Anderson's lifeless body was lying on its back on top of a canvas tarp. Allison first went through Anderson's pockets and removed his car keys. Then he removed his coat from its hook and placed it next to his body, taping them together by wrapping them with five long pieces of duct tape. He wrapped the tarp tightly around the taped-up body and coat and sealed it with five more long sections of duct tape. Next he slit a small hole in the tarp over Anderson's right ankle and attached an anchor with a pair of handcuffs. He lifted the heavy tarp-covered body up onto the rail and pushed it overboard. It slid into the lake, floating half submerged, tethered to the boat by the anchor chain until the anchor he dropped in after it dragged it beneath the surface. Finally he tossed the pistol in the water. After looking around to make sure that he was still out on the lake alone, he advanced the throttle and motored back to the dock.

He smiled to himself. There would be no more pretending, no more games. There could be no doubt about it now. This was the moment, and there would be no turning back. He *was* The Sandman.

Chapter 28

J on Kirk woke up at seven. He had spent a restless night tossing and turning, waiting for the telephone to ring. Karen hadn't called. There was no news about Lizzy. It had been a long time since her last contact with him and he was beginning to fear the worst.

Jon got out of bed. His feelings of anxiety wouldn't go away. He brushed his teeth, put on his running clothes and went outside to lose himself in the rhythm of a five-mile morning run. It was still dark, and Seattle's early morning mist pushed against his face. The shortened daylight hours of winter accentuated his feelings of impending disaster.

Lizzy was awake at seven o'clock as well, but she didn't get out of bed. Despite the heat and humidity, she kept herself covered with her bed sheet. The swelling in her face had subsided a little, but it still hurt. She was stiff all over. The heat helped her stiffness, but it still hurt her to move. She just lay there listening to the rain splash on the greenhouse windowpanes high above her cage. The sound of it was hypnotic, and it somehow carried her away far beyond the confines of her cell.

Jim Allison also awoke at seven. His alarm clock woke him up after only three hours of sleep. He had had a long night, and he had a full day ahead of him.

The previous evening, after he'd returned his boat to its dock, he'd spent over an hour meticulously cleaning up the small pool of blood that had seeped onto the deck. When he had finished and was satisfied that every trace of the crime had been eliminated, he walked over to Gil's unmarked patrol car. He put on a pair of leather gloves before opening the door, then he climbed in the car and started the engine. He checked around the parking lot to make sure he was still alone, and then he put it in drive to begin his journey south out of the city down I-5. His destination was Tacoma and its Hilltop Community neighborhood. It was an area of known and concentrated gang and drug activity.

Allison abandoned the unmarked patrol car on one of the Hilltop Community's back streets. He knew that the car wouldn't last long. It would be stripped and probably burned before the night was out. He locked the doors and then walked away. The remnants of the car would be discovered in a few days, and the search for Detective Anderson would be centered on the Tacoma gang-infested neighborhood. A few blocks away he threw the car keys in a storm drain. Allison walked towards Tacoma General Hospital, about a mile to the north. From there he took a bus to downtown Seattle, and then a cab back to his neighborhood, where he had the driver drop him off two blocks from home. By the time he reached his house it was three-thirty Saturday morning.

Allison got out of bed, dressed, and had a light breakfast. By eight o'clock he had already left the house. The sun was up, but the morning mist and rain diffused its light. He drove his Mercedes down I-5 past Olympia and then westward on a narrow two-lane highway toward the Olympic Peninsula and the Pacific Ocean. When he turned north at Hoquiam he left all traces of urban society behind. It was there that he entered the misty green world of the Pacific-Northwest rain forest.

Allison continued onward up the coast road for another seventeen miles. He finally came upon a smallish, faded sign announcing a right turn to the Rain Forest Lodge. He turned right on an even narrower road, driving ever deeper into the forest. The trees that lined the road were huge, and the ground beside them was covered with a dense carpet of ferns. Club moss hung everywhere dripping from the giant tree branches like green drapery shutting out the weak rays of the misty winter sun. The forest beyond the road was impenetrable, and the effect was claustrophobic. The twists and turns in the road restricted vision to less than a few hundred feet. Allison drove another six miles into the rain forest before coming to a clearing. There, appearing like Brigadoon out of the mists, he came upon the lake and the lodge.

The lodge was massive. It was a cedar log-and-shingle structure, and had been built in 1926 during the era of western romanticism. Franklin Roosevelt had traveled there in 1937 to establish the Olympic National Park. The ambience was simple and rustic, and it retained much of the quiet elegance of its distant past. The glacier-carved aquamarine-colored lake served as a focus for the crescent-shaped building, and it provided an opening for light to penetrate the green canopy of surrounding forest and moss. More than one guest had commented that it was reminiscent of the hotel in Steven King's *The Shining*.

Allison walked through the lobby past the huge river rock fireplace and checked himself into his usual lake-view room. After settling in, he returned to his car and drove the remaining four miles down a half-concealed gravel service road to the entrance gate of the company's greenhouse and research facility. A guard at the gate waved him through. He parked his car and walked toward the door of the research complex that he couldn't quite see, but that he knew was there.

The company's research facility was masterfully disguised by its surroundings. Constructed out of steel and green glass, it either stood out in angular contrast from the surrounding forest, or it dis-solved—chameleon-like—into its greenness, depending on how you looked at it. Sometimes, if you stared in just the right place, it would seem to materialize out of nothing, and then disappear again back into the forest.

The main greenhouse was huge, over one hundred feet tall, and it contained pirated plants and trees from Brazil. The laboratories and support facilities were housed in a single-story structure built around the greenhouse on three sides. Drug extractions were performed in the left wing, and drug synthesis in the right wing. The main entrance was through a positive-pressure airlock in the central area of the facility. Allison slid his ID card in the lock, the positive-air-pressure door opened with a whoosh, and he walked inside.

Lizzy's cage was located near the center of the greenhouse. When she'd finally forced herself to get up out of her bed, she'd gingerly explored the perimeter of her cell on her way to the makeshift bathroom. Once there she had pulled the privacy screen around her, used the toilet and then filled the sink with water. After dabbing most of the dried blood off her face with a moist washcloth, she'd washed the blood from her hair. The cuts and bruises still hurt, but she'd been able to work her way through the pain, to use the pain as a stimulant, as a mechanism to keep her alert. She'd made up her mind that she wasn't going to cry anymore.

Lizzy stood in front of the mirror for awhile, looking at the reflection of her battered face and body. When she finally walked back to her bed, she pulled off the top sheet and again wrapped it around herself. Then she walked over to the chair and sat down. She was sitting in the chair, wrapped in the sheet, when Allison approached the door to her cage.

"Good afternoon, Liz. You're looking much better today."

"Fuck you!"

"Now, now, there's no need for that kind of language. But if you insist on being impolite I'm afraid I'll have to cancel your lunch."

Lizzy didn't say anything. She just sat in the chair and glowered at her captor. The door was locked and there was nothing else she could do.

"I'll bet you're wondering about that examination table," he said. "And how about those bleacher seats over there outside of the confinement area? What do you think about them? Have you figured it out yet?"

Lizzy remained silent. She didn't move. She tried to stare a hole right through him.

"I asked you if you figured it out," he continued. "Tell me if you figured it out."

Nothing.

"Well, for your information, we're planning a little experiment here and you're going to be the star attraction, the guinea pig as it were. What do you think about that?"

Still nothing.

"Come on, Liz, you must have something to say. You've always been so talkative."

Lizzy just stared at him.

"Aren't you even a little curious about all this?"

No answer.

"OK, how about this one? Do you know who I am? You're a smart girl. I'll bet you know who I am. Deep down inside you must know."

Lizzy didn't move, she didn't blink, she didn't make a sound.

Allison roared, "WHO AM I?"

She moved her head and paused a moment before she spoke. "Sandman," she said quietly in a half whisper. "You're The Sandman." She wasn't going to cry. She had promised herself that she wouldn't cry.

Chapter 29

I t didn't take long to find Gil Anderson's patrol car. The flames and smoke could be seen from a block away. After the fire department put out the fire and identified the vehicle, word quickly spread throughout the SPD that a cop's car had been trashed, and that a cop was missing. Although it was technically the Tacoma Police Department's case, Robbie Washington was on the scene to provide assistance. Bill McCabe came into the station from his home when he heard the news. Karen was already there when he arrived.

"Any word?" he asked.

"Not yet," she answered. "We called his wife and she said he didn't come home last night. She's scared to death. June, Robbie's wife, is over there with her."

"What about Allison?"

"Haven't been able to locate him. His secretary said he won't be back for a few days. She didn't know where he was."

"Notify me the moment you hear anything," he said. He walked away into his office and shut the door.

McCabe sat at his desk and stared at the Randy Johnson baseball sitting on its stand in front of him. His shoulders sagged and his body language betrayed the heavy burden he felt over the possibility of losing one of his team. He shifted his vision to an old Seattle Mariners team photo taken in front of the Kingdome. Now the

Kingdome was gone too. It had been imploded to make way for a new football stadium. With its demise, the last vestiges of the old Randy Johnson/Ken Griffy Jr. Mariner team were blown up with it. He lowered his head into his hands.

Karen also walked to her office. She called Jon at his house. Jon answered the phone after one ring.

"Hello?"

"Jon, it's Karen."

"You found Lizzy," he said. "Tell me she's alright."

"No, we haven't heard from her yet. She's still missing. That's not why I called."

"Uh oh," he said. "Something's wrong. I can tell by your voice."

"Now Gil Anderson's missing. He didn't come home last night and his car was found stripped and burning in Tacoma."

"He had an appointment with Jim Allison yesterday afternoon," Jon said. He spoke rapidly, almost tripping over his words. "That's a little more than a coincidence, don't you think?"

"We're not sure about that," she said. "He cancelled his afternoon appointment because of a time conflict. Right now we don't know whether he rescheduled with Allison yesterday or not."

"And I suppose Allison's nowhere to be found."

"His secretary said he's going to be out for a few days."

"And she doesn't know where he is, right? Come on, Karen, first Lizzy and now Gil. Allison is The Sandman. I know it and you know it. Let's go get him, or at least call the FBI or something."

"We can't just call the FBI. They respond to kidnappings, not missing persons. And we can't just go get him. We don't have any real evidence. And in any case, we don't know where he is."

"Well I for one am tired of sitting around with my thumb up my ass. If you guys won't do your job, I will. I'll find him for you."

"Don't muck things up, Jon. We can handle this."

"Right," he said with a sarcastic tone to his voice.

"I mean it."

"Right," he said again.

"Listen, I'll call you the minute something breaks."

"Thanks a bunch."

"Come on, Jon, don't be arrogant about this. Remember what you said, we're on the same team. I'll stop by after I finish here."

"OK," he said in a softer tone. "I guess you're right," he lied. "I'll see you later." Jon hung up the phone.

Jon had no intention of sitting around passively any longer. He had had enough. Jim Allison was the connection between Lizzy, Gil and The Sandman, so that was where he would start. He walked to the front closet, put on his jacket, grabbed his keys and walked out of the front door to his Explorer. Leon wagged his tail and wondered what all the hubbub was about.

Jon drove into the south parking lot at Harborview hospital. Lizzy's car was still sitting there where she left it. Jon parked next to her car, got out and walked the now familiar route to the medical examiner's office. The doors to the morgue were open. The door to the medical examiner's office complex was closed. He tried the door. It was unlocked. He let himself in and shut the door behind him.

The outer office complex was vacant. He knew from experience that medical examiners worked weekends only on an on-call basis. He sat down in the secretary's chair and checked the drawers in her desk. They were all locked. Next he turned on her computer. No password was required so he looked through the files on her hard drive. He found one titled 'Dr. Allison's calendar.' He clicked it open. There was nothing there of value. He found nothing else of interest so he turned off the computer and moved on to Allison's private office.

The door to Allison's inner office was locked, as were the doors to all of the inner offices. Jon walked to the hallway to make certain that no one was around, returned to Allison's inner door and smashed it open with his shoulder. He stopped still, listened for a moment, and then, hearing no sound from the hallway, went inside.

Jon looked around the small office and noted that nothing had changed since the last time he'd been there. The laryngophones were still on the desk. He walked around to sit in Allison's chair, hoping he could get a sense of the man by sitting in his place. He put his hands down on the desk and looked around the room. He felt nothing at all, no vibes, no feelings, nothing. Next he tried the desk drawers. The drawers were unlocked and Jon went through them one at a time. There was nothing in any of them that linked him to The Sandman, Lizzy or Gil. Finally, after finishing with the drawers, Jon figured that he'd been in there long enough. He was getting ready to leave the office when he had another thought. Allison's telephone, like most modern phones, was equipped with a redial button. He picked up the phone and pushed the button for an outside line. He then pushed the redial button and waited. He could hear the touch-tones recall the last number. "Rain Forest Lodge, may I help you?"

He almost hung up before he thought to ask, "Is Dr. James Allison there?"

"Just a minute, I'll connect you."

Bingo.

❋

Jim Allison returned to his room in the lodge. It was old and had pine-paneled walls, but it was comfortable and the lake view was soothing. He had finished his preparations for the demonstration with Lizzy and he was ready for some much-needed rest. He was still sleep deprived from the previous night. He opened his personally stocked minibar and poured two fingers of single malt scotch in a whiskey glass. It was an indulgence he picked up from Dr. Holyoke when they were working together. Then he walked over to the window to look out at the lake and the surrounding green. It was raining a gentle rain outside. He sipped his scotch. That was when he noticed the flashing message light on his telephone.

Allison walked back to the telephone and dialed seven to

retrieve his voice mail. He sat on the edge of the bed and kicked off his shoes while he waited. He took another sip of scotch while the voice mail system informed him that he had one message. He waited some more for the recorded message to be replayed. Then he froze. He dropped his whiskey glass and spilled his scotch on the floor as the first sounds of the message were transmitted over the telephone line. A mechanical-sounding voice on the other end of the line said, "I know who you are."

Chapter 30

"Y ou did what?"

"I broke into Allison's office. I had to break the door to get in there. My shoulder's still sore."

"And after you figured out where he was, you called him."

"Yeah."

"With the Laryngophone."

"Yeah."

"Moron," Karen said.

"What?"

"You are a moron. M-o-r-o-n. That was a moronic thing to do. Ergo, you're a moron."

"You don't need to get so upset about it."

"I've been sleeping with a moron," she said to nobody in particular.

Karen had driven over to Jon's house after finishing at the station. She'd spent the day trying to track The Sandman through Holyoke's activities. There was still no word from Gil Anderson, and people were losing hope. Jon wasn't home so she'd let herself in with the hidden key. Leon had wagged his tail when he greeted her at the door. When Jon finally did come home he told her the story of how he had tracked down Allison, and how he left him a message at the lodge. He hoped it would put some pressure on Allison and maybe force him into a mistake. Jon was pumped and ready to go to the lodge. Obviously Karen didn't agree with the strategy.

"Well like it or not, it's done," he said.

"It's done all right," she replied. "You just blew away eight hours of hard detective work. We went through all of Holyoke's customs documents, and he seems to have imported a suspiciously large number of art objects from Brazil over the past eighteen months."

"So? We already knew he was a smuggler."

"So they were all delivered to a small port in Hoquiam out on the Olympic Peninsula. And that's not all. We checked out the local laboratory supply companies only to find that Holyoke ordered hundreds of thousands of dollars worth of lab equipment over the same period of time. He was obviously building a large biochemistry lab somewhere. Guess where."

"Don't tell me."

"The supplies were shipped to the same Hoquiam address."

"Somebody had to pick them up. Where'd they go from there?"

"Somebody did. Holyoke signed for them and then had them loaded onto unmarked trucks. We lost the trail from there."

"He took the stuff up to the Rain Forest Lodge," Jon said. "He had to. That's why Allison's there now. He built his greenhouse and his labs out there in the Olympic rain forest. I'll bet Lizzy's there too. We've got to go up there and find her."

"Maybe she is there, but probably not for long, not after your bone-headed phone call. If Allison's The Sandman, he knows you're onto him now," Karen said. "You threw it in his face. Now he'll either be more wary, he'll get rid of Lizzy if she's still alive and he'll be harder to catch, or he'll forget everything else and come after you."

"He'll come after me," Jon said. "First he went after Lizzy, and then Gil, probably because he stumbled onto his identity. Now he'll come after me. Or he'll expect me to come after him. You said it yourself, that's how we'll catch him."

They were sitting on the couch together splitting a Coke. They looked directly at one another.

"But now you want to go after *him*," she said.

"Yes."

"You think we can trap him."

"That's the idea."

"What makes you think he can be trapped?"

"This guy has a huge ego. He's getting bolder, more reckless. You said it yourself; he's changing. I think we can get him. All we needed was some bait."

"Let's hope you're right," she said. "I don't like this you know. I don't like it one little bit."

Karen took a drink of the Coke and passed it over to Jon. He put it down on the coffee table. He wasn't thirsty anymore.

"He's gotta know that we know, or at least suspect, that he offed Gil Anderson," Jon said. "So he can't risk coming back into town. He's still out at the lodge. I think we ought to leave right now."

"Listen, even if he's still there, which I seriously doubt after your stupid phone call, what are you going to do when we find him? He may be waiting for us for all we know."

"He's a planner, and he's probably planning something for me here in Seattle. If we go out there and surprise him, we might be able to throw him off a little. With guys like that, that's all it takes. Throw him off a little and his whole world falls apart."

"Now you're an expert on criminal psychology."

"I don't know. All I know is that I can't just sit around here any longer. We've got to do something."

Karen looked into Jon's eyes trying to get a reading. She continued, "If we go out there, if we do this, it'll be just the two of us. There isn't going to be any backup. The rain forest is way beyond the SPD jurisdiction. You understand that."

"He's got Lizzy," Jon said.

The room was silent for what seemed like a long time.

"OK," she finally said. She continued to search his eyes. "We'll do it, but we'll do it my way. You do exactly as I say."

"Sure, I'll do anything you say."

"I mean it, Jon. I can't lose you."

Her words made him feel . . . different. His chest felt tight and he felt suddenly out of breath. He returned her gaze. He tried a smile to lighten the mood, but the mood wouldn't be changed.

"Anything you say, of course."

"Then let's do it."

They both stood up. Jon walked toward the door. Karen reached to pick up her purse. Then she opened it to check her gun. It was a nine-millimeter Beretta automatic. Jon hadn't seen it before. It looked cold, and it looked deadly. She ejected the clip, checked it and then reinserted it in the handle. Then she checked her spare clip. She looked serious. He hadn't seen her this way before. It made him feel a little nervous. He turned away and grabbed a jacket out of the closet, and then he scratched Leon behind an ear.

"Let's go," he said. They walked out together.

＊

Jon drove. They followed Allison's route in his Explorer. First they drove south on I-5 and then west towards the ocean. It had been raining. The closer they got to the coast the worse the weather got. By the time they reached Hoquiam the rain and pea-soup ocean fog brought visibility down to only ten or fifteen feet. It was even more difficult to see after they made the turn northward on Highway 101. There were no other cars out on the road in the bad weather, and driving was dangerous. The opaque mist that had enveloped them diffused the beams from their headlights, creating an aura of light with no clear path ahead. Jon saw a deer just in time to hit his breaks. They had slowed to a crawl. They looked for a place to stop. Finally they spotted a widening in the road and pulled off onto the shoulder.

"What now?" Karen asked.

"There's no point going on like this," he answered. "We wait for the fog to lift." He stopped the engine, turned off his headlights and let the dark swallow them. They sat there in silence for awhile. Jon stared out the window. "She's got to be alive," he said to the night.

"I don't know," Karen answered. "I don't even know what we're doing here. I don't know anything anymore."

"Lean back and close your eyes," Jon said. "I'll wake you when the fog lifts."

Chapter 31

J im Allison awoke. It was Sunday morning and the rain had subsided a little. The Pacific front had moved inland. He could still see some patchy fog out of his window over the lake, but it looked like it was clearing. He felt well rested, alert and alive. He knew the phone call had to have come from Jon Kirk. The police would never have done such a ridiculous thing. He laughed to himself, what an amusing ploy. Maybe Kirk was on his way out to the lodge. That would be interesting. He smiled. Allison was hungry so he showered, shaved and dressed, and then he went down to the dining room for breakfast. He grabbed a morning paper and read the headlines. There was no mention of The Sandman. He was disappointed.

Breakfast at the lodge dining room was an eggs-and-bacon, pancakes or waffles kind of affair. He ordered scrambled eggs and black coffee. He noticed Sandy Rant, the board member from Hong Kong, sitting at a corner table having breakfast with Chris Bayley. They were avoiding eye contact with him. Allison was sipping his coffee waiting for his order when Paul Skinner, another board member, walked through the door and approached his table.

"Do you mind if I join you?" Skinner asked.

"Please," Allison said. "Pull up a chair."

"The chairman asked me to speak with you."

"Kate Monahan? What does she want?"

"Katherine," Skinner corrected.

"Whatever. Why isn't she here in person? The demonstration's set for Wednesday. As compulsive as she is, I would've thought that she'd be out here at the lodge by now."

"She's here," he said. "She's having breakfast in her room."

"I should've guessed." A waiter brought Allison his eggs and some toast. "Would you like something?" he asked Paul.

"No, thanks." Skinner shifted his position in his chair.

Allison put some jam on the toast and took a bite. Then he began to eat his eggs. "I hope you don't mind if I eat." He interrupted himself to take a sip of his coffee. "I don't want it to get cold."

"Of course not," Skinner said. "Finish your breakfast." He wanted to get Allison out of the restaurant as soon as possible. Allison continued to eat. Skinner continued to watch.

"So what does Ms. Monahan want," Allison asked. He emphasized the *Ms.*

"She wants to talk to you about Elizabeth Carlstrom."

"Umm," he said noncommittally.

"She wants you to make sure that our investors think that she's just a drug-addicted prostitute. She's worried about the demonstration, and she wants our investors to be pleased."

"Oh, they'll be pleased all right," he said. Allison finished eating his breakfast. Then he pushed his plate away and drank the rest of his coffee. A waiter came over to the table and asked him if he wanted a refill. "No, thank you," he said.

"Finished?" Skinner asked.

"As soon as they bring me my check."

Skinner raised his hand to attract the waiter's attention. When the waiter came back Skinner told him that they were in a hurry, and to charge the bill to his room. Then he told him to add a twenty percent tip. "Of course," the waiter told him.

"What's the hurry?" Allison asked.

"We need to get out to the lab. Dr. Monahan said she'll meet us there and I don't want to keep her waiting."

"Well, that just wouldn't do, would it?" Allison said

"No, it wouldn't," Skinner said.

"Let's go, then." They stood up and left the table.

They walked from the restaurant through the lobby to the front entrance of the lodge. Skinner's car was parked near the front door in a handicapped zone. "We'll take my car," he said. They both got in and drove down the service road to the lab and greenhouse building. The guard waved them through as they passed by his gate.

"Would you like to meet Ms. Carlstrom?" Allison asked.

"Maybe later," Skinner said. "First we're going to the conference room."

Skinner parked his car behind the trees to the side of the lab. It was the only car in the parking lot. He opened his door and got out. Allison noticed the bulge under his jacket when he bent over getting out. Skinner walked around the front of the car and looked at Allison still sitting in his seat.

"Are you coming?" he asked.

"Sure." Allison opened the car door, got out and walked with him around to the entrance of the building. He stayed close, no more than an arm's length away. He didn't want to let Skinner out of his immediate reach.

They walked into the building together through the positive-pressure airlock. The building was quiet. The laboratory complex was empty. They were the only ones there. Lizzy was in her cage out in the greenhouse.

"The place seems deserted," Allison said.

"We've closed it down until after the test," he answered. "The technicians have all left. There's nobody here but you and me."

"And the test subject," Allison corrected.

"Your little white lab rat? She doesn't count."

"What about Kate?" said Allison. "I thought you said she was waiting for us in the conference room."

"Katherine, yes, of course. Dr. Monahan is waiting for us in the conference room," Skinner said. "Come on; let's go."

"So it's *Doctor* Monahan now, is it?"

Skinner said nothing as he led Allison the short distance down the corridor to the left toward the conference room. He opened the door and motioned for Allison to precede him into the room. The room was illuminated by greenish light filtering in through the windows.

"After you," Allison said.

Skinner searched his face and, seeing nothing, he walked through the doorway ahead of him. As he reached to turn on the overhead lights Allison brought his large fist crashing down on the side of Skinner's head just behind his right ear. Skinner caught the movement out of the corner of his eye and tried to deflect the force of the punch by ducking his head forward. But the blow caught him hard, and knocked him to the floor.

Allison was on him in an instant, but Skinner was fast. He managed to roll to the side and bloody Allison's nose with an elbow. The move briefly stunned Allison, and left him reeling. Skinner managed to pull away. He stood up as he moved towards the conference table in the middle of the room. While pulling away he reached around behind his back under his open jacked and pulled his gun out of his belt. He had it in his hand and was turning to point it at Allison when Allison crashed into him from behind. He hit him hard with his shoulder and all of his bulk. Skinner crashed headfirst into the chairs around the table. The gun went flying out of his hand and the chairs fell around him as he tumbled back to the floor.

Skinner was fast but Allison was bigger and stronger, much stronger. By the time Skinner hit the floor Allison had recovered his senses and was on his feet. Skinner tried to wriggle away toward the gun, but Allison kicked him hard in the side of the chest. Ribs snapped as a whoosh of air was forced out of Skinner's mouth. He rolled over in agony onto his stomach. Allison kicked him again, then he knelt down beside him, pushed the chairs out of the way, put his right knee in the middle of his back and hooked his right arm around his neck so that his forearm was over his larynx. He grabbed his own right wrist with his left hand and began to squeeze. A pinched, choking sound came out of Skinner's mouth. Allison leaned over while he pulled Skinner's head off the floor with his chokehold, putting his lips close to Skinner's ear.

"Now what was it Ms. Monahan wanted to discuss with me?" he asked.

Skinner didn't answer. His eyes were glazed and his brain had started to fog. He couldn't breathe. His body went into an anoxic state, slowly shutting down one organ system at a time, preserving basic brain functions for the last.

"No answer?" he said. "How rude!"

With a sharp movement, Allison quickly pulled Skinner's head back with a jerk. He heard a snap. He released his chokehold. Skinner's mouth fell open and his head lolled awkwardly to the side.

Allison stood up, looked down at Skinner's unmoving body, walked 360 degrees around him one time and then kicked him again hard in the side of the chest. Skinner's limp corpse lurched under the impact. Then he walked over to the other side of the room to pick up the gun.

The gun was an old Colt-45 automatic, a World War One military issue that had proved useful for trench warfare. It wasn't the most accurate gun in the world, but it had a lot of stopping power. Allison moved back to the body, wrestled Skinner's holster out of his pants, tucked it into the small of his back, slid the gun into it, and then covered it with his jacket.

He then slowly cleaned the blood off his face with a handkerchief. He put the handkerchief back in his pocket and walked over to a closet at the far end of the room. He opened the door. There was plenty of room, so he went over to Skinner's body, picked him up by the legs, dragged him around the conference table back to the closet, stuffed him inside and shut the door. Then he carefully cleaned Skinner's blood off the chairs and floor, and put the chairs back in place at the table. He surveyed the room. It was clean.

Allison checked the room one more time and then shut the door as he left. A satisfied smile crept over his face. He walked back to Skinner's car and drove it down the gravel road to the guard station. The guard waved him past. He continued on to the lodge parking lot. He parked the car, left the keys in the ignition where he'd found them, re-entered the lodge and walked through the lobby toward the elevators. There was a twinkle in his eye and lightness to his step. He'd decided to keep his appointment with Katherine Monahan. The elevator doors opened.

✳

Katherine Monahan had finished her breakfast. She'd scheduled a board meeting in the lab conference room at eleven to go over plans for the drug test demonstration scheduled for Wednesday. She double-checked with the lodge manager to make sure that all of the board members had arrived.

Katherine was standing at her window looking out over the lake. She was staying in her usual room, the best room in the hotel. She was comfortable in her navy Chanel pants suit, but she felt she needed something more severe, something more authoritarian for the board meeting. She was thinking Armani when she heard the knock on her door. The lodge was old and, unfortunately for her, the doors weren't equipped with peepholes that allowed guests to screen their visitors. Katherine opened the door to her room.

"Hello, Kate." Allison smiled at her. She tried to slam the door in his face but the door hit his foot and bounced back open. "I'm sorry," he said. "You prefer Katherine, don't you. Or should I call you Dr. Monahan?" She backed up a few steps and then stood her ground. "May I come in?" he said after he had walked into the room and shut the door behind him.

"What do you want," she said more than asked. "I've got a board meeting over at the lab in an hour, and I don't have time for conversation."

"Groovy," he said. His eyes were unblinking. She involuntarily shuddered and then backed up a few steps.

"Listen," she said. "I've got to get dressed. Whatever it is that you want, we can take care of it later."

"I don't think so." His eyes narrowed as he kept her firmly fixed in his gaze. He started to move forward. She backed up to the window. "Paul sends his regards," he hissed.

"You son of a bitch," she yelled. She bumped against the table next to the window knocking down a vase of fresh flowers. She grabbed the vase in her right hand and threw it at him. Flowers and water spilled all over. Allison easily deflected it away. "You God damned crazy son. . . ."

That was the last word she spoke. Allison had her in his large hands. He grabbed her by the throat, threw her down on the bed and crushed her larynx. She kicked and struggled but he held firm. He was strangling her. He kept up the pressure until he had squeezed the last drop of life out of her limp body.

Allison sat on the side of the bed for a few minutes just looking at her. Then he got up and he found the key to her room on her desk. Finally he walked out into the hallway and let the door close and lock itself behind him.

He searched the hallway until he found the linen closet. The door was unlocked and the hall was deserted. He found the extra bedspreads on one of the shelves, and he took one.

He returned to Katherine's room and unlocked the door. The room was a mess. He picked up the flowers and put them back in the vase. Then he wiped the spilled water from the table and other hard surfaces. He spread the spare bedspread out on the floor, placed Katherine's body on top of it and then wrapped it tightly around her. He remade the bed and tidied up the rest of the room. He looked out of the window. The rain had started again and was falling through the mist. Finally he opened the door and looked outside. The hallway was still empty.

Allison picked up Katherine's body wrapped in the bedspread and threw it over his shoulder. She wasn't heavy, and he easily carried her through her doorway down to the end of the hall. The door to her room again closed behind him. He opened the end window and looked outside. He was alone. Then, with Katherine over his shoulder, he stepped out onto the fire escape. He felt the rain on his face. It felt cool. Finally he carried her down the steps, out onto the grounds and into the mist.

Chapter 32

At 10:45 AM the remaining members of the board gathered in the lobby. General Jeffers was talking to Joshua Green, and Bayley and Dyer were arguing about something or other. Rant was fussing with his bow tie. Runstad was leaning against a large cedar pillar drinking an espresso. After milling around for a few minutes, the six people left to proceed in two cars to the green-house, labs and conference room.

The meeting had been planned to review Wednesday's test. The financial stakes were high, and the board members all felt pressure to assure a successful demonstration of their new drug. The future of the company depended on it. They were scheduled to review the details of the test at the meeting, and they wanted to make certain that the test subject would appear to be a drug-addicted prostitute, as advertised.

The laboratory conference room had been prepared for them before their arrival. There were three places set on each side of the table and a seventh at the end, with bottles of mineral water and glasses, agenda booklets, blank tablets and pens for taking notes. The chairman's seat was at the head of the table. There were no tablets, booklets or bottled water at her position. She would speak from memory without notes, and it was her style to never drink or eat anything during a meeting.

The two cars containing the board members were checked out thoroughly before being waved through the control gate by the guard. The conference room was empty when they arrived, and they all took their customary seats. Paul Skinner's seat near the foot of the table was empty, and so was the chairman's. No one expected her to arrive until precisely eleven o'clock.

Clarissa Dyer was particularly concerned about investor reactions to the drug demonstration. She had demanded that a mannequin be brought to the meeting to help the group review the test in detail. She wanted to visualize every detail in sequence, and to predetermine the reactions of the audience. A mannequin had been brought to the room as she had requested, and it was situated in the center of the conference table covered by a white sheet.

At 11:00 the board members looked toward the closed door to the room. At 11:01 they began checking their watches. Katherine Monahan was never late. At 11:02 whispered conversations developed around the table, and at 11:03 the door opened. The group was ready to welcome their chairman when Dr. Jim Allison walked into the room.

Surprise registered on several of the faces, at least on those who couldn't conceal it. Allison wasn't supposed be here. As a matter of fact he wasn't supposed to be anywhere. The chairman had informed all them that Allison was no longer involved with the project. There were inadvertent glances toward Skinner's vacant chair. No one spoke.

Jim Allison stood at the head of the table in the chairman's position. He looked down at the six seated members of the board and smiled a wicked half smile. His eyes flashed back and forth. He broke the silence and addressed the group.

"Ladies and gentlemen, members of the board, welcome."

He heard only silence in response. Finally Clarissa Dyer spoke. "What in the hell are you doing here? This is supposed to be a closed meeting. Where's the chairman?"

"Surprised to see me?" he asked. "Why is that?"

There was another silence, then she continued, "I demand to

know what happened to Katherine Monahan."

Again there was a pause. The room was expectantly quiet. All eyes were on Allison. "All right," he said. "Since you asked." Allison reached over the end of the table to grasp the corner of the sheet on top of the mannequin. He paused a moment for dramatic effect. Then he pulled the sheet off the table with a flourish and tossed it on the floor behind him. Dyer gasped at the sight of Katherine Monahan's naked body.

"Jesus," Bayley half whispered.

Allison laughed out loud.

General Jeffers started to stand. He didn't get to finish.

Allison reached behind his back and withdrew Skinner's gun from his belt. He fired a single shot. The retort from the large caliber weapon was deafening in the enclosed room. The bullet entered Jeffers' head just below his left eye. It flattened as it went through his ethmoid sinus and started to tumble when it penetrated his cranial cavity. Then it exploded out of the back of his skull in a cloud of red mist, brains and bone. Jeffers lurched backwards as if kicked in the face by a mule. He crashed over the back of his chair hard to the floor. The chair tumbled over backwards to the ground with him.

Judy Runstad started to scream. Allison shot her through the lower neck, shattering her spine and nearly decapitating her in the process. The rest of them started to scramble to their feet, duck down under the table, or try to get away any way that they could. The room was all movement, screaming, chaos and noise. The large gun fired repeatedly. Bodies went flying. Blood was everywhere. The savage slaughter went on and on until the carnage was complete. Then the room was quiet. It all stopped as quickly as it had started. The smell of burning gunpowder and death hung heavy in the air.

The glass walls of the building couldn't contain the noise from the old military weapon and when the guard at the gate heard its somewhat muffled retort he electronically closed the perimeter and then walked toward the lab complex to investigate. He walked through the main entrance, disarming all the locks on the way in. He continued until he saw Dr. Allison walking towards him in the hallway.

"Dr. Allison, I heard something that sounded like gunfire. Is everything alright?"

Allison raised his gun and pointed it at the surprised man. He shot him once in the center of the chest. The guard flew backwards, and then died on the spot where he fell. Allison watched him with a minor degree of curiosity. Then he walked back to the conference room. He had made certain that there were no support personnel in the greenhouse or elsewhere at the facility.

Allison looked in the door and surveyed the bloody scene. A feeling of satisfaction swept over him. It was almost sensual. He walked into the room not caring where he stepped, not caring what he touched. The world would soon know he was The Sandman. He pulled Skinner's body out of the closet to join the others. He surveyed the slaughter. He made some adjustments. Then he left the room for the greenhouse, and Lizzy.

Chapter 33

A logging truck rumbled by them at high speed. It woke Karen up with a start.

"Jon, wake up. You fell asleep."

"What?" he said. He rubbed his eyes. It was barely light outside. "What time is it?"

"It's almost nine o'clock. We've got to get going." With the clouds, rain and low winter sun it was still relatively dark outside.

"I'm sorry, Karen. I must have dozed off. I remember that I was awake at 6:30." He started the car and pulled back onto the highway. Karen checked her gun again. Both ammunition clips were full, and the chamber was empty. Jon watched her as she put it back in her purse.

"That thing looks dangerous," he said. "Are you sure we're doing the right thing?"

"It was your idea, remember. And no, I'm not sure that we're doing the right thing."

"Lizzy's still out there somewhere," he said.

"Let's go get her."

Jon stepped on the accelerator. They were driving faster than they should on the old coast road, and they almost missed the faded sign for The Rain Forest Lodge. When Karen saw it they skidded to a halt, backed up a little ways, and then turned right. After another quarter mile the world changed. Civilization became a distant memory.

The access road snaked its way into the old growth of the Olympic rain forest like a twisted, black viper. An overcast layer of clouds hung low, below the tops of the trees. Trees and dense vegetation lined the edge of the asphalt, eroding its edges in an unrelenting effort to reclaim its lost territory. The trees formed a barrier, with only forest and dark beyond the margin. Jon and Karen followed their ribbon of a road for another twenty minutes. Finally they reached the lodge.

"What a great old place," Jon said. "It looks like it belongs here, like it's been here forever."

"It's creepy," she said.

A panel truck came from somewhere behind the lodge and drove past them in the parking lot. A sign on the side read *Aberdeen Medical Glassware.*

Jon parked his Explorer. The rain was getting worse. They jogged to the front entrance of the hotel and walked in. There was a roaring fire blazing in the oversized fireplace in the center of the lobby. They brushed off the rain and stood in front of the fire to warm themselves for a moment.

"What now," she said.

"Now we find Allison."

Jon walked up to the registration desk and to the clerk standing behind it. His nametag read David Wyman. "Is Dr. James Allison staying here?" he asked.

"Yes, he is," he said without needing to check his computer.

"Would you ring his room please?"

"He's not in his room. He left earlier this morning."

"He checked out?" Jon asked.

"No, he's just not in his room. Is there anything else I can do for you?"

"Did he say when he'd be back?"

"He didn't say."

"I don't suppose he said where he was going."

"No, he didn't." The desk clerk smiled an officious smile.

"Thanks," Jon said. He walked back over to Karen by the fireplace. "He's here somewhere, but he's not in his room."

"Why don't you check out the hotel public areas. I'll call SPD and get his license plate number to see if his car's in the parking lot," Karen said.

"OK, I'll meet you back here in the lobby in fifteen minutes."

The old hotel had three floors of guestrooms. Jon walked the hallways of all three floors. He checked out the restaurant and bar on the ground floor, and then a room converted to show old vintage movies, and the gift shop. He walked out onto the large porch overlooking the lake on the lobby level, and then down to an old two-lane bowling alley and the spa in the basement. He searched the place as thoroughly as he could. Then he met Karen back in the lobby.

"Any sign of Allison?" she asked.

"None. Unless he's in one of the guestrooms, he's not in the hotel. How about his car?"

"It's in the parking lot. He's got to be around here somewhere."

"Let's check out the grounds," Jon said.

They walked outside to check around the perimeter of the hotel. Allison wasn't there. There was a boat dock on the lake, and there were several marked trails leading through the moss-covered trees, but only dense forest beyond. For all practical purposes the hotel was completely contained by nature. It was a primitive and primal place, a place from another time.

"He could be out on the lake," Karen said.

"Maybe, but I don't think so," Jon answered. "It's too rainy. I don't think he's out hiking in the woods either."

"Remember that truck that drove past us in the parking lot?" He didn't. "Where did it come from?"

✳

Lizzy was sitting in the large, white chair with a sheet wrapped around her body. She didn't hurt anymore, at least not all of the time. Her pain had improved to the point where she could move around without too much difficulty. The cuts and bruises on her face, while still disfiguring, had started to heal. She stared out into the surrounding vegetation of the greenhouse. A movement and rustling of the vegetation caught her eye. The moving vegetation gave way to the form of a man. The Sandman was approaching. Lizzy willed herself not to move.

Allison approached the door to her cage. "Hi, Lizzy. What's new? She didn't look at him and she didn't answer.

"You're really a beautiful girl, but then you know that, don't you. Sorry about the face." Allison walked over to the bleachers and sat down.

She wanted to be defiant. That was the only way she could gain a measure of control over the situation. She'd spent every waking moment of the last twenty-four hours convincing herself that she still had some control. But she felt vulnerable and she hated it. She fought to push down her anxiety and maintain a defiant stance that she didn't really feel.

"You've cleaned yourself up. That shows pride. That's good."

Lizzy didn't say anything.

Allison just looked at her for a few minutes. "I hate these one-sided conversations, don't you?" He paused. "Oh, well," he said. "I guess there's no point beating around the bush. I've got some good news and I've got some bad news. Which would you like to hear first?"

Lizzy was not going to acknowledge his presence. She looked straight ahead through the walls of her cage toward a spot in the trees that she could see only with her mind.

"Nothing? No preference? OK then, we'll start with the good news. Pay close attention. You'll want to hear this."

Silence.

"The big drug demonstration's been cancelled. You're no longer a human guinea pig. We no longer need your services as a test subject." He paused to watch her reaction. "What do you think about that? Isn't that great?"

She wouldn't look in his direction although she flushed with fear.

Allison noticed her reaction and smiled. "Oh yes, of course, the bad news," he said, as if they were having a real conversation. He paused again for effect.

Silence.

"It's the same as the good news, really. We no longer need your services as a test subject."

Allison's words hung in the air. Lizzy did her best not to reveal her fear, but The Sandman knew fear when he saw it.

"I promise I won't hurt you," he said. "I promise it won't hurt."

✳

The rain came on and off in spurts, always through an ever-present background of mist. Clouds descended to cover the tops of the trees. Jon and Karen explored the back of the property away from the lake, looking for a place from where the panel truck could have come. They followed a wide rock and moss-covered path from the parking lot to the edge of the forest. There were occasional tire tracks on the moss leading to an irregular opening in the wall of trees. They followed the tracks. After a few hundred twisting yards, gravel replaced the moss and rock and outlined a road through the old growth forest. After hiking a quarter of a mile they found a sign that read:

DANGER, ROAD CLOSED
KEEP OUT

They stopped. The gravel service road appeared to penetrate the trees and hanging sheets of club moss ahead of them with a tunnel-like effect.

"What do you think?" he asked. "Should we go back and get the car?"

"In for a penny, in for a pound," she answered. "It can't be much farther, whatever it is. Let's keep going." They continued on down the road.

After another half-hour or so they came upon the guard station and security perimeter. The guardhouse was empty, and the security gate was closed. They could see the road continue for a short distance beyond the gate, but only forest beyond that. Then, with only a slight movement of her head, Karen saw it.

"There's a building out there," she said.

"Where?"

"Just beyond the road, in front of the trees. It's big."

"I don't see it."

"Tilt your head from side to side. Look for angles; don't look at colors."

There it was in front of them, standing out from the green and shadows of the forest and sinking back into it at the same time.

"Wow, that's weird," he said.

"No kidding "

"I think we found what we're looking for."

"Let's be careful," she said.

The gate across the road completely blocked their way so they walked into the trees to get around it. Jon was in front of Karen, pushing his way through the chest high ferns when he inadvertent-ly touched a hidden wire. He was jolted backward onto the ground. "God damn it! It's electrified."

"Not anymore. Not after you touched it," she said. "It'll take a few seconds to recharge the capacitors. Let's go." She found the wires and spread them apart to climb through. She could feel the tingle from the continuously discharging current as she touched them. Jon followed. They walked on to the only door on the front side of the building.

The gate guard had left the airlock door unlocked. It really was-n't a door in the usual sense of the word. It was more like a seal of some kind. They walked inside and it automatically shut behind them. They took a few more steps and then saw the guard's body on the floor of the corridor to their left.

"Shit!" Karen drew her gun out of her purse and chambered a bul-let into firing position. She pushed off the safety and held the weapon out in front of her. Jon rushed over to the body on the floor. The guard was lying on his back in a large pool of blood. His eyes were open. Jon felt for a pulse with two fingers on the side of the guard's neck.

"He's dead," Jon said.

"Don't touch anything else, and try not to track the blood around. Let's find a phone and call the police."

Karen caught up to Jon, briefly looked at the body, and then quickly returned her searching gaze back to the spaces around them. She advanced down the hall with her gun extended in front of her. Jon followed close behind, looking over his shoulder every few seconds to check the hallway behind them. The building was silent. They came to the open door of the conference room.

Karen gasped.

Jon moved to look over her shoulder. "Jesus Christ!" He felt like he was going to be sick. He bent over and swallowed hard. He fought through the feeling and again looked at the scene before him. Karen advanced through the doorway and into the room with her gun at the ready. Jon hung back by the door. Nothing moved. There wasn't a sound. There was only death. "Don't touch anything," she whispered loud enough for him to hear.

Blood was splashed on the walls and pooling on the floor. Sitting at the conference table in the center of the room, members of the board were posed in their chairs around the table. They had been shot to pieces, and they were covered in blood and gore. But their hands were on top of the table. Some of their hands held pens to paper, others were wrapped around a glass of water. Judy Runstad's head hung to her side, and it was attached to her body by only half of her neck. The back of General Jeffers' head was completely gone. With the exception of Paul Skinner, the rest of the board members were in equally bad shape. Skinner's body was relatively un-bloodied, but his neck was broken and his head was resting on his shoulders several inches to the side of where it should be. He was posed at the foot of the table. Thirteen lifeless eyes seemed to be focused on the pale body resting lifelessly at its center.

The table was spotless. All traces of blood had been wiped away. The clean lines of its chrome inlay and maple wood grain stood out in dramatic contrast to the bloody mess in the rest of the room. Katherine Monahan's nude body lay posed peacefully on its back, feet together and toes up. Her hair was neatly combed, her eyes were shut and her hands were crossed mummy-like across her chest covering her breasts. It was The Sandman's signature.

Karen advanced to the closet with her gun in front of her. She flung the door open and found that it was empty. Then she moved back to join Jon by the doorway. He was bracing himself on the door. The color had drained from his face

"Who are these people?" she asked.

Jon fought his nausea. "I think the woman on the table's Kate Monahan, although I can't be sure. She look's different from the last time I saw her."

"Who is she?"

"She's a naturopath from Orcas Island. I have no idea about the rest."

"I'm going to have nightmares," she said. They both continued to stare at the scene that was so carefully set before them.

Karen broke the spell. "We've got to find a phone and call the police. My cell phone's not working out here."

"We've got to find Lizzy," said Jon.

They left the room, Jon closed the door behind them and then they started down the hallway to check the labs.

Chapter 34

Jon and Karen searched the two laboratories and the remainder of the lab complex. They found sophisticated laboratory equipment and glassware, but no more bodies or other evidence of The Sandman's presence. Karen lowered her gun to her side. She flicked on the safety but did not put her weapon back in her purse.

"Do you think it's safe?" Jon asked.

"No, it's not safe," Karen answered. "Allison could be anywhere. And we have to find a phone immediately."

"What about Lizzy?"

"I saw another building behind this one. If she's out here, it's the only place she could be."

"We've got to find her."

"I know we do," she said.

"Then what are we waiting for?"

Karen took a deep breath. "Don't get in front of my line of fire."

They walked back into the hallway and looked for the connecting corridor between the greenhouse and the labs. Karen found it. Jon opened the door and stepped out into the lush vegetation. The heat and humidity hit him like a sledgehammer. Karen walked up beside him. She raised her gun and clicked off the safety.

✸

Jim Allison was still sitting on the bleachers looking at Lizzy. She was in her chair in what looked to him to be an almost catatonic state. She looked small, wrapped in her sheet the way she was. She looked to be completely broken. He'd seen it before. He stood up and walked deliberately from the bleachers over to the door of the confinement cage. Lizzy followed him with her peripheral vision. Her body remained still.

Allison looked at her through the door. Then he reached into his pocket and removed a syringe still in its sterile plastic wrapper. He also removed a medical vial containing a clear liquid. He unwrapped the syringe and pulled the plastic needle guard off the needle. Then he thrust the bare needle through the rubber stopper cap into the vial and withdrew some of the fluid. After he filled it he expelled all of the residual air from the syringe. He did it out of habit. A little air with the drug wouldn't make any difference to Lizzy. He replaced the needle guard over the needle, and finally he put the loaded syringe back in his pocket along with the vial.

Lizzy tensed her body. Her heart rate rose as she steeled herself for whatever was to come next. She wanted him to think that she was helpless, but it was difficult to stay still as she channeled all her fear into fury.

Allison smiled. He was excited. He wanted to prolong the feeling. He slowly unlocked the door.

Lizzy tried to control her breathing. She forced herself to be still. She didn't move a muscle.

Allison opened the door and stepped inside. Lizzy looked pitiful. She looked sad, scared and pitiful. He left the door to the cage open behind him.

He approached, taking his time. His smile had turned menacing.

Allison stopped a foot in front of Lizzy, just twelve inches away. He reached inside his pocket and removed the syringe containing its fatal contents. He looked down from the full height of his large frame at her, small in the chair. She didn't look up. He stared at her. He didn't look around the room. He didn't look at the examination table in the center of the room. He didn't notice that only one of the stainless steel gynecology stirrups was still attached to the end of the table.

"Lizzy," he said. "You've been a good patient. This won't hurt; I promise." He put out his hand. "Give me your arm."

Liz didn't move at all, so he reached down to grasp her left elbow to give her the injection. As he lifted her arm, the bed sheet fell open a few inches showing him her nakedness. He paused just a moment.

As he turned his head to look at her body, she violently thrust the one-foot-long steel gynecology stirrup she had been hiding under the sheet hard into his face. He fell backwards, but not to the ground. She bounded to her feet, swung the stirrup and hit him again, this time on the side of the head. He went down. Then, using all of her strength, she raised the steel bludgeon high over her head and brought it down with both hands hard on the base of his skull. A scream came out of her mouth as she hit him. He was out like a light. Lizzy dropped the stirrup and ran from the cage as fast as she could.

✳

Jon and Karen both heard the scream through the trees.

"It's Lizzy " Jon exclaimed. "Lizzy," he yelled as loud as he could. "It's Jon! Can you hear me? Where are you?"

Karen dropped to a crouch; her gun out in front of her pointed in the direction of the scream.

"Lizzy, we're over here," he yelled.

They heard a crashing of branches somewhere in front of them. Karen had her finger on the trigger. She scanned bushes and trees, and started to apply pressure, bracing for a shot. "Lizzy," Jon screamed.

Liz came running toward them, toward the sound of Jon's voice. She tripped and fell in the dirt, rolled, got up and started running again. She didn't feel a thing. Adrenaline had completely shut off her pain. Then she saw Jon. Karen was in a shooting crouch to his left and a little in front of him. She cried out.

Lizzy came bursting through the trees. She was naked and smeared with dirt from her fall. She ran to Jon. He grabbed her and enveloped her in his arms. She sobbed uncontrollably. Tears came to Jon's eyes as well. Karen kept her gun trained in the direction from whence Lizzy had come.

"I killed him," she said through her sobs. "I think I killed him."

She couldn't stop crying. Jon tried to comfort her. Karen scanned the trees for any sign of movement.

"You killed The Sandman?" Jon asked.

Karen spoke without taking her eyes away from her gun sight. "Was he alone?"

"There's no one else here," she said still sobbing. "I think he's dead."

"Where," Karen asked. "And talk quietly, please."

"Over there, through the trees." She was talking through her tears. "There's a room. He's on the floor. He's dead. I killed him."

"You stay here with Jon. I'll go check." Karen started to move forward with her gun extended in front of her. She disappeared into the foliage.

Lizzy slid to the ground. She was spent. The adrenaline was wearing off and she started to hurt. She huddled up into herself. Jon knelt down next to her. He put his arm around her shoulders. He gently covered her with his jacket. Her tears wouldn't stop.

Karen saw the containment cage through the trees. She carefully approached the cage, gun in hand. She saw the open door and worked her way towards it. She looked through the door; then she stepped inside.

She surveyed the room, but Allison wasn't there. He was nowhere to be seen. Then she heard Lizzy's scream.

Allison had regained consciousness and was in the trees when he saw Karen moving toward the containment cage. He waited for her to pass, and then circled around toward the entrance door to the labs. He spotted Lizzy and Jon huddled on the ground near the door and he carefully moved towards them.

When he was close enough he sprang out of the foliage in a rush. Lizzy saw him and screamed. Jon turned just in time to get hit in the face with Skinner's heavy gun. It knocked him out cold.

Allison pointed the gun down at Lizzy. He pushed the barrel down through her hair above her forehead and onto her skin, twisted the gun barrel from side to side so that she could feel the cold of its tempered steel, and then he pulled the trigger.

Click.

Nothing. It was empty. A look of disgust came over his face as he removed the gun from her head. He stared at her for a moment as she huddled near his feet. "Poor Lizzy," he said. He slammed his gun into the side of her skull. She toppled to the ground. Blood started to ooze out of her left ear. Then he turned his attention to Jon.

Allison reached into his pocket and retrieved the still-loaded syringe. He grabbed Jon's head and popped the needle cap off the end of the needle with his thumb.

Karen burst through the trees, gun extended in front of her. "Stop! Drop the needle and put your hands up where I can see them!" she barked.

"Oh I don't think I can do that," he said, and then he roughly jabbed it into Jon's carotid artery.

BANG!

A bullet struck the earth a foot to his right. "Drop the fucking needle," she yelled.

He pushed the plunger halfway in. Jon went limp. "Drop the fucking gun," he answered. Karen didn't say anything. "If you don't drop the gun I'm going to inject the rest of this fluid and he'll die."

They stared at each other. It was a stand off. Neither flinched. Then Allison said in a calm voice, "There's a muscle relaxant in this syringe. It's Compound-7, one of Dr. Holyoke's mistakes. It's already paralyzed Jon. A little more and he won't be able to breathe. It'll kill him. Now, put down the gun."

Karen stared at him an agonizing moment longer. Then she lowered the gun and dropped it. Her shoulders drooped. She looked defeated. Allison smiled.

"Now kick it away into the ferns."

She did as she was told.

"That's better," he said. "Now listen very carefully. Jon's life will depend on it." He looked down at Jon and pushed the plunger in a little farther. Karen swallowed hard. She watched the plunger move. She looked up into The Sandman's face and pleaded for Jon's life with her eyes.

"Compound-7's a short acting drug," he said. "It's effects only last a few minutes. During that time Jon won't be able to breathe. He'll suffocate and die unless you breathe for him. Do you understand?"

"Yes," she said in a quiet voice. She nodded her head.

"Now I'm going to inject the rest of the drug.

"No," she cried in anguish.

"He'll be alright, but only if you do exactly as I say." He looked at her to make sure she understood. "Once the drug's in his system you'll need to give him mouth to mouth resuscitation until it wears off. It'll take ten or fifteen minutes. During that time I plan, as they say, to take my leave." He paused again for effect. "You can't stop or leave him for any reason. If you do, he'll die. Do you understand?"

"Yes."

"Take good care of him," he said. "I have a vested interest in his welfare, you know." He looked down at Jon, then back at Karen. "He gave me my name. In a way, he made me who I am." He pushed the plunger in to the hilt. Then The Sandman stood up and walked away.

Karen rushed over to Jon. He wasn't breathing. The syringe was on the ground beside him and blood was leaking out from the site of the injection. Karen turned him on his back. She took a deep breath, clamped his nose with her fingers and placed her mouth around his. Then she exhaled. His chest rose. She leaned back and heard the air escape from his mouth. His chest fell. She did it again.

She did it again and again, six times a minute. When Lizzy regained consciousness, Karen told her between breaths to find a telephone and call the police. Then she breathed into Jon again. Finally he started to move.

Chapter 35

The late afternoon crowd at the Blue Moon Café was smaller than usual. Karen and Jon were sitting with Janet Saunders in a corner booth. Bobby Arnold had just joined them. Bobby's favorite country western song, *Gol Darn Your Wife, She's Cheatin' On Us*, was playing in the background. They were discussing The Sandman murders.

"It's an amazing story, isn't it," Karen said.

"And it's all about money," Saunders added. "What a surprise." She took a drag from her cigarette, tilted her head back and blew a smoke ring into the air.

"Holyoke, Allison and the company were trying to get around the FDA and the federal rules for drug development. The prostitutes were only incidental," Karen said. "Kate Monahan must have known what was going on, but it's not clear how many of the other board members were in on the plan."

"They didn't foresee Allison's insanity," Jon said.

"What a lucky bastard," Bobby said. "You were handed the story of a lifetime. Several of them. Stories that is."

"What's so lucky about almost getting killed?"

"Jon's even more famous now than he was before," Karen said to Saunders. "*The New York Times, The Washington Post, The Miami Herald, The Los Angeles Times, The San Francisco Chronicle,* they all picked it up. His story made every newspaper in the country." She turned to Jon. "Have you thought about your Pulitzer acceptance speech yet?"

"Oh, please " Bobby rolled his eyes.

"Come on," Jon said. "I'm not the only famous journalist around here. Lizzy's account of her abduction and imprisonment made all the name papers, too, and all the talk show hosts are going crazy to get her in front of their cameras. She's the real star."

"How's she coming along?" Bobby asked. "She got banged up pretty bad."

"She's doing well," Jon said. "She had her nose and her teeth fixed, and the rest of her injuries seem to be healing OK. She's had some nightmares and psychological problems, but who wouldn't? She's seeing a counselor."

"Writing that account of her experiences seems to have helped," Karen said. "It gave her a way to get it out and get rid of it. It provided her with some measure of release. And anyway, she is one tough cookie."

Saunders blew another smoke ring and then put out the remainder of her cigarette. She leaned over to say something in Bobby Arnold's ear. They both laughed.

"I wonder what ever happened to him," Saunders asked. "The Sandman. Nobody knows, right?"

"He disappeared," Jon said. "The last time I saw him I was lying on the ground, paralyzed by his drug, looking up at him. He just walked away. That was right before Karen started mouth to mouth."

"Enjoyed that, did you Karen?" Bobby asked.

"You bet," she said. "It's not often you have a man totally at your mercy, totally helpless at your feet."

"Honey, they're all totally helpless," Saunders said. She cackled at her own joke as she lit another cigarette.

Jon laughed and then continued, "I think he got away."

"No chance," Karen said. "We had dogs out there. We had helicopters with infrared viewing devices so we could see through the clouds. The Indian police force from the Quinault Indian Nation searched the area. Nobody found a thing. He's dead. Lizzy gave him a pretty good whack on the back of the head, you know." She looked into the faces of the group. She wanted to believe what she was saying. "He crawled under a log somewhere and died."

"Maybe," Jon said. "But the rain forest's a difficult place to find a man who doesn't want to be found. There are a gazillion places to hide, and the rain washes away your trail. I'm not surprised the dogs couldn't find him."

"And the infrared cameras?k" Karen asked.

"I don't know," Jon answered. "Can they tell the difference between a man and bear? How about between a man and a goat?"

A voice came into the booth from over by the bar. "What do you have to do to get a little service around here? What kind of a joint is this anyway?"

"Lizard," Jon said. "Come on over."

Lizzy walked over to the booth. Her nose was bandaged and she still had a few healing cuts and abrasions on her face, but otherwise she looked pretty good.

"It's nice to see everyone together again," she said. She looked at Jon and Karen sitting next to one another. "How are you guys doing? Have you two moved in together yet?" she asked.

Janet Saunders answered, "Yeah, we thought we'd give it a shot. She looked at Bobby and blew him a smoke-filled kiss.

"Bobby?" Jon said. He raised an eyebrow as he looked at him.

"What can I say," he said. "She's special." He smiled back at her.

"Well I'll be damned," Jon said.

Lizzy turned to Bobby and asked, "How about a margarita?"

Acknowledgements

Writing a first novel is an interesting endeavor, one that draws on a lifetime of experience and human interaction, and there is no way to acknowledge the many influences that contribute, for better or for worse, to its development. Nonetheless, I will try.

First of all I want to thank my wife, Vicki. She listened, criticized, cajoled, chided, encouraged, researched, inspired, collaborated, comforted, and in the end provided me with what I needed most. She loved. Words hardly seem enough.

Eric and Andrea read the chapters as they developed, one by one, and kept me going with their help and suggestions.

Lois McCabe, my eighty-five-year-old mother-in-law, (she'd try to tell you that she's only eighty-four), told me to spice up the sex scenes. I should have listened better.

A multitude of friends provided me with a multitude of inspirations, inputs, editorial comments, and suggestions, but Jim, Bobby, Karen, Judd, Barb, Kate, and Liz deserve special thanks.

I want to thank Colleen Daly for her professional help, guidance, and editorial expertise. Without her, this book would never have seen the light of day. That, by the way, is a cliché that she would have mercilessly cut from the body of the book. She doesn't get to do it here.

The medical schools at the University of Nebraska and The University of Washington provided me with more material than I could possibly use.

And finally, I'd like to thank my father and my mother for giving me the tools I needed to complete this work. Unfortunately, it's a little late for that. I should have done it when I had the chance.

Author's Note

I took a small amount of literary license with the University of Washington Medical Center and Harborview Medical Center, mostly for my own amusement and for that of my friends. Likewise I rearranged some of Seattle's more prominent streets and lesser landmarks.